BLUE PROMETHEUS

BLUE PROMETHEUS SERIES #1

NED MARCUS

ORANGE LOG PUBLISHING

Copyright © 2014, 2017, 2019 by Ned Marcus.

3rd edition (paperback).

ISBN 978-986-95833-2-9

All rights reserved.

No part of this book may be reproduced in any form or by any electronic or mechanical means, including information storage and retrieval systems, without written permission from the author, except for the use of brief quotations in a book review.

This book is a work of fiction. The characters, places and events are products of the author's imagination or have been used fictitiously and are not to be construed as real. Any resemblance to persons, living or dead, is entirely coincidental.

Published by Orange Log Publishing

Cover Design by Damonza

To my mother

CONTENTS

Prologue	1
Chapter 1	3
Chapter 2	18
Chapter 3	32
Chapter 4	45
Chapter 5	58
Chapter 6	73
Chapter 7	84
Chapter 8	95
Chapter 9	104
Chapter 10	116
Chapter 11	127
Chapter 12	140
Chapter 13	151
Chapter 14	159
Chapter 15	175
Chapter 16	183
Chapter 17	189
Chapter 18	198
Chapter 19	206
Chapter 20	215
Chapter 21	220
Chapter 22	232
Chapter 23	243
Chapter 24	251
Chapter 25	256
Chapter 26	268
Chapter 27	276
Chapter 28	282
Chapter 29	288
Chapter 30	297
Chapter 31	302

Chapter 32	314
Chapter 33	321
Chapter 34	330
Chapter 35	335
Chapter 36	343
Chapter 37	350
Epilogue	356
Free Stories	359
Please Leave A Review	361
Books By Ned Marcus	363
About the Author	365
Acknowledgments	367

PROLOGUE

A thought disturbed the darkling sea. From beyond our universe, it rippled through the millions upon millions of galaxies and on through the many planes of the universe that lay together so closely intertwined that few could distinguish between them.

The thought vibrated through millions of lives, unseen but not unfelt. Plants withered, animals lashed out in fear, and the moods of man changed. The emotional states of those unaware of the darkness within fluctuated wildly.

The thinker of the thought sensed a change and a possibility it didn't like. In a far corner of the universe, a consciousness had awoken; one that could grow to threaten it. It felt an intense hatred towards this newly awoken life.

Far away, a kindred creature sat deep within his cold dark moon and listened. He heard a whisper of a threat. He waited, hoping for a return of his second sight. It came suddenly. He saw his distant colony, surrounded by the wilderness of the frigid blue planet. The wild magic of this world disturbed him. However, it was not that magic he had been shown. It was something else. The Emperor's Isle, the only civilization on that primitive world, was threatened. The Emperor had long delayed putting the final pieces of his imperial jigsaw into place. Now was the time to act.

But on a distant shore of the darkling sea, one other creature had heard and recognized what had passed. A shiver ran down the Mariner's strong black and red back. This brave creature felt dread, not at his coming death, but at the disturbance in life. He followed the thought back through the darkling sea to the very edges of the universe.

Beyond this, even he could not venture. He sensed the malevolent presence that dwelt there and recognized its intent. The Mariner was the last of an ancient race. With his passing, they would evolve beyond the physical, but before they passed to a higher plane of existence, there was a final task.

The Mariner breathed deeply and began his song: a song that had not been heard in the universe for ages. Ghostlike, a strange ship appeared beneath him. Sailors stood around him, and they sang together as a chorus. The song they sang was of the deepest magic, and their music and poetry altered the fabric of existence. The sails filled with wind and the brig set out into the darkness of space. The stars swam in the black sky, and he stood still on his deck and focussed his thoughts on a man and a woman who had the power, if they chose, to alter the destiny of the universe. This was the final voyage of the ancient Mariners.

1

Thomas Brand was a realist; he didn't believe in superstition of any kind. He certainly didn't believe in fortune telling or that the level you vibrated affected your future. That was like believing in religion, only worse. Yet here he was, standing outside a small independent bookshop in Clapton Pond, late on a warm Sunday afternoon. A sign in the window said, Intuitive Tarot for Beginners.

He hesitated outside the bookshop; he'd been once before and disliked the New Age feel. A new book on spiritual awareness sat next to a second-hand copy of a book on psychic self-defence. This was a bad idea. Lucy was a good friend, but he now regretted letting her persuade him to come to her class. He should've just met her after so they could visit a friend of theirs who had just had an accident. But she'd been insistent, even saying her intuition had told her he must come today; she'd had a dream of him embarking on a voyage of discovery.

The bookshop appeared to be closed. He couldn't see anybody inside, and he felt some relief at the possibility that he'd missed the class. So when a middle-aged woman in purple waved at him from inside, his heart sank. A bell rang as he opened the door and walked inside. Now he could see the class—and Lucy—sitting around a rectangular wooden table at the rear of the shop.

She smiled at him, and as he sat in the empty seat next to her, she addressed the class. "My name's Lucy Thomson, and I'd like to introduce you to intuitive tarot card reading." She picked up the pack of cards and began to shuffle. "Has anyone here used tarot cards before?" About half of the class raised their hands. The woman in purple said she occasionally read for her family and another woman said she sometimes dabbled.

Lucy introduced the tarot deck and went through the meanings of some of the cards. There were the major and minor arcana. The major arcana each had a picture; the minor arcana consisted of the court cards and the numbered cards. "Intuition comes from within, not from the cards themselves. They're just tools to help us."

Thomas wondered how anybody could believe that tarot cards could predict your future. But the class was utterly captivated by Lucy and her colourful cards.

"Would you like to be first?" Lucy said.

"What?" He'd been absorbed in his thoughts, and he looked up to see everyone watching him.

"Would you like a reading?"

"Why not?" Although he knew it was all superstition, at least now he'd be able to disprove it scientifically.

"I'll use a simple four-card spread," she announced to the group. She gave Thomas the cards, and he shuffled the deck. Then she took the cards and laid them out on the table.

Four cards lay upside down in front of him. "Let's take a look," she said. She turned over the first card. "This card represents your situation now." The card showed a knight sitting on a horse with a pentacle in his hand. "You're on the edge of a great journey. You have a spirit of adventure, but you need a push to get you started."

She pointed at the next card. "This one shows what you'll have to overcome on your journey." She turned the card over, and some of the students tittered. The devil stared up at Thomas from the tabletop. "Don't worry," she said.

He wasn't worried. After all, it wasn't real. But he'd always respected Lucy, despite her strange ideas, and he decided to play along. "Will I meet the devil?"

"It doesn't mean that. It means the obstacles you face could be self-imposed limitations. To gain freedom, you must let go of what's holding you back." She pointed at the chains that bound two naked humans to a giant devil. "These represent the chains to the material world, or ideas, which can prevent you from moving forward." Some of the students were taking notes.

Lucy pointed to the third card. "This card shows you what action you should take to overcome the difficulties you face." She turned it over. There was a picture of a magician with one arm pointing into the air and the other pointing to the ground. "You need to overcome the obstacles in your path by developing your intuition. You need to understand the unseen forces within the universe. Trust your higher self."

He looked around and saw several people nodding at the advice, but he had no idea what she was talking about. "Higher self?"

"Your imagination or intuition. Believe in what your inner self tells you."

Thomas nodded; although he didn't believe in higher

selves, he didn't want to upset Lucy. "What about the final card?"

"The last card shows the most likely outcome." The class waited for Lucy to turn over the card. Even Thomas felt a little tense, which he knew was ridiculous.

"Well, let's see the future." She turned over the final card. The class stilled. Death rode a white horse and around him lay dismembered bodies. The card disturbed Thomas a little, but he reminded himself that it was all just superstition. Lucy began to speak when a brick shattered the shop window.

The woman in purple screamed. The bookshop owner dropped his book onto the counter and rushed to the front of his shop. Shouts came from the street, and Thomas walked to the door. A parked car across the road was on fire, broken glass lay along the pavement, and a gang of young men ran down the street.

Lucy joined him by the door. "What's happening?"

"I don't know."

The sound of breaking glass came from around the corner, quickly followed by shouts. He could hear a police siren in the distance.

"Let's finish early for today," Lucy said. The members of the tarot class left without goodbyes and the bookshop owner began to close the shop. Lucy gathered her things and joined Thomas on the street. The old metal shutter screeched shut behind them.

Her face was pale. "It should be me who's feeling nervous after the reading you gave me," Thomas said.

She smiled. "That was an interesting reading. I think it's portentous."

"I hope it's not too portentous," Thomas said. Some of

the men were now running back along the middle of the road. There were police lights in the distance.

A red double-decker bus pulled away from the bus stop. The passengers peered out of the windows. Several young men clustered around the vehicle. A solitary female stood amongst them. She threw a full can of cider into the side of the bus and then opened a second one.

The bus driver braked hard to avoid hitting a man who had run across the road, and he received screams of abuse. The man he had just missed kicked the side of the bus and tried to force open the passenger door. The girl laughed between swigs of cider, while the driver tried to move forward again, very slowly.

"He's trying to run us over," the boy shouted. "Open the door." The bus driver refused.

"I wanna drink!" the girl said. She dropped her empty can and walked towards a grocer's shop. The gang lost interest in the bus, which accelerated down Lower Clapton Road.

"Thank God for short attention spans," Thomas said, as the men followed the girl into the corner shop. The elderly owner watched helplessly as the gang helped themselves to drinks and snacks.

"I know that shopkeeper," Lucy said quietly.

A young couple walked out of the shop, each had two bottles of wine in their hands. "Help yourself, it's free," the man said.

"What?" Thomas asked.

"London's rioting," he said. The girl laughed, and the couple was gone. The sounds of police sirens became louder.

"They stole the wine from the corner shop," Lucy said.

"We have to find somewhere safe," Thomas said. He

watched the lines of police draw nearer to Clapton Pond. When he turned round, his friend had gone. "Lucy?"

She was crouching by the broken pet shop window.

"What're you doing?"

She held up a kitten. "It escaped through the hole." She put the animal back inside.

"It'll just get out again," he said.

"I've got an idea. Help me." She dragged a sack of garden fertilizer through the broken window of the garden supplies shop next to the pet shop.

"Lucy?"

She began to explain, but he stopped her. He understood but didn't think it was a good idea. Despite that, he helped her lean the bag against the hole. The kittens began to scratch the sack from the inside. "That should keep them safe for a while," she said.

A woman leant out of a third-floor window and screamed down at them. "She thinks we're stealing the fertilizer," Thomas said.

Lucy tried to show the woman what they were doing, but he could see she didn't care. Three police vans were driving along Lower Clapton Road.

"Lucy, if we don't go right now, we'll be caught up in the riot."

"How about the park?" she said.

As they crossed the road, a man approached them; he smelt strongly of alcohol, and Lucy pulled away from him. "Have a drink, mate," he said to Thomas. He held a bottle of cheap brandy in one hand and removed a tube of plastic cups from his coat pocket. Several of them dropped to the ground, but he managed to clutch one of them in his hand. He gave Thomas the plastic cup and began to pour the brandy onto the tarmac. Some splashed into the cup.

"Cheers!" The man then turned and staggered down the road.

"Community spirit," Thomas said as he threw the cup and its contents into the gutter. Lucy smiled.

A vandalized notice board stood at the entrance to the narrow park surrounding the pond. "I'd always meant to visit this park. It must have been beautiful once," Lucy said. She looked at the information board. "But we're a century too late. Swans on the water. I'm glad they're not here now. I'd be worried about them." A small wooden bridge arched over the corner of the pond closest to them; it was partially concealed by the drooping branches of a large weeping willow. They walked onto the bridge and looked into the shallow water.

"I'm glad you're here, Thomas. I mean, if there's trouble, at least you know how to fight. Perhaps you really are the knight in the cards."

Thomas smiled. "Learning a martial art is one thing, fighting my way out of a riot is another. I hope it doesn't come to that."

From the peace of the park, they watched the chaos unfold around the edges of the pond, but in the middle, a polite queue of looters waited patiently in line outside an electronic appliance shop for their turn to steal flat-screen TVs, DVD players, and various other appliances.

"The eye of the storm," Thomas said.

Their peaceful world vanished when police charged into Clapton Pond. Some looters escaped, including three men who ran through the park, but many were caught and handcuffed. They were placed in line by the vans. More vans arrived, and more police officers milled around Clapton Pond.

"Do you think they'll arrest us?" Lucy asked.

"Yes."

"But we didn't do anything."

Thomas knew that they were just in the wrong place at the wrong time. "We took a sack of fertilizer from a shop."

"We didn't steal it."

"They won't see the difference."

"They're in there," a female police officer said. A line of blue uniformed police moved along the outside of the bushes towards the park entrance.

"Let's go to that bench, over there," Thomas said. They walked along the path. The bench was opposite a small island. Pigeons wandered in and out of the birdhouses. They seemed completely unaware of the events happening around them.

"Stop!" the female police officer shouted. They sat and waited while the police officers ran along the circular path. They came from both directions and held batons in their hands.

"Thomas!"

"If we explain what happened, it should be all right." Thomas hoped, but he didn't really believe it.

"You're under arrest," the police officer said.

"What for?" he asked. "We're sitting in the park."

"Two people of your description were seen breaking and entering a shop on the high street."

"We only wanted to put a bag of fertilizer against a broken window. The kittens were getting out," Lucy said.

"So you admit to theft?" another constable asked.

"We took it to block the hole in the pet shop."

He nodded. "What did you want the fertilizer for?"

"We've already told you. To block a hole," Thomas said.

"Block a hole? What did you really want it for?"

"He's telling the truth," Lucy said.

"Where is it now?"

"We didn't steal anything," Thomas said. His heart sank as the direction of the conversation became clear to him.

"Breaking and entering is a crime," the female police officer said. "You must come with us." They were handcuffed, marched from the park, and placed in a line of rioters, looters, and others caught up in the disturbance. A young constable moved them to near the front of the line and looked at them suspiciously.

The sky was darkening, but there was still enough light to watch the police activity around Clapton Pond. Thomas looked at the line of people next to them.

A pair of girls bumped into him. "It's not our fault," one of them said.

"It's all their fault. The government and the rich," her friend said.

"We showed them that we can do what we want. It was a good laugh."

A man nodded and grinned at Thomas, as if in search of approval. What did he want? For Thomas to pin medals on the girls' jackets?

This was the last place on earth he wanted to be. And he was bored. An hour or more passed, but the police were in no hurry. They seemed to be waiting for something. He looked up into the sky at the stars. Then he saw something. "Lucy." She didn't hear him. "Lucy," he said louder.

"What?"

"There's something out there."

She looked up. "Stars," she said.

"No, not stars. It's moving."

"Then it's a plane." She looked away.

Thomas watched the light; he was sure it was getting closer. If it was a plane, it was a strange plane. Its motion seemed wrong. His attention was distracted when one of the girls next to him vomited on the ground. He pulled his foot away just in time. When he looked up again, it was bigger than before. "It's flying straight towards us," he said to Lucy, who was checking that none of the vomit had landed on her pants.

Lucy watched the dribbling girl next to her. "The light again?" she asked. "A UFO?"

"No, but something's flying towards us."

She looked up again. "Where?"

Thomas pointed. "Look. It's moving."

"You're right." Her expression changed from annoyance to interest. "I wonder what it is?" She studied it for several more seconds. "Thomas, it may be a UFO."

Together they watched the bright light move towards them, and he wanted to laugh at the surreal situation.

"Thomas! It's really coming straight for us. It's going to hit us!"

Their police guard looked at them suspiciously. He'd not looked up into the sky but had kept his gaze firmly on his charges.

"Lucy, we have to move. Get ready to run," Thomas whispered. "Now!" he shouted. The constable lunged at them, but Thomas pushed the man's arm away. They ran back across Lower Clapton Road. They had surprised the impassive constable. He hadn't expected anyone to attempt an escape.

"Stop!" the constable who'd arrested them screamed in a high-pitched voice. She and several other police officers chased them, while the crowd cheered them on.

The light above them intensified, and finally the crowd noticed it. A woman screamed, and the waiting line of arrested rioters, looters, and others scattered in every direction, single-mindedly pursued by the police.

Thomas and Lucy jumped through the hedge and back into the small park as light illuminated Clapton Pond. Thomas ignored the scratches from the bushes. He planned to wade across the shallow pond and escape through the hedge on the far side.

Just as they reached the edge of the water, there was a bright flash of light, followed by a loud bang. They stood still as windows shattered along the high street. For a few seconds there was silence. Then the contents of Clapton Pond fell on their heads. Lucy, who had had her mouth open, spat out part of the pond, including a few strands of weed.

"Oh my God, Thomas. Look!"

Thomas looked up, and what he saw made no sense. Mist covered the pond and partially obscured their view, but what lay within the mist was unmistakable. A sailing ship floated gently on Clapton Pond. It was attractive, in a ghostlike kind of way, and it glowed with blue and silver light. Two square-rigged masts rose above them. The strange mist hung closely around the dark wooden hull. The illuminated sailing ship took up most of the pond, including the small island with the birdhouses, which had now completely disappeared.

"What is it?" she asked.

"A brig, I think," he answered.

"Thomas!" She looked at him. "I meant what's it doing here? How can a boat fly?"

"I've no idea."

A crowd slowly approached the pond to look at the floating brig. Thomas looked up and saw dozens of martial artists in white staring at the sailing ship from the shattered windows of their martial arts studio.

The female police officer and the sergeant pushed their way through the crowd towards them. Thomas heard the police reporting a possible terrorist incident on their phones. "Do you know anything about this?" the woman asked.

"It flew out of the sky," Thomas said.

"Sky?" The woman's voice rose. He knew this was going to be difficult.

Across the street there was an explosion; light followed by darkness. An electricity blackout. All the streetlights went out. The only light came from the police floodlights and the illuminated sailing ship.

Lines of police marched into the small park and soon removed the crowd, most of whom were too surprised by the arrival of a brig in Clapton Pond to resist. "How did it really come here?" the sergeant asked.

"I saw it in the sky. It flew down and landed in the pond," Thomas said.

"Sailing ships don't fly."

"I think they're terrorists, Sergeant," she said. "They've shown the classic signs: stealing fertilizer, suspicious and out of place behaviour, followed by attempts to get into position here in the park."

"We're not terrorists. We thought the ship was going to hit us," Thomas said. But the police were not listening.

"Something's not right about them." The sergeant glared at Thomas. They were in a park full of police, some of whom were armed, and they were surrounded. More police milled around the outside of the park. Thomas wondered whether this was going to be one of those notorious acts of police brutality on citizens that he'd read about in the newspapers.

One of the constables pointed. "There's a lorry parked over there. It wasn't there earlier." They looked to see the parked truck. "It might've come off the lorry," he said.

"Come off a lorry? Are you insane? It came from the sky!" Thomas said.

The sergeant punched him in the stomach, catching Thomas by surprise. He gasped for breath. "Don't insult a police officer."

"Shall I put them with the others, Sergeant?"

"Not yet. I want to keep them separate for now." A sound came from the boat.

"Someone's onboard, Sergeant."

"Did you see anyone, Constable?" The man shook his head.

Thomas leant close to Lucy and whispered. "Let's climb onboard."

"Are you crazy?" she whispered back.

"Maybe, but they've forgotten about us for now." He glanced at the police who stood huddled together in conversation. "I don't think this is what they think."

"What do you think it is?"

"I've got no idea, but I want to find out. If they really are aliens, then this is really big. Bigger than just being arrested." The more he spoke, the more he convinced himself that his idea was good. "I know one thing, it didn't come off the back of a lorry."

"What about the handcuffs?" she asked.

"We can still climb."

"I can't see a ladder," she said.

"There are footholds."

The wooden hull was smooth, except for a series of

footholds that had been carved into it. Each one had a small iron rung inside.

"I didn't see those before."

For a few seconds, a burning car blazed more brightly on Lower Clapton Road. "Now!" he whispered. He slipped into the shallow water and grasped a metal rung with both hands. As he heaved himself up, his handcuffs dropped into the water. Faulty, he thought. He climbed quickly, and he was pleased that Lucy was right behind him.

"Stop!" the constable screamed. She rushed forward to stop them.

He pulled himself over the edge of the hull and immediately turned and reached down for Lucy. Her handcuffs were gone, too. Lucy grasped hold of his hand. The constable jumped up in the air and grabbed hold of Lucy's leg. She kicked out reflexively, hitting the woman's jaw, causing her to tumble into the pond.

The sergeant shouted threats, and two armed police constables began to climb the hull. Thomas heaved Lucy over the edge of the hull, and they stood on the deck together. "That was close," she said.

"It still is." There were shouts and a splash. He looked over the side. "Lucy, the footholds have disappeared."

She leant over to look. "That's odd."

"So was our handcuffs just falling off."

One of the armed police officers had managed to hold on and was dangling from the side of the hull. Below them the crowd of blue-uniformed men and women stared up. Some of them had weapons drawn. "Arrest them!" the sergeant screamed to the constable, who was now pulling himself up the side of the hull.

Lucy poked him. "Uh, Thomas."

"What?" He shook his head. There was no way they could get up without the holds he and Lucy had used.

She poked him again. "Thomas. I think you should look."

"What?" he repeated. He was trying to estimate how long it would take the man to board the ship. They'd need ladders now that the footholds had disappeared.

"There's something standing behind us, and I don't think it's human."

Thomas turned and felt the hairs on his neck stand up. The police and everything else beyond the deck of the sailing ship was forgotten.

2

The creature watched them. It had black eyes and jet-black skin with red patches on its face and body. Its skin shimmered. It could have been the light, Lucy wasn't sure. It was tall, around eight feet, naked and male, and had no hair whatsoever. Lucy looked down at the six toes on each foot. The alien was handsome but definitely not human. Lucy blushed.

"Thomas. There are more of them." They were similar to the one in front of them, but less substantial. Several of them glided around the deck, while a few were climbing above in the rigging.

"I know."

She inched closer to Thomas. Her legs felt weak, and she now wished she hadn't followed him. She watched the wraithlike figures walk through solid objects. The brig was haunted. She felt like sliding back down into the pond below. She didn't care about being arrested, nor did she care that a police officer was now clambering over the side of the hull.

"Thomas, what should we do?"

"Say hello," he said.

"Hello?" The constable had managed to climb aboard. His eyes were fixed on Lucy and Thomas. "You're under arrest."

"Are you going to arrest the terrorists, too?" Thomas asked.

"I knew you were terrorists," the constable said. He looked quickly around the deck for the others. Then he saw the alien. "What's that?"

"A good question," Thomas said.

The constable faced the alien. "What are you?"

The alien stood still on the deck.

"Thomas, I don't want to be here. The ship is haunted," she whispered. She moved to the side of the hull.

"Get down!" the police officer shouted. He drew his gun.

"I am getting down!" she shouted back.

"Lucy, no!" Thomas yelled as the officer raised his pistol. Thomas knocked the gun away and tripped the man. The constable fell heavily to the deck, and the gun discharged, firing into his foot. The police officer swore and reached for his gun, but Thomas picked it up.

"You're in serious trouble." The constable was examining his bleeding foot.

"You were going to shoot her," Thomas said.

"Thank you," Lucy said quietly. She looked at the pistol in his hand. "What should we do?"

"First, drop this in the pond before anyone can use it." He dropped the gun over the side of the hull. As it splashed into the pond, the police in the park fired at the ship. Thomas pulled Lucy down, and they crouched on the deck.

Lucy looked at Thomas. "We're really in trouble now, aren't we?" He didn't answer, but her usually calm friend looked more worried than she'd ever seen him.

The creature turned to the constable, who now leant against the side of the hull, and raised its hand. The man edged back and made an odd, choked sound. Strangely, his terror gave Lucy a little more courage. The alien opened his palm, and the police officer screamed and tumbled over the side of the hull, splashing into the pond below. Lucy laughed nervously.

She looked again at the insubstantial figures, similar to the very real looking creature standing in front of them. All of them were naked and were more attractive than she'd imagined ghosts to be, but still quite uncanny. One of them, a female, glanced at Lucy and Thomas but said nothing. Lucy turned back to look at the alien standing in front of her. He was the most imposing, and he appeared completely solid.

"Hello," Lucy said. The creature watched them impassively. "He's examining us."

"I can see that. Be ready to jump over the side if it makes any sudden movements."

"What about the police?" she asked.

"We might have to risk it."

"I wonder if he speaks English," Lucy said.

An image flashed before her mind. In the blackness of space, she saw a bright sailing ship flying fast from a deeper, inky darkness that reached towards it. She glanced at Thomas. His eyes were wide, and he was staring at the creature. She guessed he was experiencing something similar. A deep voice reverberated in her mind.

"Welcome to my ship. I am the captain; I have travelled from a distant shore of the universe to find you." Lucy glanced back to the park, worried that the police would try to board the boat a second time and possibly even shoot them. *"Your*

police will not disturb us." They carefully stood and moved away from the side of the boat.

"Who are you?" Lucy asked. Although she believed in many strange things, she could hardly believe that she was speaking telepathically to an alien in Clapton Pond.

"I'm the Mariner, the last of my race. These you see are my crew. The projections of their deeper selves; their bodies have long since disappeared from the physical world. They cannot speak to you, although they are aware of your presence. After our work is completed, we will cease to exist in your world."

"What work?" she asked.

"A thought has disturbed the universe. It has rippled through many worlds causing imbalance."

Lucy saw an image of London burning—death and terrible destruction were all about her. Her friends were walking barefoot along a smoking street; they carried the body of the girl she and Thomas had planned to visit today. "No!" Tears came to her eyes, and Thomas held her hand tightly; his face was pale and set in a grim expression.

"Will what I just saw happen?" she asked.

"If the evil is ignored, then it's a likely future. You, however, have the potential, if you choose, to restore balance to the universe. I'm here to give you passage to another planet in another plane of the universe, where this disturbance has found a home. Your help is needed."

Lucy shivered. What she'd just seen in her mind's eye had shocked her. "Whose thought is it?" she asked.

"A demon from outside our universe. Its only power in the physical world is that of suggestion, but its power of suggestion is strong."

"So you want us to leave Earth and travel across the universe with you?" she asked.

"To another plane of our universe," the Mariner said.

"What are these planes?" Thomas asked.

"The universe consists of countless planes, each existing in the same space."

"And the thought?" Thomas asked. "What type of thought is it?"

"An undeveloped thought; you'd call it evil. This is a harbinger of what will come." The alien creature raised his hand towards the police lines surrounding his brig and the smouldering buildings in the background.

"Why us?" Thomas asked.

"You chose this work before you were born."

"That's a strange thing to say," Thomas said.

"What're we supposed to do?" she asked.

"You're needed to help counter the imbalance in the universe."

"What exactly does that mean?" Thomas asked.

An image of a giant blue planet flashed into their minds. *"A young woman awaits you; she will be your guide. It's from her that you must learn your tasks. Heed her words, but make your own decisions. For you to succeed, you must awaken your inner magic."*

"How do we awaken our magic?" Lucy asked. She noticed Thomas frown, but she was curious.

"Your guide can show you. Once your magic has awoken, my task will be finished, but your work will continue."

"Only one person on a planet to help us?" Thomas asked.

"One is enough; however, you will be four. Your guide has a companion," the Mariner said.

Lucy had no idea what to make of this conversation. She believed in all kinds of strange things, but this was really strange.

"How can we trust you?" Thomas asked.

"Trust your intuition and make your own choice." Lucy watched Thomas's frown return at the mention of intuition.

"What if we refuse?"

"You're free to choose as you wish. I will leave this planet soon. With or without you."

"How free are we with the police waiting for us in the park?" Thomas asked. Lucy glanced back at the small park. A medical team was attending the wounded constable.

"There is always freedom of choice, however small." Thomas shook his head at that.

"What about the demon?" Lucy asked. She felt uncomfortable at the thought of such a creature existing.

"It lives beyond the universe. You will not see it, and it cannot directly harm you, but its workers are powerful, and they propagate its evil. If you decide to stay, the universe will receive a great setback. It will be millennia before the next conjunction of spheres when the conditions are right again. I will not be here to guide those future beings."

Lucy was not sure she was really following this. "What are our chances?" she asked.

"That depends on you, but you have a chance."

Thomas raised his eyebrows. "I can't believe this is true."

"That's your challenge, Thomas. You need belief."

"Can you guarantee our success?" Thomas asked.

The Mariner laughed. *"The future is indicated, not predetermined."*

"Which planet are you talking about?" Lucy asked.

"The seventh."

"Which is that?"

"Uranus," Thomas said.

"You call it Uranus, but there it is also called Prometheus."

"It's an ice giant. It can't support life."

"In this plane of the universe that may be so, but in other planes, it's teeming with life."

"Are these other planes parallel to ours?" he asked. "Are there other Lucys and Thomases?"

"Millions upon millions of planes lie closely together within our universe, and in each, the evolution has been different. There is no exact copy of you in any world, although there may be beings close to you. Sometimes these planes share ideas, names, and have histories with striking resemblances. There may be altered versions of London, but never an exact copy, and often there is something very different indeed."

"There's evil on this world, too. What about sorting that out first?" Thomas asked.

"Your work is there; whatever happens there will affect all the universe. To help your world, you must first leave it."

"If it's so important, why don't you do it yourself?" Thomas asked. "I mean, you're so powerful."

"Thomas," Lucy whispered. She thought that he was being too closed—she wanted to listen to more of what the Mariner had to say.

"I'm not permitted to interfere in human affairs. I can only guide."

"Isn't guiding helping? What's the difference?"

The Mariner stepped closer to them, and Thomas backed up a little. *"The universe seeks balance. The demon stepped beyond its domain; therefore, I'm permitted to act. If I were to step beyond my role, I, too, would invoke an opposite force."*

"Will you bring us back after we've done whatever we're supposed to do?" Lucy asked.

"One day you will be able to choose to return or remain, but first you must choose to go. I'll allow you time to decide, but one

more thing. If you agree, you must know that you will change. It is necessary."

"How?" Lucy asked.

"Your bodies will strengthen, and you'll begin to awaken." Lucy noticed Thomas's eyes brighten at the idea of strengthening, but she was more interested in what the Mariner meant by awakening. *"Call me when you are ready, but do not delay for long."* The Mariner left them alone on the deck of the strange wooden brig.

"What do you think?" she asked.

"I think we're in serious trouble, whatever happens. Can we really believe any of this? I mean an alien sailing ship landing on Clapton Pond."

"So it fell off a lorry?"

"No, I didn't say that." They watched a naked ghostlike sailor walk through the mast.

"If that's a hoax, then it's a good one," Lucy said.

"Okay, that would be hard to fake."

"Do you trust him?" she asked.

"I don't trust any of them. How about you?"

She thought carefully about her feelings towards the alien. She certainly knew she had more trust than Thomas, but sometimes she worried that she was too open-minded about things. "If he can fly a ship like this, then I think he could force us if he wanted, but he's not forcing us. He's giving us a choice. Also, he's doing a good job of stopping the police from boarding the ship."

They looked down from the boat. The small park had been transformed into a security village.

"I don't like the look of that at all." Lucy pointed at another group of men with rifles who walked across the park. She noticed others, in plainclothes, possibly detectives, talking to the sergeant and a constable. Dozens of police vans were parked on the roads around the park. A TV camera pointed towards them. "We're on the news," Lucy said.

"Surrender now!" the police sergeant shouted.

A man in plainclothes took the microphone. "You're in serious trouble. You've shot a police officer, possibly committed terrorist activities, disturbed public order, looted, avoided arrest, and assaulted other officers. Refusing to surrender will only make your situation worse."

"Terrorist activities?" Lucy said. She looked at the broken windows around the park. "That's not terrorism," she said.

"I'm not a member of your college debating team, miss. You can start by climbing down and bringing those men with you."

"I don't have a debating team," she said to Thomas.

"We know who you are and where you live," the plainclothes officer said.

"We're not terrorists. The crew of the ship are aliens," Lucy said, gesturing behind her. She was interested in what the Mariner had said, but she wasn't sure she wanted to leave her home. But at this point, she was losing hope that she had any choice at all.

"Enough of this nonsense. Come down." The officer turned away briefly as another uniformed officer walked up to him.

"We've spoken to the captain. He's peaceful." At least she hoped he was.

"Captain?" The plainclothes officer turned back to face her. "Who is this captain, and what does he have to say for himself?"

"He's from a distant galaxy." She stopped herself when she saw Thomas shake his head. She knew that much of what she believed possible sounded ridiculous to others. Not many people were as open as her.

"Tell the wizard to beam himself down here for a chat. Do you think I was born yesterday?"

Police carried ladders into the park. "They're going to try to board us," Thomas said.

"Do you think they'll hurt the Mariners?" She'd noticed a few of the sailors were in the rigging above the deck.

"I doubt if they can, but it'll be interesting."

Lucy didn't think it'd be interesting at all. The sergeant blew his whistle, and the line of police charged. The ladders banged against the hull. Lucy jumped back when the top of the closest ladder almost hit her in her face.

"What should we do?" she asked.

Thomas reached for the top of the ladder. "Don't you dare touch that!" the female police officer screamed.

A man in the park aimed a rifle at Thomas, and Lucy pulled him back. The men climbed fast, and the nearest one raised his baton at them. Lucy stepped back and almost screamed as a ghostlike female walked straight through her. The female alien turned and smiled at her. Lucy would never forget that smile, nor the look of horror on the constable's face. The sailors lined the side of the boat. They shone with a faint light, and as they moved their hands forward, the light intensified. The ladders fell back, and the police splashed into the shallow, muddy water. The sailors looked down at the sea of police officers.

Lucy leant over to look at the fallen police officers, too. "Their faces," Lucy said. She smiled for the first time.

The police looked up at the naked aliens, open-mouthed. "That's disgusting!" the constable who'd arrested them said. The inspector glared at the ghostlike figures and then at Thomas and Lucy.

"I think he's angry," Lucy said.

"Talk about understatement."

"You'll regret that," the inspector said.

"We didn't do anything," Lucy said.

"We all know that's not true. You've shot a police officer, and you're aiding and abetting terrorists."

"They're not terrorists. This is a first contact between species." Her mobile phone rang. "Excuse me," she said.

Thomas laughed.

She frowned at him. "Hello? I'm in Clapton Pond. I'm ... Oh. Really?" She looked at Thomas. "It's Rosina. She says we're the main story on the news." Lucy hung up. Seconds later, they were watching the news on her smartphone.

"Terrorists thought to be part of a terrorist cell operating in London have parked a stolen sailing ship on Clapton Pond. They've shot a police officer and are believed to be responsible for a series of explosions in the vicinity. Police have sealed off Clapton Pond and have tried to board the vessel, but were repelled by naked terrorists wearing black and red masks." The reporter grinned briefly. "That's apparently not a joke."

A panel of experts appeared on the TV. A distinguished male professor from a renowned institution discussed the nature of terrorism and gave a series of predictions on how the terrorists would most likely act now that they had been surrounded and all possibilities of escape had been removed. "This was obviously part of their plan. There's a serious danger that they'll attempt to blow up the boat and kill as many of our police officers as possible."

A female professor explained that the reason for the display of nakedness by the men and women onboard was to show their lack of fear and their contempt for our society.

On one point, all the experts agreed. The terrorists were each facing thirty years in prison, if convicted.

Lucy turned it off. "They can't," she said. "We have to explain."

"I'm sorry, Lucy. I never imagined it'd become this serious."

"This isn't your fault, but surely we can explain. I don't want to go to prison for the rest of my life for what I haven't done. What about justice?"

Thomas shook his head. "I don't think anyone will believe us if we talk about aliens and a spaceship that looks like a brig. If we surrender, and they really are terrorists, then we may be locked away for the rest of our lives. And if what the Mariner says is true, and it just takes off, then we'll still be in serious trouble. I shot a police officer, remember?"

"That was an accident," Lucy said.

"Will anyone believe it?"

Lucy stared at the scene below. How could things have become so bad? "Let's try. One more time."

He shrugged. "It's worth a try."

She could tell that he didn't believe it. She gripped the side of the hull tightly and took a deep breath. "This is a spaceship, and these are aliens, not people in masks," she shouted to the officers below.

"Do you think I'm a fool?" the sergeant shouted back at the boat. "You're surrounded and are not going anywhere. There are marksmen in the buildings and around the park. Surrender now, and tell your terrorist friends to put some clothes on and climb down with you."

A shot rang across Clapton Pond. Lucy was too stunned to move. "Thomas, they're shooting at us." Her voice began to crack. Thomas pulled her down. A bullet flew straight through one of the crew. Three more shots rang out, but they had no effect on the sailors.

"Don't shoot," Lucy said. Tears formed in her eyes as she thought about her future, which seemed to be rapidly disappearing, and her parents who she might never see again.

The police sergeant ordered his men to stop shooting. He shouted up at the sailing ship again. "Tell those perverts in frog masks to come down!"

Thomas stood and stared defiantly at the man. "They're not wearing any masks, and they don't look anything like frogs. They're aliens."

"And I'm your fairy godmother."

Lucy pulled herself up and stood close to Thomas. "Well, they look quite alien to me. I've never seen a man that size," Lucy said suddenly. Despite the tense situation, Thomas laughed aloud and Lucy blushed. "I meant their height," she added quickly. "They must be eight foot tall."

The police were not amused. "You joke? You're on a boat with strangely painted naked people who are probably perverts or terrorists with masks who've just crashed into a public park, demolishing the island below, and you laugh? Unless you do what we tell you right now, I cannot guarantee your safety."

Lucy turned to Thomas, who looked back and forth between the ship and the ground below. "What should we do?" Lucy asked.

"I think we've run out of choices." Thomas frowned and met her eyes. "We face prison or a voyage to another planet. I've always wanted to travel."

"The reading I gave you did show a journey," Lucy said. "And what these police could do frightens me more than the Mariner."

"I might miss work tomorrow because I'm exploring another planet," he said.

"This is your final chance," the sergeant said.

"Captain," Lucy called. The Mariner appeared besides the ship's wheel. "I don't want to be here anymore. I'll come with you to the other world."

"Me, too," Thomas said.

The Mariner nodded and took hold of the ship's wheel. The sailors stood around him, and again they sang as a chorus. The ancient song of the Mariners echoed through the streets of London, and the sailing ship vibrated to the magic of their music.

"What do you make of that, sir?"

"I've got no idea, Sergeant."

"They could be suicide bombers," the sergeant said.

Orange light appeared beneath the vessel. It cast a rich glow through the water. The ship vibrated.

"They're going to blow it up! Fall back!" the inspector yelled. The sea of blue fell back as if pulled by a huge tidal force.

A blinding flash of light illuminated Clapton Pond. It was followed by darkness. Around the pond, thousands of people were blinded. Several minutes passed before their sight returned. When it did, they looked around in confusion. The ship was gone. The island in the pond, with its little wooden houses, was as it had been before the sailing ship had appeared. A pigeon casually flew around the small island as if nothing had happened.

3

The remote sun and the four visible moons cast a dim light that illuminated the planet's surface in shades of blue and grey. A mist rolled down the mountains towards the blue lake. A solitary figure moved unseen through the woods. The fierce cold of this planet penetrated her protective clothing, but within her, a fire burnt as intensely as it did within the fire-breathing creatures that hunted the frozen forests and wastelands of Blue Prometheus.

It was with these wild creatures of Prometheus that she felt a bond, a shared hatred of the intruders. Aina Kay was one of only two living humans who had travelled deep into the wilderness beyond the Silvan Mountains and returned alive. The other she was sworn to kill.

As she approached the village, which lay several miles from Rime, she looked with affection at the collection of shacks that had been built on stilts by the side of the lake. This was her childhood home. A well-wrapped child played outside, searching for the strange, flat Promethean arthropods that inhabited the planet's lakes, but the girl's father called her back inside their roughly-built shack. At these temperatures, Aina wasn't surprised that the father wanted his daughter inside.

Or perhaps he was scared of what she may find beneath the surface. The lake was within the mountainous rim and protected from much that lived in the wilderness beyond, but some wild creatures still lived in the lakes, swamps, and rivers of these mountains. Not the great leviathans of the planet's vast oceans, but there were stories of children being taken and eaten by the inhabitants of the deeper lakes.

A shadow moved through the trees ahead of her. Aina froze. She watched the creature in disbelief. This should not be possible, not outside a battlefield or the experimental stations on the moons of Neptune. An ice demon, its long tail flicking from side to side, watched the village, its back to her. Then she saw another of the black and green lizards. It stood at about eight feet tall; its frilled neck was expanded.

These were callous, genetically-designed reptiles: the killing machines of the Deep Space Trading Company and the Empire. So this was how they'd cleared the villages in the mountains so fast. She moved slightly, and one of the creatures looked in her direction.

In this materialistic world, few believed in the kind of tricks that kept her alive. Although her tricks were pitiful in comparison with the wild magic of the creatures in the wilderness beyond the mountain wall, she shared enough of that magic to keep her alive. She focussed her mind on nothingness and visualized a grey shield; she physically ceased to exist in her mind, and, she hoped, those of the reptiles. She blended into the landscape, and the creature returned its gaze to the village.

She counted a score of them. Her plans had changed: she was no longer returning to Rime. Her younger sister and grandfather still lived in the village. What she had long feared had begun.

Aina stood within the trees and watched the creatures move through the forest. She knew that this many ice demons could destroy her village. Some villagers had guns, but guns were of limited use against creatures such as these, and no one would be expecting an attack. She was armed with a hand cannon, pistol, and knives. Not much but more than most of the villagers.

If she could create a distraction and draw them away from the village, then at least the villagers would be alerted. Perhaps they could escape. She'd kill as many of these monsters as she could. She looked for a defensive point from which she could shoot the reptiles. The two large boulders by the lake were the best place. She moved silently through the trees towards them.

As she crept forward, she felt a lump under her foot. She froze and cursed herself for not being more careful, but she knew that there had never been anything there before. She slowly crouched down. She'd stood on a whiner: a company device that alerted their security force to intruders in the area. They had no right to plant such devices on Silvan territory, but week by week they encroached on her country.

At least it was a whiner and not a land mine. She took out her knife and slid it slowly under her foot. She pressed down and looked around for something heavy to put over it. There was a large stone on the ground in front of her. She carefully leant forward and pulled it. The stone broke free, and she breathed out in relief. She put the stone over the knife and pulled the knife out.

Aina stood up and looked down in horror to see that the frost-covered stone had stuck to her glove. It dropped to the ground too late. The whiner began to whine. The volume was low at first but slowly increased. Aina ran towards the boulder; her hope of a surprise attack had gone. The sound of the siren rose and fell and rose again. Then she heard a long screech, followed by another, closer screech.

Lights appeared from the shacks. The villagers had been warned, at least. She took out her hand cannon and waited. Aina guessed she had about a minute before they attacked. As she waited, she rubbed her gloved hand over the hardy Promethean lichen and watched the sparks jump up.

Ariel and Miranda hung low in the dark sky above her. Beyond them was Puck. She'd never been to the moons of Prometheus. That was one of the very few regrets she had. A beetle appeared in front of her. The green scarab was the size of her hand. It opened its shell, and a beautiful set of wings emerged. Despite the screeching reptiles that approached, Aina was curious. They were said to be lucky; perhaps this meant her sacrifice would ensure the survival of the last of her family. The scarab lifted into the air and rose above her, and then it flew out over the lake. Aina smiled, then turned to the approaching ice demons.

At that moment, a large shadow passed low above her. She dropped to the ground and cursed. Spacecraft were rarely seen in the Silvan Mountains. How could the Company have sent a ship so quickly? It must have been patrolling the area. Aina felt sick, as if all her luck had left her.

An orange light came from the middle of the lake. It hovered about ten yards above the lake's surface. She looked at it carefully but couldn't make out the design. She felt the heat from the spacecraft. Aina glanced back at the lizards. They were still, apart from their long tails, which flicked from side to side. The lead lizard had now appeared from the cover of the trees. The leaders were larger than the others. The ice demons stared at the spaceship. She wondered whether they'd known it was coming.

She waited, hidden in the hollow space between the rocks. Out of habit, she pulled her coat around her, although she no longer felt cold. The heat from the spaceship was causing the water to evaporate, and thick clouds of mist rolled towards her. She expected the spaceship to move to the shore and search for her.

The orange light burnt intensely. Then it descended, landing in the middle of the lake. Why? There was nothing there. The water boiled and mist rose all around it. Aina strained to see the craft. This made no sense, and from the looks of the ice demons, it made little sense to them, either. She wondered whether this could be a lost merchant ship or even a private boat. Perhaps they were lost tourists. She pitied them if they were.

The steam began to settle as the cold Promethean wind blew across the lake's surface. A small wave caused by the spaceship's landing rippled towards her. Aina climbed a little higher on her rock and waited while the water lapped below her, then rushed back into the lake. The orange light had disappeared, and the vessel was now illuminated in shades of blue and silver. She looked carefully, scarcely believing what she was seeing with her own eyes. "Impossible," she whispered.

A sailing ship floated gently on the lake. The mist still obscured her view, but there could be no mistake. A sailing ship had landed on the surface of Prometheus. Aina knew every type of vessel in existence in the solar system, but she'd never seen anything like this outside of history books. A screech from one of the reptiles turned her head. "You'd better be able to look after yourself, whoever you are," she said aloud. She knew that like many Promethean creatures, the lizards were able to swim through freezing water and survive.

One of them was already wading, knee-deep in water. There was a movement near the sailing ship. The waiting ice demons saw it, too. They stopped moving and watched. A lizard pointed out into the lake and screamed. Aina followed the reptile's crooked finger. A small boat was moving away from the sailing ship and towards the shore. Although the boat didn't look anything like any imperial vessel she had ever seen, there was still a chance it was a trap, whether the ice demons knew about it or not. There were three figures inside: two humans, perhaps, and something else. If you really are aliens, then good luck with the reptiles. This won't make the most diplomatic first contact between species, she thought.

There was no more time to think. Three of the ice demons ran at her. They were males and heavily built. She raised her heavy hand cannon and fired. She hit the first lizard. The shell exploded in its chest. Despite her strength, the recoil of the cannon knocked her back onto the rock. The creature died. Two more rushed her and two more died. She cursed again and threw the now-empty gun into the lake. They'd not expected her to have that type of weapon. Otherwise, it wouldn't have been so easy. She pulled out her pistol. "Now it's your go," she said quietly. "Let's make it quick."

The ice demons now approached her more warily. They were not used to humans who fought back.

One of them, a female, hissed, "Die!"

"You too!" she shouted back.

"Enjoy," it hissed, its mouth twisting into what Aina thought may have been a smile—with reptiles it was hard to tell. The creature ran at her, and she fired her pistol. But this was not a cannon, and the bullets just bounced off its armoured body. However, it must have stung, as it swung away and tried to circle around her, keeping its distance.

Her gun had twenty bullets that supposedly were able to penetrate an ice demon's hide, but either the lizards were growing tougher skins, or the gun had never been powerful enough. A single lizard was usually equal to three or four humans, even if armed. There were still seventeen in the woods.

She felt calmer than she'd ever thought she would when facing her death. She'd make sure she killed as many of the lizards as she could before they overpowered her. She waited with her back to the lake. The lizards approached her at their own pace. They were still partially protected by the trees. She waited for the creatures to make their move. She knew that once they attacked, it'd be fast.

The green and black ice demon that approached from behind the rock in front of her hissed, and its frilled neck expanded, increasing the apparent size of its head dramatically. It was a female and about seven feet tall, a little shorter than the males. Aina looked at the frilled neck and the flicking tongue. So this is how you scare your victims, she thought. As if you need anything to do that. She waited for her death and hoped it'd be quick. The ice demon hissed and slithered backwards; its long tail flicked from side to side. Aina was confused. "What's wrong?"

Aina waited, but nothing happened. "What are you waiting for?" There was a splash behind her, and she knew. A shiver ran up her spine as she saw a shadow on the ground next to her. Her stomach sank, and she felt sick. *Just as I was ready to die, something worse happens,* she thought.

She tried to imagine what was worse than them, and the

thought was extremely unpleasant. She span round, dropping to one knee, her pistol pointing up. What she saw made her lose balance and almost fall back onto the frozen ground.

Three creatures stood by the edge of the lake. The largest was unlike anything she'd ever seen. It was as tall as an ice demon but broader. Its skin was black and red, and it was naked despite the frigid conditions. She looked the creature in the eyes. It appeared intelligent, possibly very intelligent, but not Promethean, she was sure. Next to the black and red creature were two humans. A young man and woman, a little older than her. Their skin was paler than hers, but nothing that would draw a second glance in Silva. Their drab, inadequate clothes were something else. The clothes they wore were hardly sufficient for the Promethean surface; then she noticed something about them and looked more closely—there were traces of magic around them, not much but enough to explain their lack of protective clothing. They watched her and appeared to be shocked by what they saw. She didn't blame them, she was shocked, too. Aina now looked backwards and forwards between the ice demons and the odd band of creatures from the lake.

One constant with the ice demons was their arrogance. They were not used to being challenged, and it wouldn't take them long to get over their shock. What intelligence they did possess, they used poorly. Their shock would turn to indignation, then to anger. Aina knew all their typical behaviour patterns. They would likely attack soon.

She looked back at the alien. The black and red creature looked strong and would probably prove formidable in a fight, although it didn't seem to be armed. The two humans were unarmed and therefore helpless—the little magic they had was unlikely to be enough help, if they were even aware of it. Still, appearances could be deceptive, as she knew when others sometimes misjudged her.

Aina tried to speak to the humans, but they answered in a strange language. The naked black and red creature didn't speak at all, but began to hum. The lights on the ghostly illuminated ship flickered.

The small hairs on Aina's body stood up. She looked at the alien in awe. She shivered as she felt an odd vibration pass through her body. Neither of the two humans seemed to understand what it was doing, and neither did the waiting reptiles, but she did. Her gift was not like this. She hadn't felt this kind of power since she'd been a child and alone in the forest; perhaps it was even greater. If this alien wanted to kill her, there was nothing she nor the waiting lizards could do about it. Strangely this thought relaxed her. She had nothing more to fear.

The leader of the ice demons stepped forward. "What are you?" it asked the alien. Its long tail flicked from side to side. Aina waited.

The alien creature continued to hum.

"You trespass on the land of the Deep Space Trading Company." When the three newcomers failed to respond, it continued. "The Company represents His Imperial Highness on the Outer Planets. Surrender yourselves."

For several seconds, the ice demons watched in silence. Then they attacked. The black and red alien raised his arms and fire came from his hands. The ice demons began burning. Every one of them. One tried to escape, but the fire followed it. The bodies of the lizards soon lay smouldering on the damp ground.

Never in her life had Aina ever seen anything like this. She turned to the tall alien. "Who are you?"

He spoke in the True Language. *"I am the Mariner."* He

was telepathic. She wasn't surprised, but she was surprised at the clarity of sounds, thoughts, and images that flooded through her mind. *"The Conjunction of Spheres takes place, the ancient prophecy begins. You are called to play your part."*

Aina listened quietly. Few knew about the ancient prophecy, although her father had told her the story when she was a child. The black dragon had spoken of her part when she'd lived in the ancient forest, and her guardian had trained her since childhood, but she'd never expected it to come about.

"Your part is to guide the Bright Ones on their journey." He motioned to the humans next to him.

"But their magic is latent," Aina said. She was sure of it now she'd had a chance to study them.

"Help them awaken it. You know the steps."

"I know the steps to natural magic, but if they're the ones, they'll need more: according to the prophecy, the Bright Ones take the Spirit Keys. I always thought they were mythical."

"They're real."

"Where are they?"

"The Empire holds them."

"Where exactly?" The creature didn't reply, and she shook her head. *"That won't be easy then."* She looked again at the man and woman. If they were the legendary pair, she'd have expected them to be more ready than they appeared. *"I'm no teacher."*

"You're their guide. They come from another plane of the universe; they need your help."

She'd once looked into another plane, but she'd never travelled to one. As far as she knew, she was the only human who even knew of their existence—until now. *"The Bright Ones of the prophecy deliver us from evil. Can we defeat the emperor?"*

"It's possible. But there will be sacrifice."

"That's what I thought."

"Aina, your life has been hard, but you have the strength to succeed."

Aina knew the decision would change her life and that of others forever. She also knew that the right choice was to fight. All her life had been a fight, and she wasn't scared of sacrifice. The alternative was to die quietly. *"I accept."*

The creature nodded. *"You're important, Aina Kay."* He turned and waded to his boat, leaving the two humans standing on the shore.

The Mariner halted in the lake. *"Do not delay. This opportunity will not arise again for a thousand years."*

Aina wanted to ask more questions, but the alien was already in his boat, gliding over the lake to the illuminated brig. The Mariner's boat gradually disappeared into the mist. "I didn't have the chance to thank you," she said to the already-distant figure.

An orange flame came from the hull and a deep rumbling sound echoed across the lake. The spaceship lifted into the air and vanished.

She glanced back at the dead demons and felt very pleased with the outcome, even if she wasn't sure what she'd do with the two humans. She looked up. Villagers walked from the trees. They stared in amazement at the dead ice demons and the disappearing spaceship. She saw the familiar red mask her sister always wore.

"Aina!" Her younger sister ran to her and threw her arms around her.

Her grandfather approached. "Aina, we thank you yet again."

She hugged him tightly.

"Who're these people?" her grandfather asked.

"The Bright Ones." She felt foolish as she spoke. Few on Prometheus believed in such things.

"How do you know?"

"The alien. The creature of power told me. Grandfather, I pray it's true."

"And we all pray for you and your new friends." The old man nodded to the two humans.

"Come," Aina said. She led the man and woman away from the village towards her lighter, the vehicle she'd hidden in the usual place. Although they were both a little older than her nineteen years, they appeared younger, softer, and rather helpless, but perhaps she would appear the same if she'd just been transported from another plane of the universe. She wanted to question them, but that would have to wait. Whatever their story was, she was sure it was interesting.

The siren had stopped, but the company police would soon come to investigate. She smiled to herself at the thought of the confusion on their faces when they came and found the burnt bodies of the ice demons. They would suspect a small army had attacked the lizards.

The path led away from the lake and the village, and soon they were alone together. Aina noticed the man glance at her as they walked back. He looked stronger than she'd first thought—they both did. She studied their magic. The man's was harder and had a feeling of the earth; the woman's was in some ways closer to her own. Twenty minutes later, they reached her lighter. It was still where she'd hidden it; well away from the imperial settlements in the mountains that she'd been monitoring for the Resistance.

Once inside, Aina pulled off the mask that was more for appearance than practical use—she had her own protection against the cold. Her long black hair fell down to her shoulders. She loosened her jacket and pulled back the sleeves and turned to look at her new companions. They'd have to start wearing protective clothing so as not to attract attention in public. Few people believed in magic in the nine planets, and she didn't want to draw attention to them.

The lighter started on her voice command and rose from the ground. She span it round and accelerated fast down the rocky road to Rime. She grinned at the look of shock on their faces.

An hour later, they reached the city. "Welcome to Rime." She watched them look at her in the mirror. "You don't understand anything I'm saying, do you?" They spoke quickly in a strange language. She switched from Silvan to standard Dnassian, the imperial language and common language of the nine planets. Then she tried Venusian and both dialects of Martian. The pair stared at her blankly. Finally she tried her limited Noish. She wasn't surprised when they didn't respond to that.

"So what are you?" she said quietly to herself. "You really are from a different world, aren't you?"

The young woman leant forward, touched her arm, and smiled. "Lucy," she said, pointing at herself.

"Thomas," the man said.

"Aina," she said. They repeated her name. "It looks like I've just made two new friends, and they're a long way from home." Aina smiled at the two young aliens.

4

Thomas and Lucy sat by the window in the common room of the Amber Tulip. Three months had passed since they'd arrived in Rime, and the district of Sunna, where Aina lived, already felt like home. The street outside bustled with people. Yellow lights, like little suns, radiated heat from the false sky that protected the city from the harsh exterior environment. The little suns alternated with oval windows that looked up at the real sky.

Glasses of steaming golden tea sat on the table in front of them. Thomas watched Lucy take her tarot cards from her pocket. "Put them away," he said. He took a sip of the hot tea and quickly put it down, the tulip glass was hot to his fingers. Although he wouldn't admit it, the first reading in London had had some truth in it.

Lucy shuffled the tarot cards. "Aina's not due for half an hour." She held out the deck to Thomas. "Shuffle." Reluctantly, and only to keep her quiet, he did. She took the pack and laid out three cards before him. "The past, present, and future," she said. She turned over the first card: the past.

"So, I used to be a fool."

"You were a free spirit."

"And now?" he asked, unsure why he was continuing with her game.

"The ace of cups is for love." She grinned at Thomas. "I see opportunities for romance."

"Lucy, please." She was right, though. He did like Aina, but this was hardly a true reading. "You're making this up."

"No, I'm not. The lotus blossoms also indicate an awakening of the human spirit."

"Don't start on magic again," Thomas said. "I've seen no evidence whatsoever." He could have said more, but he stopped himself; she was just playing. "And the future? It looks better than the last one you showed me."

Lucy smiled. "The king of wands—an opportunity is presenting itself, but don't get too full of yourself."

"I'll try not to." They were distracted when Old Morris entered and sat at his table.

"He looks more grumpy than usual," Lucy whispered. Thomas liked the irascible old man and had learnt some surprisingly earthy Silvan from him.

"What do you think of our Aina?" Old Morris asked.

"She's interesting," Thomas said, trying to both ignore Lucy's grin and to pronounce the Silvan words correctly.

"Interesting?" The man's face was red.

Before he could continue, Thomas spoke. "She's pushy, but she gets things done. I never expected to learn a language so fast."

"Your Silvan's getting better every day. Credit to you and Aina. Three months ago you were as dumb as a rock." He slapped the stone table. A few of the patrons glanced at the old man. "And you're right about her being pushy. She's important, you know. In the House of Chance."

"House of Chance?" Lucy asked.

"She hasn't told you? She speaks for us. The No-Head of Sunna." The man laughed and drank his tea. Then he carefully poured more into his narrow tulip glass."

"No-Head?" Thomas asked. He'd heard Aina mention something about heads. And about a house she visited.

"Not like the brainless blockheads. Bickering away while we lose our rights."

The door of the Amber Tulip swung open. A grey bot flew into the room followed by four men. Three of the men were green. The robot flew to a table, knocking a plate to the floor, and the two young men at the table stood hurriedly and moved away. The fourth man to enter was plump, white, and wore yellow and white robes. He thanked the young men and sat down.

Old Morris spat on the floor.

"Who are they?" Lucy asked.

Thomas had no idea, but he was curious to see the green-skinned people who were apparently so common outside of Silva. He recognized the uniforms from an image he'd seen. "Imperial Order."

"How do you know?"

"From a picture on Aina's computer." Thomas wasn't exactly sure what the order was, but he'd seen Aina's reaction to the picture, and it wasn't good.

"I don't like the feeling of those men," Lucy said quietly.

Old Morris nodded at her. His face was like stone.

The men became engrossed in conversation. Their bullet-shaped metal robot rested on the floor beside them. Imperial attack dogs, Aina called them. And as Thomas had found out, they didn't move out of the way for a human, unless that human was a lord.

"To the Empire," the large man said.

"The Empire!" the others repeated.

"How dare you utter those words in Silva!" Old Morris said.

"Imperial Uranus is the future," the large man in white and yellow said. "The future of our children. That's the most important thing. There are no jobs here. The company offers prosperity to all. Surely you wouldn't want to deny that to future generations. Silva's the only place on this frigid planet that lies outside the Empire."

The teahouse door slammed shut, and the man in yellow spilt tea on his white pants. "Blockhead Topper. Spreading your lies again. You're a disgrace to the Silvan government." Aina's bad mood was clear. Thomas had found out that his new friend had many qualities, but moderation was not one of them. She stood before the four men.

"Aina Kay. I'd expect you to deny the truth. Can you specify exactly which part of this planet the Empire does not control?"

"Ninety-nine percent."

"All Uranus belongs to the Emperor. Just because most of the planet is primeval forest doesn't make it any less a part of the Empire," a lord said.

Aina looked at the man, and Thomas thought she was going to spit on him. "Pat C. Ocio, company man. You know nothing of Prometheus."

"On the contrary, Ms Kay. I know a great deal. More than you, it would seem. I know that its correct name is Uranus. I also know how the wealth of the planet can benefit the Empire, and how the Empire, via the Deep Space Trading Company, can benefit the region of Silva."

"The wealth of this planet doesn't belong to the Empire."

"And who exactly does it belong to?" Lord Ocio asked.

"To the intelligent species of Prometheus."

Topper and the lords laughed. "Intelligent species? Wild animals, you mean. We've been on this planet for more than thirty years. Enough time to know if we share it with any intelligent species," Lord Ocio said.

"You've forgotten the war you fought with the intelligent species when you arrived thirty years ago."

"A few skirmishes with herds of animals, that's all," Lord Ocio said. "I'll grant you that some of them are big, but hardly intelligent."

"Well, Silva's been here for over a hundred years. And I can assure you that we're not alone on this planet. And you, Blockhead Topper, I can tolerate your ignorance and stupidity but not your treason."

"I'm the Honourable Member Topper of the House of Blocks. Please use my proper title, Ms Kay."

"Then use mine."

"I'm afraid you no longer have a title. The House of Chance was abolished this morning."

"You can't do that."

"We already have," Lord Ocio said. "The House of Blocks has already signed an agreement with the First Lord of Imperial Uranus, Lord Own. Silva has returned to the Empire. The day-to-day running of the Special Administrative Region of Silva will be under the control of the leader of the Blocks and the Deep Space Trading Company."

"Silva's never belonged to the Empire, nor to the Federation before it. Silva's a free country."

"The region of Silva is historically a part of the glorious Empire. Later today the new lord of the manor will make a speech in Scarlet Square announcing some changes," Lord Ocio said.

"Just because the emperor announces that Silva is a part of the Empire doesn't make it so."

"I can assure you that it is so. Our laws are your laws. It's a great honour for you to be accepted as imperial subjects."

Old Morris cursed.

"We're tolerant of differences of opinion, of course," Lord Ocio said, "but our laws protect you from the untamed region beyond the mountains. Rest assured, the company will fully exploit the region of Silva and bring prosperity to this backward area." The lords and their blockhead left the teahouse.

"What if it's true?" a man asked.

"Then we'll fight," Aina said. "But remember, just because someone says something's true, it doesn't make it true." Many in the Tulip nodded in agreement.

"Aina, we need to speak. There's still too much we don't know about this world," Thomas said.

Aina sat down with Thomas and Lucy. "I agree. I've been waiting for your Silvan to reach the right level; I think now's the time."

Lucy asked the first question. "You've told us some people are green, but why?"

"Most people in the solar system are green."

"But in Silva they're brown," Thomas said.

"We have many white people, too," she said with a smile. Silvans originally come from Venus, like all humans, but we migrated over a century ago when Prometheus was even more remote than it is now. We existed before the Emperor's Isle was established. We were far removed from the fashions of the inner solar system."

"Fashions?" Thomas asked.

"Humanity was originally the same as on your world. But when we began to explore the solar system, someone had the idea of changing the pigment in human skin so we could obtain energy directly from the sun. Imagine the benefit of not needing food supplies when colonizing new worlds," Aina said.

"Did it work?" Thomas asked.

"No, it failed. But the idea caught on. When the rich and famous changed their colour, others copied, and then almost everyone changed. It was supposed to bring about a new era, an end to racial discrimination."

"Did it?" Lucy asked.

"Yes, but other forms of intolerance quickly took its place."

"So everyone in the inner solar system is green?" Lucy asked.

"More or less. But Venus and the large cities are more mixed, of course."

"Why is the Deep Space Trading Company here?" Thomas asked.

"It's taking over Silva. Our country's rich in mineral deposits, and the company wants them. They plan to bring more soldiers here. Silva has no army; we never needed or wanted one. We have a police force, but that's not enough. The company has a royal charter to administer large parts of the outer solar system, and they have a standing army that almost equals the size of the imperial army. The president of Deep Space is Lord Martin Anlair."

Thomas noticed a slight frown on her face when she mentioned his name. "Who are these lords?"

"The Empire runs a feudal system, and the Imperial Order administers it. Peter Own is the first lord of the Emperor's Isle, as they call the imperial colony. And he's placed Maun Somder, a rich Dnassian, as the lord of the manor for Silva."

Thomas suddenly had the feeling that there was a lot

about Aina that he didn't know. "How do you know all of this?"

She leant forward and spoke in a low voice; both he and Lucy listened carefully. "I've been a member of the Silvan Resistance since the beginning. Do you remember when we first met?"

Thomas grinned. "It's hard to forget."

She smiled in return. "But did you ever wonder why my lighter was hidden outside the village?"

"I thought it was strange," Lucy said.

"I was carrying out surveillance in the mountains. Too many people had reported being forced from their mountain homes, and I went to investigate."

"What did you discover?" Thomas asked, his respect for her increasing as she spoke.

"What I just told you. The largest village in the mountains has now become a rich man's estate." A few drinkers in the Amber Tulip looked up as her voice rose with emotion. She sipped her tea and then continued. "We've never had a lord rule over us. Silva's not that type of country. This is Lord Somder's first time in the outer solar system, and he's trying to make an impression."

"How?" Thomas asked.

"It's rumoured that he's going to introduce the compulsory fitting of tags."

"Tags?"

"Nano-computers. They're placed in the brains of almost all imperial subjects at birth."

"Why?" Lucy asked.

"They allow the Empire to monitor the thoughts of its subjects."

"They can read people's thoughts?" Thomas thought of his thoughts being read by others, and he shuddered.

"We don't really know. They're better at interpreting emotion. The Empire downloads mental software into them every day."

"And people accept this?" Lucy asked.

"Most imperial subjects love them. They love their convenience, especially their instant downloads and free mental movies."

"You said almost all imperial subjects," Thomas said.

"Some people live outside the law. And parts of the military have exemptions."

"It's appalling. I wouldn't be surprised if there was rioting," Thomas said. He and Lucy exchanged a look, and he knew she was remembering the riots the day they left Earth, too.

"That's why the company army's here. So far there are only a few hundred soldiers and police, but more will come."

"Who is this emperor?" Thomas asked.

"He used to be the president, until he dissolved the old federation."

"By force?"

"No, by choice. The people were sick of corrupt governments, and they hated the politicians. The people became disillusioned with democracy and voted for a change."

"For an emperor?" Lucy asked.

"Not an emperor at first. He helped engineer the mood of the people to suit himself. He created the Imperial Order, his closest supporters and much more. The Order fomented fear, then offered a resolution. Tags were becoming popular and were influential in forming opinions. They selected the news, exaggerated the parts they liked and lied about the parts they didn't. His agents manipulated the situations on Mars and the Jovian Moons to his advantage. He used special mercenary forces to resolve the problems he had either encouraged or initiated. The imperial resolutions were bloody but popular. He was a saviour who offered a secure alternative. At least if you were not a Martian or Jovian colonist."

Thomas poured another glass of tea. All of this was depressingly reminiscent of politics on Earth. "What happened next?"

"The people voted to dissolve the elected government and replace it with a life-term presidency. This was a popular move, and it was later followed by a referendum to choose between a presidential or imperial system. A glorious empire stretching across the solar system was the romantic choice and one which allowed the squabbling political parties to disappear. The people voted and democracy died. Most people wholeheartedly approved."

"I'd like to say that that was unbelievable," Thomas said, "but it's not. How long ago did this happen?"

"Forty years ago."

"How old is he?" Lucy asked.

"That's the strange thing. He's been forty something for the past forty years. Since the implementation of tags."

"He lies?" Lucy asked.

"Of course he lies, and he has access to the best medical technologies. If you have the money, you can extend your life. Also, he controls the media and influences how his subjects see him through the tags. There are rumours of black magic, too."

"So he uses science and superstition to get what he wants. How influential are these tags, really?" Thomas asked.

"They influence and suggest rather than control, but most of the time that gets him what he wants."

"Which is?" Thomas asked.

"Complete control seems important to him, but he's recently become more interested in Silva. But I don't think it's only about mineral deposits, not for him."

"How organized is the resistance to the Empire?" Thomas asked. He drained his glass of hot tea.

"We're small but organized. But we need to expand after what's just happened. I hope that both of you can attend our next meeting."

"The blockhead mentioned the House of Chance. What's that?"

"A lower house in our government. It's a house where all the members are randomly chosen from a list of all Silvans, and each serves for one year. I've been a no-header for six months. We're all equal in power; there's no head to the house."

"That sounds anarchic," Thomas said.

"That's its strength; the House of Blocks is more organized."

"And now they've closed it," Thomas said.

"Illegally. I must challenge the lord of the manor."

"Is that safe?" Lucy asked.

"No, but Scarlet's a poor district, and I don't think he'll find a lot of support there."

"What about us?" Lucy asked, meeting Thomas's eyes briefly. "You've mentioned that the Mariner said we should search for something, but you weren't very specific. What do we need to search for?"

"Keys," Aina said.

"To what?" Thomas asked.

"To your inner power." Thomas glanced at Lucy, who was nodding, but Aina was looking at him. "To your magic," she said.

Thomas shook his head; he couldn't accept this. "Aina, there is no magic."

"Haven't you noticed how you're less affected by the cold than other people?"

"The Mariner said our bodies would change a little when we came here," Thomas said.

"Yes, it's awoken your magic." Thomas grinned at her as her face grew more serious. "It's true, Thomas. I lived for years in the ancient forest, and I learnt to survive. I could never have survived in a place like that without it." Thomas wasn't really sure how to respond. He could see she was sincere and believed everything she was saying, even if it was obviously not true.

"And there's more I've not told you," Aina continued. "When we first met, the Mariner told me that I was about to play a part in an ancient prophecy. And he told me that you are a part of the prophecy, too."

Thomas laughed. "Ancient prophecies?" He was amazed by the advanced technology that had brought them to Prometheus, but believing in magic was too much—and possibly dangerous.

Lucy looked at him with annoyance. "What does the prophecy say?" she asked.

Aina rested her hands together on the table in front of her and was quiet for a few moments. Then she spoke. "When a darkness spreads across the stars, and when the shadow of a dark leader stretches throughout the nine planets, a force shall arise to counter the evil. From the stars, Bright Ones shall come and claim the keys and counter the darkness with fire."

"And you think we're these Bright Ones?" Lucy asked.

"The Mariner told me you were."

"With all respect to the Mariner," Thomas said, "this is

just an old story." He looked from Aina to Lucy, and he could see that they were losing patience with him, but he had to state the truth. "We must act on what's real."

"Why couldn't it be true?" Aina asked.

"How could someone centuries ago, or whenever it was, know what's about to happen now?"

"They might have caught glimpses of the future," Aina said. Lucy nodded her agreement. Thomas decided to let it pass.

"What do these keys do?" Lucy asked.

"As far as I know, they'll amplify your natural magic. There's a longer version of the prophecy that few know: "The Bright Ones shall descend to the inner sun, where their strength shall be tested and forged in fire. They shall raise the Fire of Prometheus, thereby raising the consciousness of all.""

"Nothing small then," Thomas said.

"No, it's very big," Aina said, apparently not noticing his sarcasm. "But first we must find and take the keys.

"Will it just be the three of us?" Lucy asked.

"I've been thinking about that. Our journey could be dangerous. I'd like a fourth companion," Aina said.

"The Mariner mentioned a fourth member," Lucy said.

"Do you have anyone in mind?" Thomas asked.

"I know someone. He lives on the outskirts of Rime, a few hours from here. He was my guide and teacher when I was young. I'd like to take him to the speech this afternoon. Then we can begin our search."

5

A few hours later they took the tram to the Old Manding Mine. "It's very different here," Thomas said. He rubbed his hand on a mossy wall. "It has a rural feel."

"Rime has many faces."

Old Manding Mine was deep beneath the surface of the planet, and the light was muted. They walked from the tram stop, and there was a stillness about the street. Grass grew from the derelict buildings; moss and lichen covered the walls.

"Orange lives here," Aina said, pointing down a desolate street.

"Orange?" Lucy asked.

"You'll understand when you meet him."

"Does anyone else live on this street?" Thomas asked.

Aina looked at the handful of boarded-up doors. "I've never seen anyone else here." They came to a doorway.

"There're no windows," Lucy said.

"Orange is a little strange, but he has a good heart. Mostly."

"Mostly?" Lucy repeated.

"I've known him since I was a child." Aina knocked, but there was no answer. She pushed the door hard, and it opened. They walked into a dark room.

"Is this okay? Just walking into someone's house," Lucy asked.

"He won't mind, and it's not really a house, more like a cave."

"You're right about that," Thomas said. He felt the stone walls as he walked in. The place had a natural, earthy feel to it. He looked at a stone statue. A creature he didn't recognize.

"He's a sculptor, amongst other things," Aina said. She walked to the fireplace and lit a fire, and then found some candles to add a little more light. Thomas felt as if he was stepping all the way back to the stone age. They looked around the bare room. There was a stone table and a few boulders that could serve as stools.

"It's a little bleak," Lucy said. "What type of person would live here?"

Aina smiled. "You'll see. He likes the simple life." Aina sat on the floor and closed her eyes.

"And we just wait?" Lucy asked.

Aina nodded. "Make yourselves at home." She smiled and fell asleep.

"So much for our guide," Thomas said. "Let's take a look around."

"Do you think we should?"

Thomas walked into the back. There were a few empty rooms that looked as if they hadn't been used in years. There were no windows. He returned to the front room.

Lucy looked up. "That was quick."

"There's nothing here. I don't think anyone lives here at

all; I'm not sure why we're waiting." Thomas rested his head on the table and closed his eyes. Soon he fell asleep, too.

It felt like minutes later when Lucy woke him up. "What?"

"Something's happening," she said.

Thomas sat up, his back straight. He looked over at Aina and saw she was still asleep. "Lucy?"

She pointed towards the kitchen and said, "There." He could see an orange glow where it should have been only darkness.

"Did anyone come in?" he asked.

"No."

"But you were asleep, too, right?"

"No, I couldn't sleep."

Thomas walked towards the light but quickly stepped back when a large figure appeared in the doorway.

"Oh, my God," Lucy said.

A giant stood in the doorway and stared down at them. He was over seven feet tall, and his head looked as if it had been carved out of rock. He had wild orange hair that reached his shoulders.

"Hello," Thomas said.

The giant man didn't speak.

Thomas backed up to Aina and shook her. She opened her eyes and yawned. "Hi, Orange. These are my new friends. Humans from another world."

"Does he speak?" Thomas asked.

"Sometimes." She smiled. "Orange, we need your help."

"I know," the giant said. "You bring the Bright Ones."

"He really is orange," Lucy said.

"A little. Orange hair is unusual in Nassopolis. You must have noticed people looking at your red hair. But don't mistake his silence for shyness," Aina said.

The man raised his thick eyebrows at her.

"Did you know we were here?" Thomas asked.

"He knew," Aina said.

"How?"

"He has a way of knowing," Aina said.

"I'm ready," Orange said.

They waited, but he didn't continue. Aina grinned and turned to Orange. "The cutters?" The man grunted. Orange, as Thomas soon found out, did not engage in light conversation. Aina walked to the stone wall at the back. "Orange."

He walked over and leant his large and hairy hands on the stone and pushed. A stone door, which had been hidden, slowly opened to reveal a chamber. Inside it were two large motorbikes.

"Cutters. They're like your Earth motorbikes, almost," Aina said. "The Red Bullet's mine, the Sunburst is Orange's." Aina sat on the red cutter. "Lucy?"

Lucy stared at the red bike for a few seconds, then climbed on behind Aina. Orange sat on the Sunburst and waited. His orange cutter was the larger of the two. "I guess this is my seat," Thomas said. He sat behind Orange. They rode through the living room and out of the open door. The engines roared, and they raced through the empty lanes of Manding Mines.

"It hovers!" Thomas shouted.

"They have some special features!" Aina shouted back.

An elevated highway snaked through Rime, and once they reached it, they rode the cutters hard; nothing overtook them. Thomas wondered if Rime had any speed limits. Half an hour later they turned off the highway and descended into Scarlet.

Aina's district of Sunna wasn't rich, but Scarlet was poor. Children played in the rusty metal streets, and homeless people lived in and around the derelict metal buildings. They rode slowly past Scarlet police station and then turned into a narrow alley that led to a square. "Scarlet Square and the House of Chance," Aina said. They parked the cutters.

Hundreds of people had gathered in the square. Orange waded through the crowd, and they followed in his wake. Some people nodded to Aina and many stared at Orange. They reached the front and faced the House of Chance. As Aina spoke to several people in the crowd, a line of grey-uniformed men with red stripes on their jackets emerged from the building.

"Company police," Aina said.

"And those?" Thomas pointed at several groups of police in blue.

"Local police. They still follow the lead of the Blocks, for now."

A man with light green skin and wearing a green cloak, surrounded by bodyguards and attendants, walked out of the building. He walked to a temporary podium that had been placed at the top of the steps.

"The so-called lord of the manor," Aina said.

"Why the green cloak? I thought they wore grey?" Thomas asked.

"The Mercantile Order."

"What?" Thomas asked.

"Bankers, investors, and traders," Aina said.

"Get out of Silva!" a man in the crowd shouted. Suddenly scores of grey-uniformed men rushed down the steps, forcing the crowd back.

Aina translated the speech into Silvan. It was only the second time Thomas had heard the imperial language being used in public in Rime.

"I'm Lord Somder, Lord of the Manor. I was appointed by Lord Own, First Lord of Uranus. From now on, I will administer the region of Silva on behalf of the Deep Space Trading Company."

Several people in the crowd jeered.

"I promise to protect you from danger, and I also promise to bring this isolated region of Uranus back into the heart of the Empire. Look at the city walls." Some people did glance at the rusty metal walls. "Why did the House of Chance do nothing to improve your conditions?" A handful of people in the crowd clapped.

"Company men," Aina said.

"The District of Scarlet has had many breaches in its walls. I promise to repair your city, but unlike your House of Chance, I will honour my pledges."

An explosion rocked the square.

Aina swore. The explosion created a hole in the outer wall of the city and temperature plummeted. "That was planned," Aina said. "He wants to demonstrate his power."

The people looked nervously at the hole in the wall, and they zipped up their jackets. The large pipes, which ran along the roof of the tunnel street, rattled loudly as they pumped warm air into the neighbourhood. Thomas knew that a team of beetle-sized robots would now be scuttling along the outside of the city wall. That'd been the topic of one of their Silvan lessons. The robots' job was to repair the hole by joining their bodies together, while a slightly larger beetle bot welded them into a single sheet of metal.

"Everything is under control," the lord of the manor continued. "You now have the opportunity to witness the efficiency of the company." He smiled to his staff.

"There's something out there," Lucy said.

"What do you mean?" Aina asked.

Thomas looked towards the hole, but he couldn't see anything, apart from some low shrubs that blew in the wind.

"Something's there," Lucy insisted. Aina looked at Thomas, who shrugged.

"She's right," Orange said.

Seconds later, a giant leopard strolled through the hole and snarled. The people stepped back. It stood as tall as a human.

"It's shimmering," Lucy said.

"A glimmer leopard," Aina said. "They're unusual, even on Prometheus."

"Don't be alarmed. My men will demonstrate company efficiency. I'll take this wild animal to my personal menagerie, where it'll no longer disturb the citizens of Rime."

Aina turned to Thomas and Lucy. "I need to do something. Don't follow me."

"What are you going to do?" Thomas asked.

"Talk to the leopard."

"Aina?" Thomas asked.

"I'll be all right, I hope. It's better if you wait in the crowd. I hope to do this before more police arrive. Be ready to leave fast." Orange nodded and wandered off into the crowd.

AINA WALKED towards the glimmer leopard. People in the crowd watched her. The leopard snarled, its ears pushed back flat against its head.

She stopped in front of the leopard and stood very still. She looked into its eyes, which were level with hers. Her mind touched the leopard's, and its eyes widened for a moment. Aina spoke the True Language of ideas and images, as she'd been taught as a child. Although it was not one of the intelligent species of Prometheus, it was an intelligent animal. It understood. Its ears slowly returned to a relaxed position. It watched her.

"Leave," she said, but the leopard was curious and looked around the crowd of humans. She warned again of its danger, more urgently. The creature turned back to the breach in the wall. Suddenly she sensed a change, and so did the leopard. It turned and growled lightly.

The lord had left his podium and, with his posse of police and protectors, had forced his way through the crowd. Lord of the Manor Maun Somder and his posse stood at the front of the crowd. She was badly outnumbered. Her pistol would be of little use against so many armed men and police bots.

Somder beckoned a local police sergeant, spoke a few words, and pointed at her and the leopard. He then turned away, touched his ear, and spoke on his phone.

A cold breeze blew against her as she watched the sergeant walk towards her. "Move away! The animal is the property of the company."

The glimmer leopard walked up to her and touched its nose against her shoulder. She rubbed its neck and felt its warmth. *"Come,"* she said. She wanted to get the leopard out before the tiny repair bots finished their job.

"Stop!" the sergeant shouted. She heard weapons click, and she stopped.

"Sergeant," she said loud enough for the crowd to hear.

"I'm Aina Kay, a member of the House of Chance. I'm taking a lost cat home." The sergeant hesitated.

Lord Somder glanced at the sergeant and her in annoyance but continued his telephone conversation.

"Sergeant, you don't have the authority to prevent a member of the House of Chance from performing a public service."

Finally the aristocrat interrupted his call. "Tranquilize the cat, but I want it unharmed. It'll join my menagerie." When the local police officers didn't move, Maun Somder shook his head. "The Silvan police force is not up to the job." He nodded to his men. The company police exchanged grins and pushed past their local colleagues.

They walked past Aina as if she weren't there and raised tranquilizer rifles. They'd come prepared. He must be waiting for events like this to stock his zoo, she thought. Aina touched the glimmer leopard's mind again. She showed it the men's intentions. She didn't need to do more for the intelligent creature. Its dagger claws scalped the nearest man before he saw it move. Aina kicked the tranquilizer gun from the other man's hands.

"How dare you!" Maun Somder said. "I'm the lord of the manor."

"Silva has no lord of the manor." The leopard positioned itself between her and the police and snarled at the shocked and bloody man as he picked up the top of his scalp, and with his colleague's help, stumbled back to his comrades. She picked up the tranquilizer rifle and looked at the leopard. "Shall I?" she asked.

"Tranquilize the cat," Somder said, uncertainly. She shot the man whose tranquilizer gun she held. He collapsed into the arms of a colleague. "I told you to tranquilize the cat, not the man!"

"I shot the pussy." Laughter came from the crowd, and even a couple of the police grinned.

The lord's face darkened. "You shot an officer of the Deep Space Trading Company." Aina watched him but didn't reply. "Step away from the animal," Lord Somder ordered. His voice shook, and Aina could tell that not being obeyed was a new experience for him.

"The police bots, sir," the company sergeant suggested.

"Good idea." The two blue police bots were circling over the crowd. At the sergeant's command, one of them flew towards the leopard.

"Sedate that woman, too, Sergeant."

"Yes, sir."

The blue police bot stopped four or five feet from her face. A long needle appeared from its bullet-shaped body. Aina kept very still and concentrated. Her ability to connect with minds didn't only work on animals. With the robotic computer mind, she was never sure if she was communicating or if she was simply flipping switches inside them. As long as it worked, she didn't care.

She breathed deeply and tried to ignore the needle moving towards her. Part of her mind left her body and then she saw herself through the bot's camera eyes. She was inside. It was a cold, dark place. Electricity flowed through circuits controlled by switches. She wasn't sure what she was doing; she just began to flip the miniature switches in its computer brain. The bot quivered slightly in the air and then shuddered more violently. Many of those in the crowd exclaimed aloud in surprise. Aina had little knowledge of the topography of a bot's brain. She used her intuition instead. Something seemed to be happening, even if she wasn't fully in control of it. Just as long as it didn't go mad and stab her.

The bot dropped slightly in the air and flew towards her. She ducked. "A rogue bot!" the sergeant shouted.

"Disable it!" the lord shouted.

"I can't, sir. Something has taken control of it."

"That's impossible."

She wished it to turn and point at the police. And it did. I got that bit right, anyway, she thought. Now, where does it control its weapons? Blue bots were only armed with stun guns and tranquilizer needles, but they should be more than enough.

Aina aimed at the police who were already pointing their weapons at her bot. It flew towards them with its tranquilizer needle flexing in the air. They shot at it, but she managed to hit one of the officers before the robot crashed to the ground. She pulled her mind from it just before it died. Coming out of its computer brain hurt. She rubbed her head. Next time pull out faster, she thought to herself.

"I've never seen anything like that, sir," the company sergeant said. "It must've been a faulty one."

"What about the other bot?" a company man suggested.

"Yes, use that to stun her. They can't all be faulty," Somder said.

The crowd stared at the scene in fascination. A popular member of the House of Chance was standing up to the Empire. Aina knew this would embarrass the company, but she couldn't help herself. She wanted an incident in Rime that would be talked about for years; however, she didn't expect the next event.

THOMAS WATCHED Aina's confrontation in amazement. The more he knew her, the more he liked her. She was brash and compulsive, but her courage and determination to defend what she believed in, as well as her love of the natural world, impressed him. The remaining bot flew low over the crowd towards them. He turned towards Orange and said, "I wish I had a gun. I'd shoot that bot."

The giant grinned, and as the robot flew over him, he leapt into the air and caught it as if he were playing basketball. He threw the robot to the ground and stamped on it with his heavy metal boots. The whole crowd looked up at the wild orange-haired man in awe. Then they stared down at the injured robot. It bobbed up and down like an injured insect; white fluid leaked from its body. Orange raised his hands and the crowd parted. He ran at the injured bot and kicked it at the waiting police lighter. The police moved back, but it clipped one of the men on his head, and he went down.

"You certainly have style." Thomas grinned, looking at the robot's twisted body as it lay motionless apart from an occasional twitch. The grin fell from his face as he noticed Aina standing alone in front of the police. He had to help her. Pushing through the crowd, he found the Sunburst where Orange had left it.

Thomas mounted the orange cutter and rode slowly through the crowd. He heard Aina's voice clearly above the din. She'd switched from the imperial language to Silvan.

"Maun Somder, so-called lord of the manor." The man looked at her. "Silva belongs to Silvans." There was a cheer from the crowd. "We'll resist the Empire and its company." The cheers for Aina became stronger.

Thomas saw the confusion on Lord Somder's face and realized that neither Somder nor his men could understand Silvan. The crowd became more excited and the insults stronger. Thomas recognized a few that Old Morris had taught him. When the speech turned to Dnassian, Thomas stopped the cutter and found a boy to translate for him.

Lord Somder glared at Aina. "Can't this peasant speak a real language?"

The sergeant looked nervously at the crowd. "Sir, perhaps it would be better not to upset the crowd. The police reinforcements are having problems getting through."

He can't see his danger, Thomas thought.

The lord ignored the sergeant. "Learn to speak a proper language, not this jabber!" he shouted at the crowd. More people shouted at him; someone threw a bottle.

Aina pointed at the lord. "I give you warning. Leave your manor. I revoke your right to reside in Silva," Aina said in perfect Dnassian. Loud cheers came from the crowd. Thomas rode forward again, and the boy ran by his side.

"By what right do you challenge the company?" the lord of the manor shouted.

"As Member Aina Kay of the House of Chance. The rightful government of Silva."

Somder's face turned a deeper shade of green. "This land is historically a part of the great Empire."

"Lies!" a woman called out from the crowd.

He turned to the crowd. "All of you will pay soon enough. There are changes coming."

"Company soldiers?" Aina asked.

"The Red . . ." A man in grey grasped his lord's arm and whispered something. Lord Somder managed to calm himself. He then ordered the sergeant to arrest her.

"I think we should wait for reinforcements, sir."

"I'm the lord of the manor. I was legitimately appointed in the name of His Imperial Majesty, Lord of the Nine Planets, Myriad Asteroids and Planetoids of the Solar System. I command you."

Does he know where he is? Thomas wondered. He accelerated the cutter. The boy still ran by his side, shouting translations into Silvan. Others in the crowd now ran with them, and farther away he saw the long orange hair of the giant as he ran, too.

"Silva doesn't welcome your company or your empire," Aina said loud enough for all to hear.

"Now!" Thomas shouted. He twisted the throttle, and the cutter roared. He broke through the line of police, and behind him the crowd surged. Thomas found himself at the head of a charging brigade of Silvans.

Thomas pressed the red button and the rear rockets fired just as Lord Somder took out his gun and aimed at Aina. The Sunburst took off and hit Somder, knocking him to the ground.

"Thomas!" Aina shouted. He wasn't in complete control of the machine. "To the hole in the wall!" she shouted. He had no choice as he had no idea how to turn off the booster. He flew straight at the wall. "The blue button!" she yelled. The cutter slowed. Aina ran to him, the glimmer leopard close at her heels.

"The hole's closed," he said.

"Not quite," Aina replied. She shot the wall and kicked out a plate made from the welded bodies of the tiny bots that had given their lives to protect Rime. "Sorry about that," she said to the wall. Aina jumped out into the frigid exterior, and the glimmer leopard followed her. The big cat nuzzled her and then ran into the mist.

Thomas accelerated through the narrow hole, sending a second shower of tiny worker bots into the air. He grinned. "Get on! I'll take you for a ride!"

Aina squeezed his arm as she climbed on the cutter and gave him a quick kiss on his cheek. "You did well. Thank you." She held him tight and then cried out in joy when the Sunburst's rockets fired and they flew up the misty mountain.

6

Lucy crouched in the corner of a large cage in Scarlet Station. She'd watched the incident in Rime from within the crowd. Thomas, Aina, and Orange had all surprised her, but it was the incident with the glimmer leopard and the robot that fascinated her. It was as if Aina had really spoken with the animal. When Aina had approached the leopard, Lucy had felt something. A cat's mind, perhaps.

When the police reinforcements had arrived, they'd arrested those too slow to escape, and Lucy'd been one of them. Now she was locked up. Nobody had told her what was happening, and she didn't want to draw attention to herself through her poor Silvan.

Her friends had had the strength to stand up and publicly challenge the lord of the manor. Lucy regretted her lack of courage. She'd put herself and her friends in danger. She'd been too scared to move and too easy to catch. She wondered if the Mariner made a mistake in choosing her.

Looking absently at the mixture of people milling around the cage, she concentrated on their hushed conversations. She heard the word "magic" used several times. She also understood many of the crude Silvan insults used to describe the company and the Empire.

The cage should have held about twenty people, but there were over sixty crowded inside. The metal benches were full, and the only space she had found was against the bars. She made sure she kept her body off the sticky floor. The strange mix of smells coming from it made her feel nauseous. She wondered what her friends were doing and whether they were thinking of her.

She kept her eyes downcast even though most of the people in the cage had been, like her, caught up in the disturbance. It was the others she was worried about. One of them gave her a very bad feeling. She could feel him staring at her.

In the corner of her eye, she saw him walk towards her. He stopped, and she looked down at his golden shoes and the chain tattooed around his ankle. He kicked a teenage boy next to her. Lucy flinched.

"Stand up!" He kicked him again. The boy stood, and the man pulled off his new jacket. When the boy protested, the man pushed him hard against the cage bars. She didn't understand why nobody would help.

"Leave him alone!" she said, still staring at the golden shoes.

"What?"

His voice had gotten closer, but Lucy couldn't look at him. It took all her strength to reply. "Leave him alone."

He stepped on her toes and tears came to her eyes. She immediately regretted having spoken. No one else was doing anything. Who did she think she was? She wished Aina was there.

"Look at me." He grabbed her wrists and pulled her

towards him. She stood up and held onto the jacket to avoid falling onto the sticky floor. Before she knew it, he slapped her, and a stinging pain flashed through her cheek. Lucy was scared, and when he shook her, she lashed out and kneed him in his groin.

He let her go as he doubled over. "You'll be sorry," he said, gasping for breath. She nodded automatically. She already regretted it.

A deep laugh came from the metal bench.

"What?" The young man turned around. A man of about fifty sat on the metal bench and watched them. "What's your problem, grandad?"

Outside the cage, the police carried on as usual and paid little attention to those inside, but within the cage, everybody watched the drama taking place.

The man pushed Lucy against the metal bars. She struggled to get away from him, but he held her tightly. The older man stood up and walked quickly towards them. When he grabbed the bully by his neck, Lucy noticed his large and calloused hands.

"Do you know who I am?" the young man asked.

The older man tossed him away with a look of disgust.

Lucy was surprised, but when she looked closer, she saw that the man was strong, without an inch of fat on him. She was sure he'd never held an office job. "Thank you," Lucy said.

"Sit with me," the man said. He indicated two spaces on the metal bench, one of which had just been vacated by the young man, and they sat. The bully picked himself up from the floor, took one look at the man, and slunk off to the far corner of the cage.

"You've got a knack for getting into trouble." Lucy had no idea how to respond to that. "Who're your friends?"

She was confused. What was he talking about? "Friends?"

"Aina Kay of the House of Chance. I saw you with her. Half of Rime knows her, but the other two? The orange giant and the knight who led the charge."

She looked more closely at this stranger who had saved her. The more she looked, the more she realized how fit he was. What exactly did he do? His dark brown face was lined, but his eyes were kind. She didn't sense any bad intentions, but how could she be sure? Although he'd helped her, she didn't know him, and there was no way she would discuss Aina, Thomas, and Orange with someone she couldn't trust.

He nodded. "You've got your reasons for not talking. I don't blame you."

"Who are you?" she asked.

"Petty Officer Samuel Hand, Imperial Navy." The man offered his hand. The shock Lucy felt must have shown on her face because he said, "I'm a sailor, not Imperial Security."

Nodding, even though she was still wary, she said, "Lucy Thomson," and accepted his hand. Her hand disappeared inside his huge, rough palm. "Why are you here?"

"A little trouble in Scarlet Square. My commanding officer is on his way to get me out, I hope."

"What will happen to us?" she asked.

"They'll ask some questions and then let us go. What can they do?"

"But?"

"But they may have a few more questions for you. You're not from Rime, are you?"

"No." She shook her head.

"Yet you speak Silvan. Few Nassopolitans can do that."

"Are you Silvan?"

Blue Prometheus

The man nodded. He spoke in another language. She couldn't understand a word. "Stranger and stranger," he said. "You don't understand the imperial language, do you?"

She considered this safe to say. "Not yet."

"Not yet, but someone is teaching you. Aina Kay, I'd bet. The no-head."

Lucy's brow furrowed in worry for her friends, but she still didn't feel comfortable speaking about them to a stranger, especially not someone connected to the Empire.

The man seemed to guess her thoughts. "A girl like that will survive, or at least she has a better chance than most; if she doesn't keep pushing it. Does she always take risks like those?"

"I think so. Is the Imperial Navy visiting Prometheus?"

"A naval flotilla is." Samuel hesitated briefly, and Lucy realized that this big man was a little nervous. He wasn't sure whether he could trust her, either—she tried to smile. "Tell your friend that the Red Legion's coming."

"Red Legion?"

"Mercenaries."

"Why are you telling me?" Lucy asked.

"I'm Silvan. I won't betray my country."

"You," a police officer said, pointing at Lucy.

Lucy stood automatically but stopped when she felt a hand on her arm. His eyes moved briefly to the officer, and he whispered, "Act simple," to her before nodding goodbye.

She left the cage and followed the officer. Following the sailor's advice would be easy. She must be simple, or she wouldn't have got arrested. The man took her arm and guided her across the crowded room, then along a long corridor with several heavy metal doors, all closed. At least one of these cells would be better than the communal cage, at least she thought so until she heard a woman crying from behind one of the doors. The man unlocked a door. When she didn't move, he pushed her inside and slammed the door shut.

The cell was old, and the walls had crumbled enough to leave a fine white dust around the edges of the floor. This part of Scarlet Station had been built into the mountain. Escape was impossible. She sat on one of the two chairs and looked at the legs of the small table, which were firmly attached to the floor. The door opened suddenly, making her jump. A police sergeant walked in. His skin was pale green, and he wore a grey jacket with red stripes on the sleeves. A company police officer.

He sat opposite her and spoke Dnassian. She was too nervous to tell him she didn't understand. Aina had told her that everybody learnt Dnassian at school. He barked an order, but this didn't help her understand either.

"I don't understand," she said weakly. The man slapped her. Tears came to her eyes.

He pointed a small device at Lucy's head and looked at the back of the machine. He appeared puzzled. He called on his earphone. Several seconds later, a police officer in blue entered the room.

"Who are you?" the man in blue asked in Silvan.

"My name's Lucy Thomson."

"Address?" She wasn't sure she should give Aina's address to these men. "What's your address?" the local police officer repeated. He stared at her. "Refusal to cooperate with the police is an offense."

Lucy noticed a red beetle on the wall. It was strange the details she noticed, she thought.

"Why won't you speak Dnassian?"

"I can't speak Dnassian," she said.

"But Silvan's not your native language," the man continued. Lucy realized that her situation was becoming worse. She tried to calm herself—then she noticed the red beetle on the wall again. She wondered how it had got into the cell deep under the mountain.

The sergeant asked her more questions, which the man translated, but her mind wandered. It became hard for her to even keep up with the rapid flow of Silvan. She was tired, and soon the words passed over her. She saw the small red insect on the side of the sergeant's metal chair. It'd moved. She wondered what it was doing there. Was it trapped like her?

She felt dizzy. It must be the lights; they were intense and hurt her eyes. She felt different. She saw the bare arm of the sergeant, but from another place. She felt sick. Then she saw a glimpse of herself, but she looked very different. Lucy wondered if they had drugged the water she'd been drinking or whether the stress of the past few hours had affected her. Her vision was strange. They must have drugged her. She felt angry for what they were doing to her. Nothing was making sense. She could hear the men asking her questions, but she could no longer understand anything they were saying. It was as if they were in another room. The men leant over her. One of them shook her hard. She watched her body slump back in the chair. When one of the men slapped her, she rushed at him.

She had no idea how, as she was still slumped in the chair. Her wings opened and she flew onto the man's ear. Then she bit deeply into his earlobe. He jumped in his seat and swatted his ear, but she was too fast. The sergeant frantically rubbed his ear. He stood up and looked around the room. As he sat down again, she landed on his collar and bit the back of his neck. He shouted and swatted his neck, but again she was too fast for him. She could see the lower part of his body, but he was upside down. She had no idea what was happening. It was as if she were under the table. The man left the cell in a hurry. He looked concerned.

Lucy woke up. She must have passed out. She still felt sick but was pleased that she now sat alone in the cell. Bending down, she looked under the table, trying to understand what had happened. The red insect was sitting on the leg of the table. Had it bitten the man? What had she just experienced? It was as if she'd somehow entered its mind. She remembered Aina and the leopard. And the blue bot. Was this the same? Had she really bitten the sergeant?

She looked under the table again. It was still there. She stood up unsteadily and walked around the table, and then she crouched down next to it. "Was I really inside your mind?" she whispered to the beetle. It didn't move, even when she put her face very close to it. "You're beautiful," she said.

She stood and walked to the door. The sergeant had left it ajar. She looked outside. The two men strode up the corridor, towards the cell. The company man held his ear. The other followed him, holding a net.

She slipped back inside the cell. As they entered the room, she noticed that his ear was swollen. Perhaps it was poisonous. "Where is it?" the man asked.

"What?" She thought he was going to hit her, and she stepped back.

"The red assassin bug."

"I don't know. I was sick; I've just woken up." He seemed to accept that. The two men searched the room and were slowly getting closer to the red insect. It must be dangerous for two serious-looking police officers to stop their interview like this.

"There it is, Sergeant." The blue-clad man pointed at

the table leg and stepped back. The sergeant came closer, and when Lucy didn't move quickly enough, he pushed her away. Still weak, she fell against the wall, hitting her head. She slumped to the floor, feeling disoriented. She also felt anger rising, and the room began to fade. The last thing she wanted was to lose consciousness with these men standing over her. She shook her head, but the dizziness became worse. Then she saw the net moving towards her. She ran around the table leg, flew into the air, and then turned and flew straight at the eyes of the sergeant. He screamed and ducked. She wanted to laugh but couldn't. She flew through the open door, and the men ran out after her. This time the sergeant slammed the door shut.

Lucy knew she was alone in the cell, but she was also inside the mind of the red assassin. She didn't know how this had happened, but she somehow knew that she'd have to stay calm to keep the connection. She breathed deeply and relaxed. The passage outside looked strange, but she was seeing it through bug eyes. She flew towards the light.

Seconds later, she was in the public area of Scarlet Station. She landed on a wall and watched the people below her. Petty Officer Hand was at the front of a line. He stood next to a tall green naval officer. There was something about that officer, something that interested her. They spoke to a desk sergeant. The officer passed an envelope to the desk sergeant and led Samuel away. She watched the naval officer walk to the entrance.

At that moment, the doors swung open, and Aina strode in. She glanced at the sailors as she passed them and then walked to the reception desk. Lucy felt so excited that she lost contact with the red insect and sat up with a start in her prison cell. "Damn," she whispered. She moved up against the wall and tried to go back into the insect's mind but couldn't. Perhaps it was too far away.

"I have to do this," she said aloud. She concentrated, and this time she felt the insect. She was inside the public area again. She immediately saw Aina arguing with the desk sergeant when a company police officer took hold of her.

Aina pulled away from him. Lucy flew at them, and the man jumped back in alarm. The perceptual ability of the insect was very different from that of a human, but she knew it was the man who'd slapped her.

Lucy landed on her friend's bare hand. Aina froze. She sensed, rather than saw, fear in her friend's eyes. "It's me," she tried to say. Aina later told her that the insect had made a mating call. That must have been the closest thing it could do to expressing friendship. Aina tried to shake her off. She flew around Aina, calling her name. Aina looked at the red insect strangely. She was sure Aina's mind brushed hers.

Lucy flew to the entrance to the corridor that led to her cell. Aina said something, but the sound was garbled. Lucy flew back onto Aina's hand, and when the company police officer attempted to come close, she buzzed and he stepped back again.

Aina spoke to the inspector, who had walked over to see what a member of the House of Chance wanted in his police station. The man nodded and led her along the corridor towards Lucy's cell. The company police officer followed, protesting to the inspector as they walked along the corridor. The inspector opened the cell door, and Lucy saw herself slumped on the floor, next to the wall.

Aina ran to Lucy and crouched next to her. Aina spoke rapidly. Despite her tiredness, Lucy flew the insect to the wall, where she left its mind and opened her eyes. Her friend then gave her a hand and helped her to stand.

"Lucy? Are you all right? What've they done to you?"

"I feel strange," Lucy said.

Aina glanced at the red insect on the wall. "I'm not surprised. The first time I did what I think you've just done, I felt strange for hours. Lucy, the Silvan police have agreed to release you. But we must go quickly before the company police manage to change their minds," she whispered.

Aina took Lucy's hand and led her to the door.

"Wait," Lucy said.

"What?"

Lucy picked up the red insect.

"Uh, Lucy. You know what that is, right?"

"A red insect."

"It's more than that. Show him." The company police officer jumped back in alarm when Lucy moved the assassin to his face.

"I went inside it, like you do, I think," Lucy whispered.

"What do you plan to do with it?"

"I'm going to let it go outside."

Nobody stopped them as they left Scarlet Station, though the company police officer followed them to the doors. "Wait," the man said. He drew his pistol. "You must come with me."

Lucy released the red assassin bug. It flew straight at the man, and he ducked to avoid the circling insect. Lucy and Aina ran down the rusty Scarlet street.

7

Candles flickered around the chamber hidden beneath the House of Chance. Apparently the old light switches had long since ceased to work. Thomas watched as a figure climbed onto the podium; he strained to see in the dim light. "Lucetta First," Aina whispered to him.

More candles were placed on the podium, throwing more light on the woman's face. Her dark, intense eyes, long black hair, and pale skin gave her a striking appearance. Aina had already told him that this woman was one of the richest and most powerful politicians in Silva and a member of the House of Blocks. Two bodyguards stood on each side of the podium. The crowded chamber quietened.

"Everyone here has sworn loyalty to the Resistance," she said, watching her audience. "As many of you know, the Resistance was formed three years ago, after receiving intelligence of the planned invasion of Silva from one of our top agents." Thomas now knew that it was Aina who had provided that information.

A murmur passed around the chamber, but one man

raised his hand. "Then why is there no sign of an invasion?" Many of the members began talking; Thomas heard one man hiss. "The closing of the House of Chance is illegal, yes. But I see no signs of invasion." Thomas identified the politicians and other important people in Silvan society—Aina had explained each of their positions and relative influence. Everyone was watching Elton Nor, the blockhead now speaking.

Thomas and Aina stood together; Lucy and Orange were nearby. Aina whispered comments in Thomas's ear; it was clear she didn't like Nor.

"Member First, I hope you've used blocking technology to suppress the transmission of information from this chamber to the Empire," Nor said.

"I have." She looked at him coldly.

"Then, may I ask, when is this planned invasion?"

"It's already started," Member First said. "One of our agents has reported on the forced displacement of whole villages in the mountains." She looked out at the mixed groups of members from both houses. "We need people to work in many roles: some of you here will have a passive role, listening and reporting what's happening around our country; a few of you may work as field agents; and one or two may help manage our organization."

Member First waved a man over to the front and stood down to allow him to speak. "Who's willing to take an active role against the enemy?" he asked.

A few members raised their hands, and he ushered them to the side of the chamber. Member First resumed her position on the podium.

"Who will help you manage the resistance?" Elton Nor rasped.

"Aina Kay," one man said.

"No, I must take my friends and leave Silva soon," Aina said.

It seemed as if the collected politicians of the two houses had just noticed Thomas, Lucy, and Orange.

"And who're these people you bring to our meeting?" Member Jackson asked. Aina had told him about this senior member of the Blocks. She'd hoped to bring him into the Resistance. "They're not members of either house."

"And how do we know we can trust them?" a woman asked.

"That's Member May of the Blocks," Aina leant closer and whispered in his ear.

"I've run checks on these people; they don't exist. Who could make that happen apart from Imperial Security?"

"Member May, you didn't find anything because there's nothing to find. That's a gift to the Resistance," Aina said.

"There's always something," Member May said.

"They're neither from Silva nor the Empire."

"As much as I regret to say it, almost nothing is outside of the Empire," Member First said.

Elton Nor pointed at Orange. "Where does he come from?"

"I'm from Prometheus," Orange said.

"Which is not what you said," Elton Nor jabbed his finger at Aina.

Aina stood facing Nor; Thomas wondered how far she'd push it this time. "I said he's neither from Silva nor the Empire. The country of Silva and the imperial colony are only a small part of this planet."

"Speak clearly," Nor said. "Everyone knows the rest of the planet's a frozen forest."

"There's a lot you don't know," Aina said.

"For example?"

"Many of the creatures of Prometheus possess magic."

"Magic? Aina, we're not children. There is no magic. Your friend's human, if a bit wild looking," Member First said.

Thomas glanced at Orange again. He was still sore from a sparring session with the giant. Magic would be a good excuse for being beaten, but his blows had felt real enough. He wondered if some of what Aina had said could be true, not the magical part, but perhaps he was from outside Silva or the Emperor's Isle. The human parts of the planet were less than one per cent of its total surface area. A lot could live out there.

"And the other two?" Member First asked.

Thomas answered. "We're from another plane of the universe."

She waved his answer away dismissively.

Aina took a breath and continued. "Many of us know the prophecy telling of the Bright Ones. I'm to be their guide, as Orange has been mine since Anlair murdered my father. He's protected me since I was twelve. I trust him completely."

This was the first Thomas had heard of the story. He seemed to learn new things about her every day. His life had been easy in comparison.

"A terrible incident. Anlair has a lot to answer for, and you were so young. I've always wondered at your great strength after such a tragic event," the woman said. "But this ancient prophecy? Nobody believes in that. It's a fairy tale. One to comfort you as a child," she said softly.

"I believe it," Aina said. Although Thomas had serious doubts about all of this, he did respect her sincerity, and her ability to stand up for what she believed.

"And for those of us who don't have time for fairy tales. What is this prophecy?" Member Jackson asked.

"When a darkness spreads across the stars, and when the shadow of a dark leader stretches throughout the nine planets, a force shall arise to counter the evil. Bright Ones shall descend from the stars and retake the objects of power, countering the darkness with fire," Aina said.

"And you believe this mumbo jumbo?" Member Jackson asked.

"Yes," Aina said. "There's more."

"No, that's enough." The man snorted in disbelief. "And what is this fire?"

"Magic to fight the magic of the Empire."

"Magic? Are you saying the Empire uses magic?" Elton Nor asked.

"Black magic."

Many of the assembled members looked at Aina in amazement. Some shook their heads. A murmur of unrest rumbled through them.

"I don't think the people of Prometheus believe in magic any more than the people of Earth," Thomas said quietly.

"Do you?" Lucy raised her eyebrows.

"There may be strange phenomena we don't understand, but there's always a scientific explanation. There has to be. Otherwise everything we know about the universe would be put into question. What we experienced with the Mariner must have an explanation, too," Thomas whispered.

"But what if it's a magical one?" Lucy asked.

Member First smiled condescendingly at Aina. "Sometimes, when people really want to believe something, it can appear true to them, even when it isn't." It sounded to Thomas as if she was speaking to a child and not to the intelligent and brave woman Aina was—even if she did believe in magic. "There are no magicians or magical beings. Those are old stories from the old times, when the first colonists on this planet were struggling to survive. The planet is dangerous, yes. There are many wild animals, and the conditions on Blue Prometheus, as you call it, are hostile to humans, which is why the colony has never expanded beyond the Silvan Mountains."

"That's not true," Aina said. "We've not expanded beyond the mountains because the intelligent species of the planet will not permit it."

Thomas noted that the other Silvans clearly didn't share her point of view.

Member First continued. "Let's move on. You're one of our best agents, but I'm not sure you're suited to a position of leadership in the Resistance. I believe in your loyalty, bravery, and honesty, but your judgement is in question.

"These stories of magic, prophecies, guides, and guides of guides are an example of what I mean," Member First said. "You've shown great courage, but if you keep talking like this, people will think you mad."

Thomas interrupted. "The Mariner, the alien being that brought us to this planet, had real power. It wasn't magic, but it was real. He brought us from another world, and he believed we had the power to do good."

Elton Nor's voice rasped. "As to this Mariner, if this being exists, why doesn't it show itself? Why doesn't it help? If it has great powers, it could prove a useful ally."

"He said he couldn't directly interfere in the matters of other species," Thomas said.

"But according to you, he already has."

"He spoke of the balance in the universe," Lucy said. "He said that a demon from beyond our universe had disturbed the balance, and because of this, he had the right to restore the equilibrium, but if he did more than that, it would open the way for the demon to react."

The politicians had stopped listening and were talking amongst themselves.

"I have something else to say," Lucy said loudly. "I was told to tell you the Red Legion is coming."

The entire chamber fell silent, all eyes on Lucy.

Thomas saw concern in many of the politicians' faces. He'd read some of the imperial history with interest, and he too was disturbed. This mercenary legion had been involved in several imperial invasions, and they had a reputation for extreme violence against civilian populations.

"How do you know?" Elton Nor finally asked.

As Lucy explained, Thomas wondered how unified the empire really was. It sounded as if parts of the navy may, one day, be persuaded to support a different regime.

When Lucy finished, Aina leaned forward. "Somder did threaten that we'd pay—that changes are coming. And then he said 'The red,' but was stopped by his security officer."

"Hardly proof," Member First said. "Why should we trust this sailor?"

"I don't know, but I liked him." Lucy shrugged. "I think I would trust him."

"You liked him?"

Thomas had some sympathy with Lucetta First's point of view, but, if nothing else, he trusted Lucy's judgement of character.

"I think he was a good man. He warned me and told me to tell you."

"He's a member of the Imperial Navy, and as such is suspect."

"He's Silvan," Lucy said.

"If he's Silvan, what's he doing working for the Empire?" Member First asked.

Aina waved her hand dismissively. "Jobs are scarce in Silva; he wouldn't be the first Silvan to work inside the Empire. It's what he said that's important, not how nice he is."

"I agree. I'm concerned with his motives for telling your, if I may say so, rather trusting friend, this news. He asked you to tell us. Isn't that suspicious?"

"He doesn't like the Empire. Well, not that much," Lucy said.

It was clear to Thomas that the assembled politicians didn't believe Lucy. Elton Nor had been especially hostile. He wasn't even listening anymore and was holding an animated conversation via his tag phone.

"What if it's true?" Thomas asked. "What if the Red Legion is coming to Silva?"

Silence met his question, and he took in the troubled faces around him. After a few moments, Member Jackson said, "Then we'd have a problem, but there's no sign of that being true. Let's deal with the problems we have and not go looking for new ones."

"If the Red Legion comes, we'll need to stop them. You understand that?" Aina asked.

"We understand very well, Member Kay," Member Jackson said. Other members nodded. "But we require proof before we can take action."

"Somder should have it on his computer. We'll find it," Aina said.

"How will you get this information? Imperial security systems are well protected. And that's quite apart from getting in and out of his manor in the first place," Member First said.

"I have my ways," Aina said. "Our discussions here are going nowhere. We'll leave now and send you any information we find."

Elton Nor shook his head. "You're not going anywhere. You and your orange company are under arrest." Nor raised his voice so all in the chamber could hear. "Treason is a capital offence!" The chamber doors opened and dozens of company soldiers marched in.

"What's the meaning of this, Nor?" Lucetta First asked.

The politician took a pistol from his pocket. "You're also under arrest for treason against the Empire. The region of Silva has its future within the Empire," Nor said.

Thomas was considering whether he could take Nor's gun when a man rushed at the blockhead, and Elton Nor shot him dead. Silence fell across the chamber.

"Sit on the floor, everyone!" Elton Nor shouted. More company soldiers entered the room. They lined the walls of the chamber and pointed their assault rifles at the politicians and others.

"This looks very bad," Thomas whispered. Aina looked at him, worry creasing her forehead.

The blockhead next to Nor took out a gun.

"So you're involved, too, Member May," Member First said.

"The Empire will win; it's inevitable. I'd rather be on the winning side."

"You'll pay for this," Member First said to Nor.

Nor grinned. "I have been paid. And very well."

Before he could continue his speech, Orange knocked the pistol from his hand, grabbed the man's head, and broke his neck. Thomas scooped up the pistol, and Member First's bodyguards drew their weapons.

Lucetta First turned to one of her bodyguards. "Now." The man nodded and pressed a button on a device he held.

Thomas looked up in surprise as the soldiers' weapons clattered to the floor. Most of the soldiers fell with them, as did Member May. The company soldiers looked around in confusion. Thomas shared that confusion.

"Pick them up," Member First said. Her bodyguards and the assembled politicians picked up the assault rifles. Thomas, Aina, and Orange helped themselves.

"You can't win," May said.

Member First laughed. "So you had yourself implanted with a tag, too."

"What just happened?" Thomas asked.

"I hacked into their tags. We've been trying to develop this technology for years. Now seemed a good time to test it."

"You knew about the soldiers?" Aina asked.

"I suspected Nor. He implanted himself with a tag, and I wanted to expose him today, but I didn't expect this."

"This technology could be very useful in our fight against the Empire," Aina said.

"Yes, we hope so. They'll develop ways to counter it, of course. But it's promising. Make sure no one moves," Member First said to one of her bodyguards. She turned to Aina. "The Orange Company has a certain ring to it." She gestured to a table at the side of the chamber. "We need to speak." They each took one of the battered old chairs. "Do you really think you can break into Somder's base?"

Aina nodded. "Yes, he'll be distracted by events here and probably won't have all his men with him."

"There are only the four of you." She glanced at Lucy. "And perhaps not all of you are suited for this sort of thing."

"We're a team, and we also have to search for the location of the keys," Aina said.

"Do you think it'll be shown on an imperial computer?" Lucy asked.

"Perhaps," Aina said. "At least we can look."

Thomas shook his head; he severely doubted it. "They're just ancient artefacts," He just couldn't bring himself to believe that some objects possessed magic, nor that the empire would care about recording their location.

"They're more than that," Aina said, raising an eyebrow at him.

"You really believe this prophecy stuff, don't you?" Member First said.

"Yes," Aina said shortly. Thomas knew her well enough to know that she was rapidly losing patience. "I didn't just live in the ancient forest. I was a part of it. I've seen things no other human has seen."

Member First nodded, and Thomas made a note to ask Aina what exactly she'd seen. But he was becoming more doubtful about the wisdom of following this prophecy. It seemed like a dangerous distraction from the fight against the Empire, which he was becoming drawn into. But the plan to discover more about the invasion was sound. "And we can destroy the lord's base while we're there," he said.

Member First nodded slowly. "Of course, that would be good." From the slight frown on the woman's face, Thomas suspected that she didn't rate their chances.

Aina touched Thomas's arm as she glanced at him and then to Lucy. "We need to make a journey." Then she turned to Lucetta First. "We'll be in contact."

They stood and left the room. As they walked away, they heard gunfire from the old chamber.

8

The Orange Company rode along an old stone road through the Silvan Mountains. Thomas sat behind Orange on the Sunburst and thought about what had happened in the old chamber. Then Orange turned off the road and accelerated towards the edge of the mountain.

"Orange!"

The Sunburst flew from the side of the mountain and dropped. The trees rushed towards them, and a swarm of fireflies flying over the forest hurtled back into the trees. Finally Orange fired the Sunburst's rockets and the cutter rose in the air. Thomas breathed a sigh of relief.

"Tell me if you're going to do that again." They glided low over the trees and landed in a clearing next to the Red Bullet.

"Very funny," he said to Aina.

"What?" she asked innocently.

"Flying off the edge of a mountain."

Aina's grin disappeared when Lucy half fell off the cutter and stumbled away into the trees. She sat down heavily on a moss-covered log.

"Will we be flying again?" she asked.

Aina shook her head. "No, the rest of the way is through the forest."

"Thank God," Lucy said.

Aina unlocked one of the panniers on the Sunburst. Inside was a small armoury, courtesy of the company soldiers.

Orange took an assault rifle, two pistols, and two knives. Thomas took one of each. He'd practiced target shooting in Rime, but he had no idea how he'd feel when the targets were live people. Lucy refused all offers of weapons.

"It feels different here," Lucy said.

"The forest has a presence of its own," Aina said. "It can be scary at times."

After a short rest, they continued their journey. Orange and Thomas changed places. As Thomas rode the Sunburst through the forest, Orange pointed out plants that were dangerous, including some explosive varieties. An hour later, Aina stopped her cutter and turned off her headlight. Thomas stopped next to her.

"Why did you stop?"

"Turn off your headlight," she said.

The forest was dark. "Is there danger?" Thomas asked as he switched off his light.

"Wait," Aina said.

Lights appeared around them. Plants glowed, some dimly, some brightly, in shades of pink, blue, green, red, and white. In the distance, there were dimmer violet lights. Bright red and orange insects flew between the exotic flowers, some of which grew from the surface of creamy green rocks.

Seeing the forest come alive around him reminded

Thomas why he'd chosen to study geology and the environment at university. He loved being outside and close to nature. Despite later feeling slightly jaded about his studies, he'd always felt compelled to protect the natural world. "It's beautiful, but why didn't it glow before?"

"We weren't far enough in, and it didn't trust us," Aina said.

He couldn't help but raise his eyebrows at her. The idea that plants had feelings was absurd. "How can plants trust us?"

But Lucy interrupted. "Look. A red assassin. It's like a red lantern."

Thomas followed her gaze to the insect crawling up a tree trunk. "So that's the insect you possessed?"

"Not possessed, more like entered with its permission, or, at least, it didn't seem to stop me."

He'd said it as a joke, but Lucy seemed serious. He realized again how far apart their worldview was.

"Lucy is starting to speak the True Language," Aina said.

"True Language?"

"The language of ideas, symbols, and images. Some call it telepathy, but at its highest levels, it's a complex and beautiful language. The Mariner spoke it."

He remembered his interaction with the Mariner very well. Even though he didn't believe in magic, it was possible that telepathy was real. At least the idea could be tested. "Can I learn it?"

"Maybe, but Lucy's natural. The incident in Scarlet Station showed that. Your talents are different. You should work on your strengths first."

Thomas tensed a little at the suggestion that he should even consider any of this New Age stuff, which was what he guessed she meant. "Which are?" he asked, because he was fairly sure she didn't mean any of his real talents.

Orange tossed a stone to Thomas. "You've got an affinity with the rocks, with the earth."

"That's why I studied geology." He looked down at the stone. "What am I supposed to do with this?"

"Feel it, throw it, listen to it."

That made no sense, but Orange's expression was serious. Thomas put it in his pocket. In his wildest dreams he could just imagine someone communicating with an animal. Perhaps Aina and Lucy had already done this—but to a rock?

According to Aina, the forest had accepted them. If the lights went out, it meant a stranger approached. Thomas was curious to observe what actually happened. They rode for another hour through the bright forest. Eventually it began to dim. Aina waved them to a halt.

A barbed wire perimeter fence lay just beyond the edge of the trees. On the other side of the wire was a village. Nobody was visible. There were a couple of dozen stone houses, two of which were larger than the others. "The manor and the menagerie," Aina whispered, pointing at the tallest buildings. "And speak quietly. The fence watches, listens, and can defend itself."

"And I suppose that Maun Somder will be able to see us, too?" Thomas asked.

"If the fence sees anything, it'll decide whether or not to alert him."

"What happened to the people of the village?" Lucy asked.

"The Deep Space Trading Company evicted them last month. They're now homeless in Rime."

They rode for a few more minutes before Aina pointed.

"There's the entrance." From the cover of the forest, they could see a large metal gate with pillars on either side and cameras watching the road. Beyond the gate, houses were built around a square.

"Are you sure the front gate is the best way?" Thomas asked. Aina nodded.

"I can't see any guards," Lucy said.

"The pillars are sentry robots; the type that can't move, apart from their arms. They have eyes, ears, heat sensors, artificial brains, guns, and arms."

"Arms?" The ugly metal pillars were straight.

"Hug the pillar and it'll hug you back. Try it."

"No, thanks."

"I plan to trick the sentinels to open the gates without telling the manor."

"Are you sure you can do that?" Lucy asked.

"Maybe."

"Aina?" Thomas said.

"We don't have many choices. If it works, I'll find a way into the manor and Orange will create a distraction." She pointed to the trees. "Thomas and Lucy, stay here and guard the cutters."

If Aina and Orange were entering, so was he. "I'm not staying here while you risk yourselves."

"We can create another distraction," Lucy said.

"Such as?" Aina asked.

"You say there's a menagerie?" Lucy said.

"Yes, in the old schoolhouse," Aina replied.

"We could free the animals," Lucy said. "Lots of animals wandering around would create a diversion."

"Some Promethean species are dangerous."

"We're going in," Thomas said.

Aina nodded, obviously unhappy. "Red means danger

with Promethean animals. Just make sure you're not inside the menagerie when they come looking. And I need some time, so don't release them too soon."

"Half an hour from now?"

"Fine."

"We meet there after it's done." Thomas pointed at a blue house in the square.

Aina nodded. "When I have the information we need, I'll bring them running back to the manor."

"How?"

Aina grinned. "You'll see." Then she turned to Lucy. "Come with me."

"Where?" Lucy asked.

"Into the gate's mind."

Thomas watched his two friends. Their eyes were open, but it was obvious their minds were elsewhere. He waited.

A motor hummed, and the gates opened.

"Ten seconds," Aina said. They sprinted through the open gates. Lucy only just reached the buildings before the gates closed behind them. Aina waved from the opposite side of the square and disappeared between the buildings.

Thomas and Lucy walked through the deserted alleys to the schoolhouse. It was built of stone and had high walls with few windows. The imperial flag, a silver crown surrounded by nine silver planets on a purple background, flew from a flagpole.

It was cold inside the school. Almost as cold as outside. Promethean animals were able to adjust the fire within, but they preferred low temperatures. In the entrance hall, there were cages stacked on top of each other. The larger ones stood alone. In one of the bigger cages, a family of blue spiders, each one with a body the size of a rat and with legs that could comfortably span a pillow, covered the body of a dead deer-like animal.

"Stiletto spiders," Thomas said.

"How do you know?"

"I researched some of the wildlife back in Rime. They're deadly."

"Look," said Lucy. A bright blue and red bird sat on an artificial branch. As it sang, blue sparks came from its beak.

Dozens of fire-spitting cockroaches scuttled around another enclosure. Thomas and Lucy walked through the old classrooms. A ball lay in a corner, next to a cage containing a solitary and sad-looking orange-faced primate. It looked like an orangutan, except it had bristles, and it was bigger. It moved away as they approached the cage.

"What have they done to you?" she asked. She tried to open the door to free it, but it was securely locked.

Thomas looked around for something to open the cages with. A minute later he came back with a stick-like device that he hoped was an electronic key. "I found this." Thomas tried it on the primate cage, but nothing happened. "It's no good."

The animal snatched the stick from him and swiped it over the top of the lock. The cage door swung open, and the orange creature ran out. Lucy walked up to it and held out her hand. It looked at her for a few seconds before it reached out and touched her. She took the key. "Let's open some more cages."

They walked through the old school freeing the animals, except for the most dangerous ones. Some cages were stacked on top of each other, and the highest were too high to reach. Lucy gave the key to the orange creature. She pointed at the captive birds above them. It climbed the cages and swung from one to another opening them. It only left the larger insects and snakes alone.

They walked back towards the closed entrance and leant against an empty cage. "We have about six minutes before we need to let the animals outside," Thomas said.

They watched the creatures mill around them.

"Do you miss Earth?" Lucy asked.

Thomas shook his head. "Not so much." He thought of Aina and his time in Silva. "Life's more exciting here. How about you?"

"I miss my family. I worry about what they would've thought after seeing me on the news and then after the ship disappeared."

Thomas imagined that it looked very bad, and he guessed the news reports on the following day would be filled with speculation. "One day we'll go back." Although he wasn't sure that was true.

"Do you think so?" she asked.

He noticed Lucy's quietness; worry lines had formed on her forehead. He hoped to lift her mood by a change of subject. He stood. "It's about time."

"I'll take them out." Lucy opened the door and walked outside. The animals and insects followed her. Once in the open, they flew or crawled away.

"Hopefully some of them will be seen by the wall," he said. They walked back into the old schoolhouse to check. The bristly orange ape followed them.

There was almost nothing left, apart from unpleasant or vicious-looking creatures: snakes, stiletto spiders, a swarm of large black flies, and a cage of creatures that Lucy refused to even go near. The red centipedes were several feet long and each the thickness of a man's leg. They slithered around each other forming a moving red carpet on the floor. It was impossible to count their numbers.

Lucy stroked the bristly ape. "I'll take him outside with us when we leave. He can go back to the forest." Lucy turned around and froze. "Thomas. We have a problem."

9

Four company soldiers pointed guns at them. "Who are you?" one asked.

Thomas slipped the key back into the hand of the orange ape. "Lucy, you know I don't believe in this stuff, but tell our friend to start opening the cages of the most dangerous creatures. Tell him these men will kill us."

"Silence," the soldier said.

The bristly ape stared at Lucy. "He's scared," she whispered. One of the men held a stick, and he walked towards the creature. It understood its danger and ran deeper into the schoolhouse.

"Hey!" the man shouted.

"It's just an animal. We can catch it later." The soldiers took their weapons. Lucy nodded to Thomas. Several seconds later, there was a loud buzzing.

A swarm of black flies, each one the size of a fist, flew through the school room. The soldiers ducked and tried to swat the insects, some of which tried to bite them. The flies then disappeared through the open door.

"The ape," a soldier said.

One of the soldiers walked into the classrooms to look for the orange creature. Seconds later he ran back into the room. "Death gloves!" The men fled from the building.

"Death gloves?" Thomas said. "I think we should see what our bristly friend has done." They walked to the classroom door. A writhing heap of hairy red centipedes rushed along the floor. The orange ape hung from a light fitting in the middle of the room. The red centipedes were leaping into the air in an attempt to bite the nervous creature. Then they saw Thomas and Lucy.

Thomas and Lucy ran back into the entrance hall, but the centipedes were faster and blocked the exit. They were cornered by the cage of spiders.

"The spiders," Lucy whispered.

Several long centipedes slid towards them. Thomas slid open the door and stepped back. The spiders immediately stopped feeding and rushed to the doorway of their cage. He quickly climbed onto the empty cage next to the spiders and pulled Lucy up after him. It wasn't high enough, but there was nowhere higher. He found a metal bar, a part of a broken cage, to use as a weapon.

The spiders ran from the cage, and the red centipedes attacked. The spiders fought hard, but they were badly outnumbered. A minute later the spiders were only body parts to be consumed. A number of dead centipedes were being devoured by their comrades, too. Several of the centipedes leapt into the air and caught a few of the large black flies that were still in the building. A red centipede reared up and looked at Thomas and Lucy. It bared a primitive set of teeth.

"Those things can climb," he said.

"I know, be quiet," Lucy whispered. The centipedes

calmed down, and one by one they lost interest in the two of them and crawled out of the old school.

Thomas tightened his grip on the metal bar, not quite trusting his eyes. "What happened?"

Lucy beamed up at him. "I think I can speak to animals."

Thomas was, at that moment, prepared to believe anything that would get rid of them. "I hope you told them to get lost."

"No, I sent them a message of love."

"You're joking?"

"No, they love to eat, and I sent them an image of their favourite food. It was the only thought I could think of that was strong enough to affect them. I think their brains and stomachs are closely connected."

Thomas still wasn't sure whether she was joking, but she didn't seem to be. "And their favourite food is?"

"The soldiers." There were shots and shouts from outside.

"Lucy, you're becoming like Aina."

"I had to do something, and that was all I could think of. I don't really want them to eat the soldiers, but I couldn't think of anything else."

"I wasn't criticizing it. It was a good idea. Anyway, it could have been something else that made them rush outside. We should leave now, in case they come back." Thomas found his pistol on the ground outside, but the rifle was gone.

A soldier screamed. "I think I know why they're called death gloves," Thomas said. A man lay on the ground and frantically shook his arm. The red centipede had opened its mouth and crawled up his arm. It fitted like a long glove. He called out for help, but his colleagues moved back. The centipede rippled, and with each vibration, the man shrieked. "It's eating him alive."

"Why doesn't he pull it off?" Lucy asked. Her face was pale.

"I don't think he can; it seems well attached." Three more of the creatures struggled for his legs. The two winners took a leg apiece, while the third tried to swallow his head. More centipedes moved along the street.

Thomas and Lucy crept into the narrow space between two buildings. It was an open gutter, but there was just enough room to move. The sound of automatic gunfire came from the street. "The diversion worked," Thomas said.

They moved as fast as they could, trying to avoid stepping in the dirty liquid that lay at the bottom. Once on the far side of the building, they re-entered the alleys of the deserted hamlet and ran to the blue house. When they reached the house, Lucy touched the ape and pointed. It hugged her, then ran to the fence, climbed over, and disappeared into the trees.

The back door was unlocked, and they walked into the kitchen. A cake, frosted with ice, was on a plate on the table. Three pieces had been cut and placed on small plates but were untouched. Lucy stopped in front of a picture of a young family hung on the wall.

"They must have left suddenly," she said.

They climbed the stairs to a small bedroom and stood by a window. "You can see the manor from here," he said.

"Thomas, that was my fault."

"What was your fault?"

"The death of the soldier. I killed him."

He turned towards her and saw she was trembling. He wrapped his arms around her. "We saw what happened. The death gloves killed him."

She shook her head. "But I put the idea in their heads."

"I don't think it would have made any difference. Once those things were wandering the streets by themselves, no type of telepathy could tell them what to do. You said yourself that their brains and stomachs were the same thing." An explosion shook the house. Flames came from the manor house. "Aina has a flair for the dramatic."

His earphone vibrated. "Where are you?" Aina shouted.

"At the meeting place."

"Is Orange with you?"

"No."

"He may be on his way. I have to go now. The lord of the manor's not happy." Thomas heard shots in the background—Aina swore. "They're coming. Be ready for anything." The line went dead.

Lucy and Thomas looked at each other. "I think we should go downstairs," he said.

The front door was ajar. It'd been closed when they'd passed through the room a minute earlier. Thomas took out his pistol just as a man walked through the door carrying a heavy bag. When he saw them, he started and backed away. Thomas had never shot a man, and he wasn't sure what to do. Aina would have just shot him, but he wasn't her.

But when Thomas did nothing, the man smirked. He began to whistle and placed the bag on the table and opened it. It was full of weapons. He picked out an assault rifle and then fell heavily against the wall, his smirk replaced by shock. Blood trickled from a hole in his chest. He fell to the floor, and Thomas lowered his pistol.

Thomas's legs felt weak when he looked down at the dead man. He'd just killed a man. Lucy touched his arm. "Thank you. You just saved our lives."

Shouts came from the street.

"Lucy, I know you don't want to, but maybe . . ."

She nodded and chose a large pistol from the open bag. They walked to the door.

Aina and Orange dashed from a nearby street, chased by Somder and five company soldiers. They stopped in front of the blue house. They were unarmed, apart from the large knife Orange carried.

Thomas aimed at the soldiers, but his friends were in the way.

"Where are the others?" Lord Somder asked.

"Freeing the wildlife," Aina said.

"You always have a smart answer, don't you?" Somder stepped closer towards her, and Thomas aimed his assault rifle. Then a soldier shouted and pointed at four death gloves crawling along the street.

"Shoot them!" Somder ordered his men.

When the soldiers opened fire on the red centipedes, Thomas stepped out into the small square and shot two of them in the back. He tried not to think of what he was doing. They would have killed Aina. The remaining three soldiers span round, but Orange had already reached them; he cut the nearest man's throat.

The last two men raised their weapons but backed up to the building behind them. The lord of the manor stepped towards Aina and drew his pistol, but Lucy pointed her gun at the man. The heavy pistol shook in her hands.

He sneered. "What are you going to do, love? That's not even a proper gun."

"Then it doesn't matter if I shoot you." She pulled the trigger and almost dropped the pistol as it kicked back. Maun Somder's eyes widened. Then he fell to the ground. Lucy rubbed her wrist and looked at the unmoving body. "Oh no," she said quietly.

The two remaining soldiers turned and ran into the building. One of them tossed a grenade behind him and flames came from the front room.

Aina walked up to Lucy. "That was wonderful." She hugged the surprised Lucy before turning to Thomas. "You, too." She squeezed his hands, and Thomas pulled her closer, but gunfire made them both start.

Orange was shooting a red centipede; he had a big grin on his face. The noise woke Maun Somder. He sat up slowly and scowled. Lucy looked at him and screamed.

Aina grinned. "You didn't kill him. That thing you're holding is a stun gun."

"Oh." Lucy looked down at the heavy gun. "I didn't know."

"It's enough to knock the halfwit out, though." Aina turned to the dazed aristocrat. "Serves you right for laughing at her."

"You'll pay for this." Somder sat on the ground and looked at them through reddened eyes.

"Perhaps, but not to you, nor to the Deep Space Trading Company. Your company doesn't run our country."

"This region is an investment of the Deep Space Trading Company, and we have the right to exploit all our resources, including human ones. We have the law on our side."

"You're not too bright for a lord of the manor, are you? We have the guns, not you. And talking about that." She raised her gun.

"You can't just kill him," Lucy said. Somder scowled as he attempted to stand up. Orange pushed him back to the ground.

"It's the best way. He'd kill us without hesitation." The lord seemed to have lost the use of his legs and was crawling towards the burning buildings.

"I know, it's just that . . ."

"We can't leave someone like this behind."

"Can't we arrest him?" Lucy asked. Thomas wasn't sure what to say. He agreed with Aina, but to kill a man in cold blood seemed very wrong.

Somder screamed and thrashed about on the ground. Red centipedes were crawling up his legs and one of his arms, and they swallowed him as they moved.

Aina lowered her gun. "That's where they got to."

"Shouldn't we help him?" Lucy asked.

"You mean put him out of his misery?"

"No, I don't know," Lucy said.

Thomas watched the conflicting emotions on Lucy's face. "We can't take him with us. Perhaps it's better this way." Although he didn't like the idea of killing the man, saving him from the centipedes made no sense either.

"His pets need to feed," Aina said, a little too gleefully. The sight before him was disturbing, although neither Aina nor Orange seemed particularly bothered.

Once the creatures had moved into position on his legs and arm, their big red eyelids closed, Somder screamed a very long scream. It was too much for Thomas. He walked around the man, took his free arm, and pulled him towards the burning building.

"Good idea," Aina said.

"Be careful!" Lucy said.

"Don't worry," Aina said. "Once they begin to digest a victim, almost nothing can pull them off."

Thomas dragged the man as close as he could to the flames. The lord was now wriggling less vigorously. Thomas was wondering how to throw the man onto the fire when Orange walked up, grasped the man's waist, and tossed him onto the flames. The lord of the manor and the three red centipedes immediately caught fire. His eyes were already glazed over, and he did no more than flinch when the flames licked around his body. The death gloves stared at Thomas and tried to free themselves, but it was too late for them.

"He was still alive," Lucy said.

"Not for much longer, and I didn't want to leave any red centipedes wandering about," Thomas said.

Aina nodded in approval. "They breed fast; it was the best thing to do. They would never have voluntarily come off anyway." As they walked to the open gates, Aina continued. "I found what I wanted, and it's bad. The Red Legion has been hired by the Deep Space Trading Company. They'll be here in six days. Your sailor friend was telling the truth," she said to Lucy. "Thirteen thousand of them, and that's just the beginning.

"I spoke to Lucetta First." Thomas, Orange, and Lucy listened carefully as Aina outlined First's plan to stop the Red Legion."

Lucy's mouth opened wide. "You want us to destroy a flotilla of ships and kill all of those people?"

Aina's face was hard. "We must protect Silva—do you know what those types of people will do?" Thomas agreed with Aina, but the plan chilled him slightly, too. "Lucetta First will meet us at the spaceport with her team." Aina was quiet and her forehead creased again. "I've got more bad news."

"What?" Thomas asked as Lucy glanced up with concern.

"I found the keys, but they're on 28th."

Thomas studied Aina's face—he was getting more used to her emotions, and he watched her eyebrows pull together. "Where's 28th?" Thomas asked. He felt his stomach sink as he anticipated something difficult.

"How good's your geography?"

Thomas shrugged. "I watched a video of Nassopolis when I learnt Silvan. It's built in and on a mountain: the top is for the elite—all things imperial; the Hanging Cities hang from outside of the mountain; and the poor tunnelled inside—in the Inner Cities."

"Something like that." She pursed her lips. "But the video didn't show it all."

"What did it miss?" Thomas asked.

"There's a stack of twenty-eight cities underneath the mountain—the so-called New Cities—28th is the deepest."

"What's that so bad about that?" Thomas asked.

"It's home to the second largest imperial security base and a very unpleasant prison. The keys are in the base."

"Why there?" he asked.

She shrugged and looked away. "I don't know." He seldom saw her overwhelmed, but she looked it now.

"Attacking the Spaceport is enough to think about for now," Orange said.

Thomas wondered not only if it was worth risking their lives to take things with no more than superstitious value, but also if taking the keys was even possible at all.

"There's one other thing," Aina said.

"What?" Thomas asked. As if all of this wasn't enough.

"Anlair arrives on Prometheus in hours. He'd planned to meet Somder here tonight. He may be able to track us—he can smell traces of magic, and Orange and I used some." She frowned. "Thomas! Just accept it!" He realized his brows had been furrowed, but this belief in magic was becoming dangerous. She shook her head and continued. "If we get far enough away, it'll be hard for him to follow us—traces of magic fade quite quickly, and if we don't use any more magic while we're close, he'll lose us."

"We must go," Orange said.

They mounted their cutters and rode hard through the rain that was just beginning. They only stopped when they neared the edge of the forest, much farther down the mountain.

Aina stopped her cutter, and Orange pulled up next to her. They were on the edge of a wooded area at the top of an escarpment looking over a valley. "We need to go east to the airport at Stonehaven." She pointed across the valley. "From there we can fly to Nassopolis, and then travel on to the spaceport where we're meeting Lucetta First. But it's late. Tonight we should camp here."

After they'd set up their tents amongst the trees, Thomas spoke to Aina about the events since he'd arrived. She was more worried than she'd admit. He took her hand and they walked to the cliff. "Can we really stop the invasion?" Thomas asked.

"We can delay it. I'm sure of that. But stopping it is more than I can do." She moved closer as they walked. "But if you and Lucy get the keys, then who knows." She grinned. "The Red Legion are loyal to money, and Anlair's the paymaster, so killing him would be a good start."

"Who will kill him?" Thomas asked.

Aina smiled coldly.

They stopped near the edge of the cliff and watched the orange glow from the burning manor in the distance for several seconds. Then Thomas turned to her and touched her arms. "It's too dangerous." Aina was strong and driven, but even with her skills, he couldn't see how she could defeat this man. "You've told me how dangerous he is."

She stepped back and looked up at Thomas. "He murdered my father, and if he has the chance, he'll murder many more Silvans." Thomas nodded. He understood, but he just couldn't feel good about her putting herself at risk like this. "And I'm dangerous, too."

He grinned. "I know. Very dangerous."

They sat together close to the edge of the cliff. "Do you miss your home?" she asked. "You hardly ever talk about it; Lucy's told me much more."

"Not so much, really. I didn't have a lot to leave behind."

She moved closer, and he felt her warmth against his side. "Are you scared of the danger?"

Thomas smiled. "Of course, but I'm getting used to it."

"Your guide will protect you."

He laughed and put his arm around her, and she curled into his side. He could feel the heat coming from her body. He'd heard Lucy talk about Aina's natural magic, and how it kept her warm. Although he found that hard to believe, he couldn't deny that she was warm and relaxed. "You really are hot."

She laughed. "I know."

She moved closer, and he kissed her. A cold wind blew from the plains below them. He shivered, despite her closeness. "Let's go back to the tent."

Aina grinned. "My magic will keep you warm."

He knew she was playing with him. "Show me, and I'll believe."

"A deal," she said, taking his hand and leading him to her tent.

10

Four hours later, Lucy woke up. It was still dark, and she wanted to disappear inside her warm sleeping bag, but she knew soldiers would hunt them, and it scared her. She unzipped her bag and got up. Thomas and Aina emerged from the tent opposite several minutes later, looking tired. They loaded the cutter in silence. She was pleased they were together, but Aina's thin clothes puzzled her.

"Aren't you cold?"

"No, I have magical protection. I can teach you to do the same."

Aina had shown Lucy some basic magical training methods: meditations, visualizations, and breathing techniques, but nothing had happened. She'd told her it was a matter of more time practicing. Aina took Lucy's hand and put it on her arm, which gave out a lot of heat. "You're hot."

Aina grinned. "It's a type of natural magic. Most people have a tiny amount but never develop it." Aina left her and joined Thomas, who was loading the cutters.

Minutes later Aina called her over. She mounted the

back of the Red Bullet, and they rode through the widely spaced trees, the Sunburst cruising next to her. The forest ended, and this time she was ready for the drop as they flew over the escarpment and down into the featureless stony valley below. Lucy was cold, despite numerous attempts at the trick Aina had tried to teach her, and she was too tired to feel fear at Aina's high-speed flight, but the thought of their faceless enemy left her feeling anxious.

The distant sun slowly rose above the horizon, and soon the moons would rise, casting more light across the valley. Lucy preferred the bright forests to this bleak place. Here she felt exposed and vulnerable, although they moved at such a speed that she wasn't sure anyone would be able to see them clearly. The lights of Stonehaven eventually appeared ahead, but they turned away from the lights and rode directly to the airport.

They were amongst the first passengers to arrive at the airport. Lucy looked at the list of three early morning flights.

"Blue Orchid's the best option," Aina said. "It's one of the Hanging Cities of Nassopolis."

"What do they hang from?" Lucy asked.

"From the side of the mountain."

"If Anlair tracks us here, he'll know that Blue Orchid was one of our possible destinations," Thomas said.

"I know, but we don't have much choice. We do have some advantages," Aina said.

"Such as?" Thomas asked.

"Put on these earrings."

"I don't wear earrings."

"They've got tags and blockers inside. I took a packet from the manor. New identities. Look." She bent the metal, and a tiny chip flipped out. "The tag's inside the chip." She clicked it back in place. "When you're scanned, you'll have a new identity. The Empire is over-reliant on technology; we can use this to our advantage. They'll scan us and assume we're imperial subjects. Put them on."

Lucy took one of the earrings. It was more like a simple metal clasp. She attached it to her ear.

"Why would he have so many tags in the first place?" Thomas asked.

"They were intended for Silvan babies. I've created new identities. They'll have to reorder; the rest were burnt in the fire."

Half an hour later they boarded the first flight of the day. The old plane seated about eighteen people but was less than half full. It was noisy and cold, and Lucy pulled her jacket around her. Thomas and Aina quickly fell asleep while Lucy continued to stare into the clouds until her eyelids began to droop.

Three hours later, Thomas shook her awake. She was still tired and didn't want to open her eyes. "What?"

"Look."

She looked down at the mountain city beneath them. Blue Orchid burst from the side of the mountain like an exotic blue and silver flower. Hundreds of fibre rods extended from a bright blue dome on the rocky face of the mountain, and each one was alight. At the end of each rod was a crystal pod, and each pod had another hundred fibre rods sticking out of it. Within each bright pod were hundreds of lights.

"What are those lights?" Lucy asked.

"The homes of hundreds of Nassopolitans," Aina said.

The rods swayed like slender glassy stems in the strong Promethean winds. The hollow spaces within the tubular rods served as roads, connecting the many districts of Blue Orchid to each other, and to other parts of the great imperial megalopolis. Small insect-like craft moved untiringly from pod to pod, and their aircraft joined these vessels and slowly settled on top of a platform on one of the larger pods.

"It's beautiful," Lucy said.

They left the plane with the other passengers and soon reached the security check. A group of imperial police waited and watched.

"That doesn't look good," Lucy said.

"We have the false tags," Aina said. "They won't recognize us."

"What about our faces? Won't they recognize those? Especially yours. A member of the House of Chance," Thomas said.

"There're blockers in the earrings as well. They'll stop the automatic face recognition technology from working."

"But won't they recognize us? I mean the people, not just the technology," Thomas said.

"They're Nassopolitans. For them, Silva's a remote backwater. And remember their over-reliance on technology. They'll be reading our tags and looking at the data displays projected into their visual cortexes, not at our real faces. I hope." Aina glanced at Orange.

"I know," he said and disappeared into the crowd.

"Where's he going?" Lucy asked.

"He has his own way." Aina wouldn't say any more.

They walked towards the entrance. Lucy prayed they wouldn't be discovered. They nodded at the man, who stared blankly at them.

Lucy watched his eyes move from side to side. Aina was right; he was reading some mental display. He was about to ask a question when something clicked behind him. The man became distracted, and Aina tugged her arm. The three of them walked away and didn't look back.

"What happened? And what was that sound?" Lucy asked.

"A simple trick, just to be sure," Aina said.

"Trick?" Lucy asked.

"Making things click is elementary magic, and it took his attention away. He was weak minded, too much reliance on technology." Aina flashed them a grin.

"I've no idea what you're talking about," Thomas said, raising an eyebrow.

"I know," Aina replied, touching his arm. "But I hope you'll learn." Lucy noticed a slight change in the way Aina looked at Thomas—a softening in her glance.

They left the arrivals hall and walked out into Blue Orchid. The interior of the city was almost as attractive as the exterior. And unlike Rime, there was a real sky. Or at least there was a glass bubble that looked up into the real sky. It was a city of coloured glass and metal, and it had a relaxed feel. Their guide seemed to know where she was going. She cut into a narrow alley that led through a series of alleys. Several minutes later they reached a square.

"Did you know the alley led here?" Lucy asked.

"A lucky guess," Aina replied.

Lucy wondered whether Aina had studied maps of the city. She was secretly very studious sometimes. One of her hidden strengths.

The square, and the streets around it, had many hotels, from the plush Grand Commercial to a series of places that looked like fleapits.

Aina chose one of the latter. "Perfect," she said.

"Are you sure?" Lucy asked. "It looks derelict." A rat ran out of the entrance.

"At least we won't go short of food," Thomas said, watching the rat burrowing into a pile of refuse.

"We should avoid anywhere the Nassopolitan aristocracy may stay," Aina said.

As they walked in, they clicked new tags into their earrings. Lucy wondered about the new fake identities Aina had programmed in, and she hoped she would never be asked about it. Aina seemed confident that no one would ever do that.

A giant figure appeared in the doorway, and Lucy almost screamed.

"Orange," she said.

He grinned and nodded at her. Lucy was glad he was on their side.

The lift was old and dirty, and Lucy thought it very unlikely that they would ever meet an aristocrat in a place like this. Hotel Puck was cheap and hidden from view on the seventieth floor. The hotel would be invisible from the street. Aina insisted on them taking rooms on the top floor, just beneath the outer skin of the pod.

The owner of Hotel Puck was either naturally cheerful or short of guests, and Lucy only half listened as he expounded the virtues of Blue Orchid. Thomas interrupted and ordered a pot of red tea. Once it arrived, they spoke together.

"Do you think Anlair will know we're here?" Lucy asked.

"He knows we may be in Blue Orchid," Aina said.

"The Empire may be searching for us, too," Thomas said.

Aina sighed slightly. "Unfortunately, what Anlair knows, the company knows, and what the company knows, the Empire probably knows. They're all part of the same system."

Lucy just knew they'd look in Blue Orchid first—it was the obvious place to begin. "Will Anlair hunt us himself?"

"He might order the company police or Imperial Security to investigate. But..."

"But you think he might hunt us himself?" Lucy asked. "And with magic?"

"I think I've really upset him this time," Aina said. She had a smug expression on her face.

"You're good at that," Thomas said. She flashed him a quick grin but then became more serious. "He has unpleasant teams of killers who work for him. Maybe we should lay low for a few days. I could do with a rest."

"I feel tired, too," Lucy said.

They agreed to remain for two days and then go deeper into the mountain city. Thomas and Aina went to their room, and Orange wandered off to explore.

Lucy closed the door and sat alone in her room. Dreams had disturbed her sleep on the aeroplane, and she decided to take a nap. She undressed and snuggled into her comfortable bed; seconds later she was fast asleep.

The dream came immediately. She saw herself curled up on the bed below. A silver thread extended from her sleeping body to where she floated in the air. She'd never experienced a dream so strange or vivid. Then the room disappeared.

She moved over a narrow bridge that stretched towards a snowy peak, and from that peak a black obsidian tower rose. She shivered as she was drawn towards it—the dark tower gave her a sense of foreboding.

As she passed beneath an arched entrance, men looked straight through her, as if she wasn't there. Then she was alone in a room high in the tower. It was dark, apart from a crystal cabinet in the centre, which shone brightly. She looked inside and felt a shock of recognition. A golden cup was inside, and next to it was a silver pentacle; she'd found the keys.

Lucy shivered; the room had become very cold. Something was wrong. She had an overwhelming feeling of the presence of evil. Her breathing became heavy, and she could hardly move her body. A shape moved in the corner.

A burnt green head with gnashing teeth floated towards her. It watched her with cold, intelligent eyes. Despite the cold, she was sweating heavily; she knew this was not a dream. A part of herself had somehow travelled to another place. If the silver cord attaching her to her body snapped, she would die.

When the floating head was halfway across the room, she heard a voice within her. *"Take what is yours."* It was not the head speaking, nor did the head appear to have heard it.

"Take what is mine?" Lucy leant heavily on the cabinet and felt it change and give way, as if she were pushing her hand through a thick, viscous liquid. She touched the cup; she knew it was hers. It was warm and pulsed with energy. Golden light poured from it and covered her hands and arms. She looked down; her body was glowing.

The head hesitated, stopping inches from her face. It then bobbed up and down and snapped at her. Its foul breath was sickening. She noticed something trailing behind it, a thin grey trace of insubstantial mist. The head jerked forward, and Lucy raised her hands. Bright light came from them, and the apparition screamed and shrank into a tiny pinhead, which then shrivelled up along its wispy cord and vanished.

Lucy woke up with a start. Her heart was beating so hard that she was scared that she might be having a heart attack. Sweat covered her body, and her bedclothes were soaked. She rolled out of bed and gasped for breath. Still not completely awake, she stumbled into the bathroom and threw water on her face. A cold shower helped, but she still shook as she walked across the room. Lucy got dressed and picked up the phone. "Thomas, come here now!" She hung up.

Minutes later, Thomas and Aina walked into her room and found her sitting on the edge of her disarranged bed. Lucy heard them talking, but it was as if they were far away. She knew she was in shock, but it felt like a calm place to be after that dream that wasn't a dream. She knew it was real, that she'd been attacked by something evil.

She felt Aina hold her gently while Thomas looked at her in concern. Orange had reappeared, and the giant man dropped to his knees and spoke to her softly.

"We have to get out of here," Lucy said, controlling her emotions as best she could.

It took a dose of artificial sunlight and tea to calm her enough to get the words out. "I had a dream."

They waited, each looking at her expectantly.

"It wasn't a normal dream—it was real." She looked at Thomas. She knew he didn't believe in intuition or in half of the things she believed in, but he made no sarcastic comments; only concern showed on his face. She described everything that had happened in the dream.

"It was Anlair," Aina said. "I think you hurt him."

"How can you know that?" Thomas asked.

"I was there when his face was scarred by fire many years ago. This intrusion into your mind is the black magic of the Order. He chose you from the traces we left at the manor. And he saw you as his way to attack our group, but he underestimated you."

"Are you sure this wasn't just a nightmare?" Thomas

asked. "I mean, the location of the keys is wrong—we know they're underground."

"Then they've moved," Orange said.

"How do we even know that these were the keys? I mean, it was a dream," he said.

"It wasn't just a dream; it was different." Lucy was annoyed with Thomas, but she understood his difficulty in not understanding anything that wasn't right in front of him.

"Lucy's description," Orange said, "and the power released just by touching the cup has shown us something special. It's a sign."

"This reliance on intuition is dangerous," Thomas said. "Aina found the location on Somder's computer."

Lucy's face tensed. "Trusting our intuition is exactly what we need!" She looked straight at him; he glanced at Aina.

Aina nodded. "She's right, Thomas. We need our intuition as much as our reason and common sense. And Orange is right, too: the keys could've been moved. Imperial Security may have detected my search."

Thomas nodded, seeming to accept that. "So where are they now?"

"In one of the worst places in the nine planets—the Tower." Aina looked at Lucy's confusion. "The Tower is imperial headquarters in the Crown. In the citadel at the top of the mountain." Aina went quiet, then her eyes widened slightly. "We're in danger. Anlair knows we're here."

"Did he do this to find me?" Lucy asked. "I thought he wanted to kill me."

Orange nodded. "He wanted both. If he'd killed you, he'd still have learnt of our location. You did well. It wasn't a dream. You left your body and your spirit showed you what you needed to see."

"How did he find me?"

"Like a hound," Orange said. "He smells the psychic scent and follows its trail." He stood. "Aina's right. We must leave immediately."

Lucy shivered and wished she hadn't asked the question.

11

They left Hotel Puck and walked through the maze of metal and glass buildings, avoiding the main roads, with their artificially intelligent taxis, all of whom reported to the imperial police. Blue Orchid was bigger than Thomas had thought, and walking to the railway station would take longer than he wanted.

But he was pleased to be with Aina, and when she asked about his world, he soon became lost in conversation with her. He was explaining some of the differences between England and Silva and was surprised that few people in Silva understood sarcasm. "Isn't that right, Lucy?" He turned, but she wasn't there. "Lucy!"

There was no sign of her. He touched the tag attached to his ear. "Lucy?" No reply. They both tried several times, but there was no answer.

"I think we have a problem," Aina said quietly. She called Orange, who had gone ahead to scout.

A few minutes later, he ran out of an alley. "Where did you last see her?" he asked.

Aina pointed back along the road. "We have to search

for her." She spoke with a flat voice; Thomas could hear her worry—he felt the same. They each took an alley and agreed to meet further back down the road. Thomas knew she couldn't have been gone for more than ten minutes. Eventually they reached an ice cream shop they'd passed minutes earlier.

Aina asked the vendor. The man nodded and pointed in the general direction he thought she'd gone. "Can't you use your telepathy thing?" Thomas asked.

"I've already tried, but there's nothing. She's learning but not ready yet. You should try, too. People sometimes find it easier to begin with someone they know well."

"So she may speak with me?"

Aina shrugged. "I don't know." Orange pointed in a direction and ran down an alley.

Thomas nodded. "Let's meet back here in half an hour." They chose different alleys and started searching. The more he looked, the more concerned he became. There was no sign of her whatsoever. When he judged more time had passed than they'd planned, he ran back to the ice cream shop. Aina looked up hopefully, but he shook his head. "I hope Orange has found something."

They sat on a metal bench and waited in silence, watching the alleys. Thomas still hoped Lucy would walk out of one of them. About ten minutes later, Orange appeared from one of the alleys. He was holding something. He held up two of Lucy's tarot cards and the tagged earring Aina had given her. "She's been abducted."

"Show us the place," Thomas said. They followed Orange through the maze of alleys. Thomas imagined how easy it'd be to get lost here, and he silently cursed himself for becoming so absorbed in his conversation with Aina.

Orange stopped. "Here." He pointed at the wall, and

Aina walked over and touched it. Thomas noticed her shiver.

"What?" he asked.

"The feeling's bad."

Orange nodded. "A trace of magic."

Thomas suspended his disbelief for now. He only wanted to find Lucy alive and well.

"I found traces of her blood further down the alleys, but then I lost her tracks," Orange said.

Thomas tried to take this in. Until now, this journey to another world had felt like a game.

"Traces," Orange said, looking at him. "She's still alive, Thomas."

They walked quickly along the almost deserted alleys, but Thomas suddenly stopped—he leant against a wall. "Aina!"

"What's wrong?" she asked.

Thomas felt very strange. "I thought I heard Lucy's voice in my head."

ALL LUCY WANTED to do was leave. She still felt shocked by her ordeal, and she only half listened as her friends discussed their plans to reach the spaceport, which was located in a valley beneath the mountain city of Nassopolis. Aina explained that the longest way was the safest. Something about taking a train from a strange-sounding place called No. She appeared convinced that security checks at the railway station would be less strict than at airports in the Hanging Cities. Lucy was just relieved when everyone was ready to go.

She followed the others without really paying attention

to where they were going. She felt hot and tired, and when she saw an ice cream shop, she stopped. The ice cream was good, but when she turned round, they were gone. She walked quickly along the path. After twenty minutes, she realized she was lost. She tried to use her tag to call them, but it kept repeating a message in Dnassian. All her fears returned.

Lucy walked deeper into the maze of metal and glass alleys. Blue Orchid was very different from Rime, and she was scared of what she might meet around every corner. Her limited knowledge of Dnassian had vanished, and the few people she'd asked the way had looked at her as if she were simple.

Eventually she heard the sound of glasses clinking and people talking on the street. She turned a corner and saw the sign of the Imperial Orb. She felt relief. A public house would have someone who could give her directions.

A black-clad figure stepped out of the front door as she walked towards it. Lucy heard a voice within shout, *"No!"* She stopped and stood still. When her inner self spoke, she listened. Now it screamed. She reached out to the nearest wall for support. She knew that she must not, under any circumstances, meet that man. A woman passed her in the street and looked at her strangely, but Lucy hardly noticed. She felt her way back along the wall, her arms and legs shaking. She almost fell into the narrow alley behind her and leant on the metal wall to hold herself steady.

She breathed using her stomach, as she had once been taught in her yoga class, and tried to calm herself. Lucy's natural instinct was to run, but she needed to see what he was doing. She inched towards the corner and looked around. *"No!"* the voice shouted again. She wondered if she'd gone mad. The man stood in front of the Imperial Orb and stared at her. Then he began to stride along the road.

She fell back against the wall, still breathing deeply. *"Go!"* her inner voice shouted. She stood shakily and walked as quickly as she could, her outstretched hands giving her support from the walls on either side of the alley. She took the first turn and kept walking. She took turns at random; she had no idea where she was going as she went deeper into the maze of alleys.

She looked behind, but no one was following. Feeling relieved, she rested against a wall and closed her eyes. And then a strong hand squeezed her throat, another ripped her earring out—she gasped for breath and saw flashes of light. She began to faint, but he slapped her. As he pulled her through the alleys, she felt something fall from her pocket, but it was impossible to stop.

They passed two young men, both looked at her with concern, but when they saw the man, they froze with fear. The man from the Imperial Orb sneered at them and dragged her along an alley.

"Not a word," he hissed.

He pushed Lucy through a side entrance of an old building. A cockroach, the size of a mouse, searched a pile of rubbish piled in the corner, undisturbed by her cries as the man banged her head into the lift door. Her arms and legs were already cut from being knocked into walls as he'd pulled her along, and when she struggled, he pressed her head harder into the door, which vibrated her bones as the lift rattled down the building.

As the doors opened she fell inside, and the lift ascended. Eventually, it announced the sixty-sixth floor. He dragged her along a stale corridor and forced her into a private room. She collapsed onto a chair next to an unmade bed with a stained-yellow mattress and looked at the small window high up on the wall. The man locked the door, took out a pair of handcuffs from his bag, and violently forced her hands behind her back. The cuffs chaffed her skin as they locked in place.

"What do you want?" she asked.

He took another of the metal chairs and sat opposite her. He was a darker green than most and had a boyish face, but his eyes were so cold. She shivered, feeling him stare right through her. "Where are the others?"

"The others?"

He slapped her sharply, and tears came to her eyes. "Don't play with me. Where?" he barked.

"I don't know." It was true. She really didn't.

The man leant forward and put his face against her neck. Lucy had read that you should speak to people in situations like this, but she had no idea what to say. And this man was more than just disturbed. He sniffed her hair—she pulled away when he sniffed her ear.

"I can smell them."

She didn't know how. Pushing his nose against her body, he worked his way down like some sort of dog. Her feet interested him. Lucy was now terrified that he was completely insane.

"I can smell them. And what I smell, I can find."

"What do you mean?" Lucy gasped.

"I have a special sense."

She actually hoped that it was true; that his weird sniffing had a purpose. Except that if that purpose was to track the others, then they could end up here with her. But he was only one. She glanced around the room.

"Now I have their scent, I want to know more." He grabbed her hair, and she squealed as he pulled her towards him. Then she felt a pressure on her head—a terrible headache throbbed—and she felt nauseous. She screamed as he entered her mind. "It's better for you if you relax and let me take what I want," he said.

She did relax, and the pain went. "That's better," he said. Lucy followed him as he searched her mind, and she was surprised to notice that he missed certain things. She brought memories to the surface, and he quickly gobbled them, but she let other thoughts sink, and he didn't notice them at all.

Lucy showed him Hotel Puck, and his eyes brightened; she showed him Thomas standing there, and the man grinned. She saw some things she'd rather not have seen, too—the man was an imperial assassin.

He looked at her suspiciously, and she showed him the fear that she genuinely had seconds before, but which had lessened after realizing she could manipulate him. He sneered and touched her shoulder, and she suggested the need for haste: an image of Thomas getting ready to depart. Without a word, Scanlon stood and left the room, slamming and locking the metal door. She wondered how she'd discovered his name.

Scanlon had seemed sure that Hotel Puck was a forty-five minute walk; she had to escape before he returned. She knew his mood wouldn't be good, and it'd be harder to trick him again. She realized that she'd just learnt some of the things Aina had been unsuccessfully trying to teach her for weeks.

Lucy managed to squeeze her handcuffed hands under her buttocks and legs—thank goodness for yoga. A minute later, her hands were in front of her but still handcuffed together. Now she tried her magic skills again. *"Thomas!"*

She repeatedly tried to speak to him, but he kept

pushing her out of his mind; she sensed his nervousness. When she tried to speak to Aina and Orange, she got nothing at all. "I need more practice at this," she said aloud to herself.

She listened at the door for a minute, and when she heard nothing, she tried to open it. It was locked, and there was no way to force it. She pushed the bed under the tiny window, and then put the chair on the bed. She stood on it and could just reach the windowsill. Slowly, she pulled herself up, stretched out, and pulled on the handle.

"Code?" an artificial voice asked.

Lucy almost fell off the chair in surprise. "What?"

"Guest code is required to open the window. Code?"

"How do I know what the code is?"

"Code?"

She swore, but it just repeated its request. She'd learnt something of machine telepathy from Aina, especially when they'd entered the manor. She knew that simple artificial intelligence like this was the easiest to psychically hack; Aina had made her practice endless mental exercises, but she'd never been so motivated.

This time she didn't think about it; she just did what Aina had taught her. "Error. Try again." Lucy looked at the lock with wide eyes, surprised she'd had any effect. She tried again. After several more error messages, the room went dark. Lucy cursed her bad luck; Scanlon had returned. But she couldn't hear anything in the room. Then she saw flashing lights and realized she was inside the mind of the lock. It clicked open, and she pulled her mind clear. She could see the room again, and she breathed out slowly in relief.

She squeezed halfway through the space but froze when she saw a drop of almost sixty floors; it made her dizzy, and she closed her eyes. At least she was stuck so tightly she couldn't fall. After a minute, she felt calm enough to open her eyes again. A rusty metal ladder was attached to the wall—some kind of emergency exit.

She pushed harder, scratching her arms and legs. Having both her hands handcuffed together slowed her down, but eventually, most of her body was through, and she grabbed hold of the nearest rung and pulled her legs out. Carefully, she put her weight on one of the lower rungs.

She screamed as it snapped. The whole lower section of the ladder dropped into the back alley with a crash. Terrified, she hung from the bottom rung of the rusty metal ladder.

"I didn't hear anything," Aina said.

Thomas shook his head. "I must be imagining it." He moved forward and then stopped again and held his head. He was sure he'd heard her. "I don't feel well." He leant against a wall.

"What?" Aina looked at him strangely.

His vision went blurred, and he said, "I can't see properly." Then he saw the side of a building.

"Thomas, it's me!" Lucy said.

"I'm going mad," he said. "I just heard Lucy's voice again. I think she's somewhere nearby."

Aina shook him. "Lucy's learnt to speak in the True Language. Ask her where she is."

"This can't be happening," he said.

"Thomas! We don't have time for this!"

He had no idea what was happening to him, but he

knew Lucy was afraid. "She's handcuffed." Then she faded from his mind.

"Where is she?" Aina yelled.

He shook his head. "I'm not sure, but she's in danger." He had a feeling that he knew the way. Thomas pointed towards a noisy inn. When they stood beneath the building, Thomas stopped. "She's somewhere here, I think."

Aina and Orange rushed along the alleys around the building, leaving Thomas feeling a little stunned. Then he had the feeling to try the narrow rubbish-strewn alley to his left. His heart jumped, and he cried out when part of the building next to him crashed to the ground. He moved quickly backwards. A twisted metal ladder lay in pieces in front of him. He looked up and saw someone dangling from the upper part of the building.

Orange and Aina joined him seconds later. Thomas pointed up at the person swaying from the side of the building. "It's Lucy," Orange said. Before Thomas could say anything, the big man ran at the wall, leapt up, and began climbing.

"How's that possible?" Thomas asked.

A screech came from one of the nearby alleys—a second screech answered it. "No time to explain," Aina said. She pulled his arm.

"What?" Thomas was still watching Orange run up the side of the building. Thomas guessed that he must be an expert rock climber, but even so, this was extreme.

Aina pulled him harder. A man in black stared at them from the end of the street. "One of Anlair's death squads." Thomas realized their danger. They ran into the building and pressed the button for the lift. The screeches were getting closer, and he regretted the necessity of having to leave their weapons outside the airport in Stonehaven.

The lift slowly rattled down the building, and Aina rushed back to the street entrance. "They're getting closer!" She ran back and slapped the lift doors. "Come on!" He mentally prepared to fight, but the lift eventually stopped on the ground floor, and the doors opened.

They leapt inside, and Aina pressed the button repeatedly as the doors slowly closed. An ice demon slammed into the outside of the lift and scratched the metal. "Come on!" Aina shouted. It started to rise, but the screeches of the ice demons followed them from floor to floor as they raced to the top of the building—the lift was fractionally faster.

They ran out onto the top floor; screeches came from two or three levels beneath them. "This way," Aina said. Thomas prayed that she really knew the way. She ran to a metal door. It opened into a utility room with a metal ladder reaching up to a hatch in the ceiling. "You go first and open it," she said.

He climbed fast but struggled with the old metal hatch. "Quickly!" she shouted.

"I know." The ice demons; they were getting closer. He pushed the hatch again, and it opened. Aina pushed at his legs as he pulled himself up onto the roof. He helped her through, then shut the hatch. He looked for a way to lock it but could see none.

Orange climbed over the side of the building; he had Lucy in one arm. Thomas helped take her; he was shocked by her scratched and bloody appearance. The hatch opened, and Orange leapt forward and punched the ice demon. It squealed and fell back, and he slammed the hatch shut, but Thomas knew they'd push their way up eventually.

A man's voice came from the utility room below them. "Scanlon," Lucy said unsteadily. "He's an assassin."

"We have to fight," Thomas said, looking desperately for somewhere to go.

"We could fight," Orange said. "But they might kill one or two of us first. It's better if we pick our own time and place."

"We have another choice," Aina said. She pointed up at the outer skin of the pod city that protected it from the wild weather conditions outside. "It's better than fighting, and remember imperial assassins sometimes have magic, too."

"Scanlon has something," Lucy added.

"There." Aina ran to another ladder, one that Thomas hadn't noticed. It ran up to another hatchway. "Thomas," Aina said. He ran up, opened the hatch and waited for Lucy.

She climbed slowly, and Thomas was worried about her; she was still bleeding, and her clothes were torn. He helped her up into the enclosed space of a cupola on the outer surface of the city, and then he took her hand and walked along the top of the crystal pod. She moaned.

"Don't look down," Thomas said. The drop down even made him feel a little uncomfortable. Lucy collapsed onto the skin of the pod as a cold blast of wind gusted around them; she grasped one of a series of metal rungs that ran along the surface, and Thomas saw her close her eyes.

He moved just ahead and held her. With his help, she slowly crawled from one rung to the next. "Keep going to that glass dome, over there!" Thomas shouted. It was identical to their own but about twenty yards away. Another gust of wind almost blew them from the surface of the pod, and Thomas grabbed hold of her. "Lucy, keep going," Thomas repeated. "We have to move faster."

"I know, but have you looked down there?"

"No, I've not looked. If I did, I might be stuck to the surface like you."

"I'm not stuck. I just can't move."

Lucy stared at Orange as he strolled past her. He gave her a toothy grin, walked to the next door, and opened it. Aina guided Lucy from behind, and Thomas pulled from the front. They were now just over halfway across. There was a loud bang from below.

"They're coming," Thomas said.

"Now!" Aina shouted.

Thomas and Aina grabbed Lucy, who stifled a scream and pulled her the rest of the way. Thomas went straight down the hole, followed by Lucy, who was bundled in by Orange. Aina came in last. She locked the trapdoor behind her.

They were now in an adjoining building. They took the lift to the ground floor and ran to the train station—following directions fed to them from their tags. Twenty minutes later they sprinted along the platform and jumped through the closing train doors. The Night Orchid accelerated out of the railway station and along the narrow tubular fibre tunnel towards Naskopole Junction.

12

The Night Orchid rushed through the deep dark tunnels of Nassopolis, occasionally stopping at Inner City stations on its way to Naskopole Junction, which, according to Aina, was situated in the centre of the mountain.

Aina leant against Thomas, half asleep, but he couldn't sleep. Lucy sat opposite with her eyes closed, and Orange sat like an immovable rock next to her. Thomas replayed Orange's rescue of Lucy in his mind, and it made no sense to him.

"Orange?" The huge man looked at him. "How did you climb up the building?"

Lucy opened her eyes when he spoke. "Yes," Lucy said. "That was incredible."

"I have an affinity with stone and metal."

"What does that mean?" Thomas asked, hoping the conversation wouldn't turn too weird.

He felt Aina stir next to him; she rested her hand on his shoulder. "It's time you learnt about Orange," she said. "He's not human."

"What is he, then?" Thomas asked. He wondered whether she was making some kind of joke.

"He's a troll."

Thomas laughed out loud but stopped when he saw Orange's expression. "I'm sorry, but a troll?"

"I came from deep within the planet to protect and guide Aina when she was a child."

Aina grinned at Orange. "He's my guardian."

Thomas looked at the large man. He had to agree that he looked unusual. Perhaps trolls were another species of life on Prometheus. "And you can walk up walls?"

"Yes."

"That's really cool!" Lucy said.

Thomas saw no point in continuing a conversation like this. Somehow Orange had scaled the wall. Maybe he had some device to help. "Now we're hunted again. Do you think Anlair will be waiting for us in Naskopole Junction?"

"Not Anlair," Orange said. "But imperial police might be there, and his death squad will follow."

"Why not Anlair?" Aina asked.

"Lucy hurt him. He'll need time to recover."

"What?" Lucy asked. "How do you know?"

"Black magic takes its toll, even when it goes well, but this attack backfired on him. When you touched the cup, the energy surged. You said he shrank to a pinhead and then shrivelled up along his cord."

"Well, yes."

"I've seen such things before. You nearly killed him."

Lucy's eyes and mouth opened wide, and Thomas smiled at her expression, despite the mention of magic. He couldn't deny there was something to this magic; of course, it wasn't really magic, but something was happening. "So we have a short break from Anlair," he said.

"Yes," Orange said. "This is not the first time imperial lords have tested their powers in this way. They've reached out into the wilderness before and been burnt."

"I didn't know that," Aina said.

"And when he recovers?" Lucy asked.

"He's vindictive; he'll personally lead his killers in the hunt for us," Aina said. "I want to get out of the Inner Cities as soon as possible."

"I thought we were going to lay low for a while," Lucy said. "We still have over six days until the fleet arrives."

"I want to be in position before that," Aina said. "We don't want to be stuck in the Inner Cities with the death squad hunting us; the spaceport's safer. We'll soon have his squad, teams of police, and every artificial intelligence in Nassopolis searching for us."

"Won't it be the same in the spaceport if we wait there?" Lucy asked.

"No one will expect an attack on the spaceport, but they may increase security around the keys. Don't take off your tag even for a second. The moment it loses contact with your skin, you'll become visible to every AI-enabled machine—and there are a lot of them."

FOUR HOURS LATER, they arrived at Naskopole Junction, the busiest of the Inner City train stations, and the main transport hub of Nassopolis. Crowds of people pushed along the platform, bumping into them as they moved. Thomas was pleased that at least they blended in with the crowds more easily than they had in Blue Orchid, where almost everyone was green.

"Oh, no!" Lucy said. She looked at one of the giant

screens showing a news report on the attack on Lord Somder's estate.

"Don't look," Aina said, "and don't stop either. This way."

Their next destination was on the far side of the station. Trains ascended and descended inside tubes within the mountain. "Damn!" Aina said.

Thomas followed her gaze and saw groups of police, with what looked like robot dogs, standing by the entrance to the vertical train section.

"Sniffer bots—Scanlon will have sent your scent to them. Maybe ours, too, if he went to our hotel."

"Sent a scent?" Thomas asked.

"You don't have that in your world?" She raised her eyebrows. "We can digitalize smells."

"The blockers..." Lucy said.

"Won't have any effect on them." Aina shook her head. "We have a problem." The police and their robot dogs were already moving towards them.

"Back on the train!" Thomas said. It was starting to move down the platform, but the doors were still open. They turned and ran, leaping on the train as the doors were closing. The police rushed at the train, but it was already accelerating into the next tunnel. Some of the passengers were staring at them.

"We have to get off at the next stop," Thomas said.

"Why not go further?" Lucy asked.

Thomas shook his head. "We can't give them time to organize—if we wait, there'll be police at every stop, and they'll board the train, too."

About four minutes later, the train stopped in a poorer-looking station and not as big as Naskopole Junction. "Thank God!" Aina said, as they got off the train.

"There are police here, too," Lucy said.

"Not so many, and they're not prepared," Aina said.

"You hope," Thomas said.

She gave a worried grin. "It's better here; the distance to the city is shorter." She was right; Thomas could see people strolling along the street outside. She tugged at Thomas's hand as they approached the ticket barrier. The four police officers by the exit were already paying attention to them.

They walked through the ticket barrier, and an alarm rang. "I'll distract them and find you later," Orange said.

Aina squeezed Thomas's hand tightly. "Can you see that beggar?" He nodded. "When Orange does his stuff, let's run into the alleys behind him."

"I'm ready." Thomas looked at Lucy's pale face. "Can you run?" She nodded.

Lucy almost jumped into Thomas when the sniffer bot ran through the crowd straight at her. "Thomas!" It sniffed her leg and barked. Orange lifted the robot dog and snapped its neck. Passengers stared at him with open mouths. He tossed the dead robot dog at the police, forcing them to scatter, and then he rushed at them, punching a man who drew his gun.

"Now!" Aina shouted. She dashed past the police and into the street beyond, Thomas and Lucy behind her. Halfway across the street, Lucy started slowing down. Thomas took her hand. He saw Orange running in the other direction and being pursued by police officers. "Lucy!" He pulled her past the old beggar, who looked up in surprise as they ran into the alley.

After about twenty minutes, they slowed down to a walk. "Change tags," Aina said. They did so wordlessly, tossing the old ones into the piles of rubbish that lay along the sides of the street.

"What kind of place is this?" Lucy asked.

"A poor one," Aina said. "And perhaps one where not everyone's tagged." Thomas turned to watch a boy scrabbling around in the dirt behind them. "He's found our old tags."

"Why would he want them?" Lucy asked.

"Unused credits. And they have their value on the black market. We're carrying riches in our pockets."

Thomas checked his pockets, and Aina smiled. "Don't be too obvious. Not here."

The boy ran up to them. "Do you have any more of these?" He held up one of the tags.

"If you can show us a way off this level, I'll give you a dozen," Thomas said. Aina frowned at him; he guessed he'd underestimated their value.

The boy grinned. "I'll show you a way. Follow me!" He led them deeper into the maze of alleys. A gang of young men watched as they passed by.

"You shouldn't have said that," Aina whispered.

Thomas shrugged. "At least he's showing us the way."

She raised her eyebrows. "Perhaps."

They turned a corner and walked down a narrow alley. It came to a block end, and the boy whistled. Four men appeared behind them. "What have you found, Jimmy?" one of them asked.

"They'll give us a dozen new tags if we help them to another level," the boy said.

"Is that so?" The man had similar looks to the thin, dark-haired boy. "Give me the tags," the man said. He held out his hand.

Thomas regretted his offer. Without understanding the value of what he had, he'd shown their wealth and put his friends at risk. He reached for his pistol and realized he'd abandoned his weapons at the airport.

The men pulled out guns, and the boy grinned at them. "Now you'll give me all the tags."

"If I take off my tag, the police will be here in minutes," Aina said. She pointed to her ear.

The men glanced at each other. "They killed a sniffer bot," the boy said.

The man looked them up and down. He seemed unsure. "Give me the loose ones first."

Thomas noticed Orange standing at the end of the alley; he held a metal rod in one hand. The men hadn't seen him yet. "Keep their attention on us," Aina whispered.

Thomas took out a tag and tossed it in the air. One of the men caught it. For each stride Orange made towards them, Thomas flicked another tag into the air. The men caught them, with confused expressions on their faces.

Orange hit two of the men with the rod—they collapsed—and he knocked the gun from a third man's hand. Thomas wrestled the other to the ground and took his gun. Soon they were armed again.

The leader backed away with his hands in the air. "Why didn't you tell me you'd killed a sniffer bot before?" His mouth stretched into a sort of smile. "We're happy to offer Jimmy as a guide—for a price." The boy glared at him.

While the men on the ground were sitting up and rubbing their heads, Aina took back all the tags. "We're renegotiating the deal," she said. "You'll take us where we want to go, and we won't kill you." The man started to protest. "If you do it fast, you'll get six tags." She raised her gun. "And that's twice as many as you deserve."

An hour later, the Orange Company was crawling through a maintenance shaft down to a lower level. "It's a bit uncomfortable, but we'll be there soon," the man said. "And no one will know." The man had assured them that neither he nor the boy were tagged. Aina had confirmed that it was possible. Some criminals had them removed, and some people were just born into an underclass, which lived mostly unnoticed by the Empire.

Thomas noticed that his night sight had improved, and he watched the man and boy closely as they climbed down numerous vertical shafts in the dark, but he saw no attempt at duplicity.

Hours later, they stood in a room in an empty house. "We're in Musket," Alan said. "It's time to discuss the payment. The price is eighteen tags and our guns back."

Aina pointed her pistol at his head. "Six will quickly become five, and then four ... And the guns are ours." They stood staring at each other for several seconds. Then he lunged at Aina, and Thomas punched him to the floor.

The man looked up at him. "You'll regret that." Then he passed out.

"Take us to the station," Thomas said to the boy. The boy looked at the unconscious man and nodded.

"Buy us tickets with clean credits—ones that can't be traced—and you'll get your six tags," Aina said.

The boy's eyes brightened. "Follow me."

They left the house and walked down the Musket street. The morning sun lamps cast artificial light down into the streets, and Thomas realized how tired he felt. Lucy kept yawning, too. The houses they passed were coated in plastic, peeling off in places, leaving flakes of blue and white on the ground. Bare rock was exposed beneath.

"It's attractive," Lucy said, "in a way."

They entered a square—the railway station took up most of one side. "Wait here, I'll get the tickets," Jimmy said.

"I'll go with him," Orange said. The boy looked up at him, obviously scared. Orange spoke quietly to the others.

"I'm attracting too much attention here, and I can move faster by myself." Thomas was aware of the stares Orange was receiving. "I'll walk the boy to the station, and then I'll find my own way. I'll meet you in the spaceport. A troll can move in ways a human cannot." Before anyone could speak, he was striding across the square, with the boy running in front of him.

"Will he be all right?" Lucy asked.

"He's a troll," Aina said, as if that answered all questions.

While they waited, they sat on benches next to a broken fountain. Fresh air machines pumped a refreshing breeze against their faces. The square had a faded elegance. Along the sides were the facades of houses; the houses themselves had been cut out of the rock.

"I'd expected something less attractive," Thomas said.

"Musket is popular with tourists," Aina said. "I wouldn't mind being a tourist for a day after the past few days." She held his hand. "And it has the Imperial Museum."

A flock of blue and grey pigeons landed in front of them.

"Mechanical pigeons," Aina said.

"Robots?" Lucy asked.

"Sort of, but not like the bots. They're not intelligent. They're just there to look nice for tourists."

Lucy scratched her arms. "I really need a shower." She scooped some water from the pool.

"Lucy?" Aina said.

"It smells fresh; it's just the top of the fountain that's broken." She threw water on her face. "That's better."

"That's not what I meant," Aina said.

"What?" Lucy asked.

"Water's splashed onto your head."

Lucy laughed. "Water's one thing I'm not scared off. And it's only a little."

"No, not that. Your earring is wet. Apart from the tag, there's a blocker that gives us invisibility in this world. It disguises our faces from face recognition technology. But it won't work when it's wet. There's a chance that you'll be recognized by the cameras."

"But the tag? Is that affected by water?"

"I don't know. Most people have them implanted in their brains. But even if the tag's working, if the blocker doesn't work, and your true face is seen by imperial security, it'll be matched with those of their database."

"I can't see any cameras here," Thomas said. It seemed as if the whole square was camera free.

"I hope you're right," Aina said. "The boy's come out of the station. Let's go."

A mechanical pigeon hopped onto Lucy's arm. "Look at that," she said. "It's a tame robot."

"Lucy, get it off you," Aina said.

"It's all right. It's only a mechanical pigeon. You said so yourself." Lucy stroked the cooing bird. "You see, it's quite safe." She raised it to her face to get a better look and rubbed its belly.

The bird scratched her arm and flew into her face. Lucy screamed as the pigeon tried to peck her eyes. The flock of mechanical pigeons flew up into the air and then dropped onto Lucy, pecking and scratching her.

Thomas knocked them away and took her arm. "Run to the station!"

He pulled his screaming friend behind him. Lucy was becoming hysterical. She was bleeding from her arms, neck, and face. Thomas knocked one of the robot birds to the ground and stamped on it, breaking its neck. The birds now attacked him and Aina as they ran.

The station was getting busy, and a crowd of people

passed through the exit. Jimmy handed them their tickets. "What's happening?"

"Get out of here!" Thomas said. The boy quickly disappeared into the crowd. Thomas, Lucy, and Aina ran into the hall followed by a flock of aggressive robot birds. The crowd panicked.

A squadron of blue police bots flew in from the street. Thomas hoped they were only checking the disturbance. "A new tag might be a good idea," he said to Lucy.

"Oh, yes." She fumbled with her packet of tags, pulled one out, and attached it.

"Please let this work," Aina said aloud. Her eyes glazed over, and the pigeons stopped attacking Lucy.

The mechanical pigeons rose into the air, then mobbed the squadron of blue bots. The police bots responded with stunners, and the flock of pigeons soon lay motionless on the ground. Horrified tourists stared at the dead robot birds.

"I don't know why I didn't think of that before," Aina said.

Thomas pushed Lucy through the barrier and onto the waiting pod train.

13

"I hate pigeons," Lucy said.

She had wiped away the blood from her face and arms. The scratches had been mostly superficial, but she felt shaken by the attack.

"Especially robotic ones."

"The attack took us all by surprise," Thomas said. He leant forward. "What chance do we really have of destroying the spaceport?" he asked quietly.

Lucy glanced at the odd-looking passengers sitting in the carriage. She didn't think they could hear. "Thomas is right," she said. "We're four people, plus whatever team Lucetta First sends, against an army. What can we do?"

"Our aim is to destroy the incoming flotilla, not the whole spaceport. And they have a weakness."

"What?" Thomas asked.

"Pride."

"I don't like them, but they have reasons to be proud. How is it a weakness?" Lucy asked. She thought of the advanced technology in this world and wasn't surprised at all.

"I don't care if they have reasons. Excess pride is stupidity." Aina lowered her voice slightly. "No one has attacked the Empire in decades, and they don't believe it's possible. They've grown complacent.

"They assume they can read everyone's mind, but they can't. We don't have embedded tags." She tapped her head. "Imperial security depends on their ability to read minds, and almost no one steals them—it's a capital offence."

"They're still powerful," Thomas said.

"I never said they weren't, but they're not all powerful. The Mariner said you needed to believe. You must, or we'll fail."

"I hope you're right about their weakness," Lucy said. She wanted to believe they had a chance, but so few against a vast Empire felt overwhelming.

"The aristocracy believe that they're the pinnacle of evolution. They don't even call themselves human beings anymore, but new beings. Their body improvements and their nano-computer-assisted brains have made them stronger but not wiser. The emperor and his order are worse: they think magic makes them more than human."

"This may be true," Thomas said. "But how does it help us?"

"They'll underestimate us and give us opportunities, if we're ready to take advantage of them."

They looked around the carriage at the silent passengers, all of whom were dressed in drab black clothes, and all wore hats. "Why do they keep looking at us?" Lucy asked.

"They stare at outsiders; it's their way," Aina said. "We'll need to disguise ourselves when we arrive."

"Where are we?" Lucy asked. She looked through the window at the snowy mountains.

"The Valley of No." Aina glanced at their fellow passengers. "They believe in Noism. They came here to escape temptation."

"Why is it called Noism?" Lucy asked.

"No sex, no bright clothes, no laughing, no fun, no sports, no alcohol, no tea, no games on holy days, and no chocolate."

"No chocolate?" She couldn't imagine living in a world without chocolate. "Why?"

"It's a stimulant, and stimulants are sinful," Aina replied.

"I thought only Earth had this sort of thing," Thomas said.

"Humans are good at punishing themselves. We'll have to be careful in Austerity."

"Austerity?" Thomas laughed. "Is it like it sounds?"

"Apparently." Aina told them that the journey to Austerity was long and boring, and she didn't lie. For the next seven hours, they saw little but icy wasteland. Aina insisted on teaching them more Dnassian. Their level was just about functional. According to Aina, they could pass for a pair of Silvan-speaking bumpkins from the mountains.

Dnassian was not related to Silvan, which meant learning a new vocabulary. It was grammatically harder, too. Lucy was glad when the silhouettes of the cities appeared on the horizon.

"Dnassity, the spaceport city, and Austerity," Aina said.

Dnassity was a tall city coloured in shades of black, blue, grey, and silver. It was made of glass and metal, with many curves and domes. The whole city swayed gently in the strong Promethean winds. Austerity was squat and made of solid rock. The walls that faced the spaceport were without windows, and apart from the cathedral that rose from the centre, no building in Austerity was significantly larger or smaller than any other.

"They're two different worlds," Lucy said.

"They are. Dnassity is a place where anything can be bought. To the Noists, it's a place of decadence and decay. Austerity is as it sounds," Aina said.

Eventually the train stopped, and they stepped out onto a platform of black suits and hats. A woman gave them directions, and they walked through the old part of the city. Several minutes later they came to a stone building with an old sign hanging outside.

Lucy realized that she could read the Dnassian script. "Second-hand clothes," she said.

"Your Dnassian is improving." Aina nodded approvingly.

They entered the old shop and looked at the dreary clothes piled on a table in front of them. Aina pointed out the types of clothes they would need to disguise themselves as pilgrims.

"Is this really necessary?" Lucy asked.

"We need to blend in."

"What about when we get to Dnassity?"

"Dump the clothes and change identities."

Thomas nodded. "So we're pious pilgrims."

"We don't have to be too pious. Some of the kinkiest Noists travel to the spaceport to escape the rules," Aina said with a grin.

Lucy looked at the clothes with distaste, and she looked at herself in the changing room mirror with even more distaste. The only good thing was that she would no longer stand out.

Thirty minutes later, they left the second-hand clothes shop dressed as Noists. Thomas wore an old black suit. Lucy and Aina wore white blouses and long black skirts and jackets. They all wore black hats.

It was late, and they spent the night at the Guest House of the Virtuous Woman. It was spartan. The woman who ran it restricted women to the upper floors and men to the lower ones. An old woman, perhaps her mother, sat all day on a stone chair between the two floors. She enforced the rules and beat her walking stick on the stone floor when Thomas spoke to Aina for longer than was proper. The girls were taken upstairs.

The next morning they left the guest house and joined the groups of black-clad people walking along the wide stone paved street towards the cathedral. Lucy began to speak, but Aina hushed her.

"What's wrong?" Lucy asked.

"Women are not allowed to speak in public on the Sabbath. I forgot to tell you." The cathedral bell rang.

"Why not?"

"It's what they believe. Men and women have their places, and they're different. The sooner we get to the second station, the better."

"I agree with that," Lucy said.

"Where is this station?" Thomas asked.

"On the other side of the cathedral."

"Can't we take a taxi?" Lucy asked.

"Not on a Sunday. Business is banned on the Sabbath, and Austerity has deacons who patrol the streets; they're a type of religious police."

"And they enforce church attendance?" Thomas asked.

"And more," Aina said.

"And the people just accept it?" Lucy felt angry with these deacons and with the people for accepting such restrictions.

"They like it. They chose this life; the ones who stay."

"But we're not from here. Surely they won't make us go," Lucy said.

"We're Noists from the mountains now." Aina tapped her earring.

"The tags?" Lucy asked.

Aina nodded. "If we meet any deacons, don't make eye contact. Be demure. As long as we're walking towards the cathedral, there shouldn't be a problem. The problem is passing it without entering."

"Then we circle around it," Thomas said.

"We can try."

The cathedral bell tolled, and worshippers walked towards the austere building. To their right was a small square, and on the far side was a street that ran in the direction of the station. They turned and crossed the square. A few of the worshippers glanced at them, but no one said anything.

"That wasn't so hard," Lucy said. Four deacons stepped out of the shadows and stared at her.

Aina swore under her breath, and a deacon wearing special insignia rested a large stick on the ground. He stared at Aina. Lucy thought he must be the chief deacon. The man then looked at Thomas and asked a question in Noish. Thomas answered in broken Dnassian, but Lucy knew he had no idea what the man had said. A deacon scanned him with a small device.

"We have a problem," Thomas said in Silvan.

"I have an idea," Lucy said.

"Do it," Thomas said. "Whatever it is." The chief deacon shouted at him. "I think he's upset. Perhaps we shouldn't have attempted to impersonate Noists."

"I didn't think we'd have to actually speak to them," Aina said. The deacons looked from Thomas to Aina, their mouths open wide at the continued conversation between males and females in a public place. So wide that Lucy felt like asking them whether they wanted to catch flies. She swiped another fly from her face. Why were there so many?

She studied the open gutter that ran along the top of a low building. It was covered with black spots that were slowly moving. She concentrated on the flies. She heard the chief deacon shout at Thomas again as two more walked around the corner.

She imagined a deacon's head stuck in a toilet bowl, and one by one the insects rose into the air. A cloud of black flies formed beside her. The deacons looked at her strangely and watched the cloud of flies. Each fly was the size of her thumbnail. She pointed, and they flew at the deacon next to Aina. The man swatted his head in an attempt to brush them off.

"Bite," Lucy said.

The man screamed and ran off into the square, followed by a cloud of insects.

Three deacons rushed Thomas. He punched the first to the ground and threw the second on top of him, but a large deacon came from behind and wrestled him to the ground.

The chief deacon looked at the flies, which were rising into the air behind Lucy, and then he raised his stick. "I will not permit the devil to enter Austerity."

Lucy was still projecting her thoughts, and although she saw the man walking towards her, she concentrated on the flies, which rose around her. She noticed more of the black flies congregating on a water pipe that ran down the wall into the gutter, and they joined the swarm. She then looked at the chief deacon. *"Fly!"* she whispered. And they did. Hundreds of black flies flew straight at the man's face. His head became a fuzzy black ball. He screamed, dropped his stick, and then ran around in circles as he tried to frantically knock away hundreds of black insects.

Lucy saw all that was happening around her, but she also felt detached. She saw the three men move away from Thomas and stare at the chief deacon in shock. Thomas picked up the stick and hit the man on his head. She decided to try one more time with the flies, but she was now losing concentration.

The cloud of flies began to fly in different directions, but they were startling enough for the remaining four deacons to back off. Thomas thrust the long stick forward, as if it were a spear. It hit the nearest deacon in the centre of his face. He screamed, held his broken nose, and fled with the other men.

"Let's go," Lucy said.

14

The journey to Dnassity was short, but the difference was dramatic. And when Lucy saw how everybody was dressed, she wanted to dump the old clothes immediately. "It's like a shopping mall that's grown into a city," Lucy said.

"This part is," Aina said.

"I have to get out of these clothes," Lucy said. The stares of stylish Nassopolitans were making her uncomfortable.

"Bathroom," Aina said.

Once inside, Lucy dropped her black garb on the floor and changed back into modern clothes.

"Tags," Aina said from the next cubicle.

Lucy flushed the old tag down the toilet and slipped a new one into place. She was now a subject of the Second City.

The Little Empire teashop was in the twelfth basement. Lucy looked at her ticket, the one she'd needed to gain access to the spaceport. It was to the moon Titania. "Why do you call the moon Titania?" she asked.

"She was a character in an old poem. Puck was her son," Aina said.

"Who wrote the poem?"

"Willa Speare."

Lucy wondered how different Willa's work was from William's.

The imperial flag flew in an artificial breeze above the teashop. Lucy ordered tea. Thomas studied the colourful pictorial representation of the solar system on their table. The Empire was coloured purple and covered most of the solar system.

"What are these blue dots?" Thomas asked. They looked at the images of the planets and their moons.

"They're places that are still outside the Empire. I'm surprised they've even shown them. Probably nobody has noticed—if anyone complained, they'd be removed," Aina said.

"Why?" Lucy asked.

"It implies that the emperor is not all powerful."

"The Empire's almost everywhere." Thomas ran his hand over the inner planets of Mercury, Venus, Dnasis, and Mars. "They call Prometheus, Uranus. The same word that we use on Earth."

"That's the imperial name, not the true name. The Empire is almost everywhere. The almost part seems to be giving the emperor pain. Hence our problems."

"Why don't they invade Prometheus?" Lucy asked.

"They'd love to. The natural resources of this planet are exceptional, by far the richest in the solar system." Aina tapped the illustration of Prometheus. "When the Empire arrived on this planet just over thirty years ago, they attacked the intelligent species and were badly burned. The Empire plans war against them after they take Silva."

"How do you know?" Lucy asked.

"When I lived in the ancient forest, I once helped a young roc, one of an intelligent species of giant birds. He was killed by the company, but I discovered their plans. Everything I see now suggests that nothing's changed."

"Are any of the intelligent species similar to humans?" Lucy asked.

"No, they're very alien. The emperor and his Order know they exist, but they deny their existence to the people. They fear the wild magic of this planet. To the people of the imperial colony, the wilderness is populated by savage animals. They believe it's the harsh environment and the expense of exploring and exploiting it that's the problem."

"Will we meet the intelligent species?" Lucy asked.

"I think so."

"What's this blue dot?" Thomas asked. He pointed at a moon of Jupiter. "If the emperor wants everything, why hasn't he taken it?"

"It's a strange water moon, and it seems to have something in its ocean that stops the Empire."

"What?"

"Nobody knows."

They were all silent for a moment. Lucy wondered what could live in those oceans that would repel the Empire. Then her eyes were drawn to the woman who'd just entered the teashop.

The cellars of the House of Chance had been too dark for Lucy to see Lucetta First clearly, and she'd been distracted. The woman was older than Lucy had first thought, perhaps in her late thirties, but just as striking as she remembered, with intense dark eyes, black hair, and pale skin.

She walked to their table and sat down. "I think you've

proven yourselves, even to the most conservative Silvans. Imperial Security would never have burned down the lord of the manor's home and killed him so savagely."

"His pets were hungry," Aina said, her mouth curving into a smile.

The woman raised her eyebrows and continued. "Your information was well received, and the beacon was seen across Silva. A nice touch. Where's Orange? The one you claim to be non-human."

"Around somewhere. He goes where he will, but he'll return when we need him," Aina said.

"You place a great deal of trust in him."

"I do, and he's never let me down."

"Then we'll continue."

"How many are with you?" Thomas asked.

"A technical team of three and an assault team of six."

"Only nine?"

"Ten including me. If I remember correctly, only four of you managed to burn down the manor. Am I wrong?"

"True," Thomas conceded.

Lucetta First smiled. "My team's good. I spent a lot of money training them, so they should be. Anyway, for what we want to do, stealth is more useful than brute force. Now we need to go through some of the details of our plan." Lucy cringed as she listened to the details of the destruction they planned, but she couldn't see any other way to stop the invasion. "I can help you with the security systems," Lucetta said, "but you need weapons; I imagine you weren't able to smuggle any into Dnassity?"

"Weapons would be good," Thomas said. "And can you give us one of the devices you used to hack their tags?"

"Unfortunately, the Empire has already developed a way

of countering their effects. We're still working on improvements. But I'm sending my team to raid the armoury." She continued more quietly. "Our lighter will land two hundred yards southeast of the armoury. You'll have thirty minutes to reach us. We can't wait any longer."

"They'll chase us back to Silva," Thomas said. "It could mean war."

"I know. What are your plans after we return to Silva?" she asked. "We have need of resourceful and dedicated fighters in the Resistance."

"We'll return to Nassopolis and take the keys," Aina said.

"The prophecy? So you still plan to break into Imperial Security on 28th?"

Aina gave a cool smile. "We've had an intelligence update."

"Oh?" Lucetta First leant forward.

"The keys have been moved to the Tower." Aina sipped her tea.

Lucetta First sat back and shook her head; she studied their faces. "Will you reconsider. Attempting to enter the Tower is futile—it's been tried. And even if you did get in, there's no chance of getting out alive. Can I persuade you to rethink this?"

"No," Aina said.

Lucetta shook her head. "It's a waste, but we can talk more on the way back to Silva."

"We need help getting into the Crown. Can you help?"

Lucetta sighed. "I might know a way."

Aina's eyes brightened. "Tell us."

"I'm not promising anything. But I have a contact in Dnaskat. He goes by the name of the Landlord."

"A strange name," Lucy said.

"A strange man and a dangerous one. He's involved in illegal activities in the Inner Cities. He once mentioned a secret way into the Crown."

"Where can we find him?" Aina asked.

"In the old section of Dnaskat, in an inn called the Laughing Cat. But be warned, it's not a respectable establishment, and you may not be welcomed. If you do go there, tell him I sent you."

Lucy watched Thomas chat with this very controlled and doubtlessly very dangerous woman as the conversation turned to more mundane topics. In spite of this, Lucetta was charming, in a way.

She finished her tea and stood. "Be ready to move in one hour." She left without goodbyes.

"What do you think?" Lucy asked.

"She's competent. I think she can do what she says," Aina said.

"I meant about the woman."

Aina smiled. "She reminds me of a deadly Venusian snake that charms its victims with its dance before it strikes." The image remained with Lucy for a long time.

Thomas looked up. "Orange is nearby."

"How do you know?" Lucy asked.

His brows knitted, then he shrugged. "I just know."

Seconds later, Lucy started when Orange sat in the empty chair. She blinked and glanced at Thomas. "Where have you been?" she asked Orange. "I was worried."

"Trolls can move freely where humans cannot. I was safe. It's time."

Lucy felt dread at what they were about to do. She'd discussed it with Thomas, and it didn't seem right, but she couldn't think of an alternative. To do nothing was not an option.

They went into the washrooms, and minutes later they walked out disguised as cleaners, wearing the clean blue tunics and caps that Orange had found. They had inserted new tags into their earrings.

No one noticed a team of cleaners push two trolleys of cleaning gear out of the departure lounge. There were no stairs but a smooth spiralling passage, down which they raced their trolleys. Orange ran ahead, and he was already opening the door at the bottom of the stairs when they arrived. They stepped onto the special surfacing of the spaceport.

A flash of lightning lit the dark sky and illuminated a figure standing in the shadows. Lucy started, but he spoke Silvan, and she relaxed.

"Courtesy of the armoury." He placed a bag on the ground.

"Any problems?" Aina asked.

He shook his head. "They didn't expect anything. We won't always have this luck, so best to use it."

Aina nodded.

"The computerized security system went down as planned. There were two rockets inside the armoury."

"Can you use them to shoot down a spaceship?" she asked.

"Perhaps. There's an explosive device in there." He pointed at the bag. "It's not very powerful, but it'll do some damage." The man disappeared back into the mist.

They put the assault rifles and pistols into the buckets and containers on the cleaning trolley and pushed it through the fog towards the dark outline of the control tower.

When they got closer, Lucy saw a door with some sort of keypad next to it. Thomas touched the metal handle on the airlock, and his glove stuck to the metal. He cursed and pulled his hand away, leaving part of his glove stuck to the handle.

"Like this." Aina placed her hand on the specially-coated pad and entered the code Lucetta had given. The outer door slid open, and they walked into the upper maintenance area. It was empty.

The service lift opened and scanned them. As it rose, they covered the assault rifles with cloths. The control room was on the tenth floor, but special passes were needed to access any floor above the sixth, which they did not have.

The lift doors opened. The sixth floor was occupied by office workers, and nobody even glanced at them as they walked along the corridor. They hardly even looked at Orange, which Lucy thought was strange. But when she heard a supervisor berating a worker, she understood why they kept their heads down.

The supervisor jabbed his finger at a worker as they walked past to the doorway at the end of the corridor. As they had thought, it led to the stairwell, but it was locked. A sign indicated that it would only open in an emergency.

"Twenty minutes," Lucy said. She'd volunteered to keep time.

"We could force the door," Thomas said.

"That'd bring security here," Lucy said. "We should find another way."

"Hah! More slackers." They turned to see the supervisor staring at them. "You're a cleaning crew, aren't you?"

"Yes, sir," Aina said emotionlessly.

"Come here! I have some rubbish for you to remove." There was silence throughout the floor. Aina pushed the cleaning trolley along the corridor.

Blue Prometheus

A worker stood with his head down.

"Yes, sir?" Aina asked.

Lucy noticed the edge in her voice; she exchanged glances with Thomas. She knew her friend was about to do something.

"Clean my office, and then remove this rubbish."

"Sir?" she questioned.

The supervisor glared at Aina. "Are you slow? Clean my office and remove it." He pointed at the man.

"We don't have time for this. Let's show ourselves now," Thomas whispered.

"Not yet. I have an idea," Aina said.

"I was worried you might say that."

She smiled at him, then spoke in Dnassian. "We have a job, crew!" She winked at Orange and whispered to him in Silvan.

Orange stepped forward and grabbed the startled supervisor. The man struggled, but he was too weak for a seven-foot troll.

"Put me down."

Orange dropped the man in the empty bin and tossed his blue cap in with him. The troll's long orange hair fell to his shoulders. The office workers watched the strange procession move along the corridor.

"You can't do this," the supervisor said.

The lift door opened and they pushed the trolley inside.

Orange pushed the man's face to the scanner, then dropped him back in the bin.

"They'll be waiting for us outside," Orange said.

"I know." Aina took out an assault rifle. Orange and Thomas took the others. The supervisor watched them nervously.

The doors opened, and Aina shot the first security guard in the chest. The second guard drew his weapon, and Orange punched him. The man fell to the floor and didn't move. They turned a corner, and a woman bumped into them and screamed. Aina raised her rifle.

"Aina!" Lucy said.

Aina raised her eyebrows at Lucy. "I'm not going to kill her," she whispered. "Move!" Aina shouted. The woman ran back along the corridor.

A bullet hit Orange in his shoulder, and Aina shot the guard who'd attacked. Orange rubbed his shoulder, but otherwise didn't seem too bothered; his toughened jacket seemed to do its job. Two more guards attacked. Orange broke the nearest man's neck. Thomas shot the other guard.

Lucy just ran with her companions. A siren sounded throughout the building. "Sixteen minutes," she said.

They reached the control room door. It was locked. Aina hit the intercom. "Open the door, and nobody will get hurt."

A man's voice answered. "You cannot enter. Security's been alerted."

"Your security's not functioning," Aina said, glancing at the bodies. There was no further response from the control room.

"Fifteen minutes," Lucy said.

Aina studied the door. "Orange?"

The troll rested his hands on the door and then shook his head. "It's special. It would take me too long to open."

Thomas took out the explosive device.

"I don't think it's powerful enough," Aina said.

"Thomas, come here," Orange said. He still stood with his large hands placed on the doors.

Thomas stood next to him. The troll took his hand and

pressed it against the door. "Feel." Thomas looked up, startled. "Do you hear?" the troll asked.

"Yes. Two guards and two bots are on the other side of the door. The rest of the people are along the sides of the room," Thomas said. He stepped back from the door, his eyes wide. "How do I know that?"

"Rock magic." The troll made way for Aina.

"Now for my trick." Aina pressed her body against the metal door. She was still for several seconds. Lucy knew she had entered the mind of a bot. Short bursts of gunfire came from inside. Then an explosion within the room threw Aina back into Thomas's arms. She grinned and detached herself from him and touched the wall again. Then she quickly stepped away.

"Get back!" Aina shouted.

The door exploded, and pieces of metal flew past them like arrows and stuck into the wall behind them. Lucy felt Orange's hands lift her away, the troll's giant body shielding her from the blast. There were screams from inside the room and flashes of light.

Orange leapt through the large hole into the control room, and Thomas followed, holding an assault rifle.

Lucy stepped through the hole after Aina. Terrified workers crouched against the walls. The two security guards were dead. A grey bot smouldered nearby. A second bot flew erratically in circles, knocking into the ceiling as it went around.

Orange aimed his gun at the bot.

"Leave it," Aina said. "We might need it."

"What do you want?" a woman asked.

"Who's she?" Lucy asked.

"The chief controller of space traffic," Aina said.

"Twelve minutes," Lucy said.

"You must leave now. I have incoming flights." The woman glanced out of the long window overlooking the runway.

"How many?" Aina asked.

The woman stared at her. "You came here to ask me that?"

"How many flights?" Aina repeated. She pointed her gun at the woman.

"One off-world and two local."

"Land them."

The woman frowned, but she did her job.

"I want you all to act as if we weren't here," Aina said to the nervous staff. "Lucy?"

"Seven minutes."

Thomas and Orange stood by the door. The workers nervously continued, but they stole many glances at the armed intruders.

"Five minutes," Lucy said.

The radio crackled to life. "Deep Space Seven requesting permission for flotilla to land," a voice said.

"How many ships, Deep Space Seven?" the woman asked.

"Four. I've sent our details." Aina's gun was inches from the woman's head.

"Welcome to Imperial Uranus. Lord Anlair will arrive soon to meet you."

"I look forward to meeting him," a man said. The radio switched off.

"Spaceport security's coming," Orange said. Lucy could hear nothing, but she knew a troll's hearing was better than a human's.

Aina looked up at the circling bot as it flew into one of the walls. "Lucy."

She supported her friend, and when she touched Aina, Lucy also sensed her mind. Aina was already inside the robot's computer brain. The injured bot slid down the wall and hit the ground. It dragged itself along the floor before lifting into the air, sailing past Thomas and Orange and through the hole. The bot flew erratically along the corridor and fired wildly, forcing the security team to take cover. It then flew straight into an approaching bot and exploded.

"Aina!" Lucy shouted.

She felt Aina's pain as she pulled out of the robot's mind. Her eyes opened and she nodded. Lucy helped her stand. The controller glanced at them but was busy with the incoming flotilla.

Lucy checked her watch. "Two minutes."

Aina staggered over to the woman and pushed her out of the way. "Thomas," she said weakly. He ran over and restrained the controller. Orange remained by the door, taking shots at any security personnel who attempted to come closer.

"This is Deep Space One."

Lucy saw Aina stiffen.

"Is that who I think it is?" Lucy asked quietly.

"Martin Anlair," Aina said. She entered a new set of coordinates. "All clear to land," she said.

"Are you the controller?"

"The controller's been taken sick. All clear to land." She turned the radio off and leant back in the chair. She watched the approaching flotilla on the screen. "He must have flown from Silva to meet them," she said.

"How did you know that?" the controller asked.

"Thirty seconds," Lucy said.

"This is Deep Space Seven. There's been a change to our landing coordinates. Please confirm."

"What've you done?" the woman demanded, jumping to her feet. Thomas pulled her away.

"Confirmed. The new coordinates are correct," Aina said.

They waited and looked out of the window. Lucy could see the lights on the approaching space transport. It was huge and capable of carrying ten thousand men. She thought of the legionnaires onboard, but it was too late now. Once a ship of this size had committed to land it couldn't stop.

Deep Space Seven flew blind through the clouds, unaware that the altitude displayed had been altered. The lumbering transport loomed through the fog. It seemed to be moving in slow motion. Lucy looked away.

"Oh, my God!" the woman exclaimed. "What've you done?" The ship came on towards them.

Floodlights lit the foggy runway as the transport approached. At first, nothing seemed wrong, then Deep Space Seven flew into the ground, sending ripples across the runway. The tower shook violently, as if a large earthquake had hit. Lucy steadied herself on the chair. The largest transport of the Deep Space Trading Company's fleet ploughed deeper into the runway.

Larger waves of surfacing rippled out from around the ship. Its momentum carried it forward, and the ship sank below the surface of the runway. Objects flew from the control room shelves as the tower shook. Loud cracks came from the building. Two screens bounced off their desks and smashed onto the floor. Deep Space Seven exploded.

The runway was on fire, and a cloud of smoke mushroomed above them. A hail of burning metal hit the side of the control tower. The windows shattered and freezing air rushed in. The workers screamed and ran for the exit. No one tried to stop them.

Two rockets flew into the night sky, immediately followed by two bright explosions.

Aina switched on the microphone and leant forward. "The Deep Space Trading Company has been given notice to leave Silva."

"Who is this?" Lord Anlair's voice came through the radio.

"Aina Kay of the Orange Company."

"You've just murdered twelve thousand women and children."

"Red Legion!" Aina shouted.

"There's nowhere on this planet deep enough for you to hide from me. And when I find you ..."

"I will hunt and kill you Martin Anlair."

Lord Anlair hesitated, and Aina turned off the radio.

Lucy watched the monitor. Two spaceships circled overhead. Martin Anlair's personal transport—a predator class attack vessel—and a mule class transport capable of carrying a thousand soldiers. The two vessels destroyed by First's team had also been mule class, meaning that they had just prevented up to twelve thousand mercenaries from occupying Silva. But a thousand might remain in the ships that circled above.

The Orange Company stood by the controls when a message flashed on their screens. "Mission completed. Two casualties. Let's go home!"

"Lucetta First," Aina said.

Thomas took out the explosive device. "We may as well use this."

Aina nodded. "Give it to me." She placed it under the control panel. "Thirty minutes."

"Look," Lucy said. Hundreds of dark shapes flew through the night sky towards them. "What are they?"

Aina stared up into the sky. "They're what's left of the Red Legion, and they're between us and Lucetta's lighter."

"We need another way," Lucy said. "Perhaps we can blend in with the escaping office workers." Thomas and Aina nodded their agreement.

The Orange Company turned and ran.

15

The building shook as Lucy and the others ran down the emergency stairs. Screams came from the stairwells when there was an explosion outside. She hoped it was worth it and the invasion would no longer take place.

She couldn't see the security team—they must have fled—but office workers were still crowding onto the stairs as she ran. Some moved aside for them when they saw the guns they carried. Others didn't notice them at all. Each floor added more, and soon a crowd of people ran before her.

"We're not going to get down in time," Lucy said. Some of the legionnaires had been close to landing on the runway when they left the control room.

"They're using powered paragliders," Aina yelled. "We have to be fast." For a while they ran quickly, but as they approached the ground floor, the crowds slowed down. Hundreds of workers ran to the ground floor entrance, which was now visible. Lucy saw the spaceport police pushing their way towards them.

"To the basement," Orange said.

A group of men with red masks pushed against the tide of office workers.

"Red Legion," Aina said.

A police sergeant shouted at the legionnaires, but they paid no attention to him. No more than ten yards from Lucy, a female office worker ran into one of the men. He neither moved nor apologized. She swore at him in anger, and he shot her in her head. For the first time, Lucy wished she had a real gun. She shot the man with her stun gun. She hit him, but he just stared at her with blank eyes. He looked as if he was on drugs. He raised his gun, but Orange shot him. Thomas took her arm and led her down towards the basement.

They came to a metal door. Orange ran down the steps and jumped. He hit the door hard, and it flew open.

"An interesting way to open the door," Thomas said.

Lucy wondered how he could joke under these circumstances. She couldn't see anything funny about their situation or about the mad legionnaires who followed them.

Orange pushed the door back, but it no longer fitted into its frame. He pushed hard, then ran his hands along the outer edges. Orange light came from under his hands.

"What's he doing?" Lucy asked.

"Welding the door," Thomas said.

Lucy leaned closer, her eyes narrowing. Thomas was right. Orange had welded the outer edges of the door to the metal doorframe with his hands.

"How did you do that?" she asked. Orange just grinned.

An explosion shook the tower. "The explosives," Lucy said. It was followed by shouts from the stairwell.

"I think we should go," Thomas said.

Lucy looked around the basement and discovered that she could see more clearly in the dark now. She glanced at

Thomas, her brows lifted, and he nodded at her. He could see, too, she thought.

"We all can," Orange said, startling her. She had to learn how to control her telepathic skills.

They were in a very old engine room of some kind, unused in years, or perhaps much longer, judging from the dust and the staleness of the place.

"Orange?" Thomas said. "Any rock magic?"

"So you believe in magic now?" Lucy bumped his shoulder with hers, for a moment forgetting her worry, unable to keep the grin off her face.

"At the moment I believe anything that works; I'll think about it later."

As they talked, Orange wandered to the back of the room. "Here," he called.

They found him staring at a wall in the corner, next to a large machine. It appeared older than the rest of the walls, and it was made of brick.

The troll waved Thomas towards him. Thomas moved close to Orange and placed his hands on the wall. Nothing happened that Lucy could see, but Orange kept talking quietly to Thomas.

"Let's see what's happening," Aina said to Lucy.

Each bang on the door outside caused Lucy to start. With a glance back to Thomas and Orange, she followed Aina. The room was big, but not so big that they could remain hidden for long. At least it was dark. From the edge of the large machine, they watched the door. It burst open. Red legionnaires ran into the basement. They were followed by eight figures.

"Oh, I have a bad feeling," Lucy whispered.

"Me, too," Aina said quietly. "Let's go back." They crept back to the corner where Thomas was surrounded by light. "I hope you've found a way out because the death squad's here, and they can see in the dark."

Shadowy figures moved past the end of the machine and stopped. They hissed.

"Ice demons," Aina said.

One of the creatures called out. A sound between a word and a screech. The pair of giant lizards walked towards them.

"I wish I had more than this stun gun," Lucy said.

Aina gave her a pistol. "This should slow them down if you shoot them in their faces." She unslung the automatic weapon she'd taken from the control room.

"Thomas?" Lucy whispered. She glanced back. Both he and Orange were gone.

"Where are they?" Lucy asked.

"I don't know, but we've got more important things to think about. Like how to kill them." They backed up to the wall.

The ice demons stopped several yards away and waited. Lucy froze when she saw the cold eyes of the black-clad assassin in the darkness.

"The Orange Witches," Scanlon said.

The assassin's eyes were intense, and an inky substance came from his fingertips. Lucy shivered as she watched it drift towards her. She fired the gun at him, and the magic paused before advancing again.

"Good shot," Aina said. She pointed her automatic weapon at the enemy, but neither Scanlon nor the ice demons appeared concerned.

"He's wearing body armour," Aina whispered. "Bullets still sting," she said loudly. Scanlon touched his neck, and a full helmet covered his face. Aina flashed a grin at her.

"Surrender," Scanlon said. Three red legion mercenaries walked up behind the assassin.

Aina shot Scanlon. He staggered back. "I was right. He has armour," she whispered.

"Kill them!" he shouted. Aina immediately started shooting the nearest ice demon in its head. It squealed and jumped back, its tail thrashing out and knocking the mercenaries to the ground.

Lucy felt power rising from the ground and into her feet, and then up through her body. She briefly wondered whether the key was calling her. She raised her hand to the other ice demon, and for some reason, it hesitated. She aimed the pistol and shot Scanlon repeatedly in his head, while at the same time entering his mind. "It's sticky!" she said aloud and telepathically. She didn't know why she said that. Aina glanced at her, her eyebrows raised.

Scanlon screamed and fell into the legionnaires, who shoved him away. The black inky substance had pulled back into him and had stuck to his hands, arms, and face. He rolled on the floor, still screaming with sticky black energy jumping out of his body, then snapping back. The legionnaires and larger ice demon backed up.

"Lucy!" Aina shouted.

The other ice demon prepared to leap at Lucy, but at the last minute, it cried out and scampered along the sides of the basement, back to the rest of the attackers.

"What did you do?" Aina asked, as she grabbed Lucy and pulled her behind a large machine.

"I spoke to her, but I'm not really sure what I said."

"Whatever you did, it worked. Keep doing it, especially the thing with the assassin." Aina peered around the corner. "You've really hurt him."

Lucy crept to the edge of the machine and peeped

around. She was shocked at what she'd done. Scanlon's face was now a scarred, skull-like visage.

"That's good." Aina glanced at her, and Lucy guessed that her friend noticed her shock. "You saved our lives, and it's his fault the stuff stuck to him—he shouldn't be playing with black magic."

Lucy nodded. She didn't feel bad about hurting Scanlon; it was the shock of seeing the change to his face—she realized that she had more power than she'd thought.

The sound of rocks grinding came from behind them. They turned to see Orange and Thomas standing in a glowing orange archway in the wall. "Sorry we were so slow," Thomas said. "We had a problem."

"Come!" Orange said.

Lucy and Aina ran through the burning hole into a concrete chamber, which had an open doorway at the other end. Thomas rested his hands on Aina's shoulders. "Are you all right?"

She smiled. "I'm fine. Where are we?"

"Under the runway. I think this must be what's left of an old town. It looks like they built the spaceport on top of it."

"You missed Lucy's magic," Aina said.

"Speaking of magic," Lucy said, "what's Orange doing?" The troll's hands were bright orange as he closed the hole in the wall with what looked like molten rock.

"Sealing the hole. The question is how," Thomas said. "He seems to be able to manipulate rock—he can even walk through it."

"Now do you believe in magic?" Lucy asked.

"I don't believe in the name, but I believe in what works."

Lucy was pleased that Thomas was slowly changing his

point of view. She looked down at four dead bodies lay on the floor. "Who are they?" she asked.

"Company police." Thomas pointed at a jagged gap in the roof—clouds of smoke and flames came from the other side. "I think they must've fallen through the hole."

Aina knelt and studied the uniforms. "These are not company police; they were pilots."

"It makes no difference," Thomas said. "We still have the same problem. Every human and artificially intelligent machine in Nassopolis will be looking for us."

"No pressure," Aina said.

"Maybe we can take their uniforms and leave the spaceport with the others," Lucy said, pointing at the bodies.

"Good idea!" Aina said.

Lucy thought it was more a desperate idea than a good one. They took the uniforms from three men and a woman. The ground shifted under their feet. "We have to be quick," she said.

They raced across the dark room and into the space beyond; Lucy was thankful that something had changed in her body and she could see in the dark. They scrambled up over pieces of broken concrete and then climbed out into what looked like hell.

The heat was intense, and flames burst from many parts of the furrowed runway; firefighters were losing their fight against the blaze and were slowly being pushed back. "What have we done?" Lucy said aloud; she coughed when she breathed in the black smoke.

Thomas pulled her. "Run!" They ran away from the approaching flames and a thick cloud of black smoke that drifted towards them.

"Where are you going?" a police officer shouted.

"Air Force Command!" Aina shouted back.

"Wait here!" He pointed his gun at them and looked nervously at Orange.

"Idiot!" Aina yelled. "We're pilots! We were ordered by Lord Anlair to return to the command post when the runway collapsed! Now we can't even see where we're going!"

The man seemed confused, and Lucy heard whispers in the True Language. Aina seemed to be influencing his thoughts. "Then you're going the wrong way." He pointed to a line of people in the distance. They stood by one of the few buildings that wasn't burning. "They're being bussed into the city."

"Thank you!" Aina shouted.

"You'd better be fast," the man shouted. "The whole spaceport may explode."

Lucy sprinted towards the building, relieved that a way out had appeared. Aina glanced back at the man. "What?" Lucy asked.

"This way," Aina said. She changed direction and ran into a cloud of smoke. "What are you doing?" Lucy said, annoyed with Aina. "It's this way." She pointed the line of people.

"I have an idea."

"Aina!" Thomas said. "We've got to escape. We've already destroyed everything."

"The hangars are still standing."

Lucy couldn't believe what Aina was saying. "We've done enough. Let's go!"

"Copying what others do isn't the safest way," Aina said. "Quickly!"

"Do you want to set fire to the hangars?" Thomas asked.

"I want to steal a spaceship!"

16

"Hold your breath!" Thomas said as Lucy coughed on the smoke. He didn't know whether to admire Aina's audacity or curse her craziness. He stood outside a hangar, while Orange listened by placing his hands and head against the hot metal building.

"Four airmen and an officer. They're trying to decide which spaceships to save; they're moving them to Midpoint."

"Midpoint?" Thomas asked.

"A military base halfway up the mountain," Aina said.

Thomas breathed in the relatively clean air between the clouds of noxious black smoke. "Shall we start?" Aina's eyes widened slightly as she nodded. He squeezed her arm; sometimes he forgot that she was just as likely to feel nervous as anyone else.

"I'll wait here," Orange said. "It's better they don't see me. If there's trouble, I'll come quickly."

Thomas would rather have him inside, but there was no time to argue. "Let's go," he said.

They strode into the hangar, and a group of airmen looked up. "Who are you?" an officer asked.

"Pilots from Lord Anlair's command," Aina said. "He ordered us help with the removal of vessels to Midpoint."

"I've received no such orders," the officer said.

"Perhaps your tag's not functioning—an order's been sent." Thomas wondered how she came up with all of this; he'd been tempted to just rush in and shoot them, but the others had agreed with her plan.

"My tag's fine."

Aina frowned and shook her head. "You don't understand. I've had direct orders from Lord Anlair to assist in the moving of vessels to Midpoint."

The man shook his head. "You're mistaken." He reached for his pistol.

"Wait!" She raised her hand. "I'll contact him again, and he can speak to you himself."

The man dropped his hand to his side. "I'm waiting."

Thomas knew the look on Aina's face; the one she had whenever she tried her telepathy stuff. He started when he heard Anlair's voice in his head, and the airmen looked up in shock.

"This is Deep Space One." Thomas stared open-mouthed at Aina. Somehow she was replaying Anlair's voice using the True Language. Thomas was sweating as he watched her struggle. He knew that Anlair had not said anything about them piloting a spaceship.

"My Lord?" the officer said, puzzled.

"This is one from me." She was mixing his words up.

"Sir?"

"From me!" Anlair's voice boomed in their heads.

"The girl?

"Is just this." The airmen looked at each other. *"There's*

nowhere on this planet deep enough for you to hide from me, and when I find you." This time Anlair's words were clear enough.

"I apologize, my lord. I will assist these pilots in any way I can." The man was shaking.

Aina opened her eyes and breathed deeply.

"I'm afraid Lord Anlair's not in a good mood," she said. The airmen nodded. "What's loaded in these camel class transports?"

"Nothing much, Captain. 56PF has some cutters inside."

"Good. We'll take that one. All of you will take out this one." She pointed at the transport in front of 56PF.

"But the fires? We need to move more of them."

"That's an order! Do I need to call Lord Anlair again!"

"That won't be necessary," the officer said. He and the other airmen boarded the camel class transport, and a few minutes later it taxied out of the hangar.

"He's right about the fires," Thomas said. He could feel the heat building up; the wind had changed, and it was blowing the flames towards them. "The whole place is going to explode." Aina gave a broad grin as she rushed to one of the transports and turned a tap. "Aina! That's dangerous."

"I know." Orange joined her, and soon fuel poured from several of the vessels.

"Let's go!" Aina said. They jumped on board the old transport. She sat in the pilot's seat and started the engines. "Orange, can you check the hold?"

The troll looked in the back and seconds later returned. He grinned. "Five cutters."

"Perfect," Aina said. The transport taxied out of the hangar through the smoke.

"Do you know where we're going?" Lucy asked. She peered through the window.

"More or less." The screens in front of her lit up with all

kinds of displays. "Thomas, sit next to me. I want you to be my co-pilot."

"I've never flown a spaceship or any kind of plane."

"You can learn."

Lucy and Orange strapped themselves in the seats behind them, and Aina accelerated along a smaller auxiliary runway. "I hope this one's long enough," she said.

"Aina!" Thomas said. She smiled as the camel class transport lifted into the air. The hangar beneath them exploded, sending orange and red flames high into the air.

Aina flew transport vessel up the mountain. She gave Thomas the controls a few times, and he started to get used to flying the craft.

"Is anyone following us?" Lucy asked.

"Not yet," Aina said.

"Where exactly are we going?" Thomas asked.

"We're going to hit Midpoint first."

"Hit Midpoint? I don't like the sound of that."

"It's a military base," she said. "They won't let us fly past, and if we land, they'll arrest us. So the only answer is to fly straight into it."

"You really are crazy," he said. "It might be a good idea landing somewhere here." He looked at the bleak, almost vertical rocky environment through the window. "Well, perhaps not exactly here."

"That's the problem. There's nowhere around here," Aina said. "If we crash the transport into the base, they'll be occupied, and we can escape on the cutters. I know an entrance to the Inner Cities several hundred yards above the base."

Lucy stared at her with wide eyes. "I'm not flying out there," Lucy said.

"Lucy, we have little choice. Believe me, being caught by the military would not be pleasant."

"Can all of you prepare the cutters? And get mine ready, too. We're nearly there." Orange grunted and disappeared into the hold.

"This is Midpoint. Identify yourself." Thomas looked out of the window. The base was built on a platform that jutted out of the side of the mountain. "Identify yourself."

"56PF," Aina said. "We're moving the transport from the spaceport."

"ID?" Aina swore and turned the radio off. "How is a teacher from Lower Dnaskat flying a military spaceship? I'd forgotten about the tags. She took her tag from her earring and tossed it to the floor. "That's no use anymore."

"We're getting close to the base," Lucy said.

"Too close. We should go now before they shoot us down." They went into the hold. Orange had started four of the cutters.

"You can ride with me," Aina said, looking at Lucy's face.

"Where are we going?" Thomas asked.

"A place close to Dnaskat where we can sell the cutters. Follow me or Orange." Lucy seemed to have second thoughts. She sat on one of the cutters and revved the engine. It jumped forward and stalled. "Lucy, quickly," Aina said. "Get on the back of mine. The door's about to open!" Lucy started it again, revved the engine, and it shot forward. She flew out of the hold with a scream.

Thomas and the others flew out of the hold as the spaceship plunged towards the base. They raced up the side of the mountain, hugging the surface closely. The mountain shook from an explosion beneath them, sending rocks bouncing down. They followed Aina as she swung into a ravine and flew straight at a rock wall. "Aina!" he shouted. At the last minute, he saw the tunnel entrance rushing towards him, and he flew into the mountain.

17

The Orange Company walked through the streets of Old Dnaskat. It was already dark, and they hoped to arrive soon. The wealthier neighbourhoods of Dnaskat could afford to burn the sunlamps by day, and the moonlights by night, but here in the alleys of the Old Quarter, there was no light at night, apart from the little that escaped through cracks in the tightly shuttered windows. They turned into a narrow alley.

"We're being followed," Orange said. Thomas turned to look, but Orange held his shoulder. "Don't alert them." Orange ducked down a path while the others continued along the alley. Minutes later, the troll reappeared. "He's gone."

"What did you do?" Lucy asked.

"Shook him up."

"And?" Thomas asked.

"Just a mugger."

"Good." Not so long ago, a mugger would've worried him; now he only felt relief. There were worse things in the world, and he was more concerned about the type of man

Lucetta First had suggested as a contact. Nevertheless, they had little choice but to try.

Sounds of laughter and glasses clinking came from a stone house in the alley ahead.

"That sounds encouraging," Lucy said.

Thomas hoped she was right. Above the closed doorway hung a dimly illuminated sign of a laughing lion.

"This is the place," Aina said.

The Orange Company walked into the taproom of the Laughing Cat. All conversation stopped as the patrons of the Cat stared at the four strangers. Thomas read uncertainty beneath the hard stares. He looked around the room for the Landlord. A man stood behind the bar and leant slightly forward. His hands were below the bar—on a weapon, perhaps. Thomas wished he'd asked Lucetta whether the Landlord was literally a landlord.

"We're looking for the Landlord," Thomas said in the imperial language.

"So?" the man said. After a few seconds of silence, the man continued. "And who are you? Strangers here, from your accent."

"A stranger is a friend as yet unmet," Thomas said, quoting the Silvan proverb.

"Not in Dnaskat, he's not." There were laughs in the room.

"We're not from Dnaskat."

"I can see that. What do you want?"

"My name's Thomas Brand."

"I asked what you want?"

"Let it go," Aina said quietly in Silvan.

"A favour," Thomas said in the imperial language.

"So you said. Why should anyone give a stranger a favour?"

"To help them," Thomas said. There were more laughs from the room. He waited, unsure how they'd react to what he was about to say. "I heard you were no friends of the Empire." There was silence for several seconds.

"Get out!" the man behind the bar shouted.

"An enemy of my enemy might not be a friend, but at least he doesn't have to be my enemy," Thomas said.

"So you're enemies of the Empire, are you?"

The Orange Company stood impassively in the middle of the taproom.

"What if we're imperial spies and soldiers?" the man asked, sizing them up.

"Then I'll kill you," Orange said.

"That's not funny." A man with a scar on his face pulled out a large knife and put it on the table in front of him. Thomas rested his hand on his pistol. Aina pulled back her jacket and placed her hand on her gun, and Orange pulled a heavy pistol from his coat and placed it on the table beside the knife. He grinned at the man, who did not grin back.

The man behind the bar pulled a shotgun out from below the bar and then whistled. An animal appeared from behind the bar and growled. "Like I said, get out."

The hyena's head reached Lucy's chest. Its jaws were large and powerful. Thomas was sure it could do a lot of damage. Lucy looked into the animal's eyes. "Careful, Lucy," Thomas whispered.

The man laughed. "I wouldn't get too close if I were you. It's not a pet."

Thomas watched Lucy. She was doing her thing, but her head was too close to the hyena's mouth, and its eyes disturbed him. He didn't want to think about what this creature could do.

"Lady. Move away from the animal." Even the man

appeared uncomfortable. He watched the hyena move closer to her. Lucy's face was now inches from the hyena's mouth.

It tilted its head.

Lucy held out her hands. The hyena sniffed them. Then she scratched its throat and chin. "Good boy," she said.

Nice one, Lucy, Thomas thought. The animal seemed to have been completely charmed.

The occupants of the taproom stared at Lucy as she rubbed the hyena's ears. "I'd never have believed that possible," the man said.

"They're those ones on the news," another man said. "The ones wanted for the attack on the Deep Space fleet. I recognize them, especially him, the Orange Giant."

"Is that true?" the man asked, weighing them up.

"Yes." Thomas waited for his next move.

"And for the killing of a mercantile lord in Silva. This is that Orange Company," the man said. A news report came on the large screen on the wall; it showed the explosion at Midpoint.

"Impressive," the man behind the bar said. He turned the screen off.

"You follow the news in Old Dnaskat," Aina said. "Perhaps you're not so backward."

"You should have said this before," the man behind the bar said. "I'm known as the Landlord." He looked at Lucy, who was still talking to his hyena. "I'll have to train it again. I've been too soft with that animal."

Lucy looked up. "You've been too hard."

"How do you know that?"

"He told me. And let him stay inside at night. It's easier for him to guard the inn."

"He told you that?"

"Yes."

"Then ask him what he had for dinner last night."

Lucy looked at the animal for a few seconds. "He had nothing until he stole that man's pie, and you both beat him for it." She pointed at a thin man sitting in the corner.

The thin man glared at her. "Witch," he muttered under his breath.

Lucy's face reddened. She brushed the hyena's fur and pointed at the man. The animal walked across the taproom and pushed its bared teeth into the man's face.

The man froze.

The man with the knife laughed. "Dick, your mouth'll get you killed one day. Maybe today."

"Apologize," Aina said, hands on her hips.

The man pressed himself back against the wall. "Call it off."

"Not my business," the Landlord said. He started pouring drinks.

The hyena's jaws closed on the man's cheek. He screamed and cried out an apology. The patrons of the Cat roared with laughter.

"Incredible," the Landlord said, shaking his head.

He invited them to sit with him at a table in the corner; all weapons were again concealed. The hyena sat next to Lucy, and conversation resumed in the Laughing Cat.

"So Lucetta is calling one of her favours. What do you want?"

"She said you might know of a way into the Crown," Thomas said.

"I might. What do you want to go there for? It should be the last place you'd want to go."

"We have business there," Thomas said.

The man raised his eyebrows. "I'll look forward to watching on the news. Getting there won't be easy."

"Destroying the spaceport wasn't easy," Thomas said. The Landlord grinned.

"Lucetta said you may know another way," Aina said.

"Have you heard of the Pleasure Pits?" Thomas shook his head. "It's a casino and brothel. The entrance to the passage you want can only be accessed from the Gleeman's private suite, which is directly above the brothel."

"Who's the Gleeman?" Thomas asked.

The Landlord's mouth pulled back in contempt. "The boss of the Gleemen; they run half the underworld in Dnaskat. They're not people you want to mix with."

Thomas wasn't sure he wanted to mix with the Landlord's group either. "Can you help us get in?" he asked.

"I can tell you what I know, but it isn't much. Anyone can enter as a customer, but it's expensive."

"It's on the Deep Space Trading Company."

The landlord laughed. "Then enjoy the service, but I'd recommend you don't think about going any further. Getting into his private suite will be difficult, and the Gleemen aren't known for their hospitality."

"If the entrance to the passage is in his private suite, then that's where we have to go," Aina said.

"You've shown you can handle yourselves, but there are only four of you. There are thirteen Gleemen, plus bouncers and wannabe gangsters. I recommend you reconsider your plans."

"Thanks for your advice, but we've decided," Thomas said.

The Landlord nodded and sipped his water. "I can't help you gain access to the passage, but I'll help you as I can. I owe Lucetta several times over. I do know that the Gleeman's looking for a new bouncer."

"How do you know that?" Thomas asked.

"Because Erik over there," he glanced at the man who had placed the knife on the table, "killed one this morning." Erik looked up on hearing his name and nodded.

"And you think he'll hire a new one?"

"He's superstitious. He likes to keep his staff at a particular number. He's careful who he hires, but I imagine the Orange Company doesn't have imperial hardware implanted in their brains."

Thomas nodded and finished his ale. He looked at the troll. "Do you want a job?"

The troll grinned and downed his pint. "Ale!"

"I'll take that as a yes," Thomas said. "Orange can check out the Pits tomorrow, and then we can enter in the evening as guests."

"What kind of guests?" Lucy asked.

"Rich kids from New Dnaskat looking for a thrill," Aina said. She laughed at Lucy's wide-open eyes. "This is our way into the heart of the Empire on Prometheus."

The landlord stood. "I've got business to attend. Melissa." A girl of about seventeen stuck her head through a doorway. "Ale for our guests." The girl smiled and disappeared behind the bar. A minute later she reappeared with a tray of full tankards.

"What's the Crown like?" Lucy asked.

"For Nassopolitans, it's a kind of utopia," Aina said. "But from what I've heard it's the opposite: it's a plastic place of mind control and repressed emotions. But it has a shadow side, too."

"What do you mean?" Thomas asked.

"A black tower stares at the people every day, but few people talk about it."

"Why?" Lucy asked.

"Fear. This world's divided psychically as well as physically, but most people don't know it. But the Tower's where we're going." For a few moments they sat in silence. Finally, Aina said, "At least we're not going to 28th. It's the lowest part of the world in every way,"

"There's a world beneath it," Orange said. "It's the place where the human world meets the deep world of the planet."

Aina looked surprised. "The rumours are true?"

"I was there." Orange laughed and drank more ale.

Thomas clinked his tankard to the troll's. Aina leant into him. "Have you ever drunk with a troll?"

"No, why?"

"Nobody drinks like a troll."

"I can hold my own."

Aina smiled. "Yes, dear."

Lucy complained of being tired, and Aina stood. She turned to Thomas. "Enjoy your ale. And don't say I didn't warn you about drinking with a troll." They left Thomas and Orange in the noisy taproom and went upstairs.

Thomas was interested in learning more about the natural parts of the planet. He'd studied geology because he'd hoped to spend more time outdoors. It wasn't just about rocks, but about the outdoors and nature, although he'd never expected to learn about nature on another planet. He ordered more ale.

"Tell me about the deep parts of the planet," Thomas said.

"Deeper down the pressure crushes the spaces. There are no caves or rivers, but there's life."

"What type of life can live there?" Thomas asked.

"Elementals."

"Like you?" Thomas wondered again what Orange was exactly.

"Some are like me. Others are different. In the centre of Prometheus, there's a second sun."

Thomas guessed that he was talking about the inner core of the planet. "And things live there?"

The troll nodded and drank more ale.

"What can live there? It must be as hot as the sun."

"Tropical creatures." Orange grinned. Thomas remembered very little after that.

18

The next morning he woke up when he heard Aina moving about the room. He felt sick and his head hurt. He was on the floor, but he definitely remembered getting into bed the night before.

"You look terrible," she said.

"Why am I on the floor?" He was fully clothed and wrapped tightly in a blanket.

"You fell onto the bed last night, and I kicked you out. You stank of stale ale and snored. Unfortunately you rolled up into my blanket."

"Your blanket?" He felt nauseous. She left the room before he could start an argument, and he immediately fell back asleep. Hours later he woke again to hear Aina and Lucy in the corridor.

"What are those strange noises?" Lucy asked.

"A pair of trolls snoring."

"Do you think they're okay?" Lucy asked.

Aina laughed. "No, I expect they're very much not okay, but as long as they're up by this evening, it doesn't matter too much."

Thomas staggered out of the room, pushed past Aina, and stumbled into the bathroom. He slammed the door shut.

"Never drink with a troll!" she shouted through the door.

"I feel great," Thomas said. He threw up in the toilet.

Hours later they met downstairs. Orange ordered a fresh jug of ale and Thomas drank tea. The troll drained the jug and stood. "I'll see you tonight." Orange left, and Thomas spent the rest of the day resting.

THAT EVENING the Landlord's long black lighter glided down the streets to the Pleasure Pits. The place was in a derelict section of the city. The lighter stopped by an unmarked entrance. All three of them wore the clothes of the young rich, apart from their boots, which were designed for walking. The clothes came courtesy of the Landlord, and Lucy and Aina's morning trip to the street market. Several bouncers watched as Thomas gave the orange-haired doorman their bags.

"I'll follow you later," Orange said.

They walked up the spiral staircase to the large lifts on the second floor, all eyes on them. Only the rich visited the upper floors. The lift attendant welcomed them into her plush machine. There were no buttons; the lift answered to her voice.

When the doors opened on the upper floor, a beautiful girl bowed and guided them through the opulent yet primitive surroundings. Gilded cages with domed tops hung from the high ceiling of the palatial chamber. Naked girls and boys of all colours were chained to a central pole inside the cages. A group of businessmen sat on the couches in front of the first cage. They were loud and drank heavily. Deeper in the room a group of women laughed and commented on the naked boys.

The bouncers were blank faced and muscular. Thomas imagined that few people would refuse to pay their bills, however expensive. Waitresses wearing crimson thongs served the tables.

"Number Three," Aina said.

The girl led them to the third cage. Aina threw herself on the soft red couch and demanded drinks. The waitress bowed again and left.

"It's terrible," Lucy said, sitting next to Aina as she surveyed the room around them.

Aina shrugged. "It is what it is."

"How can you be so casual? We should do something."

"We can't help every lost puppy we meet."

"These are humans, not puppies."

"They're not free." Thomas looked around the palatial room. "There are guards on every door. I doubt those people are ever allowed to leave this building," he said.

"I don't like it either, but remember why we're here," Aina said. "We have the chance to ensure a million Silvans remain free. That's more important than freeing a few unlucky girls and boys. Assuming we could."

"But we should do something," Lucy said.

"Such as? We can't just ask nicely. Not with the type of men who control this business."

Thomas hated what he saw, but Aina was right.

The waitress came back just then and set down their drinks. Once she left, Lucy said, "Can't Orange help us?"

"How? Lucy, people will be hurt if we try to help them. What do you want to do, go around every brothel in the

Inner Cities helping girls, many of whom might not even want your help?"

"There must be something we can do," Lucy said.

"We're fighting the company. Isn't that enough?" They spent a few minutes in silence. Lucy stared at her drink. Thomas watched the rotating cages, feeling uncomfortable. A few of the girls looked at him, and he quickly averted his eyes. He'd never been in a brothel before, and the experience was strange, but having Aina next to him made it stranger.

"Which one do you want?" Aina asked. When he didn't answer, she said, "That one's hot," and pointed to a green, tattooed girl with rainbow hair.

Thomas shook his head. She was right, the rainbow-haired girl was hot. That was exactly the type of distraction he wanted to avoid; he wanted to stay focussed on the task.

"I've already chosen," she said, touching her glass to her mouth.

"Who?" Lucy asked.

"That one." Aina pointed at a girl of about fifteen, the only brown-skinned one in the cage. "She'll do us both. I think it looks better if Thomas takes his own."

"She's so young," Lucy said.

"She's Silvan." Aina nudged Thomas. "Which one do you want?"

Thomas had no idea. He pointed at a green girl of about twenty.

"So you like fat girls?" Aina asked.

"She's not fat. None of them are." Although compared to Aina's athletic body, the girl looked soft.

An older woman approached. "More drinks?"

"We're ready." Aina pointed out the two girls.

The woman nodded and gave instructions to a man and a woman.

A young woman stood before them. "I'll take you to the chambers. Your girls will be brought to you shortly." They followed her to a second lift, which slowly rose to the next floor.

"Where's Orange?" Thomas whispered as they walked along a corridor. "Will they just let him in this part of the place?"

"A rock troll doesn't need permission. He'll know where we are. Be ready for him. And don't enjoy yourself too much. We may have to leave quickly."

"I'll be good," he said just before the young woman showed him inside his chamber.

AINA AND LUCY were left alone inside the second chamber. It was comfortable but claustrophobic. There were no windows, not even the kind that look into one of the interior wells used in the Inner Cities. The four-poster bed was big enough to sleep six, although Aina doubted it ever slept anyone. A minute later a man opened the door, and the Silvan girl walked in.

"She's yours for one hour. Do as you wish with her but no damage."

He locked the door and left them alone in the room with the young, slender, and very naked girl. She looked at them curiously and without any shade of embarrassment at her nudity.

"I feel uncomfortable," Lucy whispered.

The girl heard. "You speak Silvan?"

"Yes," Lucy said.

"But your accent? You're not from Silva?"

"No."

"That's unusual. My name's Nancy." The girl walked up to Lucy and put her arms around her neck. Lucy backed away. "Relax, I'll teach you. This is your first time with a woman, isn't it?"

Aina wasn't sure if the girl qualified as a woman.

"Yes, but I don't want to," Lucy said.

Nancy looked at her. "Then why're you here? I'm expensive, you know."

Aina sat on the large bed. Nancy walked up to her, took her hands, and kissed her on her mouth. Aina sat back, surprised by her feelings. "No, we can't."

"Then why did you choose me? To chat to me in Silvan?" The girl looked puzzled. Nancy then took a stick from the bed and slapped it against her palm. "Do you want to be my slave?"

Aina couldn't help but grin. "No, we want something else." Although she liked the girl, she didn't know if they could trust her.

As if by some kind of synchronicity, Lucy spoke. "We can trust her."

"Are you reading my thoughts?"

"No, it's just a feeling."

"Well, you read them well," Aina said.

What do you want?" Nancy asked.

"We just need a little of your time. We're waiting for a friend and then we'll go," Aina said.

"They won't let your friend just wander up here."

Aina didn't say anything, not wanting to tell the girl about Orange and his abilities.

"How did you come here?" Lucy asked.

Nancy shrugged. "Family problems. I came to Nassopolis to make a living."

"And here?"

"I signed a contract."

"What type of contract?" Lucy asked.

"For three years. I get accommodation, food, and a good salary."

"So you're free to go after?"

"I thought so at first, but a girl tried to leave last month, and they beat her up. She never recovered, not properly."

"Have they paid you any money yet?" Aina asked.

"They pay when we leave."

"Nancy, that's not a good contract."

"I don't have much choice, not with the Gleemen."

"If you did, would you take it?"

"Maybe, but I don't." She paused, studying them. "I know who you are. You're the Orange Company—the Silvan Resistance," she said in a low voice. "You killed the lord of the manor." Nancy now looked at them with more respect. "Are you hiding here? I don't think it's a good place for that."

"No, we're looking for a secret passage," Lucy said.

"In a brothel?"

"On the top floor," Aina said.

"Those are the Gleeman's chambers. You can't go there. If you do, he'll kill you."

"Have you ever been there?" Lucy asked.

"Once. I was luckier than my friend. He prefers green or white girls. But you can't go. If you do, the Gleeman will kill you and then he'll kill me, too." The girl became agitated.

Aina hadn't considered that the Gleeman might take his revenge out on the girls. There was a sound outside. "Orange," she said.

Nancy jumped to her feet. "Please, don't!"

Aina held the girl's shoulders. "You can come with us. We'll take you out of this world, if you want."

The door opened. Thomas and the troll waited outside. The body of a bouncer lay on the carpet.

19

"We're taking the girls with us," Aina said.

"What?" Thomas asked.

"You said you wanted to do something. The Gleeman will kill them if they stay."

This was not how he'd imagined helping them, but there was no time to argue. "Then let them come."

Nancy stepped out of the door and looked down at the body of the guard. His neck was broken. "Did you do this?" she asked Orange. He didn't answer. "He was a bad one," Nancy said. "I'll get my friend." A few seconds later, Nancy appeared with the other girl. She was shaking.

"They need clothes," Lucy said. Thomas agreed, although he knew her shaking was not due to the temperature.

Orange dragged the body into the bedroom. "How did you get past the other guards?" Nancy asked. "Did you kill all of them?"

The troll put their bag on the bed. They took out their clothes and weapons.

"How? Oh, don't bother," Nancy said, looking at the

knives and guns. Aina stripped off her trendy disguise and dressed in her own clothes. The girl watched, a smirk on her face as the self-conscious Thomas and Lucy changed clothes in front of her. Nancy put on Aina's old clothes, but she was still barefoot.

The green girl stared at the dead bouncer. "You need clothes," Lucy said. But she shook her head. "What's wrong?"

"Perhaps she doesn't want to leave," Orange said.

Thomas found that hard to believe, but they couldn't wait for her to decide. They walked along the corridor and took the stairs to the next floor. Lucy led the green girl by the hand. A door blocked their way. "Orange, can you open this one?" Aina asked.

Orange touched the lock and nodded. It clicked open. They passed an open entranceway to the eighth floor. Men's voices came from the corridor. They crept past the opening and up the next flight of stone stairs. On the ninth floor, there was a heavy metal door. Orange put his hand against the door. "I can open it," he said quietly.

"Do you feel anything, Orange?" Aina asked. He grinned, but his eyes were wild.

"Is that a good sign?" Thomas asked.

She shook her head. "No, it's a bad one." Aina turned to Nancy. "Describe the layout of the chambers."

"There's a corridor with many doorways; they were all closed when I came. I only know that at the end of the corridor is a large door. Through that door is a long meeting room with a table and wooden chairs. The Gleeman's bedrooms and other private rooms lead off from the room."

The troll placed his hands against the lock. It clicked, and the door opened.

"How did he do that?" Nancy whispered.

"He's a troll," Lucy said, but Nancy looked confused.

They walked along the corridor. Voices came from the meeting room at the end. Orange touched the door. "Six," he said. "Are you ready?"

Thomas nodded, although he wasn't sure he'd ever be ready for something like this.

Orange pushed the door open, and they stepped into the room. For seconds it seemed as if time was suspended. Five men and a woman were sitting and standing in different parts of the room. They looked up, clearly expecting to see someone else. Aina pointed her pistol and shot the nearest man in the chest. Orange fired a shot, and a body fell to the ground. The woman rushed at her, but Aina shot her in her side. She fell to the floor cursing. Orange shot a second man. A man with green curly hair aimed his gun at Aina, and Thomas shot him in his chest. Aina walked up to the woman, who was crying in pain on the floor. Aina aimed her gun.

"No!" Lucy cried. "She's unarmed." Aina shot her, and the woman's cries ended.

"Enough," Thomas said. Orange didn't listen. He knocked a knife from the remaining man's hand and broke his neck.

"Gleemen," Nancy whispered, as he heard footsteps run into the room.

Thomas stepped out from behind the door and pointed his gun at the two men's heads. "Drop them!"

The Gleemen placed their guns on the floor. "The Gleeman is coming," one of them said. "He'll kill you."

Aina stepped towards them and raised her pistol.

"Aina, no!" Thomas shouted.

She shot the first one in the chest. The other man went for his gun, and she shot him in his neck.

"Aina? What are you doing?" Lucy asked. "They were unarmed."

"You said you wanted to free the girls. What do you think it'll take?" Aina pointed at the woman's body. "Was she a Gleeman?"

Nancy nodded.

"Then we have six more."

Lucy was looking at the bodies on the floor, her stun gun forgotten in her hand. "I didn't mean like this."

"How did you mean?" Aina raised her voice. "She's one of them, too." Aina pointed her gun at the whimpering green girl. The girl choked back her screams and fell back against the wall.

"Aina, it's over," Thomas said. He put his arm around her, and she lowered her gun.

"She enjoyed it," the green girl said, staring at Aina in concern.

Thomas wasn't sure about that, but he was concerned for Aina. They stood in the middle of the room and looked at the dead who lay on the floor.

Nancy pointed to a doorway. "Those are the Gleeman's private rooms."

They walked into a living room with a red leather armchair by a gas fire; a decanter of a dark spirit and a single glass sat on a table next to the chair. Four closed doors led out: three for them were unlocked. "Let's search the open ones," Thomas said. "Orange, can you guard the main door." Everybody, apart from the green girl, began searching.

Lucy screamed. He cursed and ran through the living room and into the room she was searching. Lucy stood in the middle of a sumptuous bedchamber, staring at the large circular bed. Thomas lowered his gun when he saw the remains of an orgy gone wrong. "It's too late for them." They left the room in silence.

Thomas pointed at the dead woman and then to the naked girl. "Take her clothes. They should fit you." The girl looked at the corpse and the bloody clothes and shook her head.

Nancy took the woman's jacket and boots and picked up a knife and pistol from the floor. "There's another doorway in that room," Nancy said.

Thomas nodded. "I want to check the last of the bedrooms first." It was the most richly furnished of the rooms with a four-poster bed and tapestries displaying naked women hanging from the walls. Most of the tapestries hung from hooks, but one of them hung from a wooden pole on the wall. He pulled it back to reveal a locked metal door. "I've found it," he said.

Aina, Lucy, and Nancy joined him in the room. "How do you know it's this one?" Lucy asked.

"I don't know. I just do." Thomas wasn't sure whether it was the size of the door or whether it was because it was hidden behind a curtain.

Aina tried the door. Then she placed her hands on it and listened. "I think he's right." She turned to Thomas with a grin. "Well done! You're learning to use your intuition." Thomas gave a tight smile. He knew she was being mildly sarcastic. "Really," she said. "Orange would know for sure. And he could probably open it."

"Do you want me to fetch him?" Nancy asked.

"Not yet." Thomas looked in the drawers next to the bed. "There should be a special key, a large one." He found mouldy bread, but no key.

The bedroom door slammed shut, and a bolt clicked into place. "Are you looking for this?"

Thomas cursed and turned to see a man holding a large key. Five other men stood around him, pointing guns at them. The naked prostitute ran to the man with the key. "I'm not with them," the girl pleaded. "They forced me to come here."

The Gleeman took a handful of her hair and forced the girl to look up at him. "You betrayed me."

"No," she said. The Gleeman pointed to the ground, and she collapsed to the floor.

"You, too," he said to Nancy, pointing at the floor in front of him. "And you can get out of those clothes."

"Why don't you drop dead!" Nancy said, spitting on the floor in front of him.

The Gleeman chuckled without humour. "A client will pay a premium to beat her." He kicked the girl on the floor, and then pointed at Nancy, "But you'll get the special." Then he turned to the others. "Put your weapons down and sit there." He pointed to a space in front of the large door. They had little choice.

"Orange," Thomas thought. *"If what you've told me about telepathy is true, come now."* Aina turned to him and nodded. Had she heard his thought?

The Gleeman took hold of Lucy's chin and moved her face from side to side. She resisted, but the man was strong. "Everything you have, including your mind, belongs to me. And I keep what's mine."

Then his tone changed. "Now tell me what you're doing in my personal quarters? And how you killed eight of my Gleemen?" When they didn't answer, he continued. "And how did you learn about my treasury?"

Thomas noticed that the Gleeman wore a ring with a ruby inserted between a circle of small spikes.

The Gleeman noticed him look. "Do you like my blood ring?"

Thomas felt its presence. It pulsed—as if it were alive.

"Shall I tickle you with it?" One of the Gleemen grinned.

Thomas's mind touched the stone, and the man's finger moved. "What?" the man said. Thomas wasn't sure what he'd done. He concentrated again on the stone in the ring.

He felt disoriented and confused about his new feelings and where they came from. He saw the bloody face of a girl. Then more faces and pain. The disturbing images seemed to be coming from the ring, as if they were its memories. When he saw the Gleeman murder a child, his temper flared.

The Gleeman screamed. He punched himself in his head. Blood ran down his cheek.

He felt Lucy lean in close. "Is that you?" she whispered.

"I think so," he said. Aina grinned at him.

"He's lost it," one of the Gleemen said.

"It's not me! It's the ring!" The Gleeman struggled to pull the ring off his finger. He threw it on the floor, and it rolled towards Thomas who quickly picked it up.

"Well done," Lucy whispered.

"What?" the Gleeman shrieked, but he was now less sure of himself. However, when Thomas didn't immediately respond, some of his bluster returned. "I'll kill you for that." He turned to his men. "Tie them up."

The men stepped forward, and Thomas raised his open palm. The ring glowed and the men hesitated. He had no idea what he could do with the thing—apart from throw it. Then more images flooded into his mind: scenes the red jewel had witnessed. He watched in shock until he felt Aina lean against him. "Share," she whispered.

Thomas breathed more easily as the mental pressure

was released. The images flowed into the minds of the watching criminals. As hard as they were, their minds were open to suggestion. They saw scenes of murder and torture, some of which had been committed against previous Gleemen. The men looked at their boss.

"We've all done bad things. You know that," the boss said nervously.

They watched the Gleeman and didn't see the form emerge from the wall behind them. Orange roared, and even Thomas started.

"Kill it!" the Gleeman screamed.

It was too late for the closest men. The troll wrapped his arms around them and pulled them back through the stone wall. A puddle of their remains formed on the floor. Thomas threw the ring at the Gleeman. It hit the man in his temple, and he went down.

The troll re-emerged through the wall and killed another Gleeman. Aina leant forward, picked up her gun and shot one of the men.

Another Gleeman, a woman, threw down her weapon. "I surrender."

"Aina!" Lucy shouted. "That's enough!"

Aina pointed her gun and shot the surprised woman in her chest. "Why?" she asked before falling to the ground dead.

The Gleeman sat alone on the floor. He looked around his bloody bedroom in confusion. "Who are you?" he asked Aina.

"The Orange Company." She shot him in his head.

Thomas pulled the key from the Gleeman's corpse. He looked around the room at his friends. Lucy was clearly disturbed by what she'd seen. She watched Aina nervously,

Aina stared at the corpses, and Nancy was trying to wipe the blood from her clothes.

"Do you want to come with us?" he asked Nancy.

She looked up, still wiping herself clean. "No. Now the Gleemen are dead, I think I'll stay.

"Will you be okay?" Lucy asked.

Nancy nodded. "The worst are gone." She picked up a pistol and an automatic weapon. "With these and the money in his treasury, I'll be fine."

"There's nothing else to do here," Thomas said. He opened the door and passed Nancy the key. "Make sure you lock up after us."

She nodded and grinned. "Don't worry."

He took Aina, who seemed shocked by the killing, by her hand and gently led her into the dark stone passage. They walked through caves filled with boxes and then into deeper, more silent tunnels. The bolt on the metal door shot into place behind them.

20

Orange led them along the dark passage through the mountain for several hours. Their progress was slow, and Thomas stung from the cuts and bruises of walking into the jagged rocks. Although his night vision seemed to have improved, it didn't help in the total darkness of the passage. But he did seem to have a sense of the rocks.

"Orange? What's happening to me? My senses have sharpened, and sometimes I know things I shouldn't be able to," Thomas asked.

"When you travelled between the planes, your latent magic stirred, and the closer you get to the keys, the more your magic will awaken. They channel power into you."

"But Aina doesn't have any keys." He glanced back at her; she'd stopped to take a drink

"She developed natural magic when she was a child. That's the first stage. The ancient forest is a place of pressure, and its magic pushes and permeates into its own—and as a child, she was a creature of the forest. It's a place where you learn quickly or die."

"She once mentioned a dragon." Thomas had thought her story innocent and childlike, but now he was less sure.

"The black dragon saved her life and breathed a special fire on her," Orange said. "The kind of fire a dragon breathes on its own young to awaken their magic. I've never heard of this happening outside of a dragon family before, and certainly not to a human."

"I didn't know that about her," Thomas said. He felt Lucy's presence behind him.

Orange's deep voice became louder. "I'm going to scout the tunnels. I'll be back later. Use your feelings to find your way."

"Wait," Lucy said. Orange turned to face her. "You talked about natural magic. Does that mean there's an unnatural magic?"

"Natural magic flows in harmony with the universe, while black magic forces itself on life." Orange turned and disappeared into the darkness. The four of them were alone deep inside the mountain.

"Something to think about while we grope our way through the darkness," Thomas said.

"He does things like that," Aina said. She squeezed past Lucy and took Thomas's hand.

"Can you sense him?" Lucy asked.

Thomas stood quietly for several seconds. He wasn't sure, but he did have a feeling that he knew where Orange was. "This way." He also felt the rocks and minerals around him; excitedly, he noticed the types of rocks just from their feel. He seemed to have developed a sixth sense. He held Aina's hand, and they walked through the dark passage in silence.

Orange was absent for much of the journey, although he returned each night. When he did appear, he showed

Thomas things that he'd never imagined possible. Thomas realized that if he doubted his own experience, then he'd be as illogical as those he'd once condemned for their lack of reason.

One incident affected Thomas more than any other—it was on the third night. They were deep within the mountain. Aina slept, but Lucy was missing, which was unlike her. Thomas got up and walked back down the tunnel. He moved confidently through the darkness now, sensing the rock around him. He was drawn to a cavern they'd passed earlier but hadn't entered.

A light came from the cavern. He stopped at the entrance and watched the shadows dance on the wall.

"Hello," Lucy said. She crouched in the corner of the cavern with Orange. The troll moulded a substance in his hands.

"What's that?" Thomas asked.

"Molten rock," Lucy said.

Thomas came closer as the troll continued to mould the substance in his hands; he hummed as he worked. The substance glowed. His hands moved faster and faster. Thomas thought he saw sparks jump out of the cracks between Orange's fingers.

The troll opened his hands and threw a steaming mass of molten rock into Lucy's face. The molten rock stuck to her face and blood welled up. Thomas rushed to Lucy. Her head hung down, and blood dropped onto her lap in a lump. But when she looked up, her face was normal. There was no sign of blood or scarring.

A dark thing flew at him. He pulled back, and then the shadow was gone. "What happened?" he asked.

"What did you see?" Orange asked.

"A glowing red butterfly," Lucy said.

"You didn't see that, did you?" The troll looked at Thomas.

"No, I saw you throw something at Lucy, and then I saw her bleed."

"Lucy stared at him, her eyes wide, and Thomas realized that something outside of his experience was happening. Again.

"You saw an illusion because your mind couldn't accept the truth." Thomas looked again, and this time he saw a bright creature on the cavern wall. How could he have mistaken a red butterfly for blood?

Thomas sat on the floor of the cave. What he'd just seen shouldn't have been possible. Lucy and Orange were talking, but he didn't listen. He sat still, and he soon ceased to feel his body. He felt as if he had sunk into the rock and had become one with it. The rocks vibrated around him, the small spaces within the rock, the empty spaces and the forces that held them together. He felt Prometheus all around him. It was bright, energetic, and full of life. He didn't know how much time had passed, but when he looked again, he saw his friends in front of him as they had been before.

"Something just happened to me," he said.

Orange scooped another fistful of rock from the wall of the cavern. He placed the strangely viscous rock in Thomas's hands. It was hot but didn't burn. He moved his hands around the bright rock; he didn't speak for several minutes. He opened his hand to reveal a turquoise stone.

"A beautiful egg," Lucy said. The red butterfly then fluttered towards her and landed on her arm. She lifted it up. "Have you created life?"

"I created a body. Life chooses whether or not to inhabit it," Orange answered.

"What kind of life is it?" she asked.

"A rock spirit."

The foundations of Thomas's world view had been shaken. His old beliefs didn't explain the strangeness of this world, but he was unable to uncover an adequate set of beliefs that would explain it.

21

On the morning of the fourth day, they followed the rock troll through a winding series of caves. Thomas noticed a greyness framed by darker rocks and a biting cold. They'd reached the mouth of the cave.

Thomas stepped onto a narrow rocky ledge and stopped. On the far side of a deep abyss was a citadel: the Crown of the Empire. The Crown seemed to grow out of the rock itself. Hundreds of lights shone from crystal windows. Its outer walls were only thirty yards away, but a deep chasm prevented any direct access. From deeper within the Crown, a black tower rose.

"It's beautiful!" Lucy said, stepping up next to him. Then she looked down and began to sway. "Thomas!"

He pushed her back against the rock wall. Something had definitely happened to him. He was attracted to the rock face like a piece of iron to a magnet.

Lucy's eyes were closed. "Thomas, I feel dizzy."

"Stay close to me. I won't let you fall."

Aina came out next. Unlike Lucy, she didn't seem to

notice the drop at all—he wasn't sure which reaction disturbed him more. Orange came last.

To their left, just beyond Aina, the ledge crumbled away and disappeared. To the right, it formed a path of sorts. Perhaps one suitable for mountain goats, if such an animal existed on Prometheus. A cold wind blasted the mountain, making walking along the ledge even more treacherous.

"The wind's increasing. We should go," he said.

"Go?" Lucy asked, looking nervously over the ledge.

"We only have one choice. Unless we want to go back," Thomas said.

"No way," Aina said.

Orange strolled along the narrow rock path, his long orange hair streaming out behind him in the strong gusts of wind. He walked past the others so close to the edge that his feet were only partially supported by rock. He grinned as he passed Thomas.

"This path will take us down, eventually," Orange said.

Lucy looked away, her face pale. "Or very quickly," she added.

Aina smiled for the first time in three days, and Thomas breathed out a sigh of relief; she was recovering from the shock of what had happened with the Gleemen. Orange moved ahead and then disappeared around an outcrop of rock.

"Great," Thomas said.

"That's a troll for you," Aina said.

"But not when we're on an icy ledge on the side of an abyss."

Thomas walked along the ledge. He firmly held Lucy's hand. Aina walked close behind Lucy. Over the next hour, Lucy slipped three times: each time she was caught by either Thomas or Aina.

On one of their frequent rests, Thomas commented on Aina's ability to walk along the narrow path. "Orange told me about your natural magic. Is that how you stick to the rock?"

She smiled. "I'm pleased you've changed your mind on magic. And yes, it helps me climb, but your affinity to earth magic will make you stickier than me. It's already working."

"I thought it was rock magic?"

"That's Orange's speciality. But rock magic is only one type of earth magic."

She was right. Thomas could feel his affinity to the rock growing. But despite his increased confidence, it was painstaking and painful work. A few times, gusts of frigid wind forced them to stop and press close to the rock for fear of falling.

"There's Orange," Thomas said. They looked at the distant troll; he waved at them. "He's stopped." It took another hour of slow movement along the path before they reached him.

Orange stood next to a rusty footbridge that extended to about two feet from the ledge. "How odd," Lucy said.

There were several more footbridges of various designs that stretched out from the citadel's outer wall across the abyss. Only a few of them completely spanned the chasm. One bridge stopped halfway across the drop. "Extending footbridges," Aina said.

"Why?" Lucy asked.

"For Nassopolitan aristocrats to experience the wilderness in safety."

"This bridge is old and hasn't been used in a long time," Orange said. Thomas noticed that much of the paint had already peeled off. "I sense no life within the rooms."

"Then it's a good place to enter," Thomas said. "Can you open the door?"

Orange raised his eyebrows. "There are few human doors that can withstand a rock troll."

"Just asking," Thomas said. He stepped onto the bridge, and it creaked under his weight. He quickly crossed to the red door on the other side, Lucy, Aina, and Orange following. Orange placed his hands on the door, and several seconds later it swung open.

They walked into a reception room with old couches and low tables. It had a musty smell. Lucy wiped dust from a table. "Don't leave signs that we've been here," Thomas said.

"Oh," she said, moving her hand away.

"I don't think anyone will be back soon," Aina said. They quickly explored the apartment: it had three bedrooms, all of which had wardrobes of clothes. "The last occupant was a mercantile lord."

"How do you know?" Thomas asked.

She pulled out a green jacket with brown trimmings. "Mercantile Order, third class."

Thomas raised his eyebrow. "And?"

"We need a disguise, and this order is as good as any, perhaps better because merchants are looked down upon in the Empire."

"How is that good?" Lucy asked.

"Most aristocrats will ignore us because of our lower rank. We'll be freer to explore."

Thomas was very aware of their ignorance of the layout of the Crown—particularly of the Tower. He turned on a computer and searched for plans of the citadel. "Here." He general plans of the groups of buildings around the peak, but he could see nothing about the Tower, which lay on a smaller peak nearby.

"Don't even search for it," Aina said. "They'll notice."

"Well, at least we have something."

They dressed as members of the Mercantile Order and were wondering what to do when Lucy pointed at the screen she'd activated. "The Empire Day celebrations."

"Empire Day," Aina said. "I'd forgotten about that."

"There are events every day for a week," Lucy said. She looked up excitedly. "There's a special event this evening in the Tower."

Thomas stood next to Lucy and examined the screen. "She's right. Aristocrats are being taken from receptions all over the citadel this afternoon. There's one in this building in three hours from now."

"Let's party," Aina said.

They sat down with bottles of a chemical tasting beer—almost the only thing in the kitchen—and discussed their plans in more detail. Most of what they knew about the Tower came from Lucy's dream. She was sure they had to go to the top of it.

"I can feel the key," she said. "And the feeling's getting stronger. I've noticed I can hear thoughts, too."

"That's possible," Orange said. "It senses you and can help, even at a distance."

"What about Thomas's key?" Aina said.

"They're together," Lucy said.

"I don't think so," Thomas said. Everybody looked at him, and he wondered why he'd just spoken. After all, he had no idea where it was. It was usually Lucy talking about feelings and intuition. "I'm not sure, but I have a gut feeling it's somewhere else."

"Where?"

"In the earth." He had the sense it was deeper, but that

made little sense. "I think it's underground. I hope they didn't leave it in 28th."

"I know what I saw," Lucy said, "but they may have moved it again."

"I'll visit the Tower tonight," Orange said. "It's time we discovered its secrets."

"Won't they sense you enter?" Aina asked.

"A troll can be quiet when he wants."

Holding his breath, Thomas entered the Great Hall with Aina and Lucy. He felt uncomfortable in the stiff green costume, but no one gave them a second glance. Other aristocrats of various orders milled about the ballroom. The mood was of excitement, and guests took drinks and snacks from the long tables. Lucy picked up a star-shaped cake and bit into it. She spat it into her hand and dropped it under the table.

"What's wrong?" Thomas asked.

"It tastes like sweet cardboard," Lucy said.

Aina laughed. "That's basically what it is. Nassopolitans don't eat natural food. I've always suspected their mental software dulls their taste."

Thomas looked at the lords and ladies of the Empire. They were distinguished by the colours and styles of their costumes, and as each order had many ranks, the reception was colourful. A lady of the Star Order walked past and muttered "interplanetary merchants" in a disapproving tone. Thomas was pleased; the fewer people they spoke to the better.

"I don't like it here," Lucy said.

"What do you mean?" Thomas asked.

"It's unnatural. There's no life apart from the lords and ladies, and they only seem half alive. Everything's plastic, including the flowers and the stupid budgerigars."

"It's not the utopia they think it is," he said. "Lucy, have you noticed a feeling?"

"A tingling, electric sort of feeling?"

"Yes, that's it." She'd described it perfectly. "Do you think it's the keys?"

"I do," she said.

Aina nodded. "Magic can work like that."

"What exactly is magic?" Thomas asked. He couldn't accept that the things happening to him were unexplainable. Just as Aina began to reply, he had a strange sensation. "I think we need to stand over there." He nodded towards one of the walls.

"Why?" Aina asked.

"I don't know."

"Thomas, you need to work on examining your feelings more," Aina said. She took his and Lucy's hands, and they strolled over to the place he'd indicated.

A woman smiled as they approached, and they smiled back. Several cages of brightly-coloured robot birds had been placed on a long table by the wall. They chirped, turned their heads and fluttered their wings, but did little else, Thomas hoped, remembering the mechanical pigeons. They pretended to take an interest them, until the lady wandered off into the crowd.

"Now what?" Lucy asked.

Thomas had no idea, but he still had a feeling he couldn't explain. "I just have a feeling that someone wants to speak to us."

Then Aina looked at the wall and grinned. "Orange," she whispered.

Thomas and Lucy followed her gaze. He started, and Lucy spilt some of her drink, prompting a robot beetle to scuttle from beneath the table and wipe it up.

Orange's face pushed out of the stone wall like a moving mask. "I walked around the Tower and sensed a basement."

"Why didn't you enter?" Aina asked.

"The Tower's sentient and malevolent. I didn't wish to alert it to my presence."

"How can that be?" Thomas asked, his forehead creasing slightly.

"I sense black magic and a melding of unwilling souls."

Lucy wrinkled her nose in disgust. "That's appalling."

"Yes," Orange said.

"Can we help them?"

"The sorcery is beyond my powers to undo. We have our own concerns." Thomas felt a little surprised; he'd started to think of Orange as being almost invincible. The troll continued. "I'll meet you in the Tower, but you must remain invisible to the many eyes within its walls."

"This is getting worse," Thomas said. "What if the transport won't take us to the Tower?"

"Find a way to enter," Orange said. Lucy glanced at Thomas, her eyes wide. "If we become separated, continue with the plan. If only one of you takes a key, then the tide may still turn in our favour. But leave the Tower as soon as you can. It's both evil and dangerous."

"What if they take the keys?" Aina asked.

"The keys alone will not defeat these sorcerers—and remember that Thomas and Lucy need time to learn how to use them. You'll need to lure the sorcerers out of the Tower, which is their ally, to the ancient forest, which is yours. There, the power of Prometheus will be with you." Then his face faded from the stone wall, leaving it as smooth as it had been minutes earlier.

"I feel like I've got a hangover without having drunk anything," Thomas said. Both Aina and Lucy looked at him with sombre expressions. He wanted this dull reception to end, and the narrow buses he saw through one of the rare windows to take them to the Tower.

The room lights dimmed and spotlights lit a stage. A lord of the Imperial Order stepped up, and the audience applauded. The man was accompanied by a young woman. They both wore dark grey cloaks. The clapping slowed down. When the room became silent, the woman spoke.

"Lord Locke." Again the audience applauded.

The lord watched the crowd. Thomas noticed the hypnotic effect he seemed to have on his audience. Lord Locke looked around the room without speaking. Suddenly everybody laughed and burst into applause. Something very strange was happening. He looked at Aina, who was applauding. She indicated that he and Lucy should do the same.

"A herd of cows," Lord Locke said. The lady laughed and the audience applauded.

The Empire was downloading a speech directly into the minds of the people. The applause stopped suddenly, but Thomas gave an extra clap. Lord Locke looked in his direction. Thomas silently cursed. The lord studied the audience, then gestured to a company police officer standing at the side of the room. The man leant close and listened before nodding and leaving the stage. There was another burst of applause.

Aina pulled his arm. He didn't need encouragement. There were about a hundred people between them and the lord, but the police were already pushing people aside to get to them.

The odd audience reactions continued, even when they bumped into the insensible aristocracy as they hurried towards the back of the room. The audience was completely unaware of what was happening around them.

The programmed speech didn't last long. Although Thomas had no idea how long it had appeared to the rapt audience. Suddenly the applause became varied. The audience was smiling, and some had turned around to comment, others were clapping harder.

"They have their minds back," Thomas said.

"I didn't know they could do that," Aina said. "It's worse than I thought."

"Yes, much worse," Thomas said. "We've lost our way into the Tower."

"Then we find another way." They reached the edge of the crowd and ran. After a short sprint, Thomas turned back. All he could see was an empty passageway.

"Lucy," he shouted. She'd fallen behind. "We could stop and fight them."

"There are too many," Aina said.

Lucy appeared from around the corner. "I'm here." She was breathing heavily. Thomas didn't think she was unfit, but compared to himself and Aina, she was. When she'd caught up, they ran again. Loudspeakers announced the presence of the Orange Company in the citadel. Citizens were advised to use extreme caution if they were seen. Thomas cursed.

They ran for several minutes and seemed to be pulling away from their pursuers. Thomas glanced back. "Damn! Lucy's gone again. She's not as fast as us. We should've known better. He called her on the tag, but it wasn't working.

Aina cursed. "The Empire could've blocked them. Mine's not working properly either." She pulled out her pistol, and they ran back to the last junction in the path. Men ran along the corridors towards them. Apart from the path they had already taken, there were three other choices. Aina gave him a worried look, then ran straight down the middle path. He went to the right.

Thomas's path ran along the outer part of the city. Large windows to his right showed the icy peaks around the citadel, and in the distance, he could see the Tower shrouded in mist. He was a faster runner than Lucy, and he knew he'd catch her up if she'd come this way.

He ran for about fifteen minutes—far enough to have caught up with her if she'd taken this passage. He prayed that Aina had chosen the right path. Several police officers followed him, and they were getting closer. As he passed a turn, a maintenance worker said something to him. Thomas ignored him and continued to run along the passage until he saw an attack bot flying down the corridor towards him. He sprinted back to the turn. The worker moved out of the way and then shouted for help. There was a small door into a maintenance area that looked like it was used for bots to repair the outside of the city. He opened the door, crawled inside, and slammed it shut.

He opened the outer door and stepped onto the snow. The Tower rose on a smaller peak a little away from the main part of the citadel. Hailstones hit him hard as he walked in the direction of the Tower.

The storm increased in intensity, but he kept walking until he slipped and fell over an edge, dropping onto a flat area five or six feet below. In this weather, he'd be invisible to his pursuers as long as he could put enough distance between himself and them.

Shivering in the freezing wind, he thought of heat, and he felt the same tingling sensation Lucy had talked about. Heat radiated through his body and into his chilled limbs. As it did, pain wracked his body; he'd been too quick.

He heard the police behind him. He had seconds to hide. An attack bot flew out of the building and down the mountain on the far side. It'd be back soon. There was a drift of snow in front of him, and he crawled into it. Thomas desperately tried to scoop the snow up to cover himself, but it was frozen. He slipped and fell onto the surface face down. A second bot flew from the building.

His chest was wet. He cursed and looked down, but there was no blood. The heat he was drawing into his body had melted the ice. He sank into the thick drift of snow that was now melting all around him. He kept sinking, and within seconds he was covered by a layer of ice and protected from the gale. He sank deeper and finally came to rest on a rocky floor. He turned around and looked up. He was hidden in an ice room. Steam rose from his clothes. At least the hailstones couldn't hurt him here. Thomas watched the shadows of the bots on his ice ceiling as they circled above. Tiredness came over him, and he fell into a deep sleep, wet but warm within his icy chamber.

22

Aina's only thought was to find Lucy. She paid no attention to the squeals of the aristocrats she knocked and sent spinning into walls as she ran past. Her hope of concealment had gone; now she needed speed and luck.

Ahead of her, a plain metal door was slightly ajar. She stopped, curious. Would Lucy have gone inside to hide? She pushed the door open wider. It was a large storage area with many crates and boxes. She slipped inside. "Lucy?" she said quietly. Something moved to her left. A dog in a cage watched her. It was nervous, and she sent the animal thoughts of peace. It tilted its head and watched her. *"Good dog."* She didn't want it to bark. This was the kind of place Lucy would hide. The room was big, but she didn't dare call any louder. There were footsteps in the corridor. She shut the door and moved deeper into the room.

The door opened, and the dog growled at the man who entered the room. A sergeant discussed the search with other police. A hand grasped her shoulder. Aina nearly cried out.

"Lucy," she whispered. "What're you doing here? We've been looking for you."

"Where's Thomas?"

"He's still looking for you."

"I'm sorry; I couldn't keep up."

"It was our fault. It's not the first time this has happened. But why did you come in here?"

"I followed my feelings."

For a second, Aina wished she'd never attempted to train Lucy's intuition. She needed Lucy to be focussed, not wandering off whenever her intuition called her. "Lucy, now is not the time to follow feelings."

"If not now, then when?" Aina had no answer. Lucy was right. It was her frustration at being trapped like the animals in the room. She had no answer. "You mean my feelings better be right?" Lucy said.

"We're here now."

The sergeant ordered two of the men to search the room; the others followed him down the corridor.

"And we're trapped."

"Maybe not," Lucy whispered. "I think I've found a way into the Tower." Lucy touched a large metal crate. "In here."

Aina read the label. "Lucy? Do you know what's inside?"

"A snow leopard."

Aina looked at the vents on the side; the smell coming through them was strong. "An animal for a rich lord," Aina said.

"He's going to a lord in the Tower."

"Is that your intuition?"

"No." Lucy rolled her eyes in exasperation. "The label says so."

Aina checked the label carefully. "You're right. Lucy, what happened with the glimmer leopard in Scarlet was not sure to happen, and we weren't in a confined space. This could be a very short and very bloody journey."

"It's okay," Lucy said. "I've asked him—he's willing for us to join him. I promised that I'd set him free on the mountain."

"Do you think you can do that?"

"I'll try." The wooden crate was large and inside it was a cage only slightly smaller. Lucy had already found the door. She opened it, and the leopard ran at her. Lucy merely crawled inside as the animal nosed her with curiosity. "Come in."

"Tell him I'm a friend," she said. She crawled into the crate, feeling for the animal's mind. His fierce energy almost overwhelmed her, and the young male leopard aggressively sniffed her. His eyes were inches from hers. It took all her strength to keep calm. Then their minds connected, and the young leopard relaxed.

Aina felt a mix of anger and excitement within the creature. As she brought herself into alignment with that excitement, its anger awakened her own burning hatred of the Empire. Images from the leopard's mind partially formed and then vanished from her mind. Pain, faces, one face in particular . . . the creature's new owner, perhaps. It returned to Lucy, who hugged the animal.

Someone slapped the crate, and Aina crawled deeper inside and sat next to Lucy. The leopard growled softly, its body tense. The metal slide was pulled back, and the snow leopard rushed at the narrow gap. This time it snarled in the face of a police officer, who jumped back in shock. It hissed at him, its ears flattened against its head. The officer hurriedly slid back the viewing panel. "I don't think they're hiding in there," a voice laughed nervously from the outside. The men continued to search the room, but no one came near the cage again.

They huddled in silence and listened to the sounds of the search outside. "Are they still there?" Lucy asked.

"I don't know, but we need to keep quiet until they move the crate." The collection was in a few hours. Aina was uncomfortable in the cage, and the smell of the animal was strong but not unpleasant. She'd been in worse situations, but she was concerned for Thomas. She considered leaving the cage and searching for him, but what if he'd escaped? She could put him in more danger and perhaps risk the mission.

The creature had now decided that she was a friend, and it nuzzled both her and Lucy. Snow leopards would be easier to capture than the much larger and more dangerous glimmer leopards.

"Lucy, we should be ready to leave the crate as soon as it enters the Tower," Aina said.

"I've been thinking about that," Lucy said. "It might be better to stay in the cage."

"Why?"

"It may be hard to move freely through a sentient tower." Aina was worried by exactly that. "I think the number on the outside of the cage is the floor number, which would mean that this cage will be taken somewhere quite high up."

Aina wasn't sure. "You know that as soon as the lord takes a look at his new pet, he'll discover us?"

"We're going to be discovered at some stage. This will be at a place of our choosing."

"Okay." Aina couldn't think of any better plan, and she did like the idea of being taken up to the higher levels. "I just hope this lord's sleeping when we arrive."

The three of them fell asleep but were woken when cold

water was blasted into the cage. "It still stinks," a man said. They sat dripping in the darkness while the crate was loaded onto a vehicle. The temperature suddenly dropped. They were outside and moving along a bumpy road. Lucy told her an old Earth story of a Trojan horse. Venus had similar stories. Now Prometheus had one, she hoped. The Promethean leopard. A strange situation. She was sure that no one but Lucy would have thought of, or been able to carry out, this plan for gaining entry to the tower. The vehicle stopped, and they felt themselves being unloaded.

The crate was placed on something and rolled along the ground. Aina's eyes opened wide, and she looked at Lucy. "We're inside," Lucy said. The leopard was growling softly.

Aina nodded. Orange had been right about the Tower; it was already probing the crate. She gently called on her invisibility spell: Lucy did the same—just as Aina had taught her. Aina hoped it was enough. The crate was taken deeper into the Tower. The voices disappeared, but there was movement around them. The wooden covering was ripped from the outside of the metal cage. They raised their guns, but the simple worker robots doing the labour paid them no attention.

The robots placed a black cloth over the cage. Then they pushed it along a corridor and into a lift. It rose for several minutes. Then they moved along another corridor. Sounds of conversation came from ahead.

"I don't like this," Lucy said.

Aina agreed. It sounded like they were going to be the star attraction at a lord's party. Aina had already unbolted the cage door and had her pistol in her hand. Lucy held a stun pistol she'd found in the apartment.

Music, laughter, and the sounds of glasses clinking came from the room. The robots slid the cage from a trolley and left. The cage was now only covered by a black cloth.

"It smells," someone said.

"I had it cleaned, but I daresay it could do with another wash. It's clean enough for a quick viewing. Then we can retire to the veranda for cocktails."

The lord, Aina thought.

There was a murmur of agreement from the room. "It can't escape, can it?" someone asked.

"Impossible. The cage is bolted, and I have two well-trained, armed bodyguards. You're perfectly safe, I assure you." The lord is most likely armed, too, Aina thought.

She now sat right next to the cage door, the leopard pressing up against her. She could feel the tension in the animal. Lucy had led the animal's mind towards the voice of the lord, whom they both hoped it would attack. She would shoot the security, and Lucy would wave her stunner at the guests. It should work, she hoped.

Aina and the snow leopard tensed. The lord had just used his nascent psychic skills in an attempt to pacify the leopard. The young cat was having none of it. Aina ran her hand along the creature's back.

A trumpet sounded, and the aristocrat began his speech. "I wish to present, from my hunting expedition beyond the mountains, one of my prize exhibits. A snow leopard of Uranus." There were claps and cheers from the room.

As the cloth was being pulled back, Aina opened the door, and the snow leopard slipped out. By the time the cloth had been completely pulled away, the gathered aristocracy were staring into a cage with a single girl sitting in the middle. She had a grin and a stunner in her hand.

There were gasps from the aristocratic audience. They'd not immediately noticed Aina or the leopard.

"Is this a joke?" a lady asked.

The cat pounced on the lord. He raised his hands in defence, and two of his fingers landed on the lady's dish. The leopard then slashed his throat. The lady stared at the blood decorating her finger food and fainted.

Aina shot the nearest guard, and Lucy stunned the other. The lords and ladies looked at the dead men in shock, and some of them glared at Aina and Lucy, but nobody spoke. Lucy was distracted by the heavy rain pounding the windows and the violent bolts of lightning that lit the sky.

"Lucy, give me the stunner." She took the weapon and shot into the guests until they all fell to the floor. "Here." She passed it back.

"We can't leave the leopard," Lucy whispered.

"We can't take him with us, either," Aina said. "But he can follow, if he wants."

The front door opened onto a dark corridor. They ran towards the lifts. The leopard followed, but behind them, one of the aristocrats ran out and shot the leopard. "Damn! I thought I got them all," Aina said.

"No!" Lucy shouted. The animal fell stunned to the floor. Lucy stunned the man. He hit the obsidian floor hard and lay next to the unconscious leopard.

Aina dragged Lucy along the passage towards the lifts. "Lucy, stop it! There's no way we can drag a leopard where we're going."

"You're right," Lucy said. "I'll come back later. Aina, I can feel my key—the cup. It's calling me." Footsteps were coming along the stone corridor. They ran away from the footsteps and turned onto the circular steps. Lucy went first. She climbed up four flights of stairs and out onto a silent landing. "This way. I don't know where we are, but I know where the cup is."

As she ran, Aina thought she heard the Tower groan. "Did you hear that?"

"Yes!" Lucy said. "It knows we're here—we need speed."

Aina completely agreed. "How far is the room?"

"We're close!" Lucy opened a door, and a robot challenged them; Aina shot it, and it dropped to the floor and made popping sounds. They stood in a large hall with a high ceiling. As they walked across it, the walls murmured. "I think the cup's through there." Lucy pointed at a pair of large metal doors.

"Quick!" Lucy shouted. Aina needed no prompting. They sprinted across the room. Green slime oozed from the walls, and a faint vapour rose from it.

"It's glowing," Aina said. "What is it?"

"I don't know." Lucy pulled on the large pair of doors.

"Lucy!"

She struggled with the doors. "I can't open them!"

Aina glanced at the green stream moving towards them, and the wisps of vapour reaching out. "Let me try a different way." She searched for an intelligent lock on the doors that she could penetrate with her mind, but there was nothing. "Damn!"

"What?"

"It's an old-fashioned lock."

"Then use an old-fashioned method!" Lucy said, her voice rising as a claw-like wisp of green mist separated from the stream of slime and reached towards them. Aina raised her eyebrows. "Shoot it!"

Aina shot the lock; they pushed the large doors open together. "Good. You're learning." As she turned to close the door, Aina saw a man watching her from the other end of the hall; he made no attempt to enter, and she wasn't surprised with the green stuff oozing from the walls. The claw of green mist was only yards away—she slammed the door shut.

The room was large, but smaller than the hall. It had a bare stone floor, a high-domed ceiling and a tall, narrow window placed high on the wall; there were two arched doorways leading to other rooms. A bookcase stood against one of the walls, there were two chairs, and in the middle was a crystal cabinet. "From your dream?" Aina asked.

Lucy nodded and ran to the cabinet. She peered into it: a golden goblet lay inside, but there was no sign of the pentacle.

Lucy ran her hands along the side and underneath the cabinet, looking for a way to open it but found nothing.

The door banged as if someone had pushed it hard from the other side. "The Tower's attacking us," Lucy said. She glanced up at the ceiling. "Look."

A green lattice was forming high up in the domed ceiling. Aina looked back at the door. That was the immediate problem, but nothing was seeping in—yet. Lucy pulled at and hit the cabinet but couldn't open it. "It's locked."

"Let me try," Aina said. Lucy was right, it was stuck tight. A screech came from the hall, and Aina cursed. She ran to the door.

"Don't open it!" Lucy shouted.

"I know." Aina put her head against the door and felt the life on the other side. Then she frantically pulled a bookshelf to the door; it crashed down with books, spilling across the floor. "Ice demons are crawling along the ceiling." Lucy shivered and turned back to the cabinet. "And we're so close," Aina said. "Let me try again." She aimed her pistol at the cabinet.

"No!" Lucy shouted. The bullet bounced off the cabinet and ricocheted past her. "Aina! You nearly hit me."

"Sorry, I didn't think it would do that. But we have to open it fast. We can't fight two ice demons and this green stuff with two pistols—and one of them's only a stunner." She struck the hardened glass with the butt of her pistol.

"I can feel it; it's as if it's alive," Lucy said. She rested her hands on the top of the crystal cabinet. "Aina, I feel strange, hot. Oh, my hands!" Aina looked at her. Her cheeks seemed oddly flushed.

A screech came from somewhere very close, and the door moved. Aina wedged a chair against the door and positioned herself between the door and Lucy.

The door opened, and an ice demon's head appeared. Aina shot it in its forehead. It squealed and disappeared. Its gun fell to the floor.

"Something's happening," Lucy said. Aina had no idea what she was talking about. "Oh, Aina!"

"What's happened?"

"I don't know. This is really strange. My hands just slipped through the crystal, like it melted." Aina looked back. Lucy's arms were moving freely through the gooey-glassy substance. She took the cup. The cabinet glowed for a few more seconds and then returned to its original colour. Lucy tapped it. It was warped but completely solid.

"Lucy, do something!" Aina said. The door flew open, snapping the back of the chair, and knocking books into her legs.

An ice demon spat at them as it ran into the room. It leapt to one side as she fired. She coughed on the fumes from the corrosive spit as it burnt through an antique leather-bound book. Aina fired again. A second ice demon swung under from the top of the door and dropped in front of her. It wore a heavy machine gun across its shoulder, which it unslung.

"Use the cup!" Aina screamed. Sweat dripped from her face as she glanced back at Lucy.

Lucy looked at the black and green ice demons, then down at the golden goblet, but nothing happened. "There's no training manual," she said.

Aina stared at her in disbelief. "I hope you're joking about a training manual and that you're about to kill them all!"

23

The lizards rushed Aina, knocking the pistol from her hand. It was empty anyway. The creatures smelt unpleasant, and she pulled away, pressing herself against the cabinet. "Do something!" she said.

Aina had the sinking realization that what Orange had said about them needing time to learn how to use the keys was all too true. She glanced down at the stream of green slime; at least that seemed to be receding.

One of the lizards reached out to touch Lucy. It looked at her with its head slightly to one side.

"Lucy, you're glowing," Aina said. She looked at the faint golden light emanating from her friend.

The ice demon reached out for the cup, but Lucy held it tightly. The ice demon hissed and pulled harder. A flash of light made Aina blink; the lizard fell to the floor and whimpered.

"What did you do, Lucy?" she asked.

She looked from the lizard to Aina and back to the lizard lying on the floor, her eyes wide. "I didn't do anything." The second ice demon aimed its gun at Lucy and fired. Aina screamed and kicked the creature, and she found herself flung across the room.

She sat up slowly and brushed dirt from her face. The second ice demon lay sprawled on the floor—it was dead. "What happened?" she asked slowly.

"I just held the cup in front of me. The bullets ricocheted off it and hit the demon in its face."

Aina walked over to the dead ice demon and bent over to look at its wounds. "It serves it right for using a gun like that." She removed the automatic weapon from its claws. "I should kill this one, too."

"No," Lucy said.

"Why not?"

"I'm not sure, but I think you shouldn't kill her."

"Her?" Aina looked closer. Lucy was right; this one was slightly smaller than the other and was bleeding from its face. "It'd kill us."

"I just have a feeling we shouldn't kill her. Let's access their computer system and download imperial intelligence reports to Silva."

"That's a good idea, but where's the computer system?"

"I think it's somewhere close," Lucy said. Aina watched her carefully. Apart from the glow, which had now subsided, she'd changed subtly. She seemed more confident. Lucy pointed at one of the archways. "Something's in there."

"That might not be good," Aina said. She walked in with her gun, ready for any attack, but it was just another stone room. This one had a large desk facing them; a crystal ball sat in the middle.

"What's that?" Lucy asked.

Aina had only seen them in books, but she knew what it was. "Access to the computer system." She sat at the desk and touched the crystal. A screen appeared in front of her. Then it faded away. "Damn security system," she muttered.

She looked up at Lucy, who sat in a chair and seemed to be contacting the leopard. Aina focussed on the computer; she needed an access code. She suspected only two or three people on Prometheus had this level of clearance. She tried all the codes she'd stolen from the manor house, but after minutes of trying, she was still unable to gain access. This was the most secure system she'd encountered.

Lucy joined her by the computer. "Can you get in?"

"I've tried." A screen glowed in front of her. "But it's well protected. It's nothing like the usual systems."

"What about using the other way? The way you used with the glimmer leopard and the bots," Lucy asked.

"Perhaps, but entering the minds of animals is easier because they're living. And bots are basic, but this is a complex system, and I don't know what level of protection they've put in."

"Do you think it could be dangerous?"

Aina gave a half smile. "It's the Imperial Security system, of course it could be dangerous."

"You're going to try, though?" Lucy asked.

"Yes." Aina sat and concentrated. She allowed the noises of the room to pass through her. She relaxed deeply, and in her mind the outer world ceased to exist. Aina entered the consciousness of the computer. She was used to this and had trained herself in this form of magic but had never dealt with a machine mind as complex. She felt the loops and relays of circuits within it and saw machine language flash before her.

She explored the electrical circuits and guided by her feelings, she soon found what she wanted. She began to read the imperial plans. What she found was unpleasant.

"Aina, be careful," she heard Lucy say. "There's danger inside the machine."

Aina heard her but didn't respond. She was too far inside the computer's mind. But she was alert, and Lucy's warning saved her. A cyber creature attacked her, and she recoiled in pain. Her heart beat fast and irregularly. If she broke away, she could have a heart attack. The thing guarded the machine, but it wasn't part of it; it was some sort of psychic defence. The creature trapped inside the machine stopped its attack and growled mentally like some kind of spirit hound. She felt Lucy's presence within the mind of the machine.

"I can see something," Lucy said.

"I see nothing, but I can feel it," Aina responded. Then it attacked them again. A bright, dog-like creature. Lucy saw its chains, and through her, Aina saw them, too. *"Lucy, do you think you should do that?"*

"I think I've got no choice." Her cup flared with light, and she directed the light, like a laser, onto the chains. They snapped, and the chained spirit vanished.

"Where's it gone?" Aina asked.

"I released it," Lucy said.

"You keep surprising me," Aina said.

"It was an odd experience," Lucy said.

"You're telling me. Now let's do this fast while we're in the system." Several seconds passed, then Aina spoke aloud. "The program's downloading top security files into the computer system of the Silvan Resistance. It'll take some time."

They both pulled their minds free.

"What did you find?" Lucy asked.

"I only saw a little; Lucetta First will have more time to analyse their plans. But I did see that Martin Anlair wants to hire more legionnaires—they're arguing about money. The cost's gone up significantly after the loss of Deep Space Seven."

"Does he have the money?" Lucy asked.

"The Company certainly does. We need to stop Anlair before he can make any deal. And did you see what they were downloading into people's minds?" Aina asked.

"I'm not exactly sure what I saw. Its mind was strange, and I was dealing with the bright creature in the machine."

"Just before that, I saw something. A mental program aimed at the aristocracy."

"What kind of program?" Lucy asked.

"A procrastination program." Aina shook her head. "As if people need help with that."

"We must go," Lucy said. "The leopard's this way."

"We can't help it." Aina followed Lucy into the hall.

"I have the cup, and I can feel the difference." Lucy glowed more brightly for a second.

"I thought you still needed to learn how to use it?"

"I do, but I can learn when I use it." She pointed at the walls of the hall. "The green stuff's gone. I'm shielding us from it. The Tower can't see or hear us anymore." Lucy left the hall and ran down the stairs.

Aina was forced to follow her. "Lucy, don't get overconfident." Her friend ignored her as they ran back along the corridor, towards the lord's apartment. "Stop!" Aina grabbed Lucy's arm. "At least listen to me."

"Of course I'll listen, but I promised to help the leopard, too."

"I know, and I want to help it, I really do, but this could be a trap." The doorway to the apartment was only ten yards from where they stood.

"If it were a trap, I'd be able to sense something. I can

feel emotions and thoughts throughout the Tower; I can even sense the insects hiding in the cracks in the walls."

Aina had to admit that she couldn't sense any problem inside the room, but that didn't mean there wasn't one. "The leopard's inside," Lucy said.

Lucy walked into the apartment, and Aina followed with her pistol in her hand. As soon as she entered, a man punched her hard in her face.

She lay dazed and in pain on the floor. Her nose was bleeding, but at least it wasn't broken. Lord Anlair stood in the middle of the room. Lord Locke, five imperial police officers, and a pair of black bots stood around the sides of the apartment. The leopard was back in the cage.

"Thank you for showing me how to activate the device," Anlair said to Lucy. She backed up to the large glass windows to the balcony. An imperial police officer moved towards her. A bright bolt of lightning lit the purple sky, and rain continued to pound the strengthened glass. The police officer held Lucy's arm, and several of the aristocrats stood at the back of the room and watched.

"The Orange Witches," Lord Anlair said to the gathered lords and ladies. "The males will soon be ours, too."

So Thomas and Orange were still free, Aina thought.

Anlair addressed the aristocrats. "They're responsible for the deaths of thousands of innocent children, company soldiers, and for the murder of the lord of the manor for Silva." Then he pointed at the lord and his guard who lay dead on the floor. "And now this."

"Lies," Aina said. "We've never killed children."

The aristocrats stared at her, and she wished she had her gun. She would have shot them, too. Lucy sent her a thought of peace, and she glanced at her friend in surprise.

"You're right, Lucy, we need another way," she said.

Anlair looked at Aina, a little surprised. "Punch her," he told the soldier. Aina fell back to the floor and saw stars. "I recognize you from somewhere."

She recognized her father's murderer, too, but she concealed the thought from him. Her jaw hurt, but her hatred of this man lessened the pain. She slowly stood up and thought about how she could kill him.

Then Aina felt something. She glanced at Lucy. Whatever Lucy was doing was on a level deeper than she had access to. A faint golden glow emanated from her friend. The bolt dropped from the cage, and the leopard ran at the cage door. It skidded on the floor and span round. It slashed a soldier and then attacked Lord Locke. He managed to kick it away, but his leg bled heavily.

Aina then felt Lucy turn her attention to the police officer. She was trying to mentally influence him. She took his pistol and aimed at the bot, which flew towards the leopard. She fired. Aina was pleasantly surprised when Lucy hit it, but pistol shots to a bot were like hail to a human. Unpleasant and perhaps painful, but seldom fatal. The man wrestled his pistol back.

"Witches," Anlair said. He shot the leopard dead.

"No!" Lucy shouted.

"Kill her and take the cup," Anlair said.

Lord Locke aimed his assault rifle at Lucy. He fired several short bursts into the veranda. Lucy fell back against the window. Golden light surrounded her.

Aina stared in both disbelief and with great hope. The cup was providing a shield. Then she noticed something strange about the window behind Lucy. Even the specially-hardened glass of Nassopolis had its limit. Cracks appeared in the glass, first one or two, and then hundreds.

"No!" Aina screamed.

The window shattered. Lucy, the police officer, and a black bot were sucked out into the storm. The temperature dropped dramatically as the gale whipped around the room, knocking startled nobles to their knees. Seconds later, the inner emergency shutter dropped, but it was too late. Lucy was gone.

Nobody could survive a fall like that, not even with magic. The height of the tower, the jagged rocks, the freezing temperature, and an imperial attack bot to finish the job.

Aina looked around the room, shocked. Some elderly lords and ladies had collapsed with breathing difficulties. But her only thought was for her lost friend.

"The Orange Witch is dead," Lord Anlair said, and then he stopped. "But just to make sure." He ordered the second bot to locate the bodies and return the golden goblet. The black bot flew out of the room. There were no more speeches. "Take her."

As the police dragged Aina roughly from the room, she hardly noticed the pain. She felt only a cold anger towards Martin Anlair. She might yet have one more chance to kill him. Then she wouldn't care what happened.

24

Thomas shivered, trying to ignore the voice intruding on his sleep. But when a large hand gripped his shoulder and shook him, he opened his eyes. For a few seconds, he was disoriented. Then he remembered the ice chamber. "Wake up. You'll freeze to death if you don't move," Orange said. Thomas slowly sat up, brushed shards of ice from his body. He was still shivering. "What are you doing here?" Thomas told him about Lucy, the chase, and the heat he'd generated from the distant key. "If you had it here, you'd still be warm."

Standing up was difficult; the circulation seemed to have stopped to parts of his body, and his fingers and toes were numb. "It didn't work out as well as we planned."

"We must move forward from whatever position we're in. Are you ready to walk?"

"Yes." Thomas expected Orange to lead him back to the citadel to find transport, but he walked away from the buildings and into what looked like the beginnings of a blizzard. "Where are we going?" he asked, but the troll wasn't in a communicative mood. They walked for about thirty minutes through the worsening snowstorm, then he saw another peak, and from it rose the black Tower. He knew the answer to his own question. After trudging through the snow for another thirty minutes, he saw a narrow road twisting through the mountains. It connected the rest of the citadel with the Tower via a narrow bridge. "You want to walk there? It's miles away." His feet already felt like blocks of ice.

"We're going to hitch a lift," Orange said.

Thomas became alert. He looked at the twisting road. A single line of caravans moved slowly along it. "Who are they?"

"Let's find out."

They walked through the snow and wind for the next hour but hardly seemed any closer. Thomas slipped and slid down an icy slope. The wind was stronger now, and the snow was blowing straight in his face. They stopped to rest while the blizzard blew around them. Thomas could no longer see the caravan. "What are we doing?" Thomas shouted above the wind.

"Waiting."

As he waited, he attempted to draw on what his friends called magic. He didn't care what it was called as long as it kept him warm. His attempts were hit and miss, and forty minutes later, he'd started to feel very cold again.

The caravan appeared out of the blizzard. Seven vehicles moved down the narrow icy road. Foot-high walls on either side of the road stopped the covered vehicles, which looked like horseless carts, from slipping into the abysses on either side.

Each vehicle was powered by an unseen engine, and none appeared to have a driver. The caravans formed a circle just beneath them. "How did you know they'd stop here?"

Orange pointed at a white circular wall below them. Thomas hadn't noticed it before—a kind of resting place by the side of the road. They moved closer to the circle of caravans. Orange had assured him that they'd remain more or less invisible—whatever that meant—as long as he performed the visualization exercise. He tried.

As they approached the caravan, they heard raised voices and walked towards them. Two men faced a smaller man who wore a jester's costume. A small white dog stood by the jester and growled at the two larger men. One of the men was almost as big as Orange; the other wore a wide-brimmed hat and had a musical instrument slung over his back.

Thomas guessed Orange's intentions. "You want to join the troupe?" he whispered.

Orange nodded.

The men's costumes would fit them, more or less. They moved closer and stood between two caravans, watching the scene unfold. No one noticed them—perhaps the invisibility spell really worked.

As they got closer, the jester asked, "Why should I pay you anything?"

"For protection," the man in the wide-brimmed hat said. The strongman stood beside his partner.

"What if I refuse?"

"Everyone pays—maybe you'll pay with your life." The strongman picked him up and dragged him towards the edge of the mountain.

"My death won't help you," the jester said.

"It'll show others the value of our protection service," the man in the hat said. "You could see it as a business investment." The dog bit his leg, and he kicked it away. "I'll kill that dog after we've dealt with you."

"We should act now," Thomas whispered. He stepped closer, pulled the man's hat off and put it on his head, then he moved back. The man span round, his eyes wide as he stared at his hat, which was now suspended in mid-air. The small white dog ran to Thomas, but all the three men saw was a dog standing on his two hind legs, wagging his tail frantically.

The man snatched at his hat, but Thomas dropped down. He rubbed the dog's ear, placed the hat on his head, and gave him a pat. The jester grinned as he watched his excited dog running in circles with the hat on his head.

Thomas stood and glanced at Orange, who had drawn his knife and was moving closer to the big man who still stood by the jester. The strongman's eyes widened as Orange materialized in front of him. The man pulled out a blade and slashed at Orange. But Orange was fast. His first strike severed the man's wrist and his second went through his throat.

Thomas realized that his invisibility had worn off when the jester called out a warning. He turned as the other man charged, but he easily evaded him, and as he passed, Thomas tripped and kicked him, sending him sprawling onto the icy ground. After sparring with a troll for the past few months, fighting a man like this didn't provide a great challenge. The man charged him again, and Thomas threw him hard onto the ground. There was a sharp crack, and he lay still. Thomas walked over. He was dead; his head had hit a rock.

"I'm much obliged to both of you," the jester said.

"You're welcome," Thomas said. "But we had an ulterior motive."

The man laughed. "We all have those, my friend." His dog ran back to him, wagging his tail. "And Lester thanks you, too." He watched Thomas and Orange strip the men and change into their clothes. They also quickly scanned the dead men's tags, copying their numbers. Orange changed quickly and dragged both men to the edge of the ridge in the time it took Thomas to put on his new outfit. The jester helped Orange throw the bodies over the edge. "Good riddance!" the man said. He then looked more closely at them. "My name's Mauricio Magna. I don't believe we've met."

"We're travellers," Thomas said as he picked up the dead man's case.

"As we all are. You're welcome to join my caravan. In fact, I've just acquired a new, more spacious caravan." The jester grinned.

"That would be more comfortable than walking," Thomas said.

"I can imagine," Mauricio said. Thomas studied the case. "It's a mandolin, and yours if you want it." The jester and his dog walked back into the circle of caravans.

They helped Mauricio move his belongings from a large communal caravan to the newly acquired one. A few of the entertainers stared when they climbed into their new caravan, but no one commented on the two missing men. Thomas imagined that few people cared about men like that.

"To the Tower!" the leader of the caravan cried out, and, one by one, the caravans lurched back onto the narrow mountain road.

25

The enigmatic jester spoke a lot but said little. He was older than Thomas had first thought—perhaps in his late thirties. Thomas remained guarded in what he said, too. The man was almost certainly tagged, and although the artificial intelligence monitoring everything the man saw and heard would not be interested in every act of human violence, it might be interested in events taking place in this caravan, especially when men appeared out of thin air. It was strange, too, that the jester hadn't even commented on their sudden appearance.

"What the jester's seen will have been seen by imperial artificial intelligence," Thomas said to Orange in Silvan. "They may develop an interest in two men appearing out of thin air."

Orange nodded. "We must leave the caravan by the bend in the road before we arrive at the Tower," Orange said.

Mauricio looked directly at them. "I'm untagged," he said in accented Silvan. "You're welcome to enter with me, although you'll need a way past the tag sensors at the gate. I was impressed by your abilities, by the way; invisibility is a trick that would've helped me on many occasions, but I didn't want to pry as to what a magician and a troll were doing, waiting on an inhospitable peak in the middle of a blizzard to join a caravan to one of the most unwelcoming places on the nine planets."

Thomas certainly didn't imagine himself as a magician, but he was curious how the man knew so much. "How did you know about Orange?"

"I've travelled to many places and seen many things, although your magic was one of the more impressive things I've seen recently—and most unexpected on this godforsaken mountain."

"You know of magic."

"A little."

Orange looked at him closely. "He has traces of magic about him."

"A very small amount. My magical ability is embarrassingly small compared to yours, I'm afraid."

"How do you know what we have?" Thomas asked.

"I know what I saw, and I know that a troll is a magical creature of the earth. I guess that you're not entertainers." He glanced at the case Thomas held. "Can you play?"

Thomas opened the case and looked at the mandolin. He shook his head. "I doubt it." He closed the case again.

"Whatever secrets you have are safe with me. But you won't be able to disguise a lack of musical ability. Your friend, however, is a true strongman."

"Why are you here?" Thomas asked.

"The woman I love is trapped inside; I've come to free her."

Thomas looked at the man differently. "I'd heard there were dungeons beneath the Tower."

The man nodded. "May I ask you the same question?"

"There's something we want inside the Tower."

"It must be important to risk your lives for— I don't take you for petty thieves." The man watched them for a moment. "Then we have similar reasons for being here." The jester's mood became sombre. Thomas guessed that he thought of the woman he'd lost. The mere thought of Aina being locked up sickened him.

"Have you been inside the Tower before?" Thomas asked.

"Once, three years ago."

Thomas wondered whether the woman he sought had been locked up for that long, but he didn't wish to intrude further into the man's affairs—he had enough secrets himself. The black obsidian tower loomed ahead in the mist, and Mauricio turned his attention to steering the caravan onto the narrow bridge leading to the Tower.

As the caravans crossed the bridge, Mauricio spoke. "Did I see you scan the dead men's tags?" Thomas nodded. Mauricio's eyes widened slightly as Thomas took out a small bag of tags, tossed one to Orange, and kept one himself. They inserted them into their earrings. "Can I offer you a couple?" Thomas asked.

"I'd be very grateful." The man put them quickly into his pocket. "These are valuable; how can I repay you?"

"You'd repay me by succeeding in your task," Thomas said. The man nodded.

Guards watched them approach. "They have no sense of humour. I don't recommend speaking to them." Mauricio turned to them as the guards scanned the caravan.

The caravans rumbled into the tower; robots showed them where to park, and then they were taken, on foot, to a large interior room—the walls were black, and there were no windows. Thomas immediately felt the Tower's probing presence as a type of pressure. It was just as Orange had said. He imagined feelings of awe and respect towards the Tower, as an imperial subject might feel, and so his emotions blended in with those of the other entertainers. Orange had told him that the Tower searched for emotions out of the ordinary.

Mauricio knew the layout of the lower part of the Tower, and he gave them directions on how to reach the basement level. Robot guards watched over them; it would be difficult to get away undetected, but Mauricio had promised to cause a small distraction to help them reach the entrance to the basement.

Thomas sat on the floor and leant against a wall while waiting for Mauricio to distract the guards. He pretended to tune the mandolin, all the time feeling the draw of the pentacle beneath him, which reached out and tickled his feet with something that felt like electricity.

The celebrations were due to begin at midday and continue late into the evening. Thomas hoped to be long gone by then. His main concern was for Aina and Lucy, and despite what Orange had said, he had no intention of leaving them trapped in the tower like Mauricio's poor lover.

Thomas wished he could just call Aina on his tag phone, but the Tower would detect and analyse any conversation within its walls. Around him the entertainers were rehearsing their performances under the cold eyes of two robot guards; the sounds of their music and songs echoed around the high-ceilinged hall. Next to him, Orange stretched.

When Mauricio reached the far end of the hall, Thomas put down his mandolin and waited, unsure what kind of distraction the jester had planned. His eyes widened when Mauricio howled in apparent frustration. The entertainers looked at him, but the robot guards didn't move. He shouted again, and when a man asked him to be quiet, Mauricio punched him in his stomach, starting a brawl. The guard robots flew towards the disturbance. "We have an hour before the start of the show," Thomas said. Orange nodded, and they slowly faded from sight and left the hall.

As they descended a narrow set of twisting stairs, they heard footsteps approaching. "It's time I gave you a new lesson on rock magic," Orange said. Thomas could only see the outline of the troll as Orange took his hand and placed it on the wall. "The earth is our friend." Thomas found this easy to accept—he loved the natural world. "And rock magic takes this attraction further. Walk with me."

The footsteps were now just around the bend. Orange held Thomas, and they walked up the wall like a pair of spiders, and as they moved, Thomas felt, through Orange, the attractive force of the rock. He looked down as two men walked beneath, completely oblivious to them.

The Tower moaned, and they quickly climbed down. "I forgot to mention that you always need to shield yourself from the spirit of the Tower whilst you're within its walls." Again it moaned. "It's sensed you, but I don't think it knows where you are. Not yet." They continued climbing down the stairs, but when they reached the bottom, the Tower murmured in many voices.

"What's happening?" Thomas asked.

"I don't know."

"Aina and Lucy?"

"Maybe." Orange seemed to guess his thoughts. "Whatever's happening, it'll be over by the time we reach them. The best way to help is for you to take the pentacle. Now listen for it."

Thomas listened. "This way." He turned a corner and

jumped back as an ice demon darted past him; its tail grazed his cheek as it passed, but it didn't stop. A second ran behind it, both had automatic weapons strapped over their backs. He wiped the blood from his face and realized that neither ice demon had seen him; both were rushing somewhere else.

"Whatever's happening is a gift for us," Orange said. Thomas raised his eyebrow, wondering how monsters attacking Aina and Lucy was a gift. "The guards leaving has made our task easier."

"Do you really think they'd send ice demons to guard the cup but leave the pentacle unguarded?"

"Not completely unguarded. I can hear voices ahead." Thomas heard nothing, but he felt the pull of the key. "Anlair has more reason to worry about the cup. After all, he knows that Lucy's seen its location," Orange said.

Thomas looked at the entrance to the chamber from which the pentacle called him. He realized that he finally believed in magic, although he still questioned its true nature.

Two guards stood outside, and in another room further along the corridor he heard an ice demon moving. The two men glanced nervously towards the room a few times; few humans liked working closely with the reptiles. Orange pressed his hands against the wall. Then he opened his eyes. "The room has its own magical protection; they will know as soon as we enter. There's one more thing." Thomas raised an eyebrow questioningly. "I checked the dungeons—there is no one there remotely similar to the woman Mauricio described."

"Perhaps she's somewhere else."

The troll shook his head. "I'd have sensed her; I was very close."

"That's strange. He seemed to be telling the truth." Then Thomas had a depressing thought. "Perhaps Mauricio's too late." He looked around the passage. "We have our own plans." They walked down the corridor and shot the guards. Orange placed his hands on the door, and it clicked open as an ice demon darted towards them.

Thomas rushed into the room while Orange fought the ice demon outside. The pentacle called more strongly, but then it gave a warning. A robot guard emerged from a doorway at the rear of the room. Thomas shot it several times before it fell against a wall and collapsed to the ground.

Screeches came from the corridor—more creatures were scampering down the stairs, and Orange was being pushed back. He was wrestling one of the lizards in the open doorway and was bleeding from his face and arms. A dead demon lay on the ground.

The pentacle called again, and he walked up to a door inserted in the wall. It was a metal safe, and the key was inside. He placed his hands on the safe door and felt magic tingling through his skin. He imagined it opening. The lock whirred and clicked repeatedly—then there was silence. He tried the handle, and it opened. A glowing pentacle flew into his hand.

It looked like a large silver coin, and it was attached to a chain. When he put it around his neck, energy rushed into him. It was intoxicating, and he leant on the black obsidian table for support, breathing heavily. When he looked down at his hands, he noticed that they gave off silver light.

Orange fell back into the room, dazed. His face, arms, and legs were bleeding. "Do you have it?"

Thomas nodded. Two ice demons rushed into the room, pushing Orange back. One of them span round, whipping him in his face with its tail. Orange fell to the ground, groaning.

Thomas wanted to help his friend, but he felt disoriented and weak and wished he'd listened more carefully to Aina and Orange when they'd tried to teach him about magic. He felt power, but he didn't know how to use it. The pair of ice demons watched him, their long tails flicking from side to side behind them; others watched the scene from the doorway.

He held the pentacle in his hands. It was hot and felt as if it were alive. The pair of ice demons walked up to him and seemed confident he wouldn't harm them. The lead one pulled Thomas closer. "What's this?" it hissed. It snatched at the pentacle, but Thomas kept a tight hold on the table; it was almost as if he'd merged with it.

The ice demon's claws tightened, but despite the creature's grasp, they didn't puncture his skin. His body felt solid, and it pulsed with magic, and then he realized that he could feel the rocks and the earth around him. As the demon pulled him, his hands stuck onto the table.

He looked down at his hands. He held a sheet of black obsidian. When the lizard pulled him again, Thomas slashed it with the sheet of black rock. It screamed and pulled away. The frills around its neck fluttered open and closed, and its neck bled. It was distressed, and Thomas knew it was going to spit.

He pushed the sheet of obsidian into its face. The rock melted over the ice demon's head. It screamed, desperately clawing at the wet rock, which quickly began to solidify. He realized it was choking. The demons in the doorway watched silently.

The other ice demon slowly raised its heavy gun. It was nervous, which Thomas knew was not a good sign.

Without conscious thought, he reached out and touched the muzzle. The demon hissed, but he kept hold. Thomas's mind travelled along the barrel of the gun. He imagined heat, and the metal heated—the barrel melted and narrowed. When the demon pulled the trigger, the gun blew up in its face.

The door slammed shut and locked, and a shadow passed behind the screaming ice demon. Orange had recovered. He stabbed the ice demon twice, and it fell to the floor. "I was overconfident," Orange said. "I'd not expected so many."

The door bulged from the pressure of the creatures. "You did well," Thomas said, looking at the cuts on Orange's face, "but they'll break the door down soon. Perhaps I can use the pentacle to fight them. Everything feels very different now."

"No," Orange said. "You're not ready yet. We need to leave. Now's not the time to fight. Fight when you know how to use the pentacle to direct and manipulate the energy, and when you're in a place of your choosing—not in the house of the enemy."

Thomas nodded. It made sense. Except for one thing. "We have no choice; there's only one way out."

"There's always a choice. It's time for your next lesson." A loud thump came from the door. Orange touched the obsidian wall, and it shimmered, appearing to melt around his hand. "This rock's hard and the wall's polluted with things that shouldn't be there. I'd prefer you begin with something different, but if you can work with this, you can work anything."

Feeling his pentacle pulsing with magic, Thomas touched the wall. He watched the troll, and he felt with his mind what his friend was doing. Thomas copied Orange, and reddish-orange light appeared from his fingertips. The rock felt sticky.

Orange then plunged his arms into the wall and moved them about, sending black waves through the obsidian. The door creaked, and the acrid smell of the ice demons' spit entered the room. But when the ice demons burst through the door, the room was empty.

THOMAS MOVED through the rock with Orange—without him, he'd be dead, pentacle or not. *"This is the toughest school to learn at, but remember what you feel. Begin slowly, feel the sticky quality of rock, then try pushing your hands in a little, but keep moving. Don't stop. Not yet. Later, if you persist, you'll be able to walk through the earth as you walk on it now."*

Thomas watched the colours change and listened to the sounds of the rock as they passed. The laws of the universe had changed, or he'd seen a side he'd never even known existed. Although the rock was hard, and he struggled to breathe, Orange provided a space in the rock for him.

Thomas heard the Tower moan again.

"It struggles to wake," Orange said.

Then Thomas thought of Aina. "I need to find her."

"I've called her, but she might not be in a position to listen."

"What?" Thomas let go of Orange and stopped moving. Pain wracked his body.

"Keep moving!" Orange grasped his hand, and Thomas started to wade through the thick rock again. *"Use your heart and head together."* He felt like a child learning to walk. He tried to frame his question again, but Orange spoke. *"I feel what you wish to ask. Your emotion's strong, but I don't know, Thomas. Rock magic does not make you omniscient; it merely*

helps you manipulate rock. But I can sense her. She's descending quickly. I think you should visit the Empire Day celebrations. Knowing Aina, I'd say that she's either in trouble or causing it."

Thomas grinned in the darkness, despite the pain of doing so. *"And Lucy?"*

"I can't feel her."

Thomas's pentacle blazed with his emotions as he waded through sticky rock. *"Dead?"*

"Don't assume the worst. I simply can't sense her. She may be unconscious, trapped, or no longer inside the tower."

Lucy would never abandon Aina, he was sure. The other options were all bad. Suddenly he fell forward. "What?" He looked around the dark space.

"You need a short rest." Orange silenced his protest. "You won't help Aina dead."

"Where are we?"

"In a space in the Tower—even in the earth, there are spaces like this." He felt the rocky cavity around him. It was higher than he could reach, but not wide enough to stretch his arms.

"I sense a gathering of power on the ground floor of the tower," Orange said. "That's where you must go."

"And you?"

"I'll come later. I have a task. Your job's to get Aina."

"Lucy?"

"If she's there, help her. Aina may know. But under no circumstances attack the sorcerers—no more than is absolutely necessary!" Thomas was taken aback by the troll's fierceness. "Not here and not yet! Whatever happens, you must escape with Aina."

"Okay." Thomas wasn't sure about this, but his elementary knowledge of magic compared to Orange was clear. Perhaps he wasn't ready to face them yet.

"She'll fight you. Be strong." Orange took his hand and led him through the rock again. That action alone made Thomas realize that he was not as independent as he liked to think; he thought carefully about his friend's words.

Minutes later Thomas stood unseen in the almost deserted players' room close to the Great Hall. Slowly he made himself visible; his body brightened and then shone. Mauricio Magna was watching from the back of the room. "It's time to begin the show," the jester said. They entered the Great Hall together.

26

The lift descended. Aina had assumed her captors would take her to the dungeons for interrogation, but the doors opened to the Great Hall, where hundreds of lords and ladies were dancing. Locke pulled her across the dance floor, and dozens of aristocrats interrupted their dance to watch. Anlair wanted her to be his trophy; he'd already arrived and watched her struggle across the floor. Next to him stood Lord Own, First Lord of Uranus.

Locke kicked her, and she staggered forward. Laughter rippled across the ballroom as the gathered lords and ladies looked on. The two most powerful and dangerous men on Prometheus watched her with amused expressions.

Lord Own took Aina by her hair and pulled her onto her tiptoes. He let go when she kicked him, but she was immediately held down by guards. "This witch is a murderous terrorist! The other witch is dead!" he announced. There were more cheers across the ballroom. "The remaining terrorists will soon be apprehended. Rest assured, we will not allow your safety to be threatened."

The Nassopolitan aristocracy applauded. "Burn her!" a lady shouted.

Aina stood and stared into the crowd of cold, hostile faces. "Wake up! You're being controlled by these men." She saw nothing, not even a glimmer of awareness of what was being done to them. "They download opinions into your minds and manipulate your emotions." But nothing she said made any difference. The upper classes of Nassopolis solidly supported the Empire.

Then she saw movement in the crowd. A musician in a wide-brimmed hat, and a brightly dressed jester with a dancing dog, led a motley procession of jugglers, clowns, and acrobats through the crowd of lords and ladies. There was something familiar about the musician.

Lord Own glared at them. "It's not time for the festivities."

Aina turned back to the two lords. "You've not won your illegal war against Silva."

"Very soon the region of Silva will be firmly under company control," Lord Anlair said.

"We'll neither submit to the Company nor the Empire. We're a free people."

"Don't underestimate the people's desire for order. Order that the Empire brings. Your House of Chance was anarchy, any fool could've been chosen."

"And the Council of the Empire doesn't have its share of fools?"

Martin Anlair laughed and then spoke in a low voice. "The Council's merely a show for the common people, no more. The Empire brings order out of chaos. We bring progress and prosperity."

"For some."

"For many. There are always losers, whichever the

system. Remember that the people chose the system they have. They chose a life-term presidency and then they voted for the glorious Empire. That was a free choice."

"I know the history, but their freedom has gone."

Lord Anlair shrugged. "They didn't value freedom. And I think you place too high a value on it. Is it worth dying for?"

"But first you'll tell us the location of your friend and the creature you keep. We have similar pets, you know," Lord Own said, looking at Aina.

"Orange is a match for either of you."

"But not for us both, I think," Lord Anlair said.

That might be true; she knew that Orange had limits and that these evil men held more power than most people could imagine. "What if he takes you off one at a time?"

"Quiet!" Lord Own said. There was silence in the ballroom apart from the appalling sounds coming from the mandolin player in the wide-brimmed hat. Aina tried to make out his face, but it was covered. Lord Own pointed to the player. "Enough!"

The mandolin player played a painful, final note, then stopped. Nearby, the jester played a whistle, and the crowd laughed as his little white dog danced to the tune. Other entertainers juggled, performed gymnastics or clowned about as they approached. She studied the mandolin player, hardly believing what she was seeing. Surely it couldn't be possible.

"Are you a fool?" Lord Own asked the player in the hat.

The player ignored him and bowed before Aina. "My lady."

"She's no lady!" Lord Own said.

Aina stared at Thomas, terrified of what might happen to him. She doubted his magic was anywhere near a match for the two sorcerers. She searched for Orange but couldn't see him. Thomas removed his hat, took a pistol from it, and shot Lord Own in his chest.

But light flashed around the lord, and the bullets fell away. The lord slapped the pistol away with a flash of green light. Thomas fell back, and the troupe of entertainers scattered across the hall.

"An assassin!" Lord Own said.

Aina used the distraction to push away from the men holding her and rush to Thomas's side. "I hope you've brought reinforcements."

"Just me."

"Please say you're joking."

Lord Own raised his hands and something passed from him, a thin, tenuous ribbon of energy. Thomas staggered back and raised his arms. A shining silver shield appeared before him; the energy cast by Peter Own fell away from the bright disc.

The lord looked at Thomas in surprise. "Take him!"

Company soldiers rushed forward and grasped Aina and Thomas. The shield vanished. Aina looked down at the ground in despair, but as she did, she felt it shake.

"Earthquake!" a woman cried. They were not so unusual on Prometheus. The ground snapped and shook again, and a crack appeared in the ballroom floor. It was straight, and it was moving towards Lord Own.

The lords glanced at each other. "Prepare a lighter immediately," Lord Own told a man. Orange light came from the crack in the ground. Aina wondered whether there had been a rupture in the planet's surface—if this were the beginning of the formation of a new volcano. She hoped so.

An orange molten form appeared from the ground. "Orange," she whispered happily. The rock troll had transformed himself into molten rock, and he was already pulling free of the hard ground and striding towards Lord Own. With each stride, he became less burning rock and more troll. Magic was alive within him. Aina shivered in appreciation. She wouldn't like to be standing against him now. Neither, it seemed, did Martin Anlair or Peter Own, but at least the first lord of Uranus was no coward.

Lord Own raised his own magic defence, but he'd been surprised, and his magic was too slow. Orange's hands were blades, and he stabbed the lord through his chest. The black magician's magic flared in desperate self-defence, then ebbed and disappeared as he fell to the ground. Aina kicked the soldier and ran back to Thomas, who'd already thrown the other man to the cracked floor.

"Get ready to run!" he said.

"No." She pulled away from Thomas, but he held her tight.

Martin Anlair had come up behind Orange and projected a dark force into the troll's body. Orange staggered. He turned to grab the man, but Anlair jumped back. "Fire!"

The imperial soldiers fired a volley into the troll. "No!" Aina cried. Orange's body was riddled with bullets. He began to fall, but as he did, he exerted himself again, and orange energy crackled from his extended hand.

Both Aina and Thomas heard the same familiar voice. *"Go!"* They followed the thin line of orange energy to the wall with their eyes. A crack had developed in the wall of the ballroom. It seemed that no one else had noticed it. Orange had told them to flee. His voice touched their minds briefly. *"I return to Prometheus."*

Aina moved towards the troll, but Thomas pulled her back. "No," he said. Thomas pulled her through the crowd of assorted nobles, shoving and kicking any that came too close. "He told me that this may happen. He told me that we must choose the time and place we stand against the Order. Not here. We must go, or his sacrifice will mean nothing."

"Sacrifice? You agreed for Orange to kill himself?" Aina couldn't believe he'd agreed to let him throw away his life. Orange had adopted her after her father's death; he'd loved her and brought her up as a little girl in the forest. And now he was dying. She was losing two fathers to the same murderer. She shook with rage. "No!"

"I tried to stop him, but he was very stubborn."

Aina turned to see Orange's light dimming. He was changing into something else. He melted like molten rock into the crack in the floor. "I'll kill you, Anlair!" she shouted. He looked at her weakly. A soldier supported him. Again she pulled hard, but Thomas wouldn't let go.

"There are too many of them, and more are coming." It was true, but she still wanted to kill the murderer.

She looked at the scene as Thomas dragged her away. Peter Own, First Lord of Uranus, lay dead on the ground. The aristocracy of Nassopolis was in shock. Lord Locke marched towards them, surrounded by several men and women: practitioners of magic—she could sense it. Thomas was still pulling her, and she was surprised at how strong he'd become, but when she saw the remains of Orange sink into the stone floor, she realized it was over. Thomas pulled her to the wall. There was a shimmering crack.

"We can't," she said.

"We can. Orange showed me."

A company police officer ran at them. Thomas punched the man in his chest. He staggered back and collapsed into a lady. Thomas stepped into the gap and pulled Aina behind him. Lord Locke ran towards them. She heard gasps as the two of them disappeared into a solid rock wall. She fell out of the other side and collapsed on top of Thomas.

"I can't see," she said quietly into the darkness. After all that had happened, blindness didn't seem too bad, except that it would make it harder to kill Anlair. "Can you lead me?"

Thomas turned on the light. "I can now," he said. She hugged him in relief.

"Where's Lucy?" he asked.

"Thomas, she's dead."

"She can't be dead. Aina, what happened? Was the story he gave true?"

She nodded. "She fell from the tower; she was blown out of a shattered window. A guard and two bots followed her."

He'd stopped glowing, and his face was grey. "Did you see her die?"

"No one can survive a fall from a mile-high tower. And a black attack bot fell with her, and another was sent to make sure. She's dead."

He took her hand. This time she didn't need any encouragement to move.

"There's a fleet of lighters and cutters under the tower." They ran down flights of stairs that ended in the concrete parking area.

A chauffeur and two guards waited by the large lighter that Peter Own called. Aina reached for her gun and cursed when she realized she was unarmed.

"It's okay," Thomas said. He reached into his pocket and pulled out a stone.

"A stone?" Aina said.

"Orange taught me a trick." The guard looked up, surprised, then pulled out his gun. Thomas threw the stone and hit the man between the eyes. He went down. Then

Thomas moved his hand to the right, and the stone followed, hitting the second guard's wrist. The man howled in pain, and his gun clattered to the ground. He looked at Thomas in fear and then ran along the road. The chauffeur ran behind him. The stone flew back into Thomas's hand.

Aina watched in amazement. "Why didn't you do that back in the ballroom? Why didn't you try to save Orange?"

"We would've been caught."

"How do you know that?"

"Orange knew that I wasn't strong enough to defeat two red lords. Especially not from within the Tower—it's trying to wake up." She shuddered as she heard it groan. "Orange said we must reach the ancient forest—it's our ally. A chauffeur and a guard are not the same as two members of the Imperial Order."

It was true. And she'd failed Lucy. Thomas had been more successful than her. But despite that, she felt a great loss—she'd loved Orange. Aina wiped the tears from her eyes as she flew the imperial lighter along the landing area.

"Where to?" Thomas asked.

"Redbol in Southern Silva," Aina said. "The Silvan Resistance now operates from there."

27

The volcano cast red light across the burning valley. Streams of orange lava flowed from the mountain and through the wide valley; fiery vents prevented them from cooling as quickly as the frozen planet would otherwise ensure. An isolated tree stood by one of the orange rivers, and on a bare branch sat a red and blue bird. It watched as they flew overhead.

"Are you sure we're still in Silva?" Thomas asked.

Aina nodded. "The South is like hell."

They flew low over the bleak landscape for the next half hour. Aina called Lucetta First and arranged a meeting. Thomas saw vehicles driving along icy roads beneath them. A city loomed through the rising smoke.

"Redbol," Aina said.

She flew the imperial lighter to a tall pink building and landed on its flat top. Lucetta First waited for them.

"Nice landing," she said through her mask. She was the only one on the roof who hadn't run for cover. "Nice vessel, too," she said, rubbing her gloved hand against the lighter. "Your attack on the Tower was unprecedented and the intelligence excellent. I'm sorry about the loss of Lucy and Orange." She patted the lighter and then nodded to her workers, who raced around the vehicle and pulled it into a small hangar.

"We need to talk," Thomas said.

"Of course. I expected that you'd want to get down to business immediately. It's best we talk as we walk. The Red Legion is searching the city for you now."

"The remains of the Red Legion," Aina corrected.

Lucetta smiled. "Quite. But Lord Anlair and his unpleasant team will arrive soon. It seems you've enraged him, and company soldiers are already moving towards Silva. Rime's been occupied, you know?"

"We know," Aina said. Their lift descended into the city. When the doors opened, the first thing Thomas noticed was the smell of smoke and the large number of torches on the walls.

"I received your message. Everything you need is waiting for you," Lucetta said.

"Where?" Aina asked.

"On the other side of the city. There's too much activity here. What do you want to do with the imperial lighter?"

"A gift to the Resistance," Thomas said.

Lucetta nodded her approval. "I'd love to learn more about your attack on the Tower. Did you find the item you were looking for?"

"We did," Thomas said.

"You paid heavily for it."

"Lucy and Orange died well," Aina said. Thomas could hear the emotion in her voice.

"I meant no disrespect to fallen comrades. They'll be missed."

Thomas thought it was a high price, but now was not the

time for regret. "Lord Own is dead, and they can no longer claim that their Tower is invulnerable. We've bought time, and we can buy more if we can lure Anlair into the wilderness and kill him," he said.

"You won't need to lure him. He'll come running. But why beyond the mountains? It's a dangerous place."

"The ancient forest is our ally as the Tower is theirs. And he can't take his army with him. Once the Red Legion is without its paymaster, the loyalty of the mercenaries will be tested," Aina said.

"Don't be too sure about where he can take his army, but I admit it's unlikely he'd take a large force there. His death would weaken the company, but funds can be gathered from other sources."

Lucetta First led them through the increasingly narrow streets, and minutes later they walked into a nondescript entrance. "Top floor," she told the old lift.

"The sooner he follows you into the wilderness, the better," Lucetta said. Thomas raised an eyebrow, and she smiled at his expression. "I wish you the best, but I don't see any point in delaying this. I want this lord out of Redbol." She hesitated for a moment. "Do you really think you can kill him?"

"He's not the only one with power," Aina said quietly.

"I believe you. But the more I learn of the Imperial Order, the more I fear its strength. The lords we've faced so far are not the worst. When one dies, you can rest assured another will replace him."

"We'll deal with that when it happens," Aina said.

On the flat roof of the building, two cutters and their riders awaited them. "They'll take you to the Western Rim. You'll have to climb the mountain and cross the wall the Empire has been illegally building on our land." Lucetta gave them a folded map. "Destroy this when you've finished with it. The Empire doesn't know of these trails, and we'd prefer it to remain that way.

"To be honest, I've thought each one of your plans risky, but each one has had a certain appeal, and they've all worked, although at a cost. Perhaps this one can, too. If it does, you'll give us even more time to organize the Resistance, but several months later we'd be faced with a similar problem. I wish you luck. You'll be remembered, whatever happens." For the first time since he'd met Lucetta First, he thought he heard concern in her voice.

THEIR RIDERS RODE FAST over the fire plains towards the mountains. Less than an hour later, they reached the beginnings of the trail. They put on their packs and began climbing up what local mountaineers called a path, but one on which their rock climbing skills were often necessary.

They climbed for hours through the wisps of mist that covered the mountains. When it was too dark to continue, they rested on the side of the mountain. Thomas lay on a narrow ledge and thought about Lucy and Orange. He hardly noticed the freezing wind or the discomfort of his cold rocky bed. Eventually he fell into a dreamless sleep.

Three hours later he awoke, numb and not rested, but ready to move. Aina was already awake. They discussed their final plans, including what to do if they became separated, and how long they'd wait for each other if this did happen. She looked more sombre than she had in the passage inside the mountain. They climbed in silence. By late morning they were just below the ridge. Figures moved in the distance along the top of the wall.

"Ice demons," Thomas said.

They waited for a thicker cloud to give them cover and then they ran to the base of the wall. Both Aina and Thomas climbed fast: both were good climbers, and both had use of magic, although Thomas's affinity to the rocks made him the more natural. He quickly reached the top of the wall, and Aina soon joined him. The ice demons were about a hundred yards away.

"We have to risk them seeing us," he said. She nodded her agreement.

They had only to cross the path at the top of the wall, jump, and pull the cords to open the gliders. Thomas pulled himself up a little higher. In the distance, an ice demon stopped and looked.

Thomas froze. "Surely it can't see me?" he whispered. The ice demon moved its head to one side.

"Their senses are not human ones," Aina said.

They dashed across the path, and the creature screeched. Seconds later, the pack ran along the top of the wall towards them.

He watched them get closer, his heart racing as Aina scrambled onto the parapet and jumped. Her paraglider opened, and she flew over the valley. He climbed the wall. The backpack was heavy and cumbersome with the weapons attached to the side. He glanced at the ice demons; the first one was almost on him.

"Go!" Aina screamed from the air.

He jumped but was pulled back hard onto the path. An ice demon had stuck its talon into his backpack and was dragging him along the rough surface. He was winded, but he kept hold of his pistol and shot the creature in its foot.

It hopped back and hissed.

He ran to the wall again, ducking when the lizard spat

acid at his head. His eyes watered as the corrosive saliva hit the wall and evaporated. When his vision cleared, he was surrounded. The lead lizard rushed forward but then staggered back, clutching its neck. A second shot hit its back. The lizards hissed at Aina.

She was circling overhead. "Jump!" she cried. An ice demon fired at her, and she was forced to fly out over the valley.

Another reptile ran at him. He fired, but at the last second the creature dropped low and span round on one leg; its tail whipped out and hit Thomas's arm and side. He flew from the wall and fell. He saw stars, and pain wracked his body. He reached for the ripcord, and then all was darkness.

28

Aina saw Thomas fall. Then a strong gust of wind pulled her further out into the valley. She struggled to return, but the wind blew her away from Silva. Soon she was lost in the clouds. After several minutes, she stopped struggling. To return would not help Thomas; it would do nothing but help their enemy kill her.

She didn't know if he'd opened the glider in time. If not, he was dead. The sheer rock wall of the mountain plunged for about half a mile into the valley below. There was no soft landing. If he'd fallen, she'd continue alone. She had no choice.

Aina sailed through the sky, thankful for the warmth from the magic that pulsed through her. She was oblivious to the time that passed. She thought of Thomas and Lucy, and how she'd failed as their guide and failed the prophecy. She'd willingly have sacrificed her life for either of her friends, but perhaps Thomas was still alive. She must hope.

In front of her, the glider's simple instrumentation showed the direction she was flying, how fast, and how high she was above the ground. She fell asleep a few times, only to wake with a start, hoping she hadn't missed the green river, which would lead her to the Tor. She was relieved when later that day she heard the roar of the waterfalls through the clouds of mist.

She soared above the clouds of spray, following the dark green river. Thick green and purple forest lay on either side. Insects began to bite her, and she rose higher into the air. Something flew from the forest. It moved fast and flew straight towards her. So many things lived in the forests of Prometheus, and not many of them were friendly. She waited, hoping it would change direction, but it didn't. She had no doubt that it was coming for her, and her instincts told her that it was not good. She continued to gain altitude, but as her glider rose, so did it.

When she finally saw it clearly, she let out a strangled scream and twisted to reach for her rifle. She fired. It dodged her shot and flew behind her, hitting her glider and making her swing violently from side to side. Her rifle slipped and fell to the forest below. She turned the glider around.

Ten blank red eyes watched her move. Aina wanted to close her eyes and imagine she was somewhere else, but she knew that if she did that, it would dart forward and inject her with venom. Once paralyzed, it would eat her slowly. She'd heard that its victims felt every bite. Not like this, she prayed as it moved closer. I don't want to die like this. Its wings clacked together, and its legs swirled from side to side. The clown edged towards her.

Its bright green oval face was wider than hers. Saliva dripped from a scarlet mouth that opened and closed in a disgusting kissing motion. It made a sucking sound and sprayed Aina with its sticky saliva. She frantically wiped it from her mask. Then, more calmly than before, she pulled out her pistol, and this time kept a tight grip. She fired and missed, then fired again. The wind jerked her glider upwards. It followed and hovered less than five or six yards in front of her. A drop of white liquid bubbled from one of its legs.

She shot again, and it backed off. Again it flew behind her. She heard its wings clapping. Aina desperately tried to turn to face it, but the wind was blowing too strongly. Her glider shook and dropped towards the forest. It had taken a bite out of it. That was another of the clown's methods of feeding—to bite lumps out of its prey until they fell out of the sky, or until it became satiated. Without being able to see it, she aimed the gun behind her and fired again, hoping she would hit the creature and not damage her glider any more. Again the creature backed off.

The clown kept circling her. She was determined not to make anything easy for it. She'd met these creatures when she'd lived in the ancient forest as a child, but Orange had been with her then, and she knew that alone, she had very little chance of escaping alive. At least it was alone. The clowns often hunted in family groups. It was now in front of her, and she aimed her pistol again. This time she hit it directly, but the giant flapping spider didn't appear to notice.

She had three shots left and then she had to reload, but her spare bullets were in her pack. If she had to, she would use the last bullet on herself. The clown's mouth opened and shut, and its red eyes brightened. If Lucy had been there, she might have made telepathic contact with the thing. Aina tried, but its mind was closed. The creature suddenly rose in the air and disappeared behind her.

She threw her glider into a deep dive, but as she struggled with the glider's controls, she lost her pistol. The clown rushed past her. She kept the glider in a steep dive. The forest was everywhere below her now. Then she saw the Tor in the distance: the pinnacle that rose from the middle of the confluence of two rivers. She pointed her glider towards it.

A huge swarm of something hurtled out of the trees. It moved in her direction. She aimed for the centre of the swarm. Whatever they were, they couldn't be worse than a clown spider, she hoped. The swarm became clearer, and it was obviously moving at an incredible speed. Out of the frying pan and into something else, she thought of Thomas's funny Earth expression.

A cloud of over a hundred giant dragonflies flew towards her. Each one had a body almost twice as long as hers and a wingspan much longer than that. She watched the red, blue, and green creatures approach. She could already see the dragonflies' large green eyes. *"Hello,"* she said. *"Please kill this disgusting clown for me!"* The swarm divided around her. Aina could hardly believe it, but she was passing though the flight of bright dragonflies. And they were loud.

She turned to look, then sighed in disappointment. The flying spider still followed her. Its front four legs were extended. She screamed in frustration and anger, and she tried to fly faster. The forest was just below her, but the trees were too densely knitted together for her to land. She looked for a hole to drop into but could see none.

Again, she called on the dragonflies for help. She knew they had no love of creatures like the clown. Then Aina heard a loud crack. The dragonflies had turned, and one had blown a jet of fire at the unhappy clown. The flames had cut through its body, slicing the flying spider in half and sending the two smoking segments to the forest below. *"Thank you."* At least she wouldn't die, chunk by chunk, in its mouth. She shivered at the thought.

As she flew lower over the forest, several predatory species of insect, and a few types of life forms she didn't recognize at all, including one that looked like a sort of flying plant, rose to investigate her. One look at the flight of bright dragonflies was enough to send them rushing back into the forest.

She was now skimming the tops of the trees. Ahead of her something rose from the treetops, apparently not seeing her escort. It was a strange kind of flying bug, about the size of a large ball, with an open mouth that was as wide as its body. It flew up at her. She reached for her gun, which was no longer there. As she prepared to kick it back into the trees, the nearest dragonfly swooped down and ate it in one bite. Aina laughed and relaxed. Only a solitary moth came close. The dark and impressive creature was twice the size of a dragonfly. It ignored both her and her protectors, as they did it, and flew straight up into the grey sky.

The flight of dragonflies flew over the green river towards the Tor. The tree covered pinnacle rose out of the swirling water from a tiny rocky islet at the confluence of two rivers. The pinnacle was a special place for the rocs and dragons. She'd planned to meet Thomas on the sandy beaches facing the Tor.

A purple dragonfly-like creature with a body about the length of her arm hovered above the surface. It dived into the river and rose with a struggling many-legged creature in its mouth. When the shadow of her glider passed overhead, it disappeared back into the shelter of the forest.

If she hadn't known how deadly almost every living plant, insect, and animal on the planet was, she would've thought the scene quite idyllic, in a surrealistic sort of way. The forest was bright: a sign of calm, perhaps. The scene reminded her of pictures of old Venus, before it had been poisoned and desecrated, although it'd probably never had the pure energy of Prometheus.

She turned her failing glider to the right and hoped she wouldn't land in the river. She was descending too quickly to make a controlled landing, so when she reached the first of the sandy beaches, she pulled the release cord and dropped. The glider flew on several yards and crashed into a patch of fire funnels. Aina rolled into a ball as it exploded and sent a plume of smoke over the river.

The flight of dragonflies now dominated the river; all other creatures had disappeared into the forest. She'd been forgotten. The creatures fished: they hovered over the river and dived into the water, plucking out more of the many-legged creatures that she'd seen the purple insect catch. Aina stood up and watched the burning glider. She waited for the flames to die out and then she salvaged what she could. At least the first aid kit was in one piece.

She felt for her knife and was relieved that it was still strapped to her side. It might not be much use against company soldiers, but it was all she had. Perhaps Thomas still had his weapons, if he was alive. She didn't want to think of the alternative.

She looked up at the vast forest and relaxed for the first time in weeks. This had been her home for half of her childhood. She spoke its language and knew it well. She remembered playing with Orange in the forest and the happiness she'd felt. Tears rolled down her face. "Thomas, please live."

29

Thomas woke up. He was colder than he'd ever been in his life. His body throbbed, and he could hardly move. He opened his eyes slowly, and everything around him appeared grey. He hung onto something. Then he remembered being thrown from the top of the wall. He also remembered the pain as he'd pulled the ripcord. He vomited into the valley below.

Flying blindly through the clouds, he passed in and out of consciousness. The pain of the freezing wind dulled the pain in his arm and side where the reptile had hit him. He hadn't realized the power of their tails.

For a long time he flew alone through the clouds. He felt vulnerable hanging in the sky, although he was aware that the pentacle gave him some protection from the environment. He wished Aina was with him. Even though she'd carefully given him directions, he had no idea how long he'd been unconscious, nor where he now was.

A dark shadow passed over him. Aina had told him of the great predatory birds that hunted in the skies of the planet, but he was too weak to fight. He tried to turn the glider away, but it followed. The dark shadow loomed through the clouds. It looked too big to be a bird, even a Promethean one, and too regular in shape.

A gunship pushed its nose out of the clouds; its pilot watched him. His rifle was strapped to the glider, but he couldn't move his right arm more than a few inches; it was impossible to reach. He hung in the sky and waited.

A door slid open on the gunship, and a red bot flew towards him, watching him with its camera eyes. Thomas would have shot it if he could have moved his arm. He wondered whether it would shoot him. Then a hatch opened on its bullet-shaped body, and a needle emerged. He had no intention of being taken alive by the Empire. Using the only hand he could move, Thomas undid the buckles that held him fast. He looked into the blank camera eyes and dropped out of the sky.

He'd won a small victory. For a second time, he waited to die, but as he fell, he thought of heat. Why shouldn't he die warm? The pentacle flared to life, and he smiled as warmth enveloped his body. Strangely, it released the pain in his side, too. Why hadn't he thought of using it earlier? As he fell, he felt the planet of Prometheus beneath and around him.

The rocky surface rushed towards him. He remembered what Orange had told him about tropical animals in the core of the planet and laughed out loud. He wondered if he was going mad. He hit the ground fast, and it rippled around him like water. He sank into the soft, viscous rock and descended deeper and deeper underground and then he began to slow down. Eventually he stopped moving.

He knew he should be dead, but he wasn't. The pentacle was a lot more powerful than he'd imagined. The lessons Orange had given him rushed back to him, including the troll's warning not to stop in one place for too long. He kept moving. Surprisingly, the pain in his side had lessened,

As he walked, he looked at the rock around him. It was warm and wet, and he noticed the different layers as he rose. He took handfuls of the soft stone, which he squeezed and watched run between his fingers. He felt as if his body was on fire. I'm becoming more Promethean, he thought. Something hard pressed against his chest. It hurt. He reached forward and felt a solid stone, which he pulled loose. It was a diamond the size of his fist. Thomas put it into his pocket.

When he stopped, the rock began to solidify. He screamed in pain and began to move again. Slowly he walked up towards the surface. Parts of the ground were harder than others, and he learnt to navigate his way around them. Once he understood this, he was able to move more quickly.

He felt the forest floor above him and climbed more quickly towards it. His head broke out of the ground, and he spat grit from his mouth. He looked around for danger, but he was alone in the forest, which shone around him. He pulled his body free from the ground and shook the dirt off. His body ached badly but didn't hurt as much as it should. Especially after the fall.

There was no sign of his glider nor of the vessel that had followed him, neither could he see the true sky, only the tops of the trees, which formed their own dark green sky. The lights shining above were a special type of Promethean starfruit.

There was a flash of red in the trees. Thomas stopped, expecting danger. A bright red bird watched him—a firebird. Aina had told him they were lucky. As he walked, he wondered how he could reach the Tor on foot when the firebird squawked loudly. It jumped from branch to branch and continued to shriek.

"What?" he asked aloud.

The vegetation moved from side to side. The bird was warning of danger. He slowly stepped back and wished he had a weapon.

A long green snake moved quickly through the tall ferns. It circled him and was partially obscured by plants, but when he saw the thickness of its body, he knew he had a problem. It stopped, then rose several feet into the air. A flattened head, part humanoid, and part serpent, looked at him through a gap in the trees. It had narrow black eyes with crossed irises, and its skin was green with flecks of black and purple. Then it crawled out of the vegetation and sat up on its long tail. The creature had two arms and in one hand was a blade. Thomas recognized it from Aina's description. He'd finally met one of the intelligent species of Prometheus. And from what he'd heard, this was the last species he wanted to meet. The basilisk hissed.

Dozens of the serpent creatures crawled into the clearing, many of them carrying bladed weapons. They moved aside for another basilisk. A serpent man with mottled skin walked into the clearing on two legs. His long tail stretched back into the forest. While all the serpents had black eyes, this one had a left eye that was different. It was blood red and glowed. The basilisks rattled and moved towards him.

"My name is Thomas Brand. I travel in peace."

They stopped, and the creature spoke to Thomas in clicks and hisses. He had no idea what it was saying. He repeated his statement in the True Language. He was not as fluent as Lucy or Aina, but he could communicate. It hissed and rattled, and then it moved closer to look at him.

"You speak our language." The creature looked him up and down. *"And you trespass within the Basilisk Nation."*

"My glider crashed. I fell from the sky."

The first legless serpent struck him with the flat of its blade. *"Address the King of the Valley as Your Majesty."*

Thomas rubbed the blood from his cheek and waited.

"You'll come to see the queen."

He didn't like the way the conversation was going. He looked at the king's strange glowing eye. It was false. He didn't question his intuition as he would have before. It was a ruby, perhaps, but certainly a red crystal. He remembered his trick with the Gleeman, and he mentally reached for the stone.

"Who are you?" a voice asked.

"What?" The voice was different from the serpents', who stared at him blankly.

"Who are you?" the voice repeated.

Thomas couldn't see the speaker, and the basilisks seemed unaware of the conversation happening within their midst.

"I'm Thomas Brand. Who are you?"

"A slave."

Thomas stared at the king's red crystal eye. Did the voice come from inside it?

"I'm trapped within the red stone."

"What are you?" Thomas asked. A blurry image of a creature he had never seen flickered in his mind. It was a doglike or a catlike creature. Its eyes were fierce but intelligent, although it was an animal, he was sure. *"I didn't know animals could speak. I mean, speak like this,"* he said, remembering what Lucy had told him about speaking to animals.

"I changed when my body was destroyed."

"Why didn't you die?"

"A basilisk spell."

"What type of spell?"

"One to enslave me."

"What do they make you do?"

"Kill."

The basilisks spoke to themselves in hisses and clicks.

"Free me."

Thomas was not sure he could, or if he did, what would happen.

"They'll kill you for entering their territory; the basilisks are not a tolerant species. You've got nothing to lose and much to gain."

"I ask for free passage through your land," Thomas said to the king.

The king watched him, his forked tongue flicked in and out. "You'll come to see the queen."

"Listen," the voice said.

And the voice showed him the king's thoughts; he had no intention of becoming a pet or a meal for the royal family.

"Help me," the voice said.

"How?" Thomas said in the True Language. This time the basilisks seemed to hear him.

"Take me."

Thomas reached out with his mind. And he felt the crystal in the serpent king's eye. The ruby pulsed with life; he mentally pulled. The king hissed. He pulled harder and raised his hand. The king screamed in pain. The red eye flew through the air. Thomas caught it. The red eye was warm and pulsed with life. He held it up to the king.

"This does not belong to you."

The basilisks shuffled back in fear, and the king wiped

his bleeding socket. Thomas sensed he had seconds before the king recovered enough from his shock to attack.

His attention turned back to the trapped spirit and how he could help it. Then he remembered the cave with Orange and Lucy. He remembered the red butterfly.

"Would you like a new body?"

"Yes."

Images rose from his unconscious, and he shaped them. He took two objects from his pocket: the green stone he'd created in the dark passage and the diamond he'd found underground. He held them with the pulsing ruby eye. His pentacle blazed, and light surrounded him. He felt as if he were holding a small sun, but one that didn't burn him. The basilisks moved further back.

A bright crystal body formed before him. The green stone pulsed with life. It became its heart, the diamond became claws. It was both doglike and catlike. He gave it wings. Thomas stepped back and looked at his creation. Its eyes were blood red and shone brightly. The creature was twice the size of a tiger, and if he hadn't just created it himself, he would have been scared.

The crystal creature looked at itself, pleased. *"Thank you."*

"What should I call you?" Thomas asked.

"I'm the Dat."

"The crystal Dat," Thomas said. It approved and then turned to the basilisks.

The king was enraged. He stared at the bright crystal creature. *"Return my eye,"* the king demanded.

"Your eye?" the Dat said.

"It's mine." Scores of basilisks slithered out of the forest. Many of them were armed with sabres.

The crystal creature laughed, and its crystal body shone

brighter. It turned fluidly, like a big cat. The basilisks shuffled back warily.

"You're wise to fear me, basilisks."

It leapt on the nearest serpents and cut them to pieces. The king cast a spell, but nothing seemed to happen. Thomas guessed that he'd relied on the black magic of the ruby eye for too long. The Dat sliced him in half.

A basilisk crashed into Thomas's side. He fell to the ground and gasped for breath. The Dat dragged the serpent away from him and killed it. Thomas noticed the energy that pulsed through him, what Aina called natural magic, and it was powered by the pentacle.

Still more basilisks appeared from the trees.

"The Queen," the serpent people hissed in unison.

The queen rushed at them. She was wrapped in magic that protected her from the blows of the crystal creature, but the Dat's fire burnt through her shield. She shrieked and retreated to a safe distance.

"I'll return and learn how to unwrap the magic of your nest," the Dat said. Then he spoke to Thomas. *"We're too close to their nest. Climb on my back."* Thomas scrambled onto his back. The Dat's body was warm, but his throat was hot. He sent another jet of fire at the serpents, and they were forced back. The crystal Dat opened his wings and lifted into the air. They flew through a small hole in green foliage and then into the grey sky above.

"Are all the intelligent species of Prometheus like that?" Thomas asked.

"These are the worst."

"Are the basilisks tribal?"

"They've got their kings and queens, towns and nations. They're jealous creatures. Their queen will seek revenge."

"Well, I won't be returning there."

"They're telepathic; they've already spoken to the other royal families. We're now notorious in the Basilisk Nation." The Dat laughed.

"That doesn't sound good."

"They'll learn to fear us. It's an honour. But first you must recover your strength. Creating my body weakened you. You must sleep when we arrive at the Tor."

"How do you know about the Tor?"

"When you created my body, we became very close. I've seen much of what you've experienced. To fight your enemies, you must regain strength. Those you fight possess even more power than the basilisks."

"What will you do?" Thomas asked.

"I'm free and serve no master. I'll kill serpents, but I'll guard you while you rest. I'm grateful for what you did, Bright One. I will remember you."

Thomas struggled to remain conscious during the flight, and he was relieved to see the Tor rise from the wide green river below. As they approached, his vision began to fail. But as they descended, he noticed the vegetation on the Tor and the jungle below and was very pleased that he didn't have to trek through it.

30

Aina rested within the trees close to the edge of the beach. She stared at the green Tor and the swirling water that washed around it. There were caves higher up that were supposed to be the home of hermit rocs or dragons. She looked hard but couldn't see any sign of life, other than the many trees and flowers that grew from the column. She waited, ready to escape along the path at any sign of danger, but she already knew that she'd wait longer than the day they'd agreed on. Yet again, she prayed he was safe.

Something glittered in the distance. It was large enough to be one of the great predatory birds of the mountains, but birds didn't glitter like jewels in the sky. It flew directly towards her, and there was a rider on its back. She stood and watched. It circled the Tor. Then it swooped across the river to the beach. It landed only yards from her.

"Thomas!" She ran towards him.

Aina had no idea what the crystal creature was, but she gently pulled Thomas from its back. He was alive but injured. She pulled him some distance from the creature before she turned back to it and spoke.

"What are you?"

"The Dat," it said. The creature rested on the beach with its legs elegantly stretched out in front of it and its wings folded against its back. It faced the Tor.

"What happened to Thomas?"

"Basilisks," it said with a growl. And then it was silent.

She dragged Thomas's unconscious body under the cover of the trees. At the press of a button, the tent self-erected. She pulled him inside, taking another look at the crystal catlike thing. She didn't like such a dangerous creature to be so close, but it had brought Thomas to her. And she had little choice. Thomas was too sick to move.

She opened the first aid kit and wondered how she could help him. "See what the damage is," she said aloud to herself. She unzipped his clothes, afraid of what she may find. His arm, side, and back were badly bruised. She tended his injuries as best she could. He would be in pain, but he should be able to walk. His pentacle glowed, and she carefully placed it against his chest and covered him with a blanket. Then she fell into a deep sleep next to him.

THOMAS WOKE WITH A START. His body ached, and he was unsure where he was. Then he realized that he was naked and someone was lying next to him. "Aina! Is this a dream?"

She woke up and smiled. "Only if I'm having the same one."

"Where are we?"

"In a tent near the Tor. I thought you were dead. Thomas? What's that strange crystal Dat?"

"Is he still here?" Thomas began to move but lay down quickly in pain.

"Don't move. Not yet. And yes, it's still here. Or it was before I fell asleep."

Thomas told her his story. About his encounter with the gunship, his fall from the sky, his meeting with the basilisks, and finally about the creation of the Dat.

She listened quietly. "Will it help us?"

"I don't think so." He moaned as he moved. Then he lay still as he listened to Aina's story. "Neither of us has had an easy journey then," he said.

"At least we don't have a boring life." Aina pulled back his blanket and began to feel his body. "Your injuries don't seem as bad as they did."

"Oh, I think it's the pentacle," he said. "It seems to be doing something. It aches, that's all." He pulled her towards him and gently loosened the few clothes she was wearing.

"We don't have time," she whispered.

"The Dat said to rest."

"This is not resting." He pulled her closer. "Thomas!"

THEY WOKE hours later to the roar of a spaceship's engines. Thomas cursed. He was still stiff and sore.

"They're here," she said. She looked out of the tent and then fell back inside. "Get dressed!" She was slipping into her clothes as she spoke.

"What can you see?"

She threw a pile of clothes at him. "I don't know, but Martin Anlair's death squad's coming, and we can't let them find us with our pants down." She left the tent.

Thomas struggled to get into his clothes as the roaring of the engines increased. He pressed the automatic packer as he left the tent. Seconds later, the tent had reduced itself to a small package. There were sounds all around him, but it was hard to see what was making them.

"Where's the Dat?" he asked.

"I can't see it anywhere."

They looked up between the trees. Two white gunships flew overhead. They were moving slowly towards the beach. Swarms of insects rose from the forest and mobbed the metal ships. The clangs of the insects' hard bodies striking the gunships were clear from the ground. Neither of the gunships responded.

"They're scanning the forest for life," she said.

Thomas knew that the forest emitted its own electromagnetic field that interfered with imperial scanners.

"That's the gunship that followed me in the clouds," he said. He recognized the marks on the side, probably gained in some battle.

"Two gunships could mean forty or more soldiers. I hadn't expected so many."

One of the gunships turned and flew north. "That means they haven't seen us," Thomas said.

The remaining white gunship hovered about thirty feet above the beach, blowing air down into the forest. There was a shrill sound, and the insects suddenly broke off their attack. A hole appeared underneath the gunship. Two red attack bots dropped down and circled over the river. Nine shapes fell to the beach.

"The death squad," Aina whispered.

The tall figure of Lord Anlair stood in the middle. Beside him was the assassin, Scanlon. Four ice demons sniffed the air, and their long tails flicked from side to side. Three other men, all heavily armed, searched the beach. They quickly found the remains of Aina's glider.

"Red Legion mercenaries," Aina whispered. "Their leader's Morgan Red."

Thomas felt something approach. "Aina, I think it's about to get worse." He no longer doubted his hunches; he only wished they were more informative.

"What?" she whispered.

"I've got a bad feeling."

Her eyes widened. "Me, too."

A tall, two-legged basilisk walked out of the green river, followed by a dozen walking and crawling serpents. The tattooed serpent's speckled eyes disturbed Thomas. Its forked tongue flicked in and out, tasting the air. It glanced towards them before speaking to the lord.

"Thomas, we need to go. Now!" Thomas and Aina ran into the forest.

31

Lucy flew into the freezing air. As she fell, she span out of control. She didn't resist; she saw no point. She was surprised that so many things in her life had led to fear, but facing her death did not. Whatever the power of the cup, it was less than that of the storm, which blew her about like a rag doll.

She saw the robot fly by and then it was gone. The soldier fell below her. He'd lost hold of his gun and was desperately trying to catch it. The sight was so comical that she almost laughed out loud, but then the humour vanished. He didn't see the rocks rush up towards him. He hit them with a loud crunch. Lucy relaxed, held her cup tightly and closed her eyes.

Just when she expected to die, the cup flared to life and shielded her. As abruptly as it came, the protective energy was gone. She lay still and felt the melting ice beneath her. Then she started sliding fast over the ice. She dropped onto a lower ledge of the crag.

She wasn't sure whether anyone would look for a dead

soldier, but they might look for her. She lay on her back on the ice and looked up at the Tower. It was partially obscured by a rocky overhang.

She thought she had probably broken every bone in her body, and she didn't move for fear of pain. If only it hadn't been so cold, she might have lain there for longer, but the cold was painful.

Lucy moved each part of her body to check that it still worked. There seemed to be no problem. There were tears in her protective clothing. That explained the cold. With the holes, it should've been even colder, but she remembered that the suits were self-healing. She felt the lumpy patches forming over the holes.

The cup heated her, too, but it also melted whatever she was resting on, and steam rose all around her, giving off an unpleasant smell. She was lying in a pile of imperial waste. She sat up and tried to shake the muck off, but her sudden movement broke the melting brown ice. She began to slide and fell off the edge again. She screamed but only dropped for a few seconds before she hit something hard. There was a sound above. She looked up and saw a large refuse pipe above her; it rattled and shook.

A large block of frozen refuse hit the rocks just above her. It broke into hundreds of pieces. More blocks of ice fell and smashed around her. She sat in the middle of a terrible hailstorm.

Something moved next to her. Lucy groaned, wondering what joke death was playing with her. Then she remembered the robot. Lucy tried to stand, but it moved again, and she slipped and fell back onto the ice. She looked up.

A bright bird stared down at her. It was like a giant parrot, and it must have been over fifteen feet tall. Its eyes were intelligent, and it looked at her curiously. Its head, body, and the underside of its wings were red, but she saw a flash of green, blue, and yellow on the upper part of its wings. Its talons were like sabres. It stepped closer, and she edged backwards.

It squawked loudly and shook itself, throwing more shards of ice in all directions. Lucy covered her head but kept her eyes on the giant bird. Its wingspan was enormous. It watched her, and Lucy waited, wondering what it would do.

The bird took another step towards her, and she slid back, but the ice gave way. She was right on the edge of a sheer drop. Dizzy, she wriggled away from the edge.

A vibration came from within the frozen pile of waste. The bird noticed it, too, and turned its head. The vibration increased, and there was a loud buzzing. Suddenly a black bot shot out of the heap of waste, sending fragments of brown ice into the air.

The robot hadn't seen the bird, but it noticed Lucy immediately. It flew towards her. She held her cup in front of her. The bot shot a laser blast at her, and her cup caught and flung it into the air. The robot shot her twice more. Each time Lucy's cup protected her and warmed her at the same time.

The robot then changed its tactics. A door slid open on its body, and a needle came out. The bot moved forward with its metal needle flexing in front of it. She forced herself to stand up, although she wasn't sure whether her knees would support her body for more than a few seconds.

The bot jerked forward. She jumped back. Tears came to her eyes as the cup slipped from her hand and tumbled over the side of the mountain. She'd lost everything. She knew she was going to die—or even worse be injected, paralyzed, and tortured.

When the black bot again moved towards Lucy, the bird, which had been watching silently, hopped forward and lashed out with one of its talons. It sliced through the robot as if it were butter. The upper part of the robot flew into the air and dropped beyond the rocky ledge. The giant bird kicked the lower part of the bot into the pile of frozen waste. Above them was a buzz. Another bot dropped from the tower above. It flew towards her, but because of the rocky outcrop, it didn't see the giant bird. The bird turned its head and blasted it with a burst of fire. The bot lost control and fell to the rocks below.

The giant bird lunged forward, and her legs gave way. She crumpled onto the pile of icy waste and felt all her strength desert her. Coldness embraced her, and she welcomed her death, but again, death did not come. Instead, she felt warmth returning to her body.

She opened her eyes and saw the cup in front of her. Golden strands of energy came from it and wrapped themselves around her body; she gently hugged the vibrating cup and absorbed its warmth. The bird must have caught it, but why? She lay still and enjoyed the warm feeling until she remembered where she was.

She looked up at the red bird. *"What are you?"*

The bird turned its head and looked at her.

"Are you planning to eat me?" she asked, wondering what exactly this huge bird would do. Despite being scared, she was reluctant for it to go, that would mean being completely alone in this bleak environment.

"I'm not planning to eat you," it said.

Lucy nearly dropped the cup a second time. *"Did you speak?"*

"Who else did you expect to speak?" the bird said. *"How can you understand the True Language?"*

"It just happened to me. I'm not sure," she said. "Who are you?"

"My name is hwthkls."

"Hwith," Lucy tried to repeat. "And what...?"

"I'm a roc," the bird said.

"Why were you here?"

The roc made some sounds she didn't understand. Then it spoke in the True Language. *"I heard your call."*

"My call? I didn't make a call."

"You did. A clear distress call. I was looking for you."

"I didn't know I called."

She saw no harm in speaking to him, especially if he came to help. She told the shortened version of her story from that strange day in London. The roc listened with occasional squawks.

When Lucy had finished, the roc spoke. *"Come with me to the mountain."*

"The mountain?"

The roc screeched loudly in agreement, not seeming to understand that she had asked a question. He scratched its feet on the dump, sending shards of frozen rubbish plunging down the mountainside. *"Climb onto my back."*

Lucy was scared, but she looked around the ledge and knew that to remain was a cold death.

"I won't drop you, and if I did, I'd catch you again."

She touched its red and green feathers and felt the heat generated by its body. *"You really have a fire inside you,"* she said.

The roc trilled, a sound that Lucy thought must be the roc equivalent of a laugh. He turned towards her and opened his mouth. A jet of flame shot out, making her leap back. The roc seemed amused.

She wondered about the creature's sense of humour. Lucy climbed onto his back, pulling on the bright feathers to help her. She was worried that she might hurt the bird, but like all Promethean natives, the roc was tough, a lot tougher than humans. She sat on his back, and he hopped off the side of the mountain. Lucy screamed. She was sure that Hwith laughed at her again. The roc dropped for several seconds, and then he casually opened his wings and soared into the sky.

The roc flew for a long time without any appearance of tiredness. Lucy clung to the bright feathers, desperate not to fall off. She was exhausted by the time the clouds had cleared and didn't recognize any of the scenery below, which was mostly forest, but she guessed that they had passed well beyond the Silvan Mountains.

"True."

"You're reading my thoughts."

"You show me."

A range of forested mountains appeared in the distance.

It must be a cold place to live, she thought.

"Our home is warm to us."

"You're reading my mind again," she said.

"Then don't make it so easy." A flight of several rocs flew towards them. Hwith squawked loudly. He immediately received several replies. The flight of rocs turned and escorted them to the distant mountains.

Lucy stared at them. They're beautiful, she thought. She heard laughter in her mind. "I'm going mad," she said aloud. "I'm even talking to myself."

"Not only to yourself," Hwith said.

The rocs chattered together in their own language. Only

when Hwith spoke in the True Language, to express their thanks for her compliment, could she understand. Hours passed, and Lucy gradually lost her fear of flying on the back of the roc.

Their high mountain home was covered in green and purple forest that shone with the lights of many flowers and fruits. The rocs flew low above the trees, then the flight dived into the forest. As they passed through the canopy of leaves, the branches brushed against her. A flight of large dragonflies accompanied them into the village. The rocs lived in wooden constructions high in the trees. Hundreds of them flew between the houses, and many rocs sat in rows on branches and sang.

Lucy soon discovered that roc society was sociable and noisy. She also noticed that Hwith was shown much respect by many of his companions, both young and old. She was surprised that the rocs knew of Aina. They told her a story of when, as a child, she'd defended a young roc in the forest —their affection for her was clear.

The rocs ate together every evening in the communal aerie: a platform with a thatched roof that rested on a branch as wide as a large road on Earth. She spent the evening in the aerie listening to the rocs talk and sing in their difficult language.

"Hwith," she said.

The red bird looked at her. *"Is the food good?"* he asked.

Lucy looked at the fruit, nuts, and the fat grubs that crawled across the giant leaf that served as a plate. *"I like the fruit,"* she said.

"Good."

"I need to go back to the Tower. I believe Aina was caught. I wish I could stay here and get to know you, but I must return."

"To place yourself in danger, too, won't help her."

"That doesn't matter. Will you help me return?"

Hwith chattered quickly in roc language, and all the other rocs began to squawk. Now I'll never get an answer, she thought.

"You will," Hwith said. *"If you wish, we'll return you to the Tower, but there's been activity along the wall close to Silva, and some humans have left. Aina is resourceful, even compared to a roc. We should wait to see if she's escaped with your friends."*

Lucy knew that it was possible that Thomas and Orange had escaped, but she couldn't see how Aina could have got away. *"How will you know if they come?"*

"Many rocs fly the forest, and like you, we speak to the animals. If your friends come, we'll know and help you. Now eat."

Lucy secretly dropped all the grubs onto the floor and watched them crawl away. She hoped they wouldn't crawl towards the giant birds. She ate a lot of fruit and some delicious and interesting-looking nuts. The rocs only ate raw food and were surprised that humans often didn't. One roc told her that was why humans lacked vitality.

Later, Hwith flew Lucy to his childhood nest. It was the size of a small house. A young roc called Zynt was in the house working with wood.

"She's making your bed," Hwith said.

Lucy watched the avian carpenter with interest. Her talons were strong and vicious, but also nimble. Her claws served as saws, axes, planes, and her beak a hammer. Lucy was touched by their kindness, and although the wooden bed was hard, it was better than a perch. After Lucy had explained the concept of a pillow to Zynt, the roc flew into the forest and later returned with a smooth nut the size of her head. Lucy was exhausted, and she soon fell asleep, hardly noticing the hardness of her bed or pillow.

She awoke to the sound of several rocs chattering on the

branch outside her door. She listened to their rapid speech. They spoke in a series of clicks, shrieks, squawks, song, trills and chiming sounds. The cup helped her to understand the True Language with more clarity than before, but it did nothing to help her understand their spoken language.

A metallic green beetle, the size of her thumb, crawled up the wall above her head. She spoke to it in the True Language. It stopped moving and listened. She held out her hand, and it flew to her.

She'd connected with its mind instantly and with greater clarity than she had with the red beetle in Scarlet Station. The connection she had with the creature eliminated the fear she had once had of insects. She sent it love, and it sang. As an experiment, she let go of her cup. The clarity lessened, but she could still communicate. As she touched and let go of the cup, she felt as if she were tuning in and out of a radio station using an old-fashioned radio. She put the beetle on her bed and got up.

Lucy stepped through the open doorway and smiled to see the row of rocs further along the branch. Zynt was there. She recognized others from the feast. Jzzrata, a green and blue roc, was in deep conversation with Hwith. Lucy listened to Jzzrata, who spoke in the True Language, and she understood her first roc joke. She joined them on the perch.

A grey and red roc issued a mental welcome to Lucy; musical notes came from the poet's mouth and combined with a flow of images in Lucy's mind. Understanding Old Grey was more challenging than speaking to the others, but after speaking to him, understanding the speech of the others became easier. Pzilliz Trillis, the huntress, sat next to the old poet. She was the only roc Lucy had met, apart from Old Grey, with the ability to remain silent for more than a minute. At the end of the branch sat Soonasa, the most beautiful roc Lucy had seen.

The grey and yellow huntress had begun teaching Lucy about the True Language the night before. While the other rocs spoke together, Pzilliz Trillis continued her lesson with Lucy. The roc taught her how to disconnect and turn off the constant telepathic chatter; the roc took the lesson seriously. She learnt how to regain inner peace. Pzilliz Trillis taught her how, by clearing her mind and focussing her attention on a mental shield, or by allowing her thoughts to sink more deeply, she could keep them from others. She also learnt that strong, uncontrolled emotions were the easiest to hear.

"If you learn to shield from a roc, you'll be able to shield from any form of life, apart from dragons. And the great leviathans, of course."

"What about the Imperial Order?" Lucy asked.

The roc just laughed.

The True Language used symbols, images, and thoughts. Lucy noticed that the rocs used all of these simultaneously. The thoughts of the True Language were more like "knowings." Somehow, you just knew what they meant, although this only worked when the speakers really knew what they meant. Hwith told her that the very young used only images and emotions.

They sang their language when they were in physical proximity to other rocs, but they used the True Language for when they were apart or for more serious discussions. Lucy simply didn't have the ability to sing the roc language, and she quickly realized that she'd never be able to utter more than a few words of it, but she found the True Language fascinating.

At first, she'd been tricked by the rocs' sense of humour into thinking they were sweet, but a little simple. As she sat on the branch talking and listening, she realized that they could be fierce when facing intruders and that they were deceptively intelligent. However, they were also warm and sociable creatures. Her day on the mountain was not lonely.

Despite the great cold, she felt comfortable. The golden cup's energy had wrapped itself around her body and protected her from the environment. Pzilliz Trillis had told her that her natural magic was advancing. Lucy was aware of changes to her body: she was stronger, and her skin was tougher. She was sure that her arms and legs were heavier, too, not fatter, they just felt denser, as if her bones were thickening. She wondered whether the magic of the cup was rewriting her genetic code.

Hwith squawked.

"What is it?"

"Good news. Aina's returned."

"How do you know?"

"The ancient forest welcomes its own, and it greets her. She flew into the forest with a flight of dragonflies. And there are other groups of humans."

"Who?"

"A male arrived on a strange crystal creature of a type we've never encountered. They both speak the True Language, and both have a bond with Blue Prometheus. Could they be your friends?"

"I don't know any crystal creature." She wished it to be Thomas. "What about Orange?"

"We found no creature of the type you described. There are also two gunships. From the first came a group of sorcerers, warriors, and lizards. They were met by a troop of basilisks."

"Basilisks?" Lucy remembered what she'd been told about them and shuddered. It wasn't good. "Why would basilisks meet them?"

"A good question. The second gunship has landed in the

foothills of our mountain. We go there first. Will you join our flight?"

"Of course," Lucy said. They turned to watch her. *"What, now?"*

"To immediately act upon desires is the roc way," Pzilliz Trillis said.

32

The great trees were widely spaced, and at this height, there was little vegetation growing between them. Images of the gunship and white-uniformed men appeared in Lucy's mind as the flight of rocs flew. *"Where are these images coming from?"* she asked.

"From a returning roc," Hwith said.

The flight of rocs landed smoothly on the upper branches of a tree. They must've been practicing this skill since they were fledglings, she thought.

"True," Hwith trilled. Jzzrata laughed.

"Stop it," she whispered, and she immediately visualized a mental shield protecting her privacy.

"Better," Hwith said. The rocs perched high above the humans on the great branches.

Lucy saw the imperial gunship in the clearing below. Humans and others moved around it. She recognized the white uniforms of the Imperial Navy and the crimson and khaki uniforms of the Red Legion. There appeared to be two commanders: one in white and one wearing a dark grey cloak. They both gave orders to the men. An explosion came from the forest.

Lucy wanted to get closer, to see more clearly, and perhaps even listen to what they were saying.

"We can take you closer," Pzilliz Trillis said.

"That'd be good."

Hwith dropped to the forest floor with Lucy on his back. Pzilliz Trillis followed while the other rocs remained in the trees. Lucy stood behind thick undergrowth and watched the sailors from the darkness of the forest. She immediately recognized Petty Officer Hand. He looked concerned as he spoke to the tall green officer she'd seen in Scarlet Station, albeit through bug eyes. She felt the need to speak to him—an intuition, perhaps. She moved close enough to hear their conversation. The officer had sent four bots ahead to scout. The first one had flown into a tree and exploded.

"Not a good sign," the naval officer said.

"The forest doesn't like machines, Commander," Petty Officer Hand said.

The commander smiled at his petty officer. "I think the stories of mythological beasts flying up and attacking naval ships that stray too close to the forest are just as fanciful as those of magic."

"Don't joke about this, sir. There are many stories of magic and strange creatures living on Blue Prometheus."

"So you use the old name, too. Don't let our young lord hear you. But I don't think we'll find any magic or monsters; wild animals are definitely a possibility, though," the commander said.

A third man approached them. He wore the dark grey cloak of the Imperial Order. She didn't like the feeling he gave off. For a moment, the man glanced at the forest towards her. Then he turned back to the commander.

"Commander Chance, you've lost a bot."

"It happens. When the others report back, we'll leave."

"Report what? We're in a primeval forest on a primitive planet, Commander. I don't think there's much to report. Only the path to the lord and the location of the rebels. What exactly are you looking for?"

"I'll know if I find it."

"I've just told you, Commander. There's nothing there—apart from wild animals and plants. Hardly enough to worry my men."

"Mercenaries?"

"Don't underestimate the Red Legion."

"Why did the bot crash?" Lucy asked.

"The sailor's right. The forest doesn't like technology, it confused the bot," Soonasa said.

"Is the forest alive?"

"Do you have to ask?" Hwith's voice sounded in her mind.

"No, I mean does it think?"

"It thinks like a sleeping giant, swatting gnats that disturb its dreams," Pzilliz Trillis said.

"The other bots are back, sir," Petty Officer Hand said. "The path's clear."

"As I said, Commander," the lord said.

The imperial group moved into the forest. Three attack bots flew overhead, and four ice demons ran straight into the forest. The sailors and red legionnaires followed.

Lucy followed on foot. She spoke to the forest as she'd heard the rocs do, and the plants responded, at least many of them did, and allowed her to pass unhindered. She moved quickly through the thick undergrowth, without any need to hack or cut the plants, unlike the struggling imperial party. The two rocs ran close by her, and despite their size, they ran silently, hardly disturbing the vegetation.

One of the ice demons stopped and stared in her direction. Lucy froze.

"Keep still," Hwith said. *"It senses you, but cannot see you. You're getting better, but you still need to speak the True Language more softly."*

After a few moments, the lizard turned and ran into the trees. She then resumed her jog, keeping pace with the sailors. She was sure she was getting fitter. Several minutes later, everyone stopped. A sea of fire funnels gently swayed in unison. Each plant was the size of a man.

Commander Chance cursed. "Are these those damn fire plants?"

"Yes, sir. I believe they are," Samuel Hand said.

"And there isn't any breeze."

"Sir?"

"They're moving by themselves. I don't think it's a good sign."

"I see what you mean, sir. Should we move back and take the other way?"

"A problem, Commander?" the lord asked.

"A floral obstacle."

"Commander?"

"Exploding plants. I count a hundred or more."

"We're stopping for a patch of flowers?" The young aristocrat looked at him disdainfully. "I can clear a path for you, if you want."

"No, I don't require you to sacrifice yourself yet. We'll find a way around them."

Lucy noticed the darkness. Apart from the torches, the only things that glowed were the thick stems of the fire funnels.

"It's dark here," Samuel.

"Unnaturally dark, sir."

"They're right. It is very dark," Lucy said.

"The forest is protecting loved ones," Hwith said.

"Loved ones?"

"Follies," Hwith said. *"A mother is giving birth."*

The last thing Lucy wanted was this group to stumble on some animal giving birth.

"Follies aren't animals. They're intelligent, if foolish."

"What do you mean?" Lucy asked.

"They're born with an innate knowledge of what should be: an inner map of the universe as it is intended to be. We would be wise to listen. Many navigate life with a much more flawed chart."

"If they're wise, why do you call them follies?" she asked.

"Because they're foolish to expect others to live up to what should be. They sometimes believe that all can see what they can see and are often disappointed. Because of their blindness, they can hardly defend themselves," Hwith said.

Now Lucy was concerned. *"Then we must protect them. Where are they?"*

An image of fire funnels flashed before her mind.

"That's bad," she said.

"There's another problem," Old Grey said.

Before she could ask what the problem was, the lord raised his voice.

"Any delay is out of the question. This is the most direct way to Lord Anlair. My men can cut a way through this patch of vegetables, if that's what you're worried about," the lord said.

"Our job is to flush out rebels. It's unlikely that they've gone straight through a patch of these plants. We'll cut a path around them. That's an order, my lord."

Lucy watched from the large leaves of the forest. *"He's not going to obey the commander."*

"I'm taking command of this group, as is my right as a member of the Imperial Order," the lord said. "The navy should never have been involved."

"The Imperial Navy represents the Empire, my lord. The Red Legion does not."

"I represent the Empire." He shouted an order. The mercenaries aimed their assault rifles at the fire funnels.

The red bots flew over the large plants, shooting randomly, and the legionnaires opened fire. Lucy covered her ears. A few of the plants disintegrated, but most were incredibly tough and withstood the bullets.

The whole colony of fire funnels brightened. Several swirled round and their open mouths followed the circling bots. Fireballs flew from the long funnels, and the bots burst into flames and crashed onto the forest floor starting new fires. The colony stopped swaying and bowed towards the intruders; they vibrated.

The mouths of the fire funnels gaped open. Scores of fireballs flew at the mercenaries. Half a dozen men were killed outright, and several more were covered in a flammable substance that burnt brightly. They ran screaming into the forest.

The red legionnaires ran back to the cover of the trees and continued to fire. The commander ordered his sailors to help. The fire funnels stopped firing. Flames engulfed the patch of plants, and the soldiers and sailors watched.

A creature screamed, both aloud and in the True Language.

"Looks like some animal was inside the patch," Petty Officer Hand said.

Lucy saw the folly in her mind: a burning seal-like creature with a large head lay in a shallow pool of water. It was covered in flames. *"Help it,"* she said.

"It's too late," Hwith said.

He was right. The life had gone from the poor creature. *"Why did it go into the patch of fire funnels?"*

"Usually the fire funnels protect the follies. Usually it's a safe place for them to give birth."

"But it was a male, the father." Lucy went quiet. *"There must be a mother, too."* She reached out with her mind and found another creature—alone and scared. She was about to give birth. *"We must help her,"* she said.

"The fire has attracted predators; we must deal with them first," Hwith said.

Lucy was concerned for the folly, which she sensed was a gentle and intelligent creature. She was also concerned for the sailors, or at least two of them. *"We must help."*

"The predators pose the greatest threat; we'll deal with them. It's not your duty to help either the folly or the sailors, but if you wish to, you must decide what to do," Hwith said.

"I've met two of the sailors before."

"We know."

Lucy felt a little annoyed that she was so easy to read. *"You're getting better,"* Soonasa said.

"Oh," she said aloud. Then she felt a new presence in the forest. *"I can feel something approaching. Two groups, I think. One of them feels different, darker than the other,"* she said.

"The darker group is a type of creature we cannot tolerate in our forest," Hwith said. *"The dark predators are dangerous and must be dealt with immediately. They should not be here."*

"What of the other?" Lucy asked.

"Regular predators," Pzilliz Trillis said.

"Regular predators? That doesn't sound reassuring."

"We must go," Hwith said. The rocs silently lifted into the air and flew into the forest. She was alone.

33

Her attention returned to the imperial party. She slowly counted the remaining men. She had counted thirty in total at the beginning. There were fifteen left; most of the dead were mercenaries. All of the squad's robots were gone.

"We'll wait for the fire to subside and then we'll march down into the valley," the lord said. The lord stared through the burning plants. "It looks like we've cooked an animal of some sort. A big one, too." The lord turned around when an ice demon burst out of the forest. "What've you found?"

It lowered its head before him. "My lord," it hissed. "We're being followed. The fire's attracted predators."

"Remember that we're the predators."

"Yes, my lord," it hissed.

"They're probably scavengers, attracted by the smell of the burnt flesh."

"What exactly is following us?" Commander Chance asked the lizard.

"Three groups of creatures, and something else: a solitary being of power," the ice demon said. "I sense magic."

The lord became alert. "I sense nothing, why?"

"Theirs is the wild magic of Prometheus, my lord."

Commander Chance glanced at his nervous-looking petty officer. "I hope you were wrong about monsters," he said quietly.

So did Lucy. She had no wish to meet any predators: regular or otherwise. She moved quickly around the burnt patch and thought about what the ice demon had said: a solitary creature of power. Was there something else, perhaps very dangerous, stalking them in the forest? She looked around nervously but sensed nothing in the immediate vicinity. She wanted to get closer to the folly; she'd decided that the sailors could look after themselves.

"The fire's low. We leave now," the lord said.

Lucy was on the far side of the patch when she heard the imperial party crash through the remains of the smouldering fire funnels. The soldiers stopped briefly to look at the burnt remains of the folly.

"There's another," an ice demon said.

"Good, a hunt will lift the spirits of the men."

"My lord, I don't think hunting animals is a good idea. We should move on," Commander Chance said.

"A hunt will be good for morale. We'll move quickly after that, don't worry, Commander."

But Lucy was worried. She was in the forest on the far side of the patch of burnt vegetation. She knew where the folly was. She could hear the men approaching. They were only slowed by having to walk around a few remaining fires.

The folly had followed the shallow stream of water into a tiny patch of fire funnels that still remained intact. Lucy walked to the clump of plants and spoke to them. They glowed but didn't move. They'd exhausted their energy. Lucy pushed them gently aside. A seal-like creature with a large lumpy head lay in a large puddle with a newly-born folly feeding on its milk. The mother was the same size as a human. The folly held its young one with its upper flippers. The flippers divided at the ends into four flat finger-like appendages. Its eyes were bright, and it welcomed her in the True Language, but Lucy sensed sadness.

"You must go!" Lucy urged her. But the creature showed an image of the dried-up stream. It could only move slowly over land.

"Here," a soldier said. He'd found the folly's tracks.

"Hwith, they're hunting the follies." There was no answer. She left the patch of plants, hoping that they'd conceal the creatures, but she knew she was deluding herself. She stepped into the forest and watched the imperial party approach, ashamed at her lack of courage, but she didn't know what she could do.

Screams came from the forest. The company soldiers turned and raised their weapons.

"They're fighting over us," Petty Officer Hand said.

"The thinning of the herds," the lord said. "And the better for us."

But Lucy knew he was bluffing. The young lord felt as nervous as the rest of the soldiers. An ice demon's ears twitched. It stared into the forest. She felt it, too. Something approached rapidly. A two-legged serpent with a mane of flames running from its flattened head, down its back and along its tail, ran out of the trees. The imperial group stared—shocked. A legionnaire was in the way, and the flaming basilisk cut him in half with a wisp of magic that only Lucy noticed. Then she saw the expression on the lord's face. He'd sensed the magic in the creature, too, and he was scared. The burning basilisk disappeared into the forest.

"I told you there were monsters, sir," Petty Officer Hand said quietly.

"It seems you were right, Samuel," the commander said.

The forest was silent again. The soldiers were shaken.

"What was that thing? And what type of creature could do that to it?" the mercenary sergeant asked. No one answered.

"It's here," a mercenary said.

Lucy's heart sank. She'd hoped the sight of the burning basilisk would've made them forget the folly. The imperial party surrounded the remaining patch of fire funnels. They gingerly moved them apart and looked at the seal-like creature and its young. The mother looked up at the men. Lucy could see its large head and bright eyes clearly. It greeted them in the True Language, but only Lucy could hear. The men heard squeaks and whistles.

"That's disgusting. Does it think it's human?" the lord said. "Cut it up, Sergeant. We can take part of it with us and cook it later." The red legion mercenary took out his machete.

"They're killing the follies!" she called out to the rocs.

She heard a distant reply. *"We're hunting serpents. You must help."* It was Hwith.

Lucy felt her energy fading. She looked down at herself. Her light had gone out; she was afraid. The man slashed the poor creature. It gave out a long, high-pitched whistle; it screamed in the True Language. The men laughed, and the puddle turned red.

"Act!" Hwith said.

"I can't," Lucy said.

"Then you allow sickness and death to enter the forest," Pzilliz Trillis said.

Lucy felt hurt by the words of the roc. The men were too dangerous and violent.

"This isn't right," Samuel Hand said.

"No, but much isn't right with our imperial masters," Commander Chance said quietly.

The newly-born seal creature sensed Lucy through the trees. Its mind touched hers, and it called her. Then it cried out for its mother, and the men laughed again. It was too much for her: the pain of the young creature, which she felt as if it were her own, overcame her.

Lucy stepped from the forest and exploded in light.

The sergeant stepped back. "What the . . .?" The lord and the other legionnaires moved away from the dying folly, staring nervously at her.

She sensed the lord's fear. "What are you?" he asked.

"A Bright One," Samuel Hand said quietly. "When I was a child, I heard a legend of great spirits that appear in times of need. There are not only monsters in the forest."

Commander Chance watched in silence.

Lucy felt a power she'd never felt in all her life. If only she'd known sooner. She walked to the patch of fire funnels, and the soldiers stepped back. She touched the tops of the plants, and a circle of blue flames rose. She stepped inside the circle of flames.

She poured golden energy from her cup and from her heart into the injured creature. She healed the wounds, and it breathed more steadily. She touched the young folly's large head. It spoke to her in an infant language of emotions and images. It was confused, but at least it had no physical wounds.

Lucy seldom felt anger, but now a fury rose inside her at what these men had done. Her light shone brightly as she stepped from the flames and faced the imperial party.

"It's the Orange Witch," the lord said. "Arrest her."

"I don't think that's a good idea, my lord. Even if she would let us," Commander Chance said.

"Let us? Have you gone insane? You're an officer of the Imperial Navy. Do your duty, Commander."

"If you haven't noticed, my lord, this woman's emitting bright golden light, and you've just tried to kill one of her friends. I think it'd be unwise to upset her."

"Upset her? Legionnaires, take her." The legionnaires stepped over the scorched earth towards her.

Lucy felt life all around and beneath her. She looked at the ground. It was scorched but alive. She felt the cracked pods of the burnt fire funnels. Plants that would normally protect the follies. The fire had germinated their seeds, and they were ready to grow. She called to the seeds that lay beneath the surface, her energy flowed into them, and the young fire funnels awoke.

The golden light around her increased, and the seeds stirred and shoots appeared. Lucy continued to pour energy into the young shoots, and they grew. But it was slow, and the men were close. She called again for help, more urgently. She heard a reply. Something shimmered in the earth; she didn't think anyone else saw it. A creature only inches high came from the ground and grinned at her. Then it disappeared.

The shoots of the fire funnels broke through the ground and began to twine around the ankles of the red legionnaires. The men screamed and frantically tried to free themselves, but the plants were tough. Within minutes the mercenaries had disappeared inside newly formed fire funnels. Their screams slowly choked out and were silenced.

Lucy was shocked at what she'd just done, and her light dimmed.

"Thank you," the folly said. *"Blue Prometheus is with you."*

Lucy looked at the man facing her.

"Witch!" the lord said.

She sensed terror in the man's voice. He'd lost his magic.

"Surrender and return to your ship," Lucy said.

"Surrender? I think not. You're alone, apart from a few plants, which have stopped growing," the lord said. He looked at them nervously.

She thought of what the folly had said, and the small magical creature of the forest that had appeared when she'd needed help. "Blue Prometheus is with me." Again, her light shone brightly.

The lord shook his head but still stepped back. "Superstitious nonsense." He raised his gun.

"Enough," Commander Chance said. He pushed the lord's gun down.

The lord knocked his hand away and pointed his pistol at the naval officer. "I never thought you a traitor, Aod Chance."

A bright roc dropped from a tree and sliced off the lord's arm.

"Soonasa," Lucy said in relief.

The man stared at the blood gushing from his stump. He screamed and ran into the dark forest. The sailors and the ice demons turned to Lucy and the roc.

"Thank you, Commander," Lucy said.

"No, thank you, my lady. And your avian friend."

Lucy still glowed with golden light. She walked up to Samuel Hand. "Forgive us, my lady," he said. "We meant no harm to the spirits of the forest."

She took his hands. "Samuel Hand. I'm as human as

you. And it's good to see you again, even if the circumstances are bad."

Commander Chance looked at his petty officer. "Samuel? How do you know this woman, if that's what she is?"

"I'm a woman, Commander," Lucy said. Then she showed the Petty Officer a mental image of her inside the cage."

He stood up and looked at her carefully. "We met in Scarlet Station. Although I can hardly believe it's the same girl."

"I saw you, too, Commander, but you didn't notice me," Lucy said.

"I'd certainly have noticed you," he said. He studied her face carefully.

"I looked different then. Perhaps I can tell you about it one day."

"I'd like that."

Lucy spoke in the True Language and silently expressed her gratitude to the forest for helping her save the follies. The forest lit up in shades of blue, red, green, pink, and white.

"Did you do that?" Commander Chance asked Lucy.

"In a sense, yes."

"Do you have many more surprises?"

Lucy smiled. "Perhaps."

The remaining rocs dropped from the trees. They inspected the humans.

"How many of these birds are there?" he asked.

"They're not birds, Commander. They're rocs: one of the intelligent species of Prometheus."

He nodded. "I'll remember. I suppose those two creatures we nearly killed are intelligent, too."

"More than you know."

"What now?" the commander asked.

"Return to your ship and wait. You must promise to wait in peace. Many rocs live in these forests, and if you attempt to fly your ship before we tell you, they'll attack, and there are many more than you see here.

"Don't underestimate the rocs, Commander. They're intelligent, tough, and very telepathic."

"I'd never underestimate any of your friends," Commander Chance said. He glanced up at the large rocs.

Lucy walked back to the follies. *"How can I help you?"* she asked.

"You've already helped. Thank you for saving my child. We'll be safe now. The fire plants are growing again, and the threat has gone. When the next rains come, we'll swim back to the river."

The young male folly pushed his lumpy head against her hand and sent a stream of pure love into her heart. Lucy felt overwhelmed by emotion again. *"I hope we can meet again,"* she said.

The rocs and the humans waited for her.

"Where will you go?" Commander Chance asked.

"Into the valley to find my friends."

34

Thomas and Aina ran down the narrow path, knocking away the tendrils that the crawling plants used to feel and pull their way across the forest. A chorus of shrill shrieks reverberated through the trees. Neither of them spoke; they knew exactly what the sounds meant.

The flowers of the ancient forest shone as they approached and dimmed as they passed. "Prometheus is with us," Aina said.

"I hope so because they're catching up," Thomas said. The screeches of the reptiles were now much closer.

They ran into a patch of about fifty tubular red fire funnels and stopped. Thomas slapped one of the red plants. It glowed and heat radiated from it.

"Those things are dangerous."

"I know," Thomas said. "Orange told me."

Aina looked at the patch of fire funnels. "I think I know what you want to do, but it's risky."

"Ice demons are dangerous, too."

"True."

Together they slapped the plants sharply as they walked

through the colony. The plants groaned and vibrated. The bases of their thick stems had become orange.

"They get hot," Thomas said.

"So will we if we're not quick." The fire funnels were beginning to follow their movement. They reached the edge of the clearing as the first ice demon rushed from the trees. It carelessly knocked the plants aside.

The funnel-like mouths of the plants swung in unison away from Thomas and Aina and towards the new threat. The base of their stems glowed, but the ice demon didn't notice the plants move. It ran into the patch, pushing the plants from its path. Fireballs flew from the tubular funnels, and the creature burst into flames.

Thomas and Aina slipped into the forest and watched as a second ice demon ran straight into a fireball. The third and fourth ice demons stopped on the edge of the patch and watched their burning colleagues.

"Two down," he whispered.

"Beginner's luck," Aina said.

"Knowledge of the local culture."

They walked through the undergrowth. Several minutes later, Thomas stopped and swore. "It's dark."

"Something's here," she whispered. They took out their knives.

A troop of basilisks walked and crawled through the trees. They hissed as they moved. Thomas counted thirteen of them, and they were bigger than the ones he'd met in the great valley. Most slid on their tails, but three of them walked on legs.

Aina moved closer to Thomas. "I can feel magic," she said. He felt it, too.

The basilisk leader had a large flattened head with arcane symbols tattooed across its face. Other tattoos covered its body. Scenes of ancient events, perhaps. It had crossed irises, like other basilisks, but its speckled eyes were unusual. It was the basilisk leader who'd spoken to Martin Anlair on the beach. Thomas sensed far more power in this creature than in the king of the valley. The creatures surrounded them.

"You trespass," it hissed in Dnassian.

"You speak Dnassian?" Thomas asked.

"In the Basilisk Nation, there are those with knowledge of the outer world." The basilisk moved closer to Thomas. "The pentacle around your neck is forfeit for entering our land."

"We're not within the Basilisk Nation," Aina said.

"You know something of our world, but it makes no difference. Give it to me."

"And then?" Thomas asked.

"We'll kill you."

"Not a good offer," Thomas said.

"It's better than what the sorcerer offers," the basilisk said.

"What are our chances?" he asked Aina.

She looked worried. "Not good."

"Who are you?" Thomas asked.

"I am Tnszak, high priest of the Black Nest. And you're the fabled Orange Company. A Bright One and his guide. But true Bright Ones don't hide in the woods."

Alien magic flowed through the company of basilisks. Thomas called on the pentacle; again he emitted a silver light as the power pulsed through him.

The high priest hissed. "That will not be enough."

Thomas's senses reached out around him, but there was nothing. No bare rock he could drag and fling at the serpents. Nor did these basilisks wear jewellery, as the serpent people in the Great Valley had. But then he felt a presence he recognized. A dulcet voice purred in his ear.

"Did you think I'd left you?"

Thomas looked around. Neither Aina nor the basilisks had heard. She was staring at the rattling snakes.

"I'm here."

Thomas looked up and saw the crystal Dat in a branch above. His bright ruby eyes glowed in the dark, and he grinned maliciously. Thomas smiled, and Aina looked at him as if he were mad.

"A death grin?" she asked.

"Sort of."

"Give it to me," the basilisk demanded.

"Thomas?" Aina whispered. "Your silver light. It's shining brightly. Can you fight them?"

"I might not have to."

"What do you mean?"

"Look up."

She did and immediately fell back into Thomas, her eyes round. "Is that what I think it is?"

"The Dat."

The creature dropped from the tree, and as it fell it decapitated a long purple serpent that had stretched its flattened head towards Thomas. Two more basilisks died from its diamond claws, a third bit the crystal body, then screamed through its bloody mouth.

The high priest's magic flared around him as the rest of his troop was slaughtered. "What have you done?" The high priest protected himself with magic, but he could do nothing for his comrades.

The catlike creature went berserk in its killing. A minute later, only the high priest, who looked on in fury, was still alive. His magic had been ineffective against the crystal creature. The Dat pounced on Tnszak, knocking him off his feet. The high priest slithered away into the forest.

The crystal Dat grinned like a demented Cheshire cat.

Thomas felt Aina press against his body. If he hadn't known the creature so well, he'd have been terrified, too.

"Thank you."

The Dat glanced at the forest behind them. *"You're being followed."*

"Can you help us?"

"This is not my fight. But I'll say hello." The Dat's grin returned. Aina cried out and gripped Thomas tighter as he leapt over their heads and bounded into the forest. Shouts and sounds of gunfire came from the forest behind them.

"It's definitely time to go," Thomas said.

Aina nodded. "It scares me. Thomas, what have you created?"

"A harrier of serpents."

35

Aina sprinted along a track that took them to a pale green river, which jumped and bubbled around numerous large boulders.

"I played here once," she said.

"Your playground was very different from normal children."

She grinned. "This way. I want to show you something."

They ran along the narrow path by the side of the river, jumping smoothly over the many creepers and large roots that obstructed their way. The sound of the river increased in volume. When they turned a corner, Thomas saw why. About a hundred yards ahead of them, a waterfall crashed into the river.

"Aina, it's beautiful, but how does it help us?"

"We climb it."

"Climb it? Are you crazy?"

"It's easier than it looks. Especially for you. It leads to a higher valley; it's an ideal place to ambush the death squad."

A branch snapped behind them. Thomas turned and instinctively raised his hand. He caught a globule of acid the ice demon had spat at his face. His hand stung, and he imagined fire burning, and the spit evaporated. He coughed on the acrid fumes. The lizard leapt into the air with a flying kick, its talons outstretched. He caught its leg using a circular motion and took its balance. The creature slipped down the bank.

"Run!" he shouted. Thomas pushed Aina along the path. She ran, but he slowed. Just as the reptile was almost on him, he jumped into the river and landed on a large flat rock. He picked a pebble and flung it at the demon, hitting its skull sharply. He leapt to another rock, farther out into the river, and threw another stone, again hitting the creature. Aina had stopped and was staring at him.

"Thomas!"

"I've got a plan," he shouted. "I think," he said quietly. "Come!" he shouted at the ice demon.

The ice demon laughed and dived into the river.

"Thomas, what're you doing? It's going to leap out at you," Aina cried out.

"I know."

The ice demon leapt from the surface of the river, several feet into the air, and landed next to him. Thomas stood still and watched the creature. The lizard looked puzzled. Then it snatched at him. Thomas hopped backwards and sank into the cold water; the ice demon followed.

It was dark. He felt the pull of the riverbed beneath him, and he sank quickly despite the strong current. The ice demon swam down towards him. It was very close when his feet touched the bottom. He remembered Orange's teaching and imagined that he was still sinking, but this time into the stony riverbed.

The ice demon clasped his left wrist and pulled. But he had already sunk up to his ankles into the rock, and it was he who pulled the lizard down. Thomas clasped its wrist. He continued to sink. Now he was up to his knees in viscous rock. The lizard had not yet understood its danger, and it clung to him even more tightly and pulled hard as the liquid rock sucked them down.

When Thomas had sunk to his waist, the demon realized its danger. It struggled to escape, but he held fast and continued to descend. He was soon entirely submerged beneath the rock, and he didn't let go of the ice demon until it was up to its neck in the viscous rock. Then he let go, and the rock around the creature solidified. The demon was dead.

Thomas climbed through the rock. It was strenuous work, but soon he stood on the dark riverbed next to the ice demon's head. He grasped its frill and tugged sharply. It snapped off from the rock-encased body. With the head in one hand, he rose to the surface.

Water evaporated from his body as he climbed onto the boulder. He couldn't see Aina, but he could see the death squad as they approached a small rivulet that joined the river. They moved slowly, as if expecting an ambush. They hadn't seen him.

Thomas aimed carefully and threw the bloody head. It hit Martin Anlair in his face and knocked him to the ground. "A gift, my lord!" Thomas shouted. The death squad turned in unison and opened fire.

Thomas dived into the river, a little surprised at the speed of their reaction. He swam along the bottom and moved quickly, aided by the power of the pentacle. Several creatures swam into him, but none worried him. When the river became shallow, he stopped and looked up at the surface. He couldn't see anything move. Thomas swam through the shallows and then scrambled up the riverbank.

"Here," Aina called in a low voice.

Thomas ran to her hiding place in the undergrowth on the other side of the path. "Where are they?"

"They're coming." She pointed downstream. Martin Anlair led the group of mercenaries, bots, and ice demons. "Good shot," she said. "You've really upset him. It looks like he's having a temper tantrum."

"We should go," Thomas said.

"No, perhaps not. Look."

Aina pointed to the small rivulet, but he didn't see anything at first. Then he saw something white hidden in the vegetation. "What's that?"

"If it's what I think it is, then we may have a way of killing a few more."

"What is it?"

"Throw a stone into that tree."

He raised his eyebrows at her but tossed a stone into the vegetation just along the rivulet. Something moved.

"Again."

He threw two more stones, and the noise attracted the attention of the death squad. "Perhaps that wasn't a good idea," he said.

"No, look."

Thomas saw a white face emerge from a branch above a mercenary who now investigated the upper section of the rivulet. Ten red eyes looked down at the man.

"Aina?"

"A clown."

"Is that what attacked you in the air?"

"Something similar."

Aina hadn't exaggerated in her description of the creature; he shivered. Its ten retinas swivelled in all directions as it checked its surroundings for threats. Its fat red lips opened and closed, showing its gaping mouth. All of its eyes now focussed on the man below. Its proboscis extended.

The clown spider dropped, and its proboscis pierced the man's skull. He died with a brief look of confusion. The clown then dragged his body deeper into the gully. The forest was quiet, apart from the slurping of the spider sucking out its breakfast.

Lord Anlair called his man, but there was no reply. The death squad rushed to the rivulet and stopped. There were cries of disgust, followed by gunfire. The clown spider abandoned its meal and attacked them. The creature was larger than a man, and its legs were thick and strong, but it was not a match for the death squad's guns.

Martin Anlair watched as the creature hopped from side to side.

"The death squad will win this one," Thomas said.

Aina nodded, disappointed.

The death squad continued to fire on the desperate creature. It began to weaken. The clown collapsed, and its body burst open. A sluice of white liquid flowed from the hole. As the clown's body fell apart, hundreds of clown spiders, each the size of a man's fist, scampered from their dead mother. Most ran towards the death squad.

"He didn't expect that," Thomas whispered.

"Neither did I," Aina said.

The death squad shot the creatures, but it did no good. They were everywhere. The squad of killers was forced to retreat down the narrow path, pursued by hundreds of white-bodied, red-mouthed spiders, all looking for their first breakfast.

Thomas and Aina ran along the riverbank away from the clown spiders. The noise of the waterfall became louder as they ran.

"The ladder," she said.

Thomas could only see a torrent of water pouring down from above. "Where?"

"We have to go around the pool."

They made their way around the edge of the foaming green pool. Water sprayed over them. Aina's energy pulsed through her, protecting her from the cold water. For the first time, Thomas understood what she'd been doing, and he copied her. His natural magic pulsed through him, too, but it was aided by the power of the pentacle.

He followed her along a narrow ledge on the far side of the pool. They were next to the falls. Then he saw them. Steps, of a kind, in the rock face by the falls. A few weeks earlier, climbing a rock face like this would have made him nervous. If he'd been able to do it at all, he would've moved like a snail. Now the rock was his friend and attracted him to its surface. Thomas climbed quickly, and Aina wasn't far behind.

When they were halfway up the cliff, they stopped to rest. Thomas looked down at the distant forest.

"Did you really play here when you were a child?"

"I discovered the steps myself."

"Do you mean your father let you climb rock faces like this?"

She went quiet. "He was already dead when I played here."

"I'm sorry." And he really was. "I wish I could have met him."

A bullet hit the rock face and ricocheted off only a few feet from their heads. Startled, Aina lost her grip and slipped off the rock face.

"Aina!" Without thinking, he leapt into the air and caught her wrist.

"Are you crazy?" she yelled as they fell together. Thomas hit an outcrop of rock about twenty feet below, but instead of bouncing off, his body passed through the rock. Aina fell to his side. He re-emerged from underneath the rock and hung loosely. His forearm was still within the rocky ledge. Aina dangled below him, holding tightly to his hand. "I can't believe you did that," she said.

He pulled himself and Aina up. Once his body was on top of the ledge, he lifted her up over the edge. He hugged her as more bullets ricocheted off the rock around them.

"I'd forgotten your super powers." She leaned forward, pressing her mouth to his.

"Aina!" He grinned. Then as more bullets hit the underneath of the ledge, he kissed her back.

"Thank you for saving my life. And for telling me you love me."

"I didn't." He smiled and held her close.

"Why did you leap into the air to save me?" She grinned, ignoring the bullets that bounced off the cliff.

"I think we're stuck."

"Maybe I am. But you can escape through the rock."

He shook his head. "I won't leave you."

"Thomas, be realistic."

He laughed. "You and Lucy have been telling me to stop being realistic for months."

"That's different. That was about your belief, this is about our situation."

Thomas moved slowly to the edge of the ledge and looked over. "Not good," he said, crawling back to her quickly.

"What?" she asked.

"A red bot. It'll be here in seconds."

"We can jump into the pool," Aina said.

Thomas shook his head. "It'd shoot us as we fell." He wondered what Orange would have done in this situation. Then he knew. He pressed Aina against the rock. At first she resisted. Then she just relaxed and began to speak, but her conversation was cut off as he pushed her inside the rock. That shut her up, he thought.

He imagined that Aina was a part of him and that he was a part of the mountain. He felt the coolness of the rock within, and a few of Aina's emotions, too. The sound of gunfire faded as he waded through the thick, viscous rock. Then he slipped and fell.

36

"Hey, get off of me!" Aina said.

He rolled over and looked around. Everywhere was dark.

"You did it," she said. Her torch lit his face. "You look like you've just seen a ghost."

"I thought perhaps it was me who was the ghost."

"Not yet." She gave him a hand up.

They were inside a cavern. Thomas rubbed the rocky wall; he felt the living rock around him. The waterfall was only feet away through the walls, but the cave was silent.

"Let's explore," he said. The cavern was small, but it connected with others. They walked deeper into the system of caves. He touched the wall of the cave. Seconds later he broke contact. "I think I can find a way into the valley above."

They walked for over an hour through the tunnels, slowly climbing upwards. Eventually they reached a larger cavern.

"Where are we?" she asked.

"Under the upper valley, I think. Let's rest first. I don't

think they can find us here, and I don't care if we keep them waiting." Aina agreed. They lay together on the dry floor and fell into a deep sleep.

Several hours later they woke. Thomas stretched slowly. He noticed a tiny shaft of light. "Can you see that?"

"We're close to the surface, then," Aina said.

"We might be on the surface." The light came from a narrow gap in the rock. He could see the forest beyond.

"We can't get through that," she said.

"Yes, we can."

"Thomas!"

He held her tight and pushed his body into the rock. It was a strange sensation, the centre was empty, the outsides hard. He felt as if he were walking at two speeds. They fell out into a large clearing in the forest.

"I hate it when you do that," she said, wiping her body as if the viscous rock had stuck to her. Then she looked around. "It's just as I remember it." They walked towards the forest, and then she stopped. "It's not exactly the same." She pointed. "We have a problem." The death squad had camped in the forest ahead of them. "We waited too long. Now we can't get to the best places."

They ran for the cover of the forest, and Thomas sensed something running towards them. "Something's coming," Thomas said. "Climb!"

"And you?"

"I've got an idea." He ran back into the clearing, stepped into a boulder and sank. A minute later, only his face remained on the outer surface of the rock. He watched the forest from the stone; he saw Aina climb the tall tree. Then he saw the ice demon emerge from the undergrowth.

This was the final demon. Its frilled neck flexed in and out, and its forked tongue stuck out and flicked from side to side; it could smell them. It stopped at the edge of the clearing. Thomas touched its mind. He didn't have Lucy's or Aina's skill with creatures, but he could feel its emotions. It was wary of the humans it hunted. It'd never met any like them; momentarily, it felt doubt. But when it smelt humans, its doubt faded.

AINA KEPT CLIMBING until she was hidden in the branches and leaves of the tree. From there, she watched the ice demon below. It touched her tree and glanced up but then sniffed the ground. She looked for Thomas and shuddered at what she saw on the boulder.

Two eyes watched the demon from the rock. A mouth emerged and called. The ice demon bounded towards the boulder and stopped. Its tongue flicked in and out as it tasted the air, but it didn't see the eyes watching it. Aina watched Thomas with both fascination and repulsion.

Warily, the ice demon lowered its head to sniff the rock. It screamed as a hand emerged and gripped its throat. In panic, it extended the frills around its neck. The demon's tail thrashed from side to side. Its face was already pressed up against the warm stone. It whimpered before its head disappeared into the boulder, its limp body soon following. Finally, its long tail disappeared beneath the surface of the planet.

The death squad ran through the trees and out into the clearing. "Where's the lizard?" Morgan Red shouted.

Scanlon noticed the disturbed ground. "Something happened here." He crouched down and felt the earth. "There was a struggle." Martin Anlair touched the rock. Then he moved back. "The lizard's dead."

"How?"

"The sorcerer's underground. He dragged the lizard into the earth." Martin Anlair glanced at Morgan Red and the other legionnaire. "He's beneath us." The mercenaries looked at the ground suspiciously.

"What now?" Morgan Red asked.

"There are only two of them. The one beneath the ground is trapped. He cannot rise quickly. Kill him when he begins to emerge. One of the witches is close by, too." Lord Anlair turned to his assassin. "Find her."

Scanlon nodded to his master and ran towards the trees. Aina cursed her bad luck. Very few people in the world could find her when hidden, but this was one who could. She placed the gentlest invisibility spell she could on herself, hoping that neither the lord nor the black-clad assassin would sense her magic, but if the assassin looked directly at her, no invisibility spell would help, not against him.

The assassin sniffed a tree trunk several yards from her. Aina had heard rumours of imperial assassins having genetically-modified sense organs, and Lucy had told her of the strange way Scanlon had sniffed her. He moved from tree to tree, each time getting closer until he reached hers. "She's here," the man said.

"Take her alive," Martin Anlair said.

Scanlon gave a bleak smile and slid up the tree. She held her knife and waited, unsure if he had seen her through the leaves. Several long seconds passed. She was no longer sure where he was. Then it was too late. He came from behind her and kicked her in her back. She dropped, hitting a lower branch. She was winded, but still retained hold of her knife. She turned to face her attacker.

His knife flashed towards her. She twisted to the side

and cut his wrist. It was only a surface wound, but he was surprised. She attacked without hesitation, forcing him on the defensive. Knife fighting was a skill she'd spent long hours practicing, but the assassin was good. Her first cut had partly been luck; he'd assumed she knew nothing. Now he treated her with more respect. They moved slowly towards each other, but the man suddenly jumped away to a parallel branch. She wondered why just as bullets hit her branch. It snapped, and she tumbled to the forest floor. She lay on the ground; her body hurt. She tried to sit up, but she couldn't. She heard Scanlon drop from the tree.

"You let a girl better you," Lord Anlair said, looking at the blood dripping from the assassin's wrist. Scanlon scowled.

"Shall I kill her?" Morgan Red asked.

"No, the witch is mine." Martin Anlair placed his hand on her chest. She screamed as a burst of electricity shocked her. "Real magic," he said.

He moved his hand away, and her skin stretched as if dozens of small fishhooks had punctured it and now tugged her. The swellings on her skin moved as he moved his hands. She screamed in pain as he dragged her away from the trees, yet his hands didn't touch her. The mercenaries moved away from their lord.

Her skin and muscles hurt, but she couldn't pull away. She was aware of her knife on the ground, but it was out of her reach. He moved his hand above her throat, and she felt a sharp pressure; he was choking her. She struggled to get away, but every movement hurt her more.

THOMAS MOVED in the earth below Anlair. Something was very wrong with Aina. He felt the magic and her pain. He knew the location of every person above him. He considered his choices. Any mistake could cause Aina's death.

The loose stony soil of the glade was easier to move through than solid rock, and he moved faster than he'd done before. He was inches beneath the surface. Aina was above him. He thrust his hand upwards, catching the ankle of the man holding her. Thomas pulled hard. The lord staggered, but he quickly recovered.

An electric shock stunned Thomas. He began to materialize inside the ground. Pain wracked his body; he let go. He felt Aina fall away from the lord. The assassin moved towards her, and Thomas walked through the ground towards him, ignoring the pain. He grabbed Scanlon's foot, and more pain wracked his body. They pulled against each other.

When Scanlon pulled, Thomas used the man's energy to pull himself out of the stony ground. He walked upwards as if were treading water very fast. He kept the assassin between himself and the lord. His head and shoulders emerged. He looked around at the men staring at him. Scanlon changed his tactic and slashed at Thomas's face with his knife. Thomas let go of the man's ankle; Scanlon's foot was still partly submerged in the ground. The assassin fell back and screamed. Thomas drew his knife threw it at the nearest mercenary. It pierced the man's throat.

"Use the pentacle!" Aina shouted.

Her words saved him from death. Silver light poured from Thomas. Morgan Red fired repeatedly at him, but his shield deflected the bullets. However, he felt a loss of energy as his shield weakened.

"Keep shooting. When he lowers his guard, it'll kill him," Martin Anlair said.

Thomas mentally tugged his knife, and it flew from the dead legionnaire's throat back into his hand. He then threw it at the surprised Morgan Red. It stuck into his arm. The man yelled and dropped his gun. Aina scooped up her knife and stamped on the assassin's injured foot. Scanlon screamed again, and she ran to Thomas's side.

37

A horn sounded, and all turned to look. Scores of basilisks, hissing and rattling, crawled and walked from the forest where they stopped and waited.

"The high priest," Thomas said.

The tattooed serpent walked towards them, followed by nine more basilisks. He looked at Thomas through his speckled eyes. "The Bright One and the Emperor's sorcerer. But no monsters to protect you," he said to Thomas.

"A stalemate," Thomas said.

"Not a stalemate," the high priest said. "We have an army, you have a knife." Tnszak turned to Martin Anlair. "You may leave. Your life is a gift from the Black Nest. Be grateful for my mercy."

Lord Anlair glared at the basilisk.

The serpent priest hissed. "You thought the Bright One dead. And the ancient key lost."

"It belongs to the Emperor," Martin Anlair said.

"It belongs to the Basilisk Nation."

Martin Anlair turned to Thomas and held out his hand. "Give me the pentacle, and you may live."

Aina spat in his face, and the high priest cackled. "She's right to spit on you. You're more treacherous than a silver basilisk."

Thomas felt the latent power of his enemies begin to rise, and he prepared himself to fight to the death. But then he had the feeling that something was approaching, and he looked up into the deep blue sky. "Aina."

She followed his gaze. "The rocs are coming."

"What does this mean?"

"I don't know."

Anlair's death squad and the basilisks watched the flight of bright rocs approach.

"A rider," Thomas said.

"I'd never have believed it possible," Aina said.

The rocs dived from the sky, and the remains of the death squad and the basilisks quickly moved back. Six rocs landed in a circle around Thomas and Aina. Fire belched from their beaks and nostrils.

A woman surrounded by bright golden light jumped down and stood before them.

"Lucy?" Thomas said. He smiled, relief and amazement filling him.

"I'm alive. The rocs saved me; they are with us. Prometheus is with us." She hugged them both.

The basilisks rattled in anger. "The ancient keys belong to the Basilisk Nation. Even now our nation marches to claim our ancient right," Tnszak hissed. From the trees hundreds of basilisks emerged, joining the scores already waiting by the forest's edge. Martin Anlair looked up in alarm.

"All power comes to me," the high priest said, and magic crackled around him. The six rocs lifted into the air and attacked the high priest with fire. Martin Anlair and his men backed away and watched.

The basilisk army rushed from the forest towards them; a tattooed priest led each section of twelve serpents.

"We'll fight the high priest," Thomas said to the rocs. *"Help us with the basilisk army!"*

The flight of rocs flew higher into the air and then swept down towards the marching army of serpents. Together, the six rocs created a wave of fire that rushed towards the Basilisk Nation.

"Impressive as your friends are, they're not enough," the high priest said. Magic crackled in the air as he commenced a spell.

Thomas felt his hair stand up. "Black magic," he said. He felt the land and people around him. All became one, and he became a part of it—all his doubts about magic were gone. It was then his energy flowed freely, and he felt power.

The high priest hissed and glowed black in the darkening day as he sucked the life force from the troop of serpents standing by him; they wailed and withered, falling as lifeless husks on the ground. The high priest channelled his power and directed it at Thomas and Lucy. A shadowy black energy snaked its way along the ground towards them.

It caught Aina's ankle and pulled her to the ground. Her own magic flared, and she whipped the high priest with a strand of energy. He hissed, but the black energy tightened around her ankle, and she cried out. Thomas threw his knife at the high priest's head, but the sorcerer knocked it away. Then Lucy's magic touched the black energy gripping Aina's ankle, and it loosened. Aina pulled away and ran back to her friends, but the black energy still reached towards them.

Lucy, too, shone brightly. She reached out and held

Thomas's hand, and their magic combined—he was taken aback by her power, as was she by his. Their mind was one, and they faced the basilisk together. A bright shield appeared before them. The dark worm of magic exploded and burnt when it touched the shield, and the fire crept back towards the sorcerer. The high priest of the Black Nest could not let go of his dark creation, and he desperately struggled to push the flames back, but they didn't heed him.

Tnszak was engulfed in flames, and he became a fireball that rolled back over the empty bodies he'd drained of life. Like tinder, they blazed in the dark afternoon. But still he cursed and threatened the Bright Ones. The high priest of the Black Nest screamed and rolled back towards the forest. The Basilisk Nation was in full retreat and was still harried by the six rocs that circled overhead.

Anlair rushed at Thomas—a long blade in his hand. "No!" Aina screamed. She leapt forward, thrusting her dagger into Martin Anlair's heart, but at the same time his blade penetrated her chest. Aina collapsed to the ground.

"Aina!" Thomas knelt next to her and pulled the long blade from her chest. He tried to stop the bleeding with both hands and magic. Lucy knelt by them. Bright energy flowed from her and joined with Thomas's power. They desperately tried to block the wound in her chest, but Aina bled badly.

"Thomas," Aina said from where she lay. She gasped for breath; blood trickled from her mouth. She closed her eyes, her breathing shallow.

"The Orange Witch dies," Martin Anlair said.

Thomas looked up in shock to see Anlair standing before him. A faint green light came from the sorcerer's chest; he'd healed himself with his magic. "Surprised? I have power over life and death. Give me the cup and pentacle, and all of you can live. It needn't be hard," Anlair said.

"Thomas, kill him," Aina said weakly.

Martin Anlair didn't wait for a response and attacked Thomas with blasts of cold, dark energy. Thomas parried with the hot fire that burnt within him while Lucy attempted to save Aina. It must end here. Anlair circled and attacked him repeatedly. Thomas deflected the attacks.

The black magic of his opponent was strong, but it was also isolated and fragmented. It pulled against the flow of the universe. He felt its weakness. Thomas's power came from all around him. All was one, and he was power.

He reached deep beneath the surface of Prometheus and found a river of fire. He knew exactly what to do. He called it, and the fire within the planet rose on his command. It flowed up through the gaps and cracks in the crust, and it rushed towards him.

"Come!" he commanded. Fire exploded from the surface, gushing around and over the startled Martin Anlair. The molten lava propelled Anlair into the air like a giant flare. The lord rocketed higher into the sky and exploded like a firework over the forest.

The two remaining members of the death squad, Scanlon and Morgan Red, drew back in fear. The cries of the returning flight of rocs turned their fear to panic. They fled over the scorched remains of their comrades, towards the line of trees. Nobody bothered to stop them.

Aina called weakly. Thomas ran to her side and dropped to his knees. Lucy was still pouring the healing power of the cup into their friend. Aina's eyes brightened for a few seconds when she saw Thomas, but then the power of the cup ebbed and vanished. Lucy looked at Thomas. Tears formed in her eyes.

"Lucy, it's all right. I've succeeded. You're alive, and our enemy is dead."

"Aina, it's not all right. Fight and stay with us," Thomas said.

"Thomas, it's my time. I go to the next world. It's you who has to fight."

Tears poured from Lucy's eyes. "You're making me wet," Aina said. As Lucy tried to apologize, Aina continued. "I chose my life and my death. I'm not afraid."

"Aina, don't say that. I was too slow. If I'd understood and believed earlier, I could've stopped this," Thomas said.

"My life to wake you and to free Silva. I chose well."

Aina laughed as tears welled in Thomas's eyes. But she coughed up blood and had to stop. "Laughing's not a lot of fun when you've been stabbed in the chest by a sword." She lay very still and closed her eyes. "Thomas, hold me." Aina died in his arms.

They sat by their still friend in silence, but when the moons of Prometheus shone in the night sky, Hwith's voice touched their minds. *"It's time to go."*

Thomas held Aina's body in his arms and sat motionless on Hwith's back. The roc lifted into the grey sky.

"I should've died instead of her," Thomas said.

"She was stubborn and would not have let you. She gave everything to protect you and the world she loved, and if she were here now, she'd do it again."

Thomas knew the truth of that. *"If only I'd understood and used my power sooner."* For the first time since he was a child, Thomas cried.

Hwith spoke the True Language: *"Aina lives on, always."*

EPILOGUE

The Moons of Prometheus shone a silver light onto the mountain. Thomas and Lucy stood in front of the unlit funeral pyre; Aina's body rested on the top. A roc laid a large leaf over her body, and hundreds of dragonflies flew up and down the mountain fetching wood from the forest. It was almost time.

The six rocs of the flight, including Hwith and Pzilliz Trillis, stood by Thomas and Lucy, while others flew around the peak. They sang in Aina's honour. Commander Aod Chance, Petty Officer Samuel Hand, and two ordinary spacemen of the Imperial Navy, stood a little apart. They wore their white dress uniforms. They'd been surprised but honoured when Lucy had invited them to attend.

A dark shadow moved across one of the larger moons. *"What was that?"* Lucy asked Hwith.

"Aina's childhood friend. This is the great one who saved her life as a child." Hwith's words brought Thomas's attention back to the world around him.

He looked up into the sky. Whatever it was, it was very close and very big. He felt a breeze against his face. A black dragon the size of a small whale landed gently next to them. Images, ideas, and emotions flooded their minds and hearts. The dragon spoke the True Language with a clarity they'd not experienced since meeting the Mariner. They saw Aina when she was a child, playing in the forests of Prometheus. Orange was there, too.

"Thank you," Thomas said, tears formed in his eyes.

"She lives, Thomas," the black dragon said. *"Do not doubt it."*

"She lives in spirit, I know, but it's not enough."

"Her spirit lives," the dragon replied.

Thomas sighed. *"She's dead. I was there. I'll never see her again."*

"Not as she was, but as she will be."

They turned to the pyre. It was time. Hwith spoke the True Language for all who could hear. *"May Aina's fire always burn bright."*

Thomas and Lucy threw fiery branches onto the pyre. The rocs and the dragon gave their own fire, and as the flames leapt up, the rocs sang songs of life and rebirth, as was their tradition; their music was heard across the forest.

The fire burnt brightly in the dark Promethean sky, as if an ancient lighthouse were sending its fiery message across the great planet and beyond. The fire was seen from Puck and Miranda, and word of a strange happening on this distant outer world spread throughout the nine planets.

On a deeper level, Prometheus had stirred, and a wave of hope rippled across the darkling sea. The ancient Mariner, the last of his race, had completed his task and had passed beyond the realm of the physical and vanished from this plane of existence. Thomas and Lucy sat and watched the fire, deep into the night. Eventually, they fell asleep in front of the bright flames.

FREE STORIES

Find out about Aina's young life in the forests of Prometheus. Sign-up to my newsletter at nedmarcus.com and get two exciting prequels to Blue Prometheus for free.

PLEASE LEAVE A REVIEW

If you enjoyed Blue Prometheus, please leave a review. Reviews can help a writer's work be read by more readers and help promote their career, so allowing more books to be written. Thank you!

BOOKS BY NED MARCUS

Blue Prometheus Series

- Young Aina #0
- Blue Prometheus #1
- The Darkling Odyssey #2
- Fire Rising #3

Orange Storm Series

- Orange Storm #1
- The Orange Witch #2 (forthcoming)

ABOUT THE AUTHOR

Ned Marcus is an author of fantasy and science fiction. He lives and writes in East Asia.

nedmarcus.com

ACKNOWLEDGMENTS

Thank you to my editor, Parisa Zolfaghari; my proofreader, Becky Johnson; Owain McKimm; the members of Taipei Fantasy and Sci-fi Writers' Group; and to my father for helping to proofread the earlier drafts.

www.ingramcontent.com/pod-product-compliance
Lightning Source LLC
LaVergne TN
LVHW091701070526
838199LV00050B/2238